CAVALIER
A Novel

by

K M Dudley

A NOVEL

CAVALIER

K.M.DUDLEY

CAVALIER: A Novel
Copyright © 2018 K M Dudley

ISBN-10: 1979768773
ISBN-13: 978-1979768771

Cover and interior artwork by Sydney Michuda.

First edition.

www.KMDudley.com

for Michael and Cary

CAVALIER
A Novel

by

K M Dudley

"Did perpetual happiness in the Garden of Eden maybe get so boring that eating the apple was justified?"

— Chuck Palahniuk, *Survivor*

Prologue

Gut-wrenching screams echo from behind the wooden door leading down into the underground cellar. The hallway's stone walls intensify the noise, creating a claustrophobic grasp amidst the narrow corridor. A light layer of dew from the Louisiana summer settles below the earth while the air hangs heavy and stagnant, clinging to its surroundings with no indication as to whether it is day or night.

Another gruesome scream reverberates through the bleak hall. The woman's relentless howl continues, sounding more hoarse with every wail that she agonizingly ejects from behind a secondary door at the far end of the passageway.

The hallway suddenly falls faint, beginning to calm as a new reaction emits between the cracks in the doorframe. Muffled sobs of terror ride a roller coaster of intensity; sometimes they sound of intimidation and fear, other times a melancholy surrender. This place has become a void of nothingness beneath the rich, southern soil. Time stands still with no salvation in sight.

Shocked from her stillness, a set of footsteps crashes to life throughout the cinderblock cellar. Full of force and confidence, the woman's maker has finally made his appearance and is heading in one direction. With no urgency in the stride, an ominous hollowness encroaches between each boom of the rubber soles. The woman inhales a full gasp as the tracking ceases and she can feel the presence drift through the heavy-set door. The handle turns and the latch within the knob silently sits.

The piercing vibration of the woman's heartbeat bursts through her ears as her blood burns in her veins. The room beyond the door fills with a rough anxiety and the woman's panic turns palpable as the handle does nothing but sit. Uncontrollable fear fills her like an overflowing fountain as her eyes roll back into her head and she ejects a guttural scream that rattles against the door's hinges. Her cries shift into an eerie whimper.

Abruptly swinging to life, the door exposes the man responsible for the woman's fate. A distinct connection of predator and prey. The creator and its subject. The visionary and the vision. The seeping fluorescent light washes his face with a blinding light as she attempts to look into the eyes of her possessor. She relinquishes all control and hesitantly lifts her eyes to the face of the person before her.

Harrison Bishop. Holy shit, it's Harrison Bishop. His name repeats like a metronome in her mind. *Harrison Bishop is here. Harrison Bishop is in the same room as I am. I can't believe I'm this close to Harrison Bishop!* Her eyes sparkle with excitement and her adrenaline beats to life within her chest. Finally gaining the strength to speak, she squeals out, "oh my God! You're Harrison Bishop!" Her breath is quick as she begins to hyperventilate with excitement. "*The* Harrison Bishop!"

Harrison presses his lips into a stern line and exhales a slow sigh through his nostrils. He begins to slowly pace as he examines the woman bound to her chair. Reviewing the handiwork of her restraints, he confirms that she is tied with a thick strand of nautical rope against an oversized wooden chair. The heels of her palms are tightly pressed to the chair's arms; her feet are constrained in a heavy sheet knot, her ankles uniformly restrained against the legs of the chair.

Continuing to circle, Harrison is silent in his audit as she progresses with her incessant talking. "What are you doing here? Do you know whose place this is? I just can't believe we're here together! Are you here to save me? I just can't believe it's you!" Her cheeks turn a flushed fuchsia as she nudges her shoulder, brushing a stray hair from her sight. She pulls against the restraints at her wrists only to be held by their grasp and her hands turn a ghastly shade of eggplant. Unconcerned with the binding, she continues her broad smile, causing her gums to peer from beneath her lips. She flutters her eyelashes in an attempt to appear coy and seductive despite her position.

Ceasing his prowl to stand before the woman, Harrison takes an exasperated breath and raises his left hand to her cheek. His fingertips linger as he traces the outline of her jaw. Her heartbeat is a powerful "hum" echoing off of the cellar's walls as she sinks into his embrace: *thim-thump, thim-thump, thim-thump*. His face shows a sublime mixture of annoyance and tranquility as he stares into the depths of her eyes, calculating his next move. He traces each feature of her face from her brow, to the small freckle beneath her eye, and across her rosy lips.

Taking in her beauty, Harrison admires her delicate features and thin frame. Her round eyes and raven black hair decay amidst the uneven lighting. Releasing a low sigh of wonderment, he questions to himself, *how can something so beautiful be this loud and annoying*? "Such a shame to waste such beauty," he whispers aloud to no one. His eyes flitter to life as he finally gives focus to the woman. "Can you tell me about the death of Simone Waters?" he asks, his voice murky within his throat.

Confusion paints the woman's face at the obscurity of the question. "Th-the one who died in that drunk driving accident?" she squeaks, as her heartbeat fades against the inquiry.

"Precisely," Harrison replies. "The one left for dead on the shoulder of Highway 46 while she bled out for nearly five hours until a construction crew found her mutilated body the following morning." His eyes are as dark as onyxes and his expression is completely indecipherable.

The woman forces a hard, throaty swallow, like a snake engulfing its prey in a single bite. "I tried to help her," she croaks, but Harrison raises his hand to quickly silence her.

Then, without warning, Harrison pulls a serrated knife out of his pocket. The blade is a cool and muted metal that does not deter the enthusiasm in the woman's face for her moment with Harrison Bishop. *The* Harrison Bishop. His arm moves swiftly like trapeze artist, swinging from his shoulder to his waist and then back to land gently against his hip.

A single trickle of blood drips from the woman's throat until the first wave of her ravenous heartbeat releases a cascade of hot, sticky blood down her chest. Looking up into his eyes, still gleaming with delight, the woman uses her last staggering breath to force out, "...Harrison...Bishop..."

CAVALIER: A Novel

Part One: **Summer**

Chapter One: **Mannish Boy**

The sun hangs flat against the horizon as the heat from the day idles among city streets. The summer air, now a thick mass, agonizes even the smallest of motions. The afternoon begins its descent into twilight as a deep lilac sky falls upon New Orleans.

Harrison Bishop's back is against the traffic as cars lug their way through the listless afternoon. His amber hair tousled into a polished, sun-kissed mess is now slick from the heat of the day. This time of year, temperatures easily push 100 degrees and although he his sporting his typical suit and tie ensemble, he still appears collected and at ease with his cool aura: a statuesque figure in the fleeting light.

Harrison's eyes are pursed, focused closely on a poster on the side of the withering bus stop. His stare slowly canvases the print as if he is memorizing its contents. He blinks slowly, never losing his line of sight on the image before him, his mind fixated as he becomes oblivious to the bustling world behind him.

A car slows down behind him and a high-pitched, "marry me, Bishop!" floats from the backseat as it passes. He dips his chin and turns his ear to the catcall. A smirk picks at the corner of his mouth and two slight dimples appear on his cheeks. A single exhale of laughter escapes his nose as he comes back to reality. He turns his face back to the poster and he cocks his head to the side. His smile settles into a face of content and he muses a quiet *how embarrassing* to himself as he laughs the idea out of his throat.

The poster is vivid with color and features a confident Harrison Bishop donning almost identical attire, a navy suit with caramel oxfords. His arms are strongly crossed as he powerfully stares down toward the poster's viewer. His green eyes pierce the bus stop's fogged plastic cover as if Harrison himself is standing behind the cheap material. The bright font gives details to a past event, a hospital tour featuring Harrison – a corporate meet-and-greet that predictably transformed into a fandemonium of autographs, photos, and motivational speeches, then he capped the night with nearly a barrel of alcohol until he poured himself into his bed around dawn.

"MEET THE CURE ALL KID!" the poster screams. Harrison's press manager said the phrase, which he had heard countless times, would be "catchy with not too much gloat." Now, the phrase usually goes in one ear and out the other, but tonight it takes the forefront of his mind. *What the hell was Jordan thinking? How the hell is that not gloating?* He lets out a low groan as he shakes his head in annoyance. *I'm going to start getting death threats again from church groups accusing me of acting as God.* He releases another deep laugh as he continues to shake his head at the thought.

Harrison turns on his heels to face the street. He rests his head back and allows the late afternoon sun to envelope his face. A deep sigh billows from his nostrils and he slowly opens his eyes to the street in front of him. Now alert, almost refreshed from his time spent alone with the poster, he clasps his hands and stretches out his arms in front of him to release eight small cracks from his knuckles. His hand reaches to support his chin and he turns his head sharply to either side to relieve two additional cracks from his neck.

Intensely observing the surround street, Harrison watches as people walk casually to and from the nearby shops and cafes. The city soaks up the last weeks of summer as the days begin to grow shorter. Women in their colorful sundresses drink wine and laugh loudly in unison on restaurant patios while men stand nearby, smoking their cigars in a circle. A few of the gentlemen nod in acknowledgement of Harrison, some addressing him by name. The voices blend together and begin to sound like crickets in the night, mindless chirps filling the slowly encroaching evening. The street is brightly lined with festively colored buildings bordered by white, ornate trim that accentuate their Creole and French architecture. Tourists and young professionals litter the confetti-colored storefronts and homes as Harrison makes his way to his next event.

Harrison's dark and sleek SUV is parked nearby a table of four middle-aged women, idly humming in the street. He approaches his vehicle and feels eight eyes scanning him as he walks in their direction. The voices hush as he arrives alongside their group, and their conversation takes a new movement as they begin to speak to one another with faint tones, excitedly mouthing the words, "*HARR-I-SON-BISH-OP.*" Although Harrison cannot hear them anymore, it is quite obvious that their conversation has just taken a new and enthusiastic turn.

Stopping at the car door, Harrison pauses before reaching out toward the handle and pulls a small white package out of his pocket. He can still feel the eyes of his newly found audience as the air around him lingers. Tearing the edge of the package, he removes a small white cloth from its contents; the smell of rubbing alcohol stings his nostrils. The women's eyes continue to watch him as he uses the towelette to swab the car handle's surface. When finished, he delicately folds the towelette over and over until it is returned to its original size, and he slides the towelette back into the original package. He then lightly tosses it into a nearby trash can and rubs his hands against each other.

Harrison reaches for the freshly cleaned door handle but he hesitates and peers over his shoulder at the table of women. Their eyes widen as they lean toward him. Harrison's face is pragmatic as his eyes connect with each woman. A small gasp escapes each woman's mouth as he looks into the corresponding set of pupils. He nods his head toward the SUV and he lets out an effortless, "you know, for the germs." A beat of silence fills the void between the two parties and the women's mouths, just as wide as their eyes, continue to stare into his face waiting for him to speak again.

Giving a coy wink in the women's direction, an uproar of laughter ensues as a charismatic smile crosses Harrison face and his dimples dig deep within his cheeks. The women cackle with flattery so robustly that their squeals of joy can be heard rolling down nearly a city block. Swiftly, he opens the SUV door, pausing to provocatively give the women a quick, "you ladies behave now," and lands inside, slamming the door behind him.

Harrison sinks in the dark leather of the backseat as the frigid temperatures of the cabin envelop him. "Turn it up please, Sampson," Harrison asks of his bodyguard as he recognizes the song playing on the radio. Sampson wordlessly replies with a slight nod and turns the knob of the stereo system until the music booms through the interior of the vehicle. Harrison begins to nod his head in time to the song and he silently mouths along.

Sampson, Harrison's bodyguard and most trusted confidant, was as mysterious in nature as he was unknown by Harrison. Enhanced by his dark hair and complexion, his chiseled face gave way to a pair of deep-set, kind eyes that glimmered with a touch of wisdom. However, pressing toward seven feet, his demeanor suggested he was a force to be reckoned with. He had many memorable and frightening tales of using his brute force to protect who seemed to be his only friend: Harrison.

Sampson was a military veteran, but he never disclosed to Harrison what service. This led to wild speculation until Sampson finally broke down and just agreed with whatever ludicrous idea Harrison had created in his mind. That is what Harrison always enjoyed about him, and although there were hardly any aspects of Harrison's life that Sampson didn't have at least some knowledge of, he rarely spoke, creating a perfectly balanced friendship.

"Where are we off to now, Sampson?" Harrison asks as he scans lackadaisically out of the window, continuing to sing along with the music.

"Monmount Center, sir. You have the St. John's Hospital Gala this evening," he replies in a matter-of-fact intonation.

"Speaking arrangement or social event?" Harrison questions with an irked tone.

"Both, sir," Sampson peers through the rear-view mirror to gauge his response.

"Ah, yes." A touch of concern flashes across Harrison's jade-green eyes as he momentarily pauses his singing in thought. "Time for the mannish boy to make his appearance and entertain the masses," he sarcastically croons.

Sampson reaches for the center console, waiting to trigger his next move. "Need a speech?"

"Yes, please. And a pen if you wouldn't mind," Harrison says with an appreciative but professional tone as Sampson's hand reaches into the console to produce a small stack of notecards and a pen. Reactively, Harrison kicks his right leg to land atop his left, creating a makeshift surface and scribbles amongst the elegant toast.

Thank you. It has been a pleasure having the opportunity to meet with all of you this fine evening. You sure are a lively bunch! [pause for laughter]

The work [ORGANIZATION] has provided has truly been a monumental endeavor, and I am extremely grateful to work alongside and continue to strive for [ONGOING WORK / EVENT PURPOSE.]

I'd like to take this time to thank the entire team at [ORGANIZATION], especially [ORGANIZATION LEADER] [pause for applause]. This group has worked diligently alongside my team at Bishop Enterprises, and I'd like to acknowledge their determination, patience, and most importantly, intellect to better the world around us. It is truly an honor to stand before this team, but the recognition goes to all of you. [pause, look through crowd]

Just by being here tonight, you are all telling the world that you want to better [PURPOSE OF EVENT], and that is more influential than a party or an award. This [AWARD] means the world to me, but the work you have all done means so, so much more. [raise glass to toast] This one is for all you. Cheers and have a great evening! [dispose of notecards]

As Harrison completes the notecards, he slips the pen into his breast pocket along with the stack and rolls down the window to allow the late summer air to tumble through the SUV. A sly smile touches his lips as his eyes brighten and he turns back to Sampson as they arrive to the event.

"Want to trade places tonight? You be me and I'll be you?"

"You couldn't pay me all the money in the world," Sampson replies with a slight laugh and an apathetic tone. Just as Harrison opens his mouth to snap back with a snarky remark, Sampson starts again with, "and I *know* that you think you could make that happen, sir." This stops Harrison in his tracks and causes a bellowing laugh to fill the cabin as they arrive at the final destination.

"Fair, fair. I'll trick you into it one of these days, Sampson," Harrison says as he makes his smooth exit from the backseat, but not before ducking his head back into the vehicle to remind Sampson: "Don't forget, I've only been turned down twice in my life and you're only holding a measly fifty percent of those." With a cool smile, he closes the door behind him and makes his way up the grandeur steps into the Museum of Natural History.

The Museum of Natural History towers stoically against the city block. Standing dauntingly with its oversized, cream-colored columns and surrounding emerald shrubbery, it always reminded Harrison of his childhood when he would spend hours on end combing through expansive books in his childhood library: encyclopedias, textbooks, any book he could find. The museum's brooding stonework and tremendous anterior alone could make any man feel like a small child all over again.

The traffic zips steadily behind as Harrison leisurely climbs the massive steps while his eyes fixate on his cell phone. Spotting a few coworkers and acquaintances who he greets, but nevertheless avoids until he spots his assistant, Kit Woodington, quickening his pace to meet him.

Kit a young man in his mid-twenties, looked to be barely legal. His tall, scrawny stature gave him the appearance of being easy to walk all over, but he had an honest face that made him easy to approach. His suit was too wide in the shoulders and slightly too short. His choppy hair always seemed to be in disarray, although his decisive attitude gave him a calming presence that Harrison admired and trusted to make sense of his professional career.

Harrison lands a full hand on to Kit's back as he greets him with a shoulder shake.

"Kit! You look like shit! Aren't I paying you enough to get a suit that fits you?" Harrison ribs, causing Kit's cheeks to tinge with crimson.

"No, no," Kit teases back, "you only pay me enough to make *you* look better. You know, take me down a few pegs so you don't feel threatened." Harrison stops mid-step and grips Kit's shoulder as he stutter steps in a modest stun. Holding eyes for a moment as Harrison's grip continues to dig into Kit's shoulder, he slowly pulls away and his eyes purse in response to the pinch of pain.

Kit is the first to break as he boisterously says, "got ya!" They walk in unison as Kit produces a pocket-sized notepad with a haphazard list of names strewn across the lined paper. "George Cocoran should be present this evening. You're looking to buy out his research facility in Alberta so I'll send him a drink from you later in the evening. Just play nice, don't mention the centuries between him and his wife, and the sale is yours."

"Ten-four, Kit," Harrison replies as if starring in their own budding cop episode. "Anyone else?"

"A couple. Kimberly Mason was a tentative RSVP but you're about to close down her microbial stability facility in Norway. Taller build, choppy blonde hair, and menacing stare. If you see her, steer clear."

"With pleasure. Anyone else?" Harrison asks, prodding for a specific answer.

"Just one – Charlie Meyer of the Rose Institute," Kit confirms as he slides the notepad back into his pocket. Harrison's eyes shift enough to cause Kit to snicker at the anticipation of some debauchery with his boss. "Were you hoping he'd be here? Need me to do anything special?"

"As a matter of fact, I am," Harrison broods into space. "Let's get him good and drunk. I need him to give me an offer I can't refuse." With that, the pair part ways into the night to begin their evening.

Every event Harrison attended felt like a surreal blur of politeness and half-hearted laughs. Although he knew these meet and greets were great for business, it felt like the same conversation had been had since the dawn of time.

Let's start this ballroom dance, he thinks as he waves down a cocktail waiter for his first drink of the evening. "Make it as strong as your jaw," he flirts with the man as he taps the crest of his jawline with his fore and middle fingers.

Pausing before the door, Harrison appraises the ballroom. *Bar? Check*, he lists internally. *Bland talking points? Hello Mister So-And-So. Have you been following the news lately? Something happened somewhere with someone else!* He mockingly practices to himself. *And easy exit? Check,* he mentally notes before rolling back his shoulders with a mild cough. "Let's do this."

"You've been such an inspiration to my daughter!" An unimpressive middle-aged woman in an even more unimpressive evening gown spews at Harrison through wine stained teeth. "I told her to apply to whatever university had the best schools of science and forget about partying. I want her to save the world, too!"

Harrison chews his cheek as he pushes his tousled hair out of his line of sight and replies with a generic, "our youth is really going to do great work." He takes a sip from his fresh vodka martini. Glancing through the room for his next mundane conversation, he idly pauses as he waits for his first nip of alcohol to seep into his brain like poisonous venom.

A man of about two-thirds the height of Harrison yells into his lapel, "HARRISON! Let me tell you something!" His drink spills over his rocks glass and on to the floor as he empathically thrusts his drink into the air. "This new division proposal is going to really wow you!"

Taking a step back to avoid the tidal wave of scotch, Harrison gives the small man a phony, "Is that so, Doug?" and gracefully peels the drunken hand from his suit. Once freed, he takes a long sip from his drink and with an unamused response says, "please, tell me more. I've been dying to ask you all about it," as the man starts what will certainly be nothing of interest to Harrison.

"No, no, NO!" the too skinny woman yells at the almost too fat man, "the geriatric wing of the hospital was a gift from Monica, you idiot. You cut the fucking ribbon!"

Harrison taps an impatient finger on the stem of his martini glass as his eyes move between the arguing couple. *How the hell did Martin land Sherry?*

"You don't think I would remember if I cut a ribbon the size of a python in front of Monica? Harrison, tell Sherry that you donated that hospital wing and she's being ridiculous," Martin yells redirecting his anger toward Harrison, his booming voice lost in the sound of the jazz band swelling through the massive chamber.

"You know," Harrison leans in, prodding the sleeping bear, "I heard Monica tell Doug earlier that she had asked her assistant to remove the event from her calendar. Something about a tax write-off that wasn't sitting well with her accountant and they wanted to ensure it couldn't be tied back to him." Both of their mouths hang slack as the anger in the Sherry's face rises just enough for Harrison to polish off his drink and raise a hand to nobody to yell out, "yes? I'll be right there!" With a satisfied smirk, he walks between the pair and their booming voices collide behind him.

The evening continues on with a waltz of humdrum conversation. Harrison engages in minimal small talk. He drinks vodka martinis as quickly as the wait staff can supply. He causes a little mischief as he dances through the incessant, mind-numbing chit-chat until he gives his speech about saving the world or ending world hunger. He flirts with the staff and guests in hopes of finding a companion for the evening, wondering if he'll get drunk enough to create a game with a few colleagues. These events had become so second nature to him that once his work and social lives blended together, he succumbed to his playboy lifestyle without apprehension.

After what feels like days of asinine pleasantries with barely anyone under the age of fifty, Harrison finally sections off a corner of the ballroom where he closely converses with a young, redheaded waitress. His hand presses into the wall behind her head as a nearly empty martini glass dangles in the other. Harrison touts the waitress a coy look as he finishes the punch line of a joke that causes her head to tilt with an immense chuckle, filling their private corner.

As Harrison seals the deal with a cool, "would you like to take this somewhere a bit more private?" he feels himself topple backwards, being tugged toward the crowd by the seam of his suit jacket. Skillfully, he steadies the remainder of his drink, calls out a calm, "I'll find you later!" just as Kit begins launching him up to the stage. Downing his lingering martini, Kit grabs the glass from his hand before replacing it with a flute of champagne and rocketing Harrison up by his rear to the top of the stage steps. Harrison is welcomed to the stage with an uproar of applause. With one last look over his shoulder, Kit hisses with emphasized, muted pronunciation, "*BE-HAVE.*"

The crowd's cheers die down as the jazz band dwindles to a stop. The event's host is clapping along with the audience as he motions with his free hand to Harrison to stand beside him. The host is wearing an over-the-top baby blue suit with iridescent purple trim that forces Harrison's eyes into his head as he reminds himself, *don't stare at the suit. Don't stare at the suit. Don't stare at the God-awful suit.* He continues to repeat his new mantra in his head as he balances the multiple martinis he's had.

"We are honored this evening to be accompanied by this year's largest donor, Mr. Harrison Bishop," the emcee begins, causing Harrison's cheeks to flush and to give his perfect "Who, me?" face in response – his publicist once told him that look was a "fucking goldmine." He takes another step closer knowing that he'll only need to endure a few agonizing minutes of this nitwit reciting his Wikipedia page, give the speech, and then find the redhead or another martini – whichever Kit doesn't block first.

"Mr. Bishop, while he doesn't show it, has traveled a long way from his modest home in Helena, Montana, where he spent his early years in an all-boys foster home. After a cruel childhood, Mr. Bishop worked his way through grade school, saving every penny he could along the way, and studying day and night to achieve his goals. He truly is the mentor all of our children should idolize." The emcee pauses as Harrison gives the crowd a slanted smile and a "See, I'm just like you," face that tugs at his dimples and instructs the host to continue.

"Once Mr. Bishop turned eighteen, he moved out to Illinois to attend the prestigious Northwestern University, studying in its newly founded School of Microbiological Medicine with the nation's top research scientists and practices. In his final years of graduate school, Mr. Bishop and his team of researchers discovered The Episcopus

Aerobium, or TEA, the organism that would go on to cure the common cold and that *one* modest discovery was able to rid our world of disease, cancer, and the agony that accompanied these horrendous ailments." The host pauses again as a small outburst of applause fills the room and Harrison gives a modest but proud nod, accompanied by a flat smile at the accomplishment.

I am going to skin this twat alive if he doesn't hurry this up. I have a waitress to attend to, Harrison reminds himself as he gives a doe-eye look through his fluttering lashes.

The emcee clears his throat as the crowd turns its attention back to him. "From here, Mr. Bishop established his own research operation, Bishop Research, which would begin its immeasurable good work within cancer research and grow to be the Bishop Enterprises we know today, changing the landscape of the human race as we now see it." Another applause erupts through the crowd as Harrison taps his foot in annoyance. "And that is why we are gathered here this evening, to thank *the* Harrison Bishop for his generous work within our St. John's research team. Countless lives have been saved by the hands and brain of such a wonderful, intelligent, and most impressively, young man."

The crowd now stands in ovation as they eagerly await the event they have drank so heavily in preparation for this evening: the moment to hear their duly appointed God bless their futile ears.

"Ladies and gentlemen, it is my honor to present to you this evening the wunderkind himself, the Cure All Kid, Mister Harrison Bishop," the emcee concludes as Harrison approaches the microphone.

Harrison shakes the hand of the emcee, giving him a polite smile and thanking him for the irritating introduction he has heard far too many times in his lifetime. "That was quite wonderful, sir. No one warms the mic up quite like you," Harrison lies through his pearly white teeth.

Landing at the microphone, Harrison gives a heartfelt smile to the crowd as he pulls the cookie cutter notecards from the breast pocket of his suit coat. His forced smile canvases his face as he begins his speech.

"Thank you. It has been a pleasure getting the opportunity to meet with all of you this fine evening. You sure are a lively bunch!" he recites, fawning over the crowd's scheduled laughter.

<<<

A boyish Harrison is perched on the front lawn of his childhood home. At the awkward age of thirteen, he sits cross-legged with an oversized book across his too thin thighs as his moppy hair blocks his eyes from the summer sun.

The home behind him is small and lackluster. White, vinyl siding and makeshift shutters pull away at the hinges. The yard is flooded with weeds and untouched shrubbery that questions if anyone has visited the home for weeks. The only signs of life are the dozens of broken toys littered across the lawn and driveway as a miniature Harrison hides away from the world.

Looking up to the sky, Harrison squints through his blonde hair, his bright green eyes searching for something beyond this world. He returns back to the thick textbook in front of him, readjusting the photo spreading across the withered edges. A faded night sky fills the pages and Earth's moon is positioned in the center, as if a beacon of light to the reader. Once again, he adjusts his positioning but ultimately sets the bulky book in the thick grass and stands to view the photo more clearly. Returning back to the sky, he can see the moon through the daylight sun and spins ever so slightly, readjusting his gaze. He lifts his hands to his forehead and pushes back his unkempt hair as he freezes, transfixed on the dot in the sky.

How can something so big be so small? Harrison wonders to himself, taken aback by the tiny speck far into the distance. *If I was there, I bet it wouldn't be that small.* He stretches out a lanky arm, his thumb lifted in his line of sight. Tilting his thumb, he covers the miniscule dot before him. He continues the motion, covering and uncovering, until he hears an echoing boom from the screen door of the home.

"Dinner," says a growing voice, reverberating through the tree-lined street. "Don't make me ask twice!" the man continues in his menacing tone and causes Harrison to startle then coil into himself.

Taking one last moment, Harrison leans his head back into the afternoon sun and a summer breeze tousles his hair across his face as another, "HAROLD. I'm not saying it again!" crashes through the door. A man's hand bangs against the screen of the door causing Harrison to wince and release a small shriek.

Defeated, Harrison walks toward the front door. *My name is Harrison*, he thinks to himself distraughtly. *Harr-i-son*, he overly pronunciates with protruding eyes before he is pushed aside by two older boys.

"Get the fuck out of the way, faggot!" they shout over their shoulders back at Harrison as they run inside the home, bursting through the screen door in a cacophony of commotion.

Tom and Gary were too large to be seventeen. Their broad bodies like tree trunks made them appear twice their age and at a towering six feet, there wasn't much in Helena that wasn't being overrun by the two oversized idiots. While most of their other brothers followed like their own personal lackeys, the remaining brothers were forced into a life of pain and torment. The only aspect keeping the pair from morphing into one superhuman Loch Ness Monster was

Gary's telling scar across his face, from his temple to his chin. The scar had convinced Harrison he was a villain from a James Bond film and therefore could not be trusted. The two had been expelled from the local public school and were now forced into homeschooling by Harrison's foster parents, causing anger and tension through the fifteen-person home. When they weren't avoiding their schoolwork or demonizing their siblings, they always seemed to be in trouble with local police and pinning their angst on to Harrison.

Harrison had been arrested twice by the age of twelve, and in one instance he was asleep in his bunk bed at the time of the crime, something not a soul in their home seemed to believe. The first was for spray painting the word "DICK" across the sheriff's garage door, a petty crime that made Harrison laugh until he realized he had allegedly committed the act. The second was for breaking the eye socket of a foster brother, which, in the heat of the altercation, very well could have been his undoing, but was never discussed long enough to determine.

As Harrison reaches the threshold of the dining room, his foster mother starts to sob. He watches her shoulders silently shudder as she tries to muffle her tears. Her sandy blonde hair and dreary features are famished by the years of abuse from her unruly family. She holds two bowls of a sad casserole as Tom and Gary scream at each other across the table. Gary suspends two younger brothers in the air by their collars and shouts to Tom about how he wants to, "clunk their melons together," then asks Gary if can guess the sound. Both boys cry in pain as they choke against their collars strangling their necks. "C'mon Tommy! Guess the noise! I'll bet you whatever is in their pockets that I'm spot-fucking-on!"

The other boys around the table are in a melee, attempting to stop the madness or chanting to hear the results of the bet. Harrison tightens his eyes into hard lines and pulls his hands to his temples as he crumples his hair within his fists, blocking out the world around him. *Just stop it,* he screams internally, praying for the hysteria to stop. "Just fucking stop," he says under his breath, the sound surprising him as it crosses his lips and forces his eyes open in response.

"What did you fucking say, faggot?" Gary retorts as he drops both of his siblings to the floor with a thud. Kicking one of the brothers out of his pathway, he pushes toward Harrison and repeats, "what did you *fucking* say?"

Harrison takes a steadying breath, preparing for the pain. *It won't last long,* he thinks. There isn't much room around the table and his foster father will care more about dinner than waiting to witness what will presumably go on to be called the "pounding of a lifetime." Releasing his shoulders back and lifting his chin to meet the face of his maker, Harrison opens his mouth to begin saying, "gar—" But before he can squeak out the name, Gary thrusts his arm in a swift motion up to Harrison's neck, launching him through the air. Landing on the wall of the dining room with a crash, he collapses on the floor beneath him.

As their foster father enters the room, he surveys the incident and before the others can grasp the events taking place he commands, "either eat or I'll put you all right next to Harold on the floor."

"This one is for all of you. Cheers and have a great evening!" Harrison concludes as he folds the notecards in half and slips them into the pocket of his pants before taking a smooth sip from his glass of champagne. Reaching the end of the stage, he flags down the redheaded cocktail waitress and puts in his order. "Vodka martini and meet me in the coatroom in thirty," he dictates with a subtle wink and a devilish grin. He begins to polish off the champagne as he scans the room for his next target.

Like clockwork, Harrison commends Kit as a visibly drunk Charlie Meyer approaches the stage, a glass of scotch clinking within in either hand. Tipping his head to the side, Harrison appraises Charlie. He is not unattractive, but has a bit of a paternal look to him. With salt and pepper hair and a thinning hairline, he looks to be in his late fifties, but wears a suit that most likely fit about a decade previously. He adjusts his tortoise glasses as he stumbles to land at Harrison's feet with look of excitement and urgency in his eyes.

"J-just the man I was looking for," Charlie stammers in broken speech, shoving a lukewarm scotch into Harrison's hand. "I have considered your offer and spoken with the board," he begins before slurring a drunken whistle with giddy shoulders. "Oh, boy. Do we have a proposition for *you.*"

Chapter Two: **Lolita**

"How fucking stupid do you think I am, Nicolas?" Daisy growls through her pearlescent teeth and rosy pink lips as she leans across her wooden desk to the middle-aged man sitting in an overstuffed leather chair before her. Her eyes are blazing green and her long, mousy blonde hair is thrown back into a lion's mane. Her hands are pressed heavily into the surface of the desk, a stack of contracts lying before her. "I want you to say just how stupid you think I am so I can tell that you know what an idiot you are for walking into this office thinking you'd tell me how we'd be laying out this procurement," she chides as she continues her beratement of the crumbling man.

Daisy Stone, the Chief Operations Officer of mergers and acquisitions of The Rose Institute, was always a surprise to those who entered her office. Her kind eyes and structured face felt like a ploy once she opened her mouth and annihilated the people in her path as if they were attacking her cubs. *Poor Nicolas*, Daisy muses in her mind as she watches his face visibly shake. He could barely control his emotions, feeling a prick in his eyes as he worried he may begin to tear up.

The Rose Institute was the up and coming microbiological research syndicate in the United States, and with the help of Daisy, it had recently begun branching into international territory to stretch its reach as far as its dollars would allow. Nearly at the peak of breaking into the key players in the industry, Daisy had taken it upon herself to force any competitor in The Rose Institute's path to succumb to her powers or lose what was left of their careers.

Panicked Nicolas, with his hairline quickly receding and his suit just barely fitting his growing waist, was not prepared for someone of barely thirty years of age, and especially this attractive, to admonition him this early in the day. He hadn't been subjected to such torture since his mother reprimanded him in grade school. The darkness of Daisy's office encapsulates him like an unwelcome sauna. He begins to sweat, at first sporadically across his temples, and then so profusely that he considers reaching into his briefcase for a second handkerchief. The office is too dark, much too dark for mid-morning, but by his unsettled demeanor, he may as well have been vacationing on the surface of the sun.

With the curtains tightly drawn, Daisy continues her shadowy brood into Nicolas's dampened stare. She preferred her office a dark wasteland, instilling fear in anyone who had the nerve to come to her and ask her for, well, anything. She had had the walls painted a seeping shade of navy blue and decorated the office with dark leather furniture, creating an overwhelming, nearly suffocating appearance from the intensity. The room always smelled of stale cigars and a hint of whiskey, which only contributed to the masculine and aggressive energy that did not correlate when sitting across from Daisy's angelic face. She didn't belong in this office, but her contrast in look let any occupants know that she commanded the room.

The only pops of color throughout the office are Daisy's cobalt blue dress and the many gold, silver, and crystal trophies that line the shelves behind her desk. The awards range from "Up and Coming Entrepreneur" to "Highest Grossing Acquisition of the Decade" – she even included her miniscule "The Rose Institute Trivia Champion" medal. Every word that screamed from her behind desk reinforced the importance of her career and no one was ever allowed to forget.

"Miss Stone," Nicolas pleads with a thick, German accent, "we're counter-offering with our *entire* genetics research division for 15 percent below market rate and including *every* member of our staff for free of charge. We're losing nearly half our yearly income. I can't go back to Munich with anything less than what I've provided you."

Shaking her head with a wry laugh, Daisy stands back on her heels and lowers her chin to look through her long lashes then into his eyes, now playing coy with her sparkling gaze. "Nicolas, I may look young and naive, but I didn't get my ass in this desk by taking pathetic deals like this one you dropped in my lap," her tone now apathetic and definitive as she tosses the stack of papers on to her desk for dramatic effect. She effortlessly sits herself into her chair and glances at the contracts again before looking him directly in his disoriented eyes.

"You know," Daisy begins again, drawing him in, "the moment I get my development team through your doors, your stocks will be worth fifteen times what they are now," she croons into his now fragile face. *Finish him,* she tells herself, as his throat releases a defeated sigh. She senses her words land with a deliberate intention and coolly smiles before hammering the nail into the coffin. "The Rose Institute is shelling out the best deal your team has seen in the last quarter century, Nicolas. There is no way you're saying no to me today. You and your...*nanny* will be set for life." She hisses to him as one slender eyebrow rises and a smile flickers around the corners of her lips. "Say yes to me, Nicolas. You know you want to."

Guiding a defeated Nicolas from her office, Daisy exits toward her next meeting as he mutters an angry "Lolita" between heavy breaths. Quickening to her powerful stride, her assistant Courtney appears at her side and follows in Daisy's speedy steps.

Courtney Lacelon, a cute, petite girl with a shoulder length bob of dark brown hair and a round face had may have been the only willing individual to take on the role as Daisy's assistant. Her doe-like features drew Daisy to her, and she was pleased that although she was short in stature, she could keep up with Daisy's strong personality even in the most dire circumstances.

"While I have you for just a moment," Courtney hurriedly asks Daisy as she carries an overwhelming stack of papers, eagerly trying to multitask, "anything you need before your three o'clock, Miss Stone?"

"This afternoon's agenda." Daisy commands as Courtney continues to keep pace while they tear down the sleek corridor.

The Rose Institute's corporate office was fitting of the company's personality. Formerly a shoe factory, the exposed brick and piping were softened by the frosted glass conference room and refined lighting. The hard and gentle facade was the analogy that Daisy always pitched when discussing the institute's organization: progressive technology with human instincts, or some bullshit like that.

"You're meeting with the division heads to get an update on their internal restructuring," Courtney says, reading from the tablet atop her tumbling stack of papers. "After that, you'll be meeting with *The Washington Post* for its segment on up and coming entrepreneurs. Then, back-to-back transitional team meetings and –" Daisy pauses mid-step to raise a delicately manicured eyebrow instructing Courtney explained herself. "Yeah. I've been putting off telling you this, but you'll need to let go of Warren and Bartlett's teams."

"Why the fuck would we do that? The merger was completed less than a year ago." Daisy huffs in anger, provoking a wince from Courtney.

"We've had nearly two dozen acquisitions this year. A couple of them needed to fall to the wayside, Miss Stone," said Courtney apologetically with the bad news. She did not want to go toe-to-toe with the lioness herself. She continues, "*However*, Charlie said he has some exciting news for the executive team and will present it to everyone at tonight's happy hour!" she said, attempting to salvage the moment.

Charlie Meyer, Daisy's eccentric boss and president of The Rose Institute, had become somewhat of a father to her over the last few years. With her hectic schedule and perpetual obsession with advancing her career, Daisy had put her parents on the backburner and made her work the only family she needed. His round glasses and quickly diminishing hair gave Charlie the look of an earnest professor, but his horrendous jokes and desire to meddle in his employees' lives made him the office dad. He was a lovable dork that everyone could not help but adore.

"Any chance that if I promise to double your holiday bonus that you'll handle the transitional team meetings?" Daisy proposes as they regain their strides through the hall.

Courtney gives a flimsy laugh, pulling at a distant memory that gives her round cheeks a flush. "Yeah, I don't think those people appreciated being fired by someone they'd never met, let alone me reading the notice from a bar napkin you threw at me while you finished your margarita."

"Courtney, we've discussed this," Daisy explains with a motherly tone. "That was an *amazing* margarita *and* I bought you a pitcher of them to say thank you for your hard work and dedication to this organization," Daisy sweetly hums, her eyes lighting up as the two suppress their laughter, attempting to remain professional.

Ignoring the inappropriate memory, Country presses on, "I'll leave a few wardrobe options in your office for *The Post*," she continues. Before Daisy can say anything, Courtney says, "I'll put them in the order of most to least work appropriate depending on the look of the journalist. He'll be here at 2:45, you can get a peek before you meet him."

"What would I do without you, Court?" Daisy purrs in response. "If you were a man, I would have fucked you by now."

"Well, we all saw what happened at last year's Christmas party, so I guess there's still hope for our undying love," Courtney replies in a sarcastic tone without looking up from her tablet and parting ways with Daisy as she arrives at her destination. Continuing down the hall, Daisy calls playfully after her. "Playing hard to get is only going to make me want you more!"

$<<<$

"I *promise* I won't tell Mom," a six-year-old Daisy calls from a patch of lush grass. Her hair is a blinding blonde mess of curls that billow against the summer wind, and a girlish smile reveals a barren hole from a recently lost tooth. Her haphazardly fastened jean overalls are more grass stains than denim. She raises her hands to shield her eyes from the afternoon sun, looking for Lily.

Daisy's baby sister, Lily, peers an eager face over the edge of their shabby tree house nestled away amongst the overgrown trees in their expansive backyard. Her hair is an equally vibrant shade of sun-kissed blonde, but her eyes are a luring shade of ocean blue.

"You double promise?" Lily sheepishly calls as she flashes a gap-toothed smile.

"I double, *triple* promise," Daisy shouts as she traces an "X" across her chest. "Cross my heart and hope to die that I will catch you." She gazes upward with excited eyes as Lily rises to her feet, steadying herself along an oversized limb, and braces against the edge of the worn timber.

Since before Lily could walk, she had become Daisy's shadow, a shrunken photocopy of Daisy's spirit that kept their parents in a whirlwind of mesmerizing chaos and sisterly elation. If they weren't digging up buried treasure in the backyard, they were inventing a machine to send their parents back in time or franchising a neighborhood lemonade stand while pocketing the profits. Their spunk and passion was a contagious mix that was hard to miss.

"Okay, I'm going to jump on three," Lily announces, mimicking the actions of her impending jump. Her hands grip tightly in preparation as she nervously curls her lips inward.

"I'm ready for you," Daisy affirms with both arms stretched lengthwise in preparation for the jump; a catcher waiting for the pitch, steadying herself for a fastball.

"One," Lily begins, her earnest eyes wide and lively.

"Two," Daisy continues dragging in an excited breath.

"Three!" the two yell in unison as Lily steps backward before launching herself with a barefooted leap from the wooden platform. She stretches out her arms as she closes her eyes and savors the wind across her cheeks, her unruly mane cast in disarray across her shoulders.

Sweeping past Daisy, Lily spirals in her momentum, landing not against skin but passing the warmth of her sister and falling directly into the dense grass. Daisy hears a deafening "snap," looks over at Lily, and sees her sister's lips begin to tremble.

Frantic eyes dart back and forth and the duo looks from the tree house to the grass, and then finally to the fragmented bone jutting out of Lily's wrist. The blood streams steadily from Lily, a red river amongst the green grass.

Lily takes an uneven breath, tears pooling in her navy eyes before shakily saying, "please don't tell Mom."

Daisy waits patiently at the conference room table as an intern pours two cups of coffee. The interviewer, Jason Myrtle, rifles through his list of questions in haste, obviously unprepared. The two are seated across from each other at the twelve-person table in a corner conference room of The Rose Institute, creating far too much space for the intimate interview. The views of the New Orleans' skyline is breathtaking as the summer sun caresses the city's landscape, filling the sky with an indigo hue. It was the ideal location of power Daisy was hoping to manufacture for such a meeting.

"I only have a handful of questions," Jason begins as he prefaces the interview and props his voice recorder in the center of the glass table, "but think of this as more of a conversation and less of an interview. Our lifestyle section readers prefer grit and personality to financial endeavors."

Jason adjusts his horn-rimmed glasses as he continues shuffling through the stack of papers before him. He's shorter than Daisy had expected, round and quirky, but has an inquisitive look to him. He has the look of a journalist rather than an editor. It's obvious he's a beginner, and even more obvious that he can easily be won over. His trendy attire of a bird patterned shirt and open blazer with jeans alerts Daisy that the interview will be easy. *This is going to look perfect framed in my office*, she notes to herself as she rolls her shoulders back and tosses her wavy hair over her shoulder.

"Okay, I think I'm ready!" Jason blurts out as he sets the stack of papers in front him like an ill prepared news anchor. He takes his first hard look into her eyes and pauses, feeling the awkwardness in the air, then blurts out, "I feel like I already know everything about you. You have quite the repertoire: upper-middle class family from Midwestern Minnesota, the definition of a perfect childhood, although it was quite sad to hear about your sister's illness. Though, you were able to make the most of your childhood by studying at Northwestern University under the teachings of *the* Mr. Harrison Bishop until building up The Rose Institute into the unstoppable powerhouse that it is today. Friends with almost every illustrious celebrity in town—"

"With." Daisy states assuredly, causing Jason to stop mid-sentence. The room stills as Jason does not register Daisy's correction. Her lips purse and her eyes narrow. "*With* Harry. Not under," she states, presenting a polite smile as she waits for Jason to catch up.

"*With* Harrison Bishop," Jason adjusts as he continues on. "You're the perfect mix of beauty and brains, all the while keeping up with an elusive socialite lifestyle along the coast. You live this fairytale story – it's just so cool to be speaking with you today," he gushes.

Daisy relaxes as a friendly smile tugs at her cheeks. She leans back in her chair as she waits for Jason to regain his composure.

Jason catches himself, realizing he is beginning to gush, and looks back to his notes attempting to retrieve the moment. "Tell me about Daisy Stone," he begins, immediately closing his eyes as he hears the absurdity in the vagueness of his question.

Daisy's cat eyes close as she dips her chin. She leans forward, placing her wrists on the table's edge as her hands clasp together with power. Her white, silk blouse hinting at the cleavage below causes Jason to swallow hard at the image under the fabric. Letting a delicate snort of laughter from her nostrils, she feels herself take control of the room. "What exactly would you like to know," she asks, trailing off and showing her dominance as she waits for him to repeat his name.

"J-Jason. Sorry, it's Jason," he stammers in response. "Mr. Myrtle," he says in a professional tone.

"Of course," she warmly returns. "What exactly would you like to know, *Jason*? I have a mint condition autobiography in my office if you'd like to take a look." Daisy answers facetiously.

"S-sorry. That was a dumb question," says Jason, beginning to glisten with sweat in such close proximity to Daisy's cool aura. He looks around the room to verify they are alone and whispers, "this is my first in-person interview with someone of such…" he searches for the word. "Stature. It's intimidating."

Daisy drops her head backward and releases as calming laugh as her piercing eyes return back to Jason. "Don't you worry. Let me help you out a bit," she coos. Giving him a quick wink that gives him a flush, she continues on. "How about, 'what is the greatest disparity between your career and social life, Miss Stone?'" Daisy asks herself as Jason's eyes light up and he hastily scrawls the question on the paper in front of him. Without skipping a beat, she answers her own question. "Great question, Jason! You're such a natural!" A charismatic smile uncovers her teeth. "My career is just a career. It is part of what makes me a person. It does not define me as a human. My personal life is my time. I'm not leading a team or closing a deal, so I get to do more than just be *Miss* Daisy Stone. I can be 'just

Daisy,'" she says, the idea wrinkling her eyes as a genuine smile settles on her face.

Frantically taking notes, Jason continues, "what is it that guides you to find the illustrious Daisy?"

Looking up to the ceiling, Daisy mulls over the question for a moment. "I enjoy traveling the world. You know, stepping outside of my element and challenging myself to grow on a human level. The Rose Institute has been steadily growing for the last decade and is on the cusp of taking on some of the giants in our industry. It's nice to break away from the corporate ladder and explore the world."

"Where is the most profound place you've traveled? "Jason asks, as he nods in agreement and digs further into Daisy's mind.

"Northern Scotland," Daisy responds without hesitation. "The calm and serenity is really what I desire. I spend nearly every moment of the day with people – meetings and phone calls and cocktail hours. An escape from the madness of my career is what I'm ultimately seeking so I can focus on what makes me happy."

"And what makes you happy?" Jason asks, no longer diligently note-taking, but asking with curious admiration.

Daisy delicately considers the question as she raises a pen to her lips. Rolling the tip between her teeth as the question marinates in the room before realizing the simplicity in the answer, she begins to chuckle. "Crushing every competitor in my path until The Rose Institute owns the entire free world."

The blasé answer doesn't hit Daisy's eyes and Jason holds his breath at the severe response. He opens his mouth to press further, but closes his lips knowing that his editor is going to love this raw interaction. He gives a solemn nod and scribbles down a shorthand response as he waits impatiently for her to continue.

"In all actuality, I want the world to see what a woman in power looks like in this day and age. For example, I'm being interviewed for your lifestyle section, not the financial section." Daisy continues on, ignoring the metaphorical slap across Jason's face. Her tone now harsh as she raises an eyebrow and casually tosses the pen onto the tabletop. "I'm not stupid. I know how a woman of my position is expected to behave, but I produce double, if not triple, the work that an average male does in this industry. So," she pauses as she leans ever so slightly into the table while a slack-mouthed Jason mimics her actions, as if he's joining in on a secret. Mirroring his earlier motions, Daisy looks around the room to verify they are alone and whispers with a hint of destruction, "I'm going to crush the male species into oblivion, one sale at a time. Then fill a pool with their tears and swan dive off the fucking high board."

The moment sits between the two as if Jason is frozen in time. Daisy pulls back and gives him another wink as an alluring smile fills her face. "Or I'll just start selling low calorie vodka, make a fortune, and wait until *Bravo* calls me for my own reality show. I'm fine with either at this point."

Still in awe, Jason leans back into his chair. Exhaling throatily, he regains his consciousness. He lifts his glasses atop his head and announces to no one in particular, "Holy shit. I can't tell if I should cry or buy you dinner."

Daisy's lips curl into a satisfied smirk as she straightens her back with a confident tout. She clasps her hands subtly across the conference room table before raising her brows to ask, "any other questions?"

Chapter Three: **Brandy**

Harrison stares through the table of chattering men around him, his mouth pursed and his brow furrowed as his eyes fall into an unfocused trance. Seated with six businessmen who are babbling through contracts and legalese as they eat their meal, he feigns interest while nudging a Brussels sprout from one edge of his plate to the other with his fork.

The luxurious Prise du Jour, infamous for its views of Lake Pontchartrain and historical French architecture was one of Harrison's favorite locations in the city. Sitting back in his chair, he scans the room and admires the century-old decor that he liked to imagine his ancestors built when they first came to this country. The dark crimson walls along with the ornate gold fixtures and trim, paired with the soft candles created the perfect atmosphere for interacting with the opposite sex: a romantic ambience that invited women to let their hair down and land in the arms of a welcoming Harrison Bishop.

Harrison leans deeper into his seat, stretching out his legs before him as he crosses his arms and relaxes, still gazing through the man in front of him. His boyish positioning tugs against the collar of his suit as he shifts his eyes, catching the dark pupils of a young brunette waitress cleaning glassware behind the bar.

"If Philip can handle the Prague location and Simmons can keep the Rio locations moving smoothly, I'm fine keeping Henderson here," Harrison defiantly announces to the table, all eyes now on him, but he continues his appraisal of the waitress as she continues to work.

The woman is youthful with her dark, shoulder length hair and dainty features. Her deep brown eyes, thin frame, and poor posture leave Harrison to guess she is college-aged, maybe twenty or twenty-one. She continues to stare mindlessly at the glasses she's polishing until she senses she's being watched. She quickly turns her head and locks eyes with Harrison. He holds her glance momentarily until he breaks eye contact to coolly turn his attention back to the conversation, causing her cheeks to flush cherry red.

A feeble boy carrying a teddy bear taps Harrison on the shoulder, interrupting the men's discussion. Harrison leans back so that he's balancing himself on the two back legs of his chair.

"How can I help you, young man?" he charismatically greets the boy as his mother apologetically catches up to hold his shoulders and pull him back to her. Harrison stops her with a soft "no, no," and places his hand out to stop her.

"Hello Mr. Bishop," he says shyly, looking to the floor and clutching his teddy bear closer to him. "My name is Joseph Jackson, III, and I would just like to thank you for saving my mommy and helping her get better and everything that y'all have done for us," he blurts out graciously in one long train of thought. After a noisy gulp of breath, he continues: "I wanted to give you my teddy bear to say thank you for saving my mommy." With his declaration, he thrusts the bear straight in the direction of Harrison. The boy's eyes are still glued to the floor, hair now piling across his face and covering his eyes.

Harrison gives a soft chuckle, his stern face softening as his eyes widen and his mouth curls into a smile. He swings his long legs around to sit in front of the small boy and as his forearms land on his thighs. Leaning forward, he drops his head to catch the boy's eyesight. Holding this stance, he can feel the eyes of his dinner guests and the tables around him now turning to watch the interaction, but he continues to keep his eyes fixed on the boy. Carefully, he reaches out an index finger to the boy's chin and lifts his face to meet his gaze, holding this position for a few moments.

Harrison face breaks into a magnificent grin and his dimples pull at his cheeks as he puts his hand back in his lap. Sitting up straight, he whispers, "stand up, son. Let me get a look at you," as his face beams with an adolescent smirk.

The boy brings the bear back to his chest and jumps to stand with over-exaggerated attention, as if a tiny soldier. Giving him a once over, Harrison gives him a slight nod of approval, and in a hushed but sincere tone, he says to the boy and his mother, "you know what? I'll make you a deal." The mother and son lean forward, hanging on his every word. "If you pinkie promise me that you'll stay in school and get good grades," he says, presenting a slender finger to the now gawking boy, "I'll let you keep the bear. It'll be our little secret."

With a delighted smile, the boy responds with a sheepish, "I promise!" He grabs Harrison's pinkie and gives his hand a meager shake, just as Harrison gives him a subtle wink and tousles the boy's hair.

The mother mouths a heartfelt "thank you" to Harrison and ushers the boy back to their seats as the tables around them let out a muted "aww." Realizing he has an audience, Harrison gives a bashful smile to those around him and returns his attention back to his dinner guests just as the brown-haired waitress passes their table. Holding his body still, he closes his eyes just in time to open and connect with the eyes of the waitress, maintaining contact as she passes while hiding her girlish smile.

The bar of the restaurant sparks to life as the restaurant's patrons hum with an intoxicated buzz and the dining room guests slowly migrate into the bar. The staff begins lowering the lights, setting a darker mood and giving the room a sultry feel as a nearby hostess drops tea lights into amber and crimson votives. The bar back, covered with an oversized mural of the Champs-Élysées, sets a romantic feel as the wait staff bustles about in clean white button-downs and black silk ties, transporting the patrons to Paris.

The gentlemen lounge near the end of the semicircle bar while Harrison drapes an elbow across the bar's gold surface and leans into the heavy wood front. He holds a glass of scotch as two of the men next to him argue over a sporting event that he only partially engages in, as his sights are set on other objectives. He has removed his tie and undone the top buttons of his shirt in preparation for the copious amounts of alcohol that he would undoubtedly consume in the next few hours.

Gazing down the bar, Harrison watches a young couple attempt to hide romantic kisses and nudges from the crowd. The woman leans into her date's shoulder exuding a hearty laugh, as the man continues to engage her in his story. His hands caress hers underneath the bar, and he steals a quick kiss before continuing his story. There is a shimmer of annoyance in Harrison's eyes.

Further down, what looks to be a group of coworkers celebrate as one of the men leans drunkenly across the bar to grab the bartender's attention. The man waves his arm obnoxiously in the bartender's direction. He turns his well-hidden, irritated face to the man as he shouts, "champagne for everyone! Let's celebrate Emily's promotion!" The bar's patrons give a forced yet polite clap and some send words of congratulations in the group's direction. Still leaning indecently over the bar, the drunk man looks to his left, stopping as he makes eye contact with Harrison.

"Holy shit," he bellows far too loudly for the setting. "Harrison Bishop?" he shouts as Harrison slightly purses his eyes and presses his mouth into a flat line, realizing the unwelcome scene that was destined to follow. Jumping off his stool and pushing past the romantic couple, the man makes his way to Harrison's group and drives his shoulders between two of the men at the edge of the group. "Holy shit, Harrison Bishop? Is it really you?" he drunkenly slurs.

Without flinching, Harrison gives him a short, "as I live and breathe," while a half laugh escapes his nostrils. He raises his glass to take a long drag of his drink, emptying its contents. He places the glass on the bar, gives a small nod to the bartender in a silent request for another drink, and returns his face back to the young man. "What can I do for you, sonny?" he asks, well aware that they are the same age, but setting the tone that this is neither the time nor place for his outburst.

"Boy, we're in the midst of a business engagement. Would you mind giving us some privacy?" says one of Harrison's coworkers, sensing Harrison's annoyance. Harrison nods back in a gesture of thanks and retrieves his fresh drink from the bartender.

"Man, I just can't believe it's you! The work you do – er – that you've done, it's incredible!" he disjointedly gushes out, causing the group to collectively roll their eyes and shift their weight with uneasiness. "I just wanted to come over here and—" he starts, but Harrison holds his hand up to stop him and he immediately freezes, even in his drunken state.

"Thank you," Harrison begins in a polite but authoritarian tone. "It's very kind of you to say, however, as Mr. Lyon has mentioned, we are discussing a few contract negotiations and would like to wrap things up in hopes that we can get just as rowdy as you." Harrison gives a playful smile that does not reach his eyes, and lifting a finger to grab the bartender's attention says, "astor, would you send half a dozen bottles of champagne down to..." His voice trails off as he returns back to the man: "Emily, is it?" The man mutely responds with an astonished and excited nod of confirmation as Harrison turns back to Astor. "For our dearest Emily. Please let her know that I send my sincerest congratulations for..." He trails off again, turning back to the drunk man, whose mouth is now gaping with amazement.

"What is it that she is celebrating?" asks Harrison.

The man blinks twice, completely lost in the moment playing out before his eyes and snaps back with an abrupt, "she was promoted to the head of legal."

Harrison turns yet again back to Astor and coolly says, "for her promotion to the head of legal."

"Right away, sir," Astor responds dryly, either accustomed to drunken outbursts or to Harrison's nonchalant generosity.

"Th-thank you, sir," the man bumbles. "That-that's very kind of you. My bad for interrupting." He leans forward for an awkward handshake, forcing Harrison to regain his stance and then lean in for a strong shake, causing the man to grimace in response. Astor opens one of the bottles with a "pop" that causes Emily's group to cheer in unison.

Harrison's coworkers grumble in frustration as the man saunters back to his group, but they quickly resume their conversation on sports and eventually make their way back to contract legalese. Harrison begins to disengage from the conversation, once again leaning his weight back into the bar. He looks over his shoulder and down the length of the room until his eyes land on the brunette waitress standing alone, preparing a drink. Watching her intently, Harrison drinks her in as he observes her from afar. Mr. Lyon asks Harrison a question, and without shifting his line of sight, he answers with an effortless, "Miss Knapp sent the contracts in last week, they should be finalized by the end of next." The men continue on with their conversation without skipping a beat.

The waitress begins pouring the finished drink into a glass and pauses for a moment, feeling Harrison's eyes on her. Keeping her body still, she slowly lifts her head to meet his gaze where they freeze in time. *Bingo*, Harrison thinks to himself and allows for one half of his mouth to curl into a smile, a sultry glow washing over him.

The waitress responds with a giggle and calls for Astor. Their conversation is hushed, but it is evident that Harrison is the topic. Astor clenches the martini glass by the stem and, with a clever look in his eyes, walks the glass down the bar and places it gently in front of him. "From Brandy," he announces, flashing a rare smile to Harrison.

What was once a respectable drinking hole has progressed into a boisterous late-night bar scene, and as the evening progresses, the men become increasingly intoxicated. Banter ensues as Mr. Lyon mocks Mr. Mason's golf game. Mr. Mason insults Mr. Madison's inability to solicit any new business deals this year. Mr. Madison ridicules Mr. Jefferson's lame attempt to hide his mistress. The humorous ribbing steadily escalates to deliberate prodding, and slowly the men surrender to return back to their homes or hotel rooms.

Late into the evening, Harrison finds himself alone with Ken Madison and Duncan Lyon, two of his oldest employees and closest friends. They had spent many years assisting Harrison with growing his corporation through the sales and talents team, and they had begun to feel like his own brothers. Harrison relished in their numerous nights of inebriation and debauchery – it was his favorite way to escape from what felt like countless evenings surrounded by coworkers at least double their age in during the week. Harrison would call them his best friends, but he would loathe the ridicule that would come his way from the statement.

"She can't be *that* out of my league," Ken drunkenly says to the others, referring to a gorgeous redhead at the end of the bar. Her black silk dress dips seductively down her back and a thin strap slowly slips off her shoulder as Ken says, "I'll show her my ATM receipt and we'll see how out of my league she is!" Harrison and Duncan stifle their laughs in response.

"Oh, come *on*!" Ken insists.

Ken was known for being the lovable but gullible friend in their group. His wide eyes and plump features gave him an innocent and naive look, which was not far from the truth. His sandy hair was always neatly styled as if he had appeared from a family portrait above a suburban fireplace. While he regularly attempted to play the part of a playboy bachelor, he was not known for his aptitude with women.

"I think your ATM receipt may be all she's interested in," Duncan says, holding back a deep chuckle in his throat. "Dude, come on," he adds, waiting for Ken to understand the joke.

Duncan was the tall, dark, and handsome member of their bunch. He paraded through town as if he owned everything in his path, and although this may have been true after a few well-placed investments, he was mostly a boisterous charmer that Harrison loved to prod any chance he could. While he came off as brash to many, Harrison and Ken loved him for his loyalty and spirited tenacity that made him the life of any party.

"Wh-what do you mean?" Ken answers in confusion. "You guys are dicks. What am I missing?"

"Kenny…" Harrison soothes, confining his amusement, "she may be a bit...*pricy*. Even for you." Harrison stares directly into Ken's eyes, cocking his head to the side and holding the silence as he waits for the joke to land.

"Oh, fuck me," says Ken, dropping his head in defeat as the two others burst into laughter. "Ha, ha, ha. Ken tried to take home a prostitute," he mocks as he lets out an unamused chuckle, pinching the bridge of his nose, and tightening his eyes while he shakes his head. The two men continue their boyish snickers and slap him on the shoulder. He releases his nose, pauses momentarily, then looks back to the redhead. "Eh, I've done worse," he concedes as he slips from their mockery before confidently striding over to woman, forcing Harrison and Duncan to erupt even further into their fit of hilarity.

"So, how about you Harrison? Anyone worth pulling the old Bishop charm on tonight?" Duncan asks as they peer around the bar. Harrison lands his sight yet again on the brunette waitress and Duncan follows his gaze. "Oh yeah, she's a cute one."

"Yeah, but I have an early morning. Not sure if even *I* can fit in an adequate rendez vous tonight," he laughs in response. Duncan nods in agreement with a throaty laugh, finishing off his drink.

"I've gotta pee," Harrison announces as he pushes himself off of the bar just as Duncan begins ordering a drink. "Get me another scotch and send something terrible over to Kenny," he says over his shoulder as he makes his exit to the restroom.

>>>

Adjacent to the dining room, a long corridor contains the restrooms and offices of the Prise du Jour. Dimly lit with sconces containing dripping candles and decorative deep plum wallpaper, the ambiance continues throughout the hall as Harrison emerges from the restroom's heavy-set doors. As he adjusts the collar of his shirt, he squints his eyes down the hall, realizing he is not alone. Pausing for an instant, he recognizes Brandy making her way in his direction. *Just like clockwork*, Harrison thinks to himself, adjusting his trajectory so they wind up face to face.

Standing just shy of Brandy's next step, Harrison flashes a mesmerizing grin that pulls at his dimples and causes her to let out a girlish giggle. Her face is delicate with her round features and wide eyes. She covers her mouth as she laughs, giving a look of awe and giddiness.

Crossing his arms, Harrison bends back on his heels to catch her deep, brown eyes and gives her a devilish smile as he comments, "looks like I owe you for the drink." Satisfied and knowing he has a fish on his reel, he watches her fidget and swoon in response to his perfect features.

Leaning forward, as if to lead Brandy back into the dining room, Harrison grasps her by the bicep and quickly presses her body against the wall, her eyes widen in shock and she inhales sharply in response. Harrison lowers his face to meet hers until his nose is merely inches from her own. He releases a deep breath and says, "you wouldn't happen to know of somewhere nearby a bit more private than this, do you?" The combination of his musk and sultry voice causes a slow chill to run down her spine.

Brandy attempts to speak but quickly falters as she releases a pathetic squeak. She closes her mouth and quickly nods in confirmation as her cheeks flush crimson and her breathing quickens against her chest. Harrison raises an eyebrow and leans in, further waiting her response.

"M-my apartment is just a few blocks away," she chokes out, hearing the shakiness in her voice and feeling her once confident demeanor fade.

Harrison silently answers back with an enticing smile and Brandy dips into her knees as she starts to feel her legs give out beneath her. "Let's go," Harrison purrs in response and leans out of their intimate moment before extending an arm, instructing her to lead the way.

As they head toward the exit, Harrison clutches Brandy by the hand, pulling her arm around her back as he wraps his arm around her. Nudging her at the side, she lets out a soft laugh that causes both to smile in excitement. Harrison recalls the romantic couple at the bar, and a touch of remorse glints in his eyes.

The foyer of the restaurant is now desolate compared to the full bar. Ambient classical music plays as Sampson sits at the entrance, reading a magazine. He sees the pair approaching him, and under his breath he calmly asks, "ready to go?"

Brandy slows her walk to assess the situation, both in confusion and in awe of meeting Harrison's bodyguard.

"Yes, I think we'll need a tour of the wine cellar this evening, Sampson," Harrison responds, now holding a scrutinizing stare.

Sampson quietly nods and exits through the main entrance as Brandy turns back to Harrison, her arm still trapped behind her back.

"I thought we were going back to my place?" she asks with disorientation. Harrison places his free hand on her face and gently cups her cheek in his large palm. He traces his thumb along her lower lip. Completely entranced, Brandy looks feverishly into his eyes and softly sputters, "a-are you going to kiss me now?"

K M Dudley

A soft and throaty laugh escapes Harrison's mouth that coats his cool breath across Brandy's face. His eyes comb over her features as he says, "something like that," and with his final word, he shifts his hand to the base of her neck and into her hair, pulling her into his chest as he leans her head back into his palm. Pulling her mouth to his, he plants a deliberate kiss on her lips, just as Brandy melts into his broad body. Wrapping his arms around her lower back, she allows herself to fade into his grasp and her mouth searches his as they crush each other in their embrace.

After their impassioned moment, Harrison drops his arms to her back and leans into his heels to look into Brandy's eyes, just as his fill with what appears to be a look of almost melancholy. Studying her face for a moment, she opens her mouth as if to speak, but he stops her as he cocks his head to the side and incredulously asks, "do you love me?"

Caught off-guard in her bewildered state, Brandy looks through Harrison to consider the question momentarily. She feels is hands slowly releasing their grip around her waist. Gazing deeply into his eyes, she smiles compassionately and pauses for effect as she confidently responds, "of course." The answer doesn't register, and Brandy continues her thought: "Everyone does, Mr. Bishop."

Harrison drops his hands but quickly grabs Brandy's hand and leads her toward the door. As they walk, without acknowledging her, Harrison dryly repeats to himself, "everyone does." They exit through the foyer doors and see Sampson standing beside the parked SUV.

Sampson opens the door to the backseat as Harrison releases Brandy's hand. She clumsily sits down as the door closes. Harrison stops to address Sampson, placing his hands indifferently into his pockets. "Get her ready to go in the cellar. I'll be home in an hour or so."

Sampson nods in agreement as Harrison turns to make his way back into the restaurant.

Chapter Four: **Consideration**

Stepping out of the town car and into the street, Daisy arrives at La Nuit, a swanky cocktail lounge in the financial district, as other executive members and directors of The Rose Institute check in with the hostess. Still donning her white oxford, navy blue slacks, and nude pumps, she undoes an additional button, finalizing her ensemble, and struts through the foyer to meet with the rest of her party.

La Nuit was at the top of Daisy's list of local watering holes. With its modern decor and dark lighting, the stylish and dark atmosphere made it easy for the executive team to hide within the shadows as they blew off steam on Fridays. Known for bottomless champagne and a handsome wait staff, Daisy knew she'd either go home with a work conquest, a hangover, or an attractive man on her arm, and she was happy with any result.

As Daisy checks in with the hostess, she is directed beyond the dining room toward a private room. Slinking her way through the crowded bar, she makes pleasantries with a few acquaintances, avoiding lasting conversations. As she finally reaches the private room, Daisy is greeted by a waiter ready to take her drink order, but is stopped mid-conversation as a human resources representative approaches them. An uptight woman named Angela, who had never had a pleasant conversation in her life, blocks Daisy.

"Did you make Nicolas Mader cry today, Miss Stone?" she growls, holding a petite hand in the waiter's face. "I swear to God, Daisy, if I have to write you up one more time for assailing our clients, I am going to fire you."

"Better make that a double, bud," says Daisy, winking at the waiter as he holds his laugh and returns to the bar.

Angela fumes steam from her ears as her nostrils flare. Only grazing five feet, she is short in size but her voice packs a wallop from years of reprimanding The Rose Institute's executive team.

"What is it with you people? I caught Thomas trying to *purchase* the hostess for the evening," she says, venting her frustrations to Daisy and framing the word "purchase" with air quotes. "I had to stop Charlie and Ed from explaining Monica Lewinsky to an intern, and I'm *this* close to sending Molly's drunk derriere home and we haven't even had appetizers yet!" she says, holding up her thumb and forefinger, but Daisy is preoccupied as she searches for Molly in the crowd.

Molly Jordan, Daisy's best friend and go-to partner in crime at these corporate events, would not be difficult to locate amongst the mass of middle-aged men. As the director of marketing and sales, Molly often felt the same struggles as Daisy of being a woman in a department overrun by a never-ending boys club. However, she had the unique gift of being painstakingly intelligent that rarely impacted how she was treated in their industry. At a daunting six feet with a slender frame, icy blue eyes, and cascading, jet black hair, Molly seemed to be more goddess than businesswoman. Their clients were consistently in such shock that she even considered going into any profession other than modeling, and they couldn't help but buy whatever she was selling. She did have a short stint of provocative photo shoots while living in the south of France in her early twenties, but beyond that, she took the pharmaceutical world by storm until Daisy scooped her up for The Rose Institute. The two had been inseparable ever since.

Peering through the crowd of drunken executives and bigwigs, Daisy hears Molly's sultry voice before she can see her. "Eddie, you need to listen to me. Monica Lewinsky isn't a relatable topic to kids. Half of what Monica did would be considered foreplay in this day and age," Molly says to Ed Franklin, a senile board member that Molly loved to rile up during these events. Ed was about one hundred pounds above the weight his doctor would prefer and enjoyed making his fellow board members squirm with inappropriate comments and lewd jokes. He holds his belly and laughs at Molly's crude humor, and before she continues on, Daisy steps in to finish the punch line.

"I hear that Ed was actually the one who suggested the ol' cigar trick back in the day," she quips as she ducks her head between the mismatched pair.

"Daisy Stone! Just in time for a martini and a story about my last secretary!" Ed exclaims as he prepares a story that would turn Angela the darkest shade of violet.

Standing once again atop her toes to peer through the crowd, Daisy searches for her long-lost waiter and, more importantly, her missing drink. Her eyes light up as she spots a waiter making his way toward her. "Speak of the devil," she announces to the two just the waiter passes by with a tray of drinks. She inconspicuously plucks a dirty martini off the tray and takes a long gulp from the crystal glass.

"Now, let's hear all about this secretary, Eddie."

Molly holds a martini to block her mouth as she whispers, "if he stares at your ass any longer, you might want to suggest posing for an oil painting." A playful smile fills her face as she tries to cover her obvious conversation with Daisy.

"On a scale of young to old Harrison Ford, what would you rate him?" Daisy asks, taking a sip from her martini and mirroring Molly's camouflaged stance.

Standing upright and blowing their cover, Molly quips back, "you know there is no age that you would not fuck Harrison Ford." She rolls her eyes and announces far too loudly, "either go talk to him or I'm calling dibs for eternity."

A relaxed chuckle rises in Daisy at their immature game. "What would I do without you? You're the Donnie to my Marie."

"Does that make me Donnie or Marie?" Molly muses with an intrigued simper.

Cocking her head to one side at the question, Daisy answers, "I'm not quite sure. Whoever has better tits."

They break into a fit of laughter and Daisy gives a playful, "you are zero help to me," downing the remainder of her drink in a single swig. Rolling her shoulders back and standing at attention to Molly she gives a final, "don't let Angela catch me again," before turning on her heel to strut toward the young businessman casually attempting to lean against the bar.

Giving the businessman her best what Molly calls "casual bedroom eyes," Daisy keeps eye contact as she makes her way toward him. He adjusts his stance, opening his shoulders to meet her as she arrives, but at the last moment, she passes by him and greets the woman standing directly behind him, catching him off guard. "Gillian!" Daisy exclaims as she grasps the shoulders of the nearby woman. The two embrace in a hug and quickly jump into conversation as the businessman stands stunned in his place.

Continuing their conversation, he returns to face the bar with a dumbstruck look of shame as his friends laugh at his expense and nudge his shoulder.

Daisy continues her pleasantries until she catches the bartender's attention: "Two vodka martinis, please." The businessman turns to Daisy but she holds her position facing the bar and leans into the edge with a coy look as she watches her drinks being prepared.

"After all that back and forth, I thought you knew I was looking at you," the businessman confesses as Daisy raises a single eyebrow at his attention. "You don't think I was going to let the infamous Daisy Stone grace my presence without even bothering to buy her a drink?" he asks as Daisy purses her lips, hindering a smile.

"Put it on my tab, Hector. Thank you," Daisy says as the bartender sets the martinis before her. Grasping the glasses by the stems, she turns to leave but the businessman steps in front of her and reaches his arm around her waist to grasp the bar top behind her. Skimming just the surface of her blouse to rest at her lower back, he subtly grazes her skin as Daisy's cheeks flush slightly.

Continuing to hold her smile, Daisy curls her lips inward and her eyes twinkle as she attempts keeping a serious face. The tension is palpable between the two as the businessman leans in and holds her gaze. After a moment of silence, Daisy extends one drink into the chest of the businessman, surprising him as he regains his height. "For you, Kennedy," she says, her grin continuing to grow behind her facetious facade.

"You sly fox, Miss Stone," Kennedy reprimands with a playful grin. "I was concerned that all my ass kissing at last month's conference went completely unnoticed."

Kennedy Thomas was a bit of a wunderkin as the new chief financial officer of Mendl Research Laboratories, the second largest immunology research facility in North America. His chestnut brown hair, navy eyes, and broad build always seemed to make women swoon, and at a fresh faced thirty years of age, he had recently taken over the role from his father and was quickly turning heads in the industry. It was rumored that his role was set to go to an older woman, but Kennedy had convinced her out of it after a few cocktails and a night in his penthouse, but this had never been confirmed nor denied.

Holding their gaze, Daisy and Kennedy raise their drinks in unison and quietly allow for the tension build between their tight quarters. Kennedy purses his eyes and finally announces, "let's get a few more drinks in us and see what trouble we can get into."

Eyeing Kennedy with a wicked grin, Daisy rolls a toothpick containing three olives between her thumb and forefinger as a devilish smile puckers her lips, relinquishing her amusement. Giving a slight shrug and a nonchalant sigh, she accepts with a casual, "I think I can make some time," as she raises the olives to her lips and delicately plucks the green orb from the wooden stick.

Kennedy showcases a wild smile that fills his face and holds up two fingers to the bartender.

"Hector? Two more, please."

Daisy is suspended against the wooden door of La Nuit's coat closet as Kennedy pulls her legs to wrap around his waist while he ravenously kisses her neck. The two are intertwined, all hair and hands, as they devour each other amongst the coats.

"I thought you were in Vancouver this week for the genetics summit," Daisy says as she wraps her arms around Kennedy's neck and pulls his face back to hers, impatiently interlacing their mouths.

CAVALIER: A Novel

Brushing Daisy's hair from her face and wrapping a long arm around her waist, Kennedy pops his head above water for a breath to respond. "My father went in my place," he gasps, his free hand grasping at her neck and tugging at the nape. "I'm reworking the organizational structure during our restructuring phase before Mendl goes public."

Bingo, Daisy thinks to herself as she trails a finger down Kennedy's back, causing him to shiver from the sensation. "Well they certainly have the right man for the job," she praises him as she reaches a hand up to undo his top shirt button. As the two melt further into the coats and feverishly undress, Daisy presses on. "Have you determined who you'll transition into president?" she asks as she simultaneously undoes his belt and reaches into his trousers. He drops her delicately against the balls of her feet.

Distracted by Daisy's lost hand, Kennedy closes his eyes as he loses focus, attempting to answer her. "I-I haven't decided yet. We're..." he trails off as he unbuttons her blouse, pressing his bare chest to hers. "I'm thinking it will most likely be myself or Wilson, our current vice president."

Daisy brushes a hand through Kennedy's hair and he closes his eyes against her touch as she continues to vet him. "Who are you leaning toward for consideration?" Her opposite hand plays beneath the fabric of his trousers, and he releases a moan as he again presses his mouth to hers.

Shaking his head to clear his mind, Kennedy opens his eyes at the strange question, but their hands continue to swiftly move despite the conversation. "Me, but why do you ask?"

Daisy grips below the waist and Kennedy releases a small yelp at the pleasure. She flashes a racy smile and leans into to his ear to breathily say, "just curious to see how powerful you're about to become." With that, she yanks his trousers to the floor in a single motion and they fall amongst the coats in a ravenous heap.

>>>

Leaning her back against the bar as her martini is being prepared behind her, Daisy lowers her chin to realize that she missed a button while getting redressed. A sultry smile touches her eyes and she tugs at the fabric, slipping the button through its designated hole. She tosses her hair over her shoulder as her flushed cheeks hint at her afternoon delights, but her powerful stance keeps the questions at bay.

"Here you go, Miss Stone," Hector announces as he places the delicate drink behind Daisy. "Anything else I can do for you?"

Dipping her chin to meet her shoulder without turning to meet his face, Daisy responds, "just the check, sweet Hector."

From the opposite shoulder, Kennedy stops him. "I'll take that if you don't mind, Hector," he says, tossing his credit card on to the bar. He leans into her other shoulder and discreetly whispers, "when can I see you next?"

Without adjusting her stance and swiveling her head to land her cheek just millimeters away from Kennedy's, Daisy responds with a quiet, "I bet we see each other much sooner than you would expect." Leaning back to meet his line of sight, her lips curl into a flirtatious smile and she shoots a miniscule wink back at him just as Hector sets the tab before Kennedy.

Kennedy opens the tab as Daisy turns to press her chest into him. She pulls a gentle finger to his chin to turn his gaze to meet hers. Holding their stance for a beat, he realizes their location and raises his eyebrows in amusement. "Miss Stone, don't forget this is still *your* work event. I am a mere guest! Would you like me to scoop you up in front of your entire office and take you back to someplace a bit more private?" he asks, his eyes sparkling at the idea.

"Mr. Thomas!" Ed's boisterous voice calls through the crowd, interrupting the intimate moment. "Where the hell is your father? He owes me five hundred dollars from the golf outing last weekend!"

Turning his back to the bar and warmly ribbing Ed in return, Kennedy takes a step forward and opens his arms to embrace him. "I heard you lost half a dozen balls in the water and threw a wedge at Charlie Meyer!"

"Horseshit!" Ed yells over the crowd, pulling a few looks in their direction. "Meyer threw his club at *me*!"

Daisy sinks into the bar as the old friends yell over each other. Pulling her purse to her side, she plucks a slim document and discretely folds it into thirds, flattening the edges with her manicured nails. She lays the paper atop the bar tab waiting for the conversation to die down, touching up her lipstick with her ring finger.

A pretty waitress passes between Kennedy and Daisy that catches Ed's attention. "Didn't I order a scotch from you an hour ago?" he wildly yells mid-conversation to the unfazed waitress, who stops in her tracks.

"Who? Me?" she bewilderedly responds, pointing at herself.

"Yes, you! You think I'd let a skinny thing like you take anyone else's order?" Ed drunkenly slurs as he abruptly ends his conversation with Kennedy and follows the waitress to fetch his lost drink.

Daisy drapes a casual elbow atop the bar and flashes a seductive smile to Kennedy, silently commanding him, "sign this and let's get out of here." Her eyes are fiery and inviting.

Expanding his chest with a prideful boast, Kennedy winks at her.

Kennedy approaches the bar and picks up a pen. Daisy leans into his ear and whispers, "the longer it takes you sign, the longer it takes for us to get back to my place."

A devilish laugh fills their space as Kennedy teases back, "you know I don't need much ti—"

He stops mid-sentence as Courtney approaches their cozy corner.

"We've got a situation," Courtney abruptly blurts out with a chaotic look in her eyes.

"Go, go," Kennedy says. "I need to chat with Charlie about this incredible acquisition that you're spearheading, anyway. I can't believe you bagged the beast, Miss Stone," he says, winking once again at Daisy.

The words not registering as Daisy tightens her eyes at the strange statement, she looks back and forth between Kennedy and Courtney.

"What *beast* is that?" she asks, her voice troubled and confused.

"Let's go," says Courtney, her voice poignant and harsh.

Daisy heeds Courtney's tone. She reaches her arm across the bar, grabbing the folder piece of paper and covertly dropping it into her handbag.

"Until next time, Mr. Thomas," says Daisy, giving him a mischievous smile that does not touch her eyes.

With a sultry nod, Kennedy concludes their secretive tête-à-tête. "Until next time, Miss Stone," he says, just as Courtney grabs Daisy by the elbow and whisks her away from the bar.

Chapter Five: **Night Moves**

       The night air is somber as Harrison drives the path to his estate. The sky is a murky hue of lavender; the sun has not yet reached the horizon, but its amber aurora is just beginning to crest. He rolls down the windows, filling his car with the cool breeze, knowing the darkness would be gone sooner than he hoped.

       Through the trees, Harrison recognizes his massive home amongst the seeping branches, and he emits a relieved exhaust from his nostrils as he spots the dark windows welcoming his arrival. Leaning his head back into the seat, he inhales a cleansing breath and prepares himself for his next endeavor. The long day begins to settle into his face as his eyes slightly sink. He allows a full yawn to escape his mouth, but a small squeak from his throat causes him to blink his eyes awake and shake his head back into reality. *You have an early morning tomorrow, don't let this take all night*, he thinks to himself. *Gotta look alive tomorrow. Well, today. It's going to be a big day for you.*

Built in the mid-eighteenth century and nestled along the outskirts of New Orleans, Harrison had purchased the estate in a bidding war when he first settled in Louisiana after founding what was then known as Bishop Research. In all actuality, the only other bidder was looking to tear down the ancient building and put up a resort, but once Harrison heard this, he was determined to make it his. He was captivated by the generational quality and purpose of the estate. Such a fondness had grown for the old home that nothing, other than minor upkeep over the years, had been altered since it was constructed and he instructed nothing to be changed until it crumbled to the ground.

The southern oaks' low-hanging branches created a curtain that hid the driveway from the rest of world. Even in the daylight, the extravagant estate was hard to spot between the sinuous branches and the façade's white pillars were hard to distinguish between the centuries old limbs that freckled the winding dirt road. However, when the home was lit, row after row of bright white rooms were visible for miles.

The dim windows begin to dance along the rough road as Harrison approaches in a silent whirl of dust.

Letting his shoulders fall back into his seat and taking another invigorating breath, he turns up the radio for the remainder of the drive. Bob Seger's "Night Moves" fills the car and Harrison's face brightens with a grin in response to one of his favorites. Bobbing his head to the hearty beat and tapping his thumb along to the piano, he can feel his energy perk with a twinge of excitement as he finally pulls up in front of the house. Turning off the engine mid-song, his mouth frowns knowing he has other obligations at this moment than listening to the end of the lively tune.

Harrison lackadaisically climbs the steps of the front porch, rolling his car keys through his fingers. He stops just before the double doors to lean his head back and let it fall slack to either side as a small "crack" escape his neck. He hums along to the tune in his head as he reaches for the doorknob.

Harrison opens the door and pauses momentarily in the vast foyer to assess the house. The room is desolate and dim as the morning sun tips across the sky to peer through the windows. The faint light evaporates quickly and causes him to squint as his eyes as he adjusts to the light, making his way to large table in the middle of the room.

The table is adorned with an immense white and gray marble vase that contains nearly three dozen tulips, which emit the last bit of summertime fragrance throughout the room. Flinging his suit jacket across the table, then tossing his briefcase and keys on to it as well, he clasps his hands together and outstretches his arms to feel the stretch through his broad shoulders. His throaty purr continues with more vibrato, feeling the comfort of his own home drape over him.

Walking through the back of the foyer, down the hallway, and into the kitchen, Harrison prances as the song in his mind washes over him on his way to the refrigerator. He continues on and as he opens the refrigerator door, breaking into a crackled song.

He peers into the harsh light beginning to rummage through the freezer's contents.

Setting down his assortment of items on the vast kitchen island, he grabs a frying pan from the hanging rack above him. Lighting the burner, he drops a pat of butter into the brushed metal pan and makes his way to his bedroom. Then, lighting a small table lamp, Harrison's dark room illuminates, exposing the room's muted gray tones with soft cream trim and overstuffed furniture. The four-poster bed's luxurious, white linens tempt him to slip into its divine fabric as he passes by into to his walk-in closet.

Above his bed hangs a colossal painting, difficult to view in the dim bedroom lighting, but as Harrison switches on the closet light the canvas exposes an abstract piece showcasing two vivid surfaces. On the left, a light and vibrant entanglement of brushstrokes and spirals of whites, silvers, and sheer blues. The opposite side presents a dark disarray of maroon, navy, and gold in harsh and intense streaks. The two meet in the center and entangle with a multitude of colors and mixed media, the only source of color throughout the massive space.

Harrison makes his way past the rows of suits and racks of dress shoes toward the back of the closet. Removing his white button-down shirt and undoing his belt, he continues humming the tune. He throws his shirt into a laundry hamper and shimmies out of his trousers until he is left in just his boxer briefs. Crouching down onto his toes to the drawers of the built-in cabinetry, he pulls out the bottom drawer containing a stack of worn black tee shirts and jeans. Remembering his butter on the stove, he quickly dresses with a black tee and jeans, then slips from his bedroom back into the kitchen.

Harrison's confident attitude carries on as he prepares his grilled cheese sandwich. In one fluid motion, he slips the toasty bread from the pan and on to a plate. With a tepid "crunch," he slices the bread in two and takes a sizeable bite of the corner. A small smile touches his face as he's happy to get a meal into his stomach after a night of marathon drinking with Ken and Duncan. They always seemed to coerce him into late evenings, causing him to spill back into the house around dawn.

Swallowing the last bite of his meal, he stands with his hands atop the marble countertop and pauses while the silent house engulfs him. In the stillness, he raises his ear ever so slightly upward to listen further into the calm. A muffled tone is creeping through the air ducts and his eyes narrow in a devilish smile as he remembers what awaits him.

Making his way down the aged, wooden steps, Harrison's footsteps are almost silent in contrast to the woman's voice ringing through the stone hallway. She is crying, or maybe screaming, the sound a perplexing discord that does not register on Harrison's face as he descends the damp hallway and stops just before the wooden door at the end of the hall. Allowing the heavy air to settle around him, he leans his ear toward to the door, assessing his prey. Holding his breath, he listens as the screaming continues on, then what sounds of sobs and cries continue before he pauses to study his watch. *Damn, already quarter after five. I can't dally this time,* he thinks to himself as he unlatches the large, sliding lock, as the sound behind the door hushes to a mild, raspy pant.

Springing open the heavy door, Harrison shifts his weight until he falls to lean against the open doorframe and closes his eyes in response to the vivid brightness of a single light bulb hanging from the cellar's ceiling. A moment of tranquility passes as Brandy's realization of her position connects, then, almost instantaneously, her voice booms through the cellar and knocks into Harrison's unfazed face. "Holy shit. Harrison?" she half screams, her voice cracking. "What are you doing here? Why did you let that awful man throw me down here? What is this place?" she hastily demands of an uninterested Harrison.

Bound by her hands and feet with a stiff rope and fastened to an oversized wooden chair, Brandy eagerly watches as Harrison studies her face, ignoring her binding knots. She has a small cut on her forehead, where it appears she attempted to head-butt Sampson. Her lip is also slowly swelling. Although her clothing shows a sign of a struggle, she still holds her cheerful composure at the sight of Harrison.

The annoyance in her questions pangs across Harrison's face and he glances again at his watch, silently calculating of how much time he can allow himself.

"Nice to see you again, Brandy. I hope your stay has been comfortable," he blandly responses, as if not hearing her continual questioning.

"Oh my God, this is crazy. Why are you here? I'm so excited to see you again!" she squeals through her rough face and hoarse throat.

Harrison takes his weight off the doorframe and smoothly glides his way past Brandy toward the back of the cellar. Positioned on the center of the back wall, a ceiling-high wooden armoire stands among the shelving units filled with metal baskets. He opens the console and drags a drawer from the center, revealing a row of vinyl records. Slowly flicking through the paper casings, he selects what has caught his eye and removes a record in one fluid motion, catching the vinyl between his thumb and forefinger. Finally answering her, he replies in an uninterested tone.

"Of course you are excited to see me, Brandy. Everyone always is."

Reaching back into the armoire, he lifts the center of the wood paneling and exposes a well-used record player. Placing the record on the plate, he turns the machine to life and delicately dips the needle to the disk. Bob Seger's "Night Moves" once again comes alive through the speakers hidden within the cinderblocks of the walls, and sound erupts through the cellar, causing Brandy to flinch in response.

Harrison calmly returns to the front of the cellar, positioning himself in front of Brandy's bound legs. Standing above her with his arms crossed in contemplation, he slowly lowers himself to the balls of his feet, crouching to meet her line of sight. While she continues her rambling, he holds this crouched position, appraising the workmanship of the knots. His arms stoically holding their grip as he begins to hum along to the music vibrating through the room, he finally breaks his silence and returns his lifeless eyes to meet hers.

"Are you going to talk the entire time?"

Puzzled by this question, and even more confused by why he hasn't answered her questions or explained why she is here, Brandy begins to speak.

"I don't—," she starts, but Harrison returns to his feet and interrupts.

"I always had a fascination with idols," Harrison begins, avoiding Brandy's statement. He begins to walk to the side of the cellar, where a bright blue, nylon rope clenches to a hook fastened between two silvery cinderblocks. He begins to unwind the rope and continues on. "Why would someone deem a person better than any other?" he asks. "What good does it do to begin ranking other humans?"

Harrison indifferently walks back to Brandy and stands next to her, examining her profile. Gently, he slides the rope beneath her wrist, the fabric pulling at her thin skin and causing her to wince, but she is still transfixed on his mouth, hanging on to his every word. He begins tying the rope into a thick knot and continues on, saying, "I watch television and see these actors and actresses on talk shows and watch the people in the audience fawn over a human they've never met have no true interactions with."

Pulling the knot into its final position, he takes a folding knife from his back pocket and begins to cut away at the first rope, releasing Brandy from the chair. A low chuckle escapes his throat and he continues. "You know? They're just *people,*" he says, as a more substantial laugh passes over his lips. The original rope falls to the floor, and he makes his way to the back corner of the cellar. The new rope bound around Brandy's wrist, goes up through a hook in the ceiling of the cellar, crosses the ceiling, and falls back down the cellar wall. Harrison tugs at the rope, causing the slack to dissipate from the line before Brandy's wrist lifts just increments from the armrest of the chair and slightly swing as she continues to listen on, unfazed by Harrison's actions.

"I once met Elton John at an event in London," he progresses as he makes his way to the opposite end of the cellar and begins the process anew on Brandy's opposite side, his face still apathetic to his surroundings. "He was such a lovely man. Told me a very inappropriate joke that I still laugh at from time to time," he remembers as a smile hits his eyes but not his mouth. "But a man interrupted him halfway through the joke and forced him into a photograph, then asked him to sign some items in his son's backpack," he scoffed, becoming heated by the memory. "The son didn't even know who he was. The dad just forced him around and opened the bag to grab whatever he could find and threw it at Elton," says Harrison, his eyes now annoyed and irritated. "He acted as if this man, whom he obviously did not know, owed him the world. Just for existing, he owed him...something," he says, trailing off and turning his attention to cutting the second rope.

Once he frees Brandy from her original wrist restraints, he begins on her ankles, removing the binding until her legs hang free. She has yet to remove her enthusiastic eyes from Harrison's face, still absorbed with being in such close proximity to *the* Harrison Bishop.

"Professional athletes, government officials, even news anchors. These people are still people. They may be in the spotlight, but that doesn't make any of them a deity," he jeers, now laughing at his own joke. "I mean..." He trails off, squatting in front of Brandy, snaking the rope from the chair. He shakes his head, as if to rid the memory from his mind, and looks up to finally set his eyes upon Brandy. Her pupils instantly dilate and her mouth droops as she continues to intently listen.

"No one deserves to be treated better or worse because of their character. You know what I mean?" he finally asks her, acknowledging her presence.

Brandy's mouth snaps shut and she eagerly nods in agreement. She parts her lips as if to speak but Harrison beats her to the punch.

"I'm a little shocked that you understand, Brandy," he says, beginning again, now with more vigor as he takes on a new tone. "It seems as if you wouldn't be able to discern between good and evil if it hit you the face." He snorts in laughter as he rises to his feet and towers over her, her face now confused and contorting into a grimace.

Harrison paces to the back of the cellar and softly clutches the suspended ropes, one and then the other.

"What do you know about the Kisatchie National Forest, dear Brandy?" he asks, his voice now taking on a tactical tone. "Ever made your way up north to visit the cypress trees?"

Brandy's eyes widen with concern and her breathing picks up.

"I—" she begins, fearing where this conversation may lead. "I've only visited once. F-for a vacation this spring."

Harrison lets out an exuberant laugh. He reopens his eyes and the laughter dies in his stomach. He pulls the ropes in one smooth motion, yanking Brandy arms sturdily above her head, raising her until her toes graze the cement floor.

"That is quite convenient, Miss Brandy," says Harrison, his words laced with a joke but his face possessing a serious tone. "What a great time to visit such a serene location. Wasn't that around the time when your boyfriend mysteriously went missing and then was found by hikers left for dead from a head wound?"

The air of a joke lingers against his lips. He pulls sharply at the ropes again, suspending and then dropping Brandy until her toes kiss the floor beneath her once more.

"I did love that you took the time to write 'cheater' along his chest in lipstick before he died of dehydration. Very gallant of you."

"Harrison! I can explain!" she says, her words now panicked, as if she's losing her moment with Harrison, unconcerned with her positioning. "I only wanted to scare him. I didn't mean to let things get that out of hand."

Harrison intently moves across the room to stand directly in front of Brandy, his head glowering into her eager eyes. "How foolish do you think I am?" he asks, already knowing the answer.

"I wanted to rough him up a little. Make him think that if he tried to cheat on me again that there would be consequences," she says, her words spilling out haphazardly. "I thought he would get right back up and be fine the next day," she continues, pleading as if Harrison should understand.

Harrison's mouth presses, waiting for her to stop talking. *She's about to talk over the best part*, he thinks as the final chorus of "Night Moves" booms through the speakers. Before Brandy can continue, he reaches a hand up to her face and covers her mouth, stunning her with the action. He closes his eyes, sinking into the music and giving a slight shimmy as he enjoys the melody. Turning his attention back to her, but without removing his hand, he asks, "are you going to be quiet or do I need to shut you up?" His voice sounds more stern than humorous as he raises a single eyebrow, removing his hand.

"Let me explain—" she starts again, but Harrison quickly replaces his hand to her mouth and forces an exasperated breath through his nostrils into her face. She speaks beneath his hand but produces only a soft murmur until Harrison moves his hand, dipping an ear to hear her words.

"My father was in a medically induced coma for years battling brain cancer. Your discovery. It saved him. Let me thank—"

"I think that's enough for now," Harrison jeers as he returns his palm and Brandy continues her muffled speech.

With his free hand, he reaches into his rear pocket and produces a worn roll of duct tape. Removing his hand from her mouth, the apologizing continues, but he's tuned her out with a newfound focus. Peeling off a section of tape, he raises the silver paper to his teeth before gripping between his fingers and tearing the sheet from the roll. He forcefully places it across her face until her chatter softens into silence.

"Ah, much better," Harrison says, applauding himself before taking a step back to fold his arms across his chest and decipher his next step.

Although pulled taught by the rope, Brandy does not appear to be upset or frightened.

"Aren't you scared of me in the slightest?" Harrison thinks aloud, a pang of anger skirting his question.

Brandy shakes her head in declination as an apology fills her eyes. She begins to speak but her muffled rebuttal causes her to stop short. Giving a small shrug, she shakes her head to Harrison's question.

Accepting what comes next, Harrison nods his head in agreement with Brandy. "Of course you aren't," he says in an exasperated tone. "Well, that's just too bad," he observes as he marches to the back of the cellar's many rows of shelves. Pulling at a metal bin, he peers down in search of an item but after canvassing the first bin's contents and coming up empty handed, he pushes the metal back forcefully. Pulling out the next bin and then another, Brandy's face to contorts in response to the sound of metal and wood colliding together. She attempts to speak once more, but when the tape again stops her, she attempts to scream. Harrison hushes her as her muffled attempts distract him from his search.

Finally, with an "ah-ha!" Harrison pulls a surgical knife from the bin and examines it above his head beneath the single light. He rolls it between his fingers as he walks back to the center of Brandy's vision. She watches him intently as he brushes the knife against his jeans to clean the blade. After taking a stabilizing breath, he steps forward and with one provocative motion, pulls at the hem of her black cocktail dress. Then, placing the blade at the taut edge, he slowly saws until the seam splits into two. He pulls the blade up her dress like a boat forcing its way between ocean waves, across her hips, over her stomach, and up her chest, splitting the dress into two halves that softly wilt across her body.

Brandy, now watching with infatuation, lifts her head again to meet Harrison's bewildered eyes. He takes a minor step back, pursing his eyes and tilting his head, as if reading her body for information. Again, she tries to speak but her voice sounds foreign beneath the tape. Pausing briefly in contemplation, he leans forward and extends his left thumb until it lands below the trim of Brandy's black lace bra. Pressing with focused though, he locates the base of her sternum and then uses his forefinger to trace the crest of her ribcage, his thoughts turning meticulous. With his other hand, he places the cool blade of the surgical knife just beneath the map his forefinger has traced.

Stopping short of his next action, Harrison leans his head back to meet Brandy's gaze. Her eyes are wide and her nostrils flared, but she remains silent. Gauging her reaction, the air falls still momentarily. They watch each other in cautious intensity.

Without releasing his focus, Harrison pushes the blade into Brandy's soft abdomen, causing her to release a stifled scream beneath the tape. His eyes react with a small flinch, but with his steady focus, he slowly pulls the knife downward. Her skin releases a shallow "rip" as he tugs, but it is ultimately lost amidst Brandy's suppressed wail. Continuing the motion, one hand holding Brandy's ribs steady and the other dragging the knife through her skin, Harrison continues to carve until he reaches her navel and returns to a standing position to look back into her face. Her reaction gives an air of hurt, but she remains resilient, forcing Harrison to furrow his brow.

"Are you still not afraid of me?" Harrison questions as his blood begins to boil.

Brandy, now panting from the pain as her body violently trembles, shakes her head in rejection. Harrison expels a small grunt of disapproval and reaches a bloody hand to his head, pushing his messy blonde hair away from his face, streaking blood through its dampened shine. He hinges forward to meet her stomach, and releasing another definitive breath, he forces a bloody forefinger into the newly formed mouth of her abdomen.

Brandy releases another muffled scream from beneath the tape and her eyes produce two heavy tears from their ducts. She continues to gasp for breath and closes her eyes as she attempts to push the pain from her mind.

Turning half his face upward to watch Brandy's reaction, Harrison digs his finger through her abdomen, rolling his eyes to the ceiling as he begins searching for something beneath the surface of her skin. Continuing to howl, she pants for breath until he pulls out what he has been searching for: a small tube of intestine, still attached below the surface of her skin. He releases the exposed loop and freezes his body, returning his eyes to her face to gauge her response.

Brandy continues her cries, but, yet again, shakes her head to remind him that she is still not afraid. Releasing another angry breath, Harrison grips the loop and pulls, violently, exposing nearly a foot of intestines that kick Brandy's head back into a guttural but hindered scream.

Feeling his desired satisfaction, Harrison steps back and stands again before her. He drops the knife to the floor and reaches both hands up to run his hands through his now soggy hair. He then crosses his arms proudly with a sense of accomplishment, waiting for her to return her attention to him, if at all.

After a few moments of tired wailing, Brandy calms herself and turns her eyes back to Harrison. Her breathing is rhythmic and heavy through her nostrils as she stares deep into his now black-green eyes, past his pupils and into his soul. Squinting in agony, her bright brown eyes search through him, as if speaking. Harrison's eyes mimic hers in response, and as if answering his own question, she speaks beneath the tape with a deliberate tone. Harrison reaches forward, slowly peeling the tape from her face, and the silver paper drifts to the floor.

"I'm..." she chokes through broken breaths, "I'm not afraid of you," she spits at him. "You saved my father's life. I owe you *everything*."

Harrison rolls his eyes in an aggravated response, as if a spoiled toddler. Now fed up with the situation, he marches past Brandy and to the back shelving. Selecting the correct bin on the first attempt, he removes a twelve-inch serrated knife and retreats to his previous position. Standing defiantly before Brandy, as if waiting for her to adjust her response, she holds her grateful composure.

The blade hangs menacingly in Harrison's grip as a small "pat, pat, pat" fills the empty void with sound as Brandy's blood drips into a pool beneath her.

"Well?" he asks, waiting for a response he knows will not come.

"What do you want me to say?" Brandy shallowly coughs. "Do you want me to say I hate you?" she demands, laughing back at him. Her stomach gurgles and blood spatters from her open wound. "I owe it all to you," she says with a wince.

Harrison's face flushes with anger. He reaches his hand above Brandy's head, swinging his arm down to graze her throat. Blood pours from the fresh wound against her neck. She convulses in response, but weak from the torture, she quickly falls limp. Watching her final breath rise and fall, he drops the knife to the floor and takes a step back, angrily heaving in response.

After a moment of contemplation, Harrison marches toward the cellar door, stopping short of the doorframe to push a red button on a gray intercom system.

"Sampson?" he drowsily croaks into the speaker, removing his thumb and leaving a bloody thumbprint on the button. "Call the cleaners for a full service in the cellar this morning, please."

The speaker cracks to life and Sampson responds with a calm and groggy, "you got it, sir."

With that, Harrison flips a light switch just underneath the speaker, extinguishes the light, and releases the wooden door of the cellar with a heavy thud as he makes his way into the fresh, morning air. The eerie echo of his hum lingering against the damp corridor.

Chapter Six: **Know Yourself**

The sky glints with the dawn of morning through La Nuit's lush, velvet drapery. The crowd of The Rose Institute and their guests are still in full swing as the staff attempts to close the bar every hour with no prevail. Angela is hurdling through the crowd, attempting to scold a middle-aged man as he picks out a petite waitress and parades her through the crowd. "Here she is, gents! My second wife!" he slurs, and the crowd around the unattractive man roars into laughter. The girl falls into a fit of giggles half-heartedly, trying to clamor away from her soon-to-be husband.

Courtney drags Daisy in the opposite direction of Angela. Weaving through the crowd, Daisy calls, "what is it, Court?" Her words fall on deaf ears as Courtney spots an unused side bar.

Flinging Daisy in front of her, Courtney shoves her into the small space. Daisy's hip collides with the bar top.

"What could possibly be *this* important, Courtney?" Daisy demands as Courtney surveys their makeshift room for privacy.

Leaning in, Courtney rapidly spits at Daisy in a hushed tone, "I overheard Ed blabbing about some board vote that took place just before tonight's happy hour." Daisy looks at Courtney, her expression confused and annoyed at the uninteresting news. Sensing the disconnect, Courtney says, "apparently they signed off on some big deal that you completed what sounded like *weeks* ago."

"Me? But every acquisition I've presented has been signed off by the board with..." Daisy's face tangles into further disorientation as she finishes her uneasy thought. "Me."

"Exactly," says Courtney, confirming the perplexing question between them. "I checked my phone to compare your calendar to Charlie's. There hasn't been an acquisition review meeting that neither of you have attended in the last two weeks." Daisy opens her mouth to grill Courtney further but she raises a finger to signal she was not yet finished. "I overheard Charlie and Ed discussing some event before the happy hour tonight. Sure enough, there was a board meeting set for this evening and your name wasn't on the attendees list. And, even more strange, I found a handful of private calendars that I couldn't access."

Daisy's eyes tighten at the baffling information.

"Okay," Daisy begins, but with no thought in mind. She absentmindedly looks through the bar shelving before plucking a bottle of scotch and a rocks glass. Pouring herself a drink, she muses to herself, "what do I do?"

Taking the glass from Daisy's hand, Courtney takes a swig of the brown elixir. "That's the thing," she says, handing the glass back to Daisy as she distractedly returns to filling the glass. "Charlie is about to make some big announcement before we send everyone home."

"He couldn't know about Kennedy, right?" Daisy presses as she takes a long drink from the shared glass. "I mean, I've been keeping that in my back pocket for weeks. I wouldn't have let that slip."

Once again grabbing the glass from Daisy, Courtney takes another drink, tipping her head back and emptying its contents. "I have no fucking idea. You know yourself best – could you have let it slip?"

Staring through Courtney, Daisy begins thinking aloud, "no way. Not possible. Okay, I can salvage this." Pouring herself a final drink, she downs the warm liquid in a single gulp and turns back to Courtney. "I'm going to talk to Charlie. Make sure he doesn't make the announcement until I speak with him."

"He's at the DJ booth now," Courtney says, furrowing her brow and wincing.

Scanning the room, Daisy locates Charlie and pushes both the bottle of scotch and the rocks glass into Courtney's hands, brushing past her and disappearing into the crowd.

<<<

A youthful Daisy holds her younger sister Lily's broken arm between her delicate fingers, careful to avoid the sight of the ghastly wound. The world turns on itself with a dizzying tremor as the girls drag shaking breaths through her toothy smiles, both attempting a pleasant mask.

"It's going to be okay, Lil," Daisy says with the most mature voice she can muster. Her eyes flit to the sight of the bone before they roll back into her head. "Just breathe and it will all be over soon."

Lily eagerly looks into her sister's eyes, awaiting guidance as her ducts spill over with salty tears. "Mom is going to be so mad," she chokes, the sobs building beneath her breath. She timidly watches Daisy. Her dark cobalt eyes await further instructions from her most beloved friend. "What do we do?"

Daisy ardently searches the backyard for assistance, holding on for as long as she can to her quickly dissipating all-knowing disposition. The blood of the wound cascades down Lily's arm and into Daisy's grasp as she stiffens in fear. "I don't know, but the bad part is over. I won't let anything else happen to you," she informs her sister with an anxious face, unsure if she can continue her brave facade as she senses the blood dripping against her legs. Her stomach turns on a queasy axis.

Pummeling through the private room of La Nuit, Daisy reaches into her handbag and produces a gold tube of cherry red lipstick, dabbing the center of her lips to give herself a flush of color. Shaking her hair away from her shoulders, she sashays her way toward Charlie to make her move. A waiter carrying a tray of champagne flutes passes by, and inconspicuously, Daisy plucks two between her manicured fingers then continues her stride toward Charlie who is speaking with a tall, dark haired man standing behind an unused DJ booth.

"Charlie!" Daisy calls in her friendliest voice, trying to keep her cool. "I have a present for you-u," she sing-songs, shaking the glasses in front of her.

"Daisy," Charlie says, greeting her with a comical disapproving father tone. "I heard you made Nicolas cry today?" He folds his arms across his chest and tilts his head to the side, suppressing a smile.

Stopping in her tracks, dipping her chin, and peering through her long eyelashes as she plays the part of the bashful daughter, Daisy meekly says, "I didn't mean to."

Releasing throaty chuckle and grabbing a microphone from the stand, Charlie thanks the man behind the booth. Reaching a hand to Daisy's shoulder, he silently instructs her to walk with him. "Daisy, I have some exciting news for you," he begins with a giddy tone.

"And I have exciting news for you!" Daisy counters, blocking him and hoping to stop whatever was looming in the next moment. "I think we should grab a drink and chat quickly."

"Nonsense! You're going to want to stick around for this," he says. Leaning in closely with a wild look in his eyes, he confesses, "I'm about to make you a legend."

As her mind reels, Daisy searches in attempt to barricade the freight train coming toward her. Dropping the glasses of champagne on a nearby bar table, she gnaws against her bottom lip and hastily examines the room. As the early morning sun begins its ascent through the eastern windows, the realization hits her: *Mendl*.

Without thinking, Daisy blurts out, "Kennedy Thomas signed the paperwork. The Mendl Research Laboratories is ours! Let's go chat about that first." Unbeknownst to Daisy, Kennedy is right behind her. He and Charlie stand at attention, staring at Daisy as her wide eyes survey the moment collapsing around her.

"What the *fuck*, Daisy?" Kennedy growls under his breath.

Charlie's face, now twinkling like Christmas morning, outstretches both of his arms to land a heavy hand on both Daisy and Kennedy's shoulders. "Look at our growing family!" he boasts with pride. "I just knew you crazy kids would finally recognize the potential between our organizations!"

Kennedy's mouth hangs open as fire burns beneath his navy eyes and his hands clench into fists; Daisy distinguishes that nothing can stop Charlie in this moment. He breaks free between the two and flicks the switch of the microphone as it roars to life through the speakers. An eerie squeak causes the crowd to moan with displeasure.

Stepping forward to leave the pair to their scuffle, Charlie begins.

"Could I have everyone's attention?" he booms through the microphone.

A few hoots and cheers erupt as Daisy and Kennedy stand motionless, Kennedy glaring into her eyes. Daisy's face is an unseen shade of embarrassment as Kennedy's nostrils flare. He opens his mouth to speak, but she blocks him in time.

"What did you think this was, Kennedy? Be sensible here." Her tone is unperturbed by his boiling anger.

Charlie continues with his eloquent speech despite the bickering pair behind him: "As we all know, Daisy Stone has been working diligently over the past few years to build our little Rose family to the pinnacle of research and diagnostics."

Mild cheers fill the space as Daisy perks at the mention of her name and gives a bashful wave.

Taking an aggressive step forward that does not register against Daisy's demeanor, Kennedy snarls, "you fucking *monster*." His words are more hurtful than Daisy's reaction portrays. "I should have listened to everyone, you conniving snake."

Daisy's head gives to one side as she attempts to play the innocent victim as she croons, "Kennedy, come on—" but she is stopped short as Kennedy continues his torment despite the continuing speech.

"We have been in talks with every major biological facility in, well, the world," Charlie continues as the quarrel behind him persists.

Leaning in further so that there are only inches between Kennedy and Daisy's noses, he spits in her face, "I was just another kill for you. Admit it. I heard the rumors and I told everyone that you weren't that type of person, but here we are."

His hands swing outward with an angry twitch. Daisy gently rests her palms atop Kennedy's shoulders in an attempt to soothe him.

"Please don't be like this," she whispers, her hushed tone causing his shoulders to relax at her touch. "This will be a tremendous deal for both of us."

His eyes soften as he takes a calming breath at her truthful words.

"It is with great honor that I announce our largest and final acquisition of the fiscal year..." Charlie says, his voice now boisterous and drawing the crowd into him.

"Kennedy," Daisy continues, unfazed by the commotion around them, "this is going to be the best venture of our careers. We are going to take the world by storm." Her voice acts as a velvet scarf, wrapping around Kennedy's hurt expression. "You *and* me," she whispers, her eyes hinting at a hopeful future in an unknown world.

A beat falls through the room as crowd hangs on Charlie's next words.

"It is with great pleasure that I announce The Rose Institute has been acquired by Bishop Enterprises!"

A moment of silence falls as the color drains from Daisy's face, her hands still resting on Kennedy's shoulders. Her wide eyes stare into the pits of his soul, but they do not see the sight before her. As the crowd bursts into an uproar and clink their glasses in celebration, Daisy finally turns to Charlie and growls, "what the fuck?" as he makes his way to put an arm around her to congratulate her nonexistent prize.

Daisy is pulled from Kennedy as he leans back into his heels and clutches his stomach, releasing an exuberant laugh that only infuriates Daisy further.

"The thanks needs to go to this young lady right here," Charlie announces, pulling Daisy to the center of the room. The crowd continues to cheer as she looks over her shoulder to see Kennedy topple over in laughter at her expense. "You all know Daisy is like an unruly daughter to me, but I could not be more proud of her today. Let's hear a few words from the woman of the hour!"

Daisy's jaw goes rigid as her eyes rest on Courtney, who is equally in shock. The two have a silent conversation as Courtney minutely shakes her head, signaling to Daisy that she did not know

Charlie shoves the microphone into Daisy's clumsy hands and leans in to whisper excitedly, "give the crowd a quick speech!"

Daisy stands dumbfounded as Charlie clutches her to his side. Daisy raises the microphone to her lips as she releases a hazy breath. Her mind reels and her focus fails to comprehend the room. She opens her mouth to speak, just in time to temporarily black out into Charlie's chest.

Part Two: **Autumn**

Chapter Seven: **Hey**

Suffocating her drink with her thumb and index finger, Daisy grips her wine glass tightly by the stem as she tumbles her wine to the beat of the grandfather clock in the lobby. *Tick-roll. Tick-roll. Tick-roll.* Sitting in an overstuffed leather armchair in the Douillet hotel foyer, she sinks further into the warm fabric to escape from the room, if only for a moment, as her chardonnay reverberates its yellow hue against her melancholy metronome. Already angry for having to waste a perfectly good Saturday night, she couldn't believe she was being forced into the same room as an egotistical maniac. Her blood boiling, she knows her animosity is showing as she begins tapping her perfectly manicured toe to the sound of the clock: *tick-roll-tap. Tick-roll-tap. Tick-roll-tap.*

Releasing herself from her hazy scowl, Daisy watches the mundane party spiral around her as her sights finally rest on her boss, Charlie Meyer. She now considered him nothing short of a seasoned brownnoser for forcing her into tonight's event. Watching him mingle between The

Rose Institute and Bishop Enterprises' board members with his pathetic attempts of advancement in his career as he barely covers his tracks makes her inadvertently roll her eyes.

As Charlie pushes his fake laughter at their vice president of the Americas, Daisy continues to scan the room for a potential out of the loathsome party. Her eyes canvas between droning conversations and ill-fitting suits until her view falls onto Harrison Bishop with a momentary beat. *That motherfucker*, she thinks to herself. *Shouldn't you be dead by now, Harry? I thought someone would have figured out how heartless and cold you really are and would have chopped you up into tiny bits and thrown you into the gulf by now.* Daisy reels as she continues to strangle her glass, and just as the life begins to vanish from her chardonnay, Harrison looks up from his martini to connect solely with Daisy.

Harrison's vivid green eyes dart into Daisy while his mouth perks at its corners until his dimples give way. Daisy releases a vocal sigh through her nostrils and mouths, "fuck you," before pulling her wine to her lips. She takes a long swig from the glass and gracefully sets the base against her bent knee. Although she keeps her poise, her jaw tenses in the way that her mother always willingly reminded her would "cause the most gruesome wrinkles that no medical doctor in these here Great Lakes could fix." She didn't care. *Let Harry ruin my face. What more could he possibly do?* She again sips her wine, finishing off the glass and forcefully impaling it into a senseless busboy as he passed.

Daisy watches Harrison excuse himself and take a step in her direction. *You have got to be fucking kidding me,* she thinks to herself. Reactively, she stands realizing that the wine has hit her a bit more quickly than she thought. Feeling off her axis, she extends a hand, signaling Harrison to stop. His feet freeze between steps as he waits for her next move.

Frozen in their unseen moment, two gunslingers wait for the draw. They survey the situation and wait for the other to break. Harrison narrows his eyes and Daisy flares her nostrils. The grandfather clock continues its relentless rhythm, drawing out the time in excruciating pain. They are no less than ten feet from each other, but the depth of animosity and tension crests as if an ocean is at high tide against ballroom floor. The cool waters flooding the room, both of them stand on the tide of the worst party New Orleans has ever seen. The water laps at their feet; the hatred brews and continues to flood.

When the moment feels as if it will never cease, Charlie steps in front of Harrison and earnestly reaches for his hand.

"Good to see you again, Mr. Bishop!" Charlie exclaims, with too much excitement as Harrison's brow furrows, still managing to hold his composure.

"And you and as well, Mr. Meyer. It's nice to see you in a sober state," says Harrison coolly.

"Give it a couple of hours," Charlie jokes with an exaggerated wink.

"Ah, yes," says Harrison, indifferently agreeing. "My team has been buzzing the last few weeks with the news of your group coming on board. I have a few colleagues who are itching to pick your brain on your antibodies research."

"Oh my! That would be delightful! I know I don't hold a candle to your accomplishments, but I'm happy to teach these kids a thing or two," says Charlie, ardently groveling at Harrison's pristine oxfords.

As Charlie drones on, Harrison feels himself being sucked into yet another poignant conversation. He lifts his eyes across the room to the leather armchair in hopes of continuing his internal exchange with Daisy, but she is gone. He stealthily scans the room for her angry eyes.

Just as he assumes she has fled the country, he spots her at the bar, leaning agitatedly with a dirty martini in one hand and a handsome man slightly too young for his liking on her other. Harrison raises a finger between himself and Charlie and skillfully excuses himself from whatever mundane conversation that would continue on without him.

Harrison slides his way to the bar as Daisy turns her face back to the dark haired man bidding for her attention. She gives her best "you'll wish you'd never met me" laugh that lures him in like a moth to a flame. As Harrison arrives and steps into their not-so-private moment, he pulls together a cool and aloof tone.

"Hey," he purrs toward Daisy with half of his mouth hinting at a smile as his dimples carve deep into his chiseled face. "How have you been?" he asks, completely ignoring the man who would inevitably strike out in the next few hours.

The man peers over his shoulder ready to tell off the prick attempting to pry him away from his game. Upon seeing his competition, he knocks himself into the bar and elbows Daisy in the torso.

"Holy shit. Harrison Bishop!"

Harrison does not remove his eyes from Daisy, and reluctantly, she flares her nostrils and shifts her annoyed gaze to meet his emerald eyes.

"Nice to see you, Harry," Daisy snarls sweetly though her teeth. "I'm sad to see you haven't been run over by a bus or trampled to death on safari," she continues with her best blasé "fuck you" voice.

The man snaps his head to meet Daisy's and hushes her with an urgent tone.

"Don't you know who he is? That's Harrison-fucking-Bishop," he adds under his breath with an earnest growl.

"Oh, we've met," Daisy groans back at the man without turning to meet his line of sight. "What could you possibly need, Harry?"

"It's been a while. Last I heard, you were the keynote speaker at Northwestern's graduation ceremony and—"

"And last I heard, you were acquiring The Rose Institute," Daisy retorts, cutting him off. She glares through him as Harrison's eyes tinge at the words being spat in his face. Leaning slightly in toward him, she whispers, "thank you for that, asshole."

The three sit for a beat as their standoff continues.

"Do you two know each other?" the man asks quizzically, not able decipher the strange interaction playing out before him.

"No," the old friends forcefully reply in unison. Daisy glowers at Harrison while he raises a single eyebrow and a smile tugs at his lips.

Harrison pulls his drink to his mouth but pauses before his sip.

"I heard you have the most eloquent speech prepared for me this evening," he says, his face hiding a playful and eager smile.

"I only have two words to say to you, Harry, and they're quick and to the point," she snaps back, leaning into the bar and forcing an audible breath through her nose.

$<<<$

Daisy stands in the doorway of Charlie's office with her arms crossed like a small child as blood rises in her cheeks. Her silk, navy wrap dress looks professional with her hair pulled into a sleek ponytail, but her body language reflects the contrary. She feels slightly out of place, standing in the room that she's argued her way through countless contracts, negotiations, and even spats with human resources. Her unease paints her in a hot aura of tension as she continues to agonize quietly.

"This has got to be a fucking joke," Daisy says as her green eyes pierce through a spot in the center of Charlie's forehead, laser beam piercing through his dark skin. "There isn't a single person in this *entire* building that could give the introduction for Harry? I know there are gaggles of interns on the sixth floor who would give up their trust funds to breathe the same air as him." Her tone far too aggressive, but hearing Harrison's name ring through the walls of what felt like her fortress of power for so many years gave her the stature of a child who had been caught with her hand in the cookie jar.

"You're the head of mergers and acquisitions. You should be ecstatic that The Rose Institute is finally moving up in the world, especially with your lifelong friend!" he responds in an astonished tone. "This is a big step for both of you!"

Daisy closes her eyes, releasing an audible sigh, and lets her shoulders fall as she attempts her best fake smile.

"You're right. I know this is a huge step for everyone and I'm very excited to be involved," she says halfheartedly. "I'll make sure Harry feels a warm welcome to the Rose team."

She could already feel the wheels turning in her brain as she began writing the passive aggressive toast in her mind.

"Harrison," Charlie absentmindedly corrects her as he opens a folder of contracts. "Please call him Harrison."

Daisy turns on her heels to exit, muttering, "anything to make The Cure All Kid happy" as she pulls open the door.

Once outside the office, Daisy pauses to watch her fellow coworkers casually walk along the corridor. Their happy and banal lives cause a seething tension between her brows.

"COURTNEY?" she hollers through the hallway as she marches toward her office. "Courtney. I know you're here!" Her mood quickly declines as she searches for anyone to kill in her path.

Pausing before exiting a nearby conference room, Courtney takes a steadying breath before stepping out into the lion's den.

"I'm here, Miss Stone."

"Walk with me," Daisy presses as she keeps her speed and forces Courtney to pick up her clip. "See if you can find me a transcript of the eulogy given at Joseph Stalin's funeral."

"I take it Charlie told you about the speech," Courtney says, sensing a strain in Daisy's voice. She contorts her face as she attempts to register Daisy's emotion. Courtney stops in her tracks, staring at Daisy's perfect ponytail as it swings back and forth while she heatedly walks to her office. "Is this about something else?" she bemuses to herself.

Courtney had predicted that Daisy was going to be angry, but after working for her for the last five years, she had seen her in nearly every light imaginable. Angry, sad, hurt. Even that one time she had walked in on Daisy with a Swedish diplomat. The Rose Institute signed off on a $1.9 billion acquisition with the Swedish government the next day, but this was a different side of Daisy that she rarely saw. The word sat on the tip of her tongue, but she couldn't pin it down.

"I'll do it myself," Daisy huffs as she continues past Courtney and into her office. "Cancel all my meetings, I'm on sabbatical until Monday."

Slamming the door behind her, Courtney stares at the nameplate on Daisy's door. *Miss Daisy Stone*, the duality of the name causing her head to cock to the side. "Flustered," Courtney says under her breath.

That was it, she was flustered.

Courtney arrives alongside the awkward trio. Harrison stares with a tranquil gaze into Daisy's heated eyes as the man fawns over Harrison. This was not an unusual scene for Courtney, but she was shocked to see Harrison within feet, let alone miles, of Daisy without being in a body bag.

"They're ready for you on stage, Miss Stone," she sheepishly interrupts, bracing for the beratement to come her way.

A moment passes as the group holds their positioning until Daisy breaks herself from her trance and greets Courtney with a soft smile that does not touch her eyes. "I'll be right there," she soothes as she straightens to her full height and excuses herself from the uncomfortable party.

The man swallows heavily against his throat as he musters the courage to speak. Finally breaking his silence, he says, "so, Harrison. Tell me about—"

"Please shut up," says Harrison in a cool voice without flinching.

Daisy plods away from the bar as Courtney meets her at her side.

"Are you ready? Do you need me to get you anything?"

"An atomic bomb would be nice," Daisy jokes, but the words don't register across her face. Sensing Courtney's troubled smile, she grabs her by the elbow to pull her in and reassures her, "I'll be just fine." A halfhearted smile pulls at her pale lips.

"It will all be over soon," says Courtney, offering a gentle, reassuring tap against Daisy's forearm.

Courtney directs her to the side of the stage as the ballroom hushes. The emcee warms up the crowd to begin the evening's festivities and partygoers funnel in from the outside bar into the ballroom.

Daisy stands at the foot of the stage, conscious of her breath – much more conscious than she'd like to be at this moment. She attempts to steady her breathing although she can feel the heat rise in her cheeks. She takes her small stack of notecards from her miniature purse and clenches the corners between her front teeth. Dragging her hands through her long hair, she drapes her head backward and feels the pull on her neck as her shoulders start to give. She grazes her sides as she smoothes her emerald green dress. The confidence she had originally felt when she reviewed her ensemble in the full-length mirror of her living room slowly subsides as she feels the foreign anxiety and dread build in the pit of her stomach, almost as if she had consumed a vat of vinegar.

As long as you don't tell him to go fuck himself, this will all be over soon, she repeats to herself. With a barely confident sigh, she carefully removes the index cards from her teeth and looks across the stage as the emcee continues his charade.

Beginning to feel herself let go of her frustration, she surveys the room. She finds Harrison standing directly across from her on the opposite end of the stage, his piercing green eyes drilling into her. His hair was perfectly tousled, as if he had just rolled out of bed, and he donned a thousand-dollar suit. If she didn't hate every fiber of his being, he could have been attractive.

As she stares, he pulls his bottom lip under his teeth and lets the corners of his mouth fall into that infuriating half-smile that pinches his dimples, making him look so young and carefree. Attempting to ease the situation,

Harrison gives her his best "well, here we are," look and Daisy feels herself start to spiral, glaring back with her own feverishly green eyes.

<<<

Standing in her off-white lab coat with a tray of pipettes in hand, Daisy combs through a row of samples reviewing each label on a corresponding spreadsheet on her computer. The dreary laboratory, with three laboratory stations but only enough space for two, is cramped with the towering shelves and overflowing workstations filled with samples and trays. The midday sun shines through a bleak window in the corner of the room.

Harrison, donning an identical stained lab coat, his hair an unkept mess with a too-large Northwestern tee shirt and jeans, stands up from his stool and quietly announces to the room, "It...it worked. It actually worked?"

He turns to Daisy with a look of confusion and bewilderment.

"What do you mean that it worked?" Daisy questions him as she meets his stare, pulling the pair of tortoise shell glasses from her face and placing them in her voluminous hair. Her youthful and carefree glow flickers and a curious smile touches her eyes as she makes her way toward Harrison.

"I followed the instructions just as you said and my sample worked," Harrison uncertainly answers, holding the petri dish to have Daisy confirm.

Delicately clasping the light pink dish by the rim, Daisy raises it to her face and studies its contents before dropping her arm to hang slack and giving a playfully irked face back to him.

"Wrong sample, idiot," she says, laughing at him and pushing the dish into his chest.

Harrison's face flushes with an adolescent smile that causes Daisy to chuckle even further.

"Oops," he laughs. "My mistake."

"Miss Stone?"

A man with a headset whispers into her ear, pulling her from the memory.

"Miss Stone? Are you ready to go? You're up next," the scrawny man hisses in a hushed tone. He begins tapping his pen against his clipboard, signaling he doesn't have time for her to lollygag at the stairs. Daisy returns from the thought and again locks eyes with Harrison, his lips no longer in the boyish grin, but turned into a hard line that matches his furrowed brow.

Daisy raises her sleek, nude pump to the stair and pauses on the first step. Taking a sobering breath, she drops her shoulders and slowly releases the air from her parted lips, continuing to hold her glare. Climbing up the stairs, she turns the notecards between her fingers and gracefully approaches the microphone just as the emcee concludes his monologue. The audience's polite applause and murmurs fall to a reserved hum.

Raising a finger to the microphone, Daisy taps the matte metal to test its sound. Hearing the distant "thum-thum," she feigns a confident look at the crowd, and with all the determination she can muster, she warmly greets the room, welcoming everyone to the event. After thanking the guests for their donations and generosity, she begins the portion of her tribute that she had been dreading since Charlie had assigned her this task weeks back.

"It is with great pleasure that I welcome my very old friend, Harrison Bishop, to the stage tonight," she says.

Daisy pauses, feeling the eyes of the room sit on her as she begins to gain the attention of the crowd.

After three excruciating cocktail hours and countless glasses of chardonnay, she muses to herself how the crowd is even functioning after all the alcohol. *But alas, they still could pull themselves together to see their prince*. With that thought, she thanked everyone on the board and cautiously transitioned tactics as she let her arms fall to her side, releasing herself from her note cards.

As the excess wine hit her head, she could feel herself letting go of the weight of the evening. *Fuck it, let's give him the speech he deserves,* she thinks to herself.

"Not many people know this," she coyly starts again, as if she is relinquishing a secret, "but ol' Harry and I go way back." She smirks as she glances toward Harrison, watching his mouth fuse into a dissatisfied grimace. "All the way back to Northwestern University. We actually worked on the same team that discovered TEA, and I was one of the first to be able to congratulate him on his revelation!" she exclaims, turning her well-hidden anger as she gazes back to meet his now glowering green eyes.

Harrison's cheeks flush and he uncomfortably shifts in his stance as he lets his hands fall into his pockets.

He looked small, almost childlike, as if he had been scolded for tracking mud across the family room carpet. Daisy knew exactly how to pull away the velvet curtains of "Harrison Bishop" and turn him into "Harry, The Boy Who Ruined Her Career" with just a harsh glance.

"And let me tell you," Daisy starts again, divulging more to the crowd as a few chuckles and sneers pierce the air, "when he first discovered the bacteria, he didn't even realize what he had done." More laughter now emerging from the crowd, she could feel Harrison's eyes turning from a shade of emerald to a stone gray.

"I had to point out the streaking pattern we had been looking for in the first place!" she jokes, as the crowd breaks into feverish laughter, enjoying the dry antidote. They survey the room, their excitement of extracting whatever small information they can from her about their noble prince. The boy who saved a million lives. *The fucking Cure All Kid*, she angrily thought.

"Now, if you want to hear the juicy details," she continues as their enjoyment rises and their heads lean in to hear all the salacious details, "it's almost as if he wouldn't even be here today without me back in his collegiate career!" Daisy continues her speech as the crowd roars into a bawdy thunder. Once again, she locks eyes with Harrison, not out of sadness, but out of sheer anger and enmity. His eyes crease into thin slivers and his cheeks flush in anger, a side rarely seen in such a public setting.

More than pleased to see Harrison in such an agitated state, Daisy breaks their stare and returns back to the crowd, elated with the response of her passive aggressive speech. The front row is keeling over in laughter as they slap their knees and cover their mouths at the sake of Harrison's career. Charlie mouths a silent "Oh my God" to his wife as they clink their champagne glasses, continuing their hearty laughter.

Daisy continues with fiery revenge as she mocks his pathetic career. Her eyes building to a mix of amber and emerald as she fuels her hatred for him, she pauses as the air settles in the room and the laughter begins to subside. Harrison's lips purse and he releases a slow breath from his nostrils, waiting for this torment to recede. The years of animosity and anger sit between them as the silence of the room wanes. Harrison's betrayal and Daisy's melancholy somber sit in the air like the elephant in the room, crushing the crowd with its weight.

Harrison opens his mouth, as if to right the situation and speak all the words that would conclude the years of hardship between them, but just as he raises his foot to step up the stairs, Daisy turns back to the crowd and concludes her alluring toast.

"And, with that, I'd like to raise a glass to the reason we are all here tonight," Daisy says, turning back to Harrison as he freezes mid-step, waiting for her next move. "May the venture between our two organizations be profitable and aid the human race in our quest for perfection and peace."

A quiet agreement falls among the crowd as everyone echoes a sincere "here, here," and dozens of faint clinks fill the ballroom. Daisy continues to hold Harrison's gaze, and with a serene moment of deflation, she releases a slight sigh of satisfaction, regains her posture, and turns to give a final, "your man of the hour, Harrison Bishop, the new president of The Rose-Bishop Institute, the newest subsidiary of Bishop Enterprises," she says halfheartedly, promptly beginning to move from the stage.

Harrison gracefully rushes across the stage to meet her at the microphone in hopes of having a moment of peace, but delivers a hollow "Daisy," as she reaches the final step and exits the stage. She turns over her shoulder to give a lingering look in his direction, just as the pull of the crowd tugs him into his congratulatory speech. His notecards weigh heavily in his breast pocket as he contemplates his options. This is the biggest business move of his career. Bigger than the creation of Bishop Enterprises or the discovery of TEA. He was now the president of the largest medical conglomerate in the world, and yet he is preoccupied with chasing after his collegiate love.

How could you possibly screw this up again? he asks himself slowly, surveying the crowd as he meekly thanks the rows of donors and businessmen that have supported his career. *Either let her go or give the speech, you coward*, his mind rattles.

Daisy continues her confident walk through the tables as she moves to the back of the ballroom.

"Today is one of the most momentous days in my career," Harrison smoothly confesses to the crowd through his boyish grin, his smile not reflecting in his pained eyes. In truth, this may have been the pinnacle moment of his life, but the depth to his statement rang true through the audience.

"When I was a young boy, I used to dream of the stars and space, imagining what it would be like to leave this planet. Explore outside this universe," he professes as Daisy reaches the exit, turning over her shoulder to lean against the doorframe. "But as I've aged, I am able to see that this world is just as complex as the galaxy we move within. I have witnessed the issues and dilemmas that humans face on a daily basis, and I want nothing more than to do more in this world by making a difference in what little cards I was dealt."

Harrison pauses as every person in the ballroom hangs on his every word. He drops his sight to his hands, rotating the cookie cutter speech cards between his thumb and forefingers before he coughs out a dry, singular laugh then continues on.

"In all honesty, I never imagined in a thousand years that this is where I would be standing today," he says, his jade eyes casting over the crowd to meet the distant eyes of Daisy. "I never felt that one discovery was a deciding factor in the world we occupy today," he continues, attempting to call out to Daisy in whatever lingering chance he held. "I wanted nothing more than to make those around me better, make the world around me a better place for everyone."

A small clamor of applause and the praise of his new colleagues fills the room, but this isn't the attention he is seeking.

Continuing to hold Daisy's attention as he disengages from the room around him, Harrison's eyes now deep with apprehension, he feels the distance from her. Neglecting the room around them, the suits and donors that bided so unrelentingly for his attention, he speaks directly to her, relinquishing everything he had always been meaning to say after all of these years.

"I expected only to aide as we solved whatever minuet issues we confronted and watch the world around us grow just from our gusto and devotion."

The crowd built into a roar as the speech gained speed, but still, Harrison didn't change his course.

"My life's work has come so far from the too-small Northwestern laboratory. As small as we may feel from time to time, I'm excited to have you by my side as we continue to take on the issues of today."

The crowd is standing in ovation as the speech climaxes, and Harrison takes a step back, removing his eyes from Daisy's heavy glare. He scans the room and realizes the scene growing around them as cheers come from the hordes of people beginning to rush the stage. *Come on, Daisy. Listen to me for once*, he pleads internally.

In what feels like a surreal blur, Charlie reaches the stage and grabs on to Harrison's hand to thank him for his climactic speech as other colleagues swarm the stage behind him. Harrison examines the room in a slight panic searching for Daisy, but comes up short. As Charlie continues his song and dance of thanks and praise, Harrison reciprocates with a lukewarm handshake. He hastily makes his way off of the stage and pushes through the crowd toward the back of the ballroom. The bright lights of the stage break as he enters the dim lights of the dinner tables. Guests begin pulling at Harrison's suit jacket, gripping him as he passes, yelling out, "the Cure All Kid!" and "What would we do without you?"

Holding his composure, he slides through the repugnant crowd of gratitude and phony bouts of admiration, his eyes continuing to scan the back of the room but coming up empty as he realizes Daisy is nowhere to be found.

As Harrison finally breaks through the gripping mass of people, he tears through the back doors into the quiet sanctuary of the lobby leading to the lonely bar. The doors settle behind him with a heavy thud. His eyes land on the mousy-haired blonde, her head hanging low and her elbows resting against the bar's dark stone. Standing where she confidently stood no more than fifteen minutes before, the eeriness in Daisy's shift is unsettling. Her emerald green dress rises and falls silently against her slender body and her shoulders drop as she releases an exasperated breath.

Harrison hesitantly approaches Daisy in her troubled state. He controls himself long enough to allow Daisy her moment of solace as the air dies of whatever lingering momentum once hung between them. Her body is trembling with anxiety, and as badly as he wants to move in, he reminds himself that he cannot fix this. *You are the problem, not the solution,* he says to himself as she lifts her head to her shoulders and releases herself from her anguish.

It has been years since Harrison has seen Daisy in this condition, vulnerable and upset. Daisy Stone, the ultimate oxymoron. He recalls what he would hear through the corridors of the Northwestern laboratory: "She's as sweet as flowers but she's so tough she'll kill you." Here she was, the once courageous and provocative Daisy Stone that he had always feared and pined after, slumped in defeat.

"I'm sorry," he whispers into the empty air, hoping that anyone would hear. "I... I know this isn't the way this should be playing out," he continues, knowing he should just shut up, but he cannot help himself from consoling Daisy.

You are the problem, not the solution, he reminds himself again, feeling out of his element, lost without the perfect words to mend her wounds. He lets his eyes rest softly on her as he listens to her breathing, lingering on her every move.

Suddenly, as if awoken from a dream, Daisy spins around to face Harrison, her eyes smoldering and intense, much darker than he anticipated. She holds her weight to the bar in an all too familiar scene that Harrison had never forgotten, bracing her back into the stone and stabilizing herself for her next thought. With that, Daisy repeats the same words that replayed in Harrison's mind time and time again.

"No. No, Harry. You *don't* know." Daisy repeats, pulling the pair back almost a decade into the past. Except in this instance, she does not allow herself to sink back into the bar; she pushes herself in every ounce of confidence she can gather and positions herself directly in front of Harrison. "You haven't learned a damn thing about me, and you never really learned anything about the world around you."

Her words lash across his face, forcing him to squint in reaction to the blow and push his lips into a hard line as he accepts his deserved beratement.

"You're right," is all Harrison squeaks out in a defeated whisper.

Daisy raises her hands to rest on Harrison's cheeks, forcing his gaze from the floor and into the pools of her jade green eyes. They stand in their moment, the air that hanging stagnant with every ounce of tension and turmoil they had ever experienced in their years of friendship. Daisy's eyes soften as her lips slowly part to break the silence. Before she can continue, Harrison takes his chance and grips the small of her back, pulling her lips to meet his.

Caught in the surprise of the moment, Daisy allows her hands to roam from Harrison's cheeks and into his hair. She grips the nape of his neck and pulls him closer as their mouths continue to connect. The anger and bewilderment of their speeches quickly turn into desire and fervor as Harrison's long arms wrap around Daisy's back then pluck her from the floor and push her into the bar, their breath and ache beginning to quicken.

Daisy forces her hands against Harrison's shoulders as she peels him from her body.

"Harry, wait," she huffs, the moment connecting with her consciousness. "What the fuck are we doing?"

Leaning his weight into Daisy's outstretched arms, Harrison stares deep into her eyes, his breathing ragged, forcing his chest to rise and fall visibly.

"I'm not quite sure," he confesses. Shaking the moment from his head, he lifts himself to his feet. "I've—" he begins, just as Daisy regains her footing and stops him short of his thought.

"Not now. I'm leaving. I'm sure I'll see you sooner or later," she exasperatedly announces as she pulls away from Harrison and tucks her bag beneath her arm.

"Wait, Daisy," Harrison calls over his shoulder with a half laugh, causing Daisy to stop without turning to face him. "Let me take you to dinner. We can just..." he trails off, his unplanned actions reeling in his mind. "We can just talk. I'll even let you scream at me until you're blue in the face," he offers, chuckling more intensely as the humor pangs in his eyes.

Turning to meet his face, Daisy rests for a moment, attempting to sense Harrison's sincerity. The hopefulness in his face causes him to broadcast a heartwarming smile that digs his dimples into the pits of his cheeks and his eyes to crinkle with delight. "I'll even let you stand on the table and exclaim to the restaurant how terrible of a human I am."

Daisy turns her head back toward the door as she imagines herself sprinting from the bar and into the street, running as hard as her legs would allow until she collapses in the Gulf of Mexico. Instead, she releases an unexpected sigh and she relinquishes her pride at the idea of publicly scorching Harrison to a bloody pulp.

"Fine," she breathes with annoyance. "But I'm not promising to fight fair."

A genuine chuckle crosses Harrison's lips as he realizes the air has begun to settle. "I wouldn't expect anything less from you," he croons as Daisy exits from the hotel foyer and into the evening street.

Harrison takes a step away from the bar and releases a settling breath. A young cocktail waitress approaches him with an empty tray of drinks and asks, "can I get you anything?"

Without turning to meet her gaze, Harrison keeps his eyes on the foyer door and answers, "I think I'm okay," before finally turning to lock eyes with the pretty, blonde waitress.

Realizing who he is, the waitress perks up and apologies.

"I'm sorry Mr. Bishop. I didn't realize it was you," she says.

Harrison narrows his eyes and looks over the waitress.

"Not a problem at all, Miss?"

"Highland," she says, her eyes sparkling with wild excitement. "Miss Highland."

"Well, Miss Highland," Harrison seductively rebuts, "how would you like to take a tour of my new wine cellar?"

Chapter Eight: **Redbone**

Harrison bursts through the doorway of the top floor of the Bishop Enterprises corporate office, startling Kit, who has his head buried in a heap of paperwork with another receptionist.

"Holy shit!" he squeals, realizing the source of the commotion. "You nearly gave me a heart attack, Mr. Bishop," he pants, regaining his breath and wildly blinking his eyes.

The Bishop Enterprises corporate offices, while their brooding, dark exterior provides a menacing presence to the New Orleans skyline, was surprising light and airy throughout its interior. The cement walls and cool toned lighting were unsettlingly calm. The open concept created a relaxing zen with its frosted glass and subtle electronic music humming through its halls.

"How the hell are you doing this afternoon, Kit?" Harrison calls to him in a chipper tone as he passes through the lobby, littered with receptionists and people chatting. "Walk with me," he says as Kit rises from his chair and quickens his pace to meet Harrison's side. "This afternoon's agenda?"

He's far too happy for this time of the day, Kit thinks to himself, skeptical of Harrison's cheery tone.

"You're in a good mood. Could it have anything to do with you being three hours late?" he questions, unsure of how to react and ignoring the request. "Did you skip your morning meetings to get drunk with Mr. Madison and Mr. Lyon and pretend to be foreign diplomats again?"

Harrison reaches a stern hand to Kit's shoulders and slaps him against his back with a hearty chuckle. "No, no. I'm pretty sure we could only get away with that the one time." His laugh reverberates through the hall as they arrive outside of Harrison's office.

Opening the door for Kit, a gesture that forces him to do a double take, he enters the office and takes a seat across from Harrison's desk. Ducking out of sight to open a lower drawer in his desk, Harrison begins rummaging through the contents before calling up to Kit, "drink?"

Stunned by Harrison's attitude, Kit cannot help but oblige. "Why not?" he says, still unsure of how to react.

Harrison drops two crystal glasses atop the metal desk and begins pouring from a worn bottle of scotch. "Let's hear this afternoon's agenda, Kitty. We're not getting any younger!" he warmly grins.

Yeah, he's drunk, Kit thinks as he dismisses the unusual behavior.

"You have a dinner arrangement with the executive board. Small agenda, mostly discussing The Rose Institute's transitional moves and then a few odds and ends from the sales team."

Harrison rises and circles his desk to tower over Kit, dropping a glass of scotch into his unsteady hand. Perching himself back onto the desk, he takes an exaggerated sip from his glass and savors the liquor. "Sounds fantastic! Should be a splendid evening!"

Kit drops the glass to his knee with an irked, "okay, Harrison," confronting him with a troubled inflection. "What the hell is going on? You haven't been excited for a meeting since…" the thought not piecing together in his mind. "Well, ever, if I'm being honest."

Harrison downs the contents of his glass and swings around the desk to pour another. "Kit, you worry about me too much," he says, his eyes glinting a vivid emerald as he lifts the bottle to Kit, silently asking if he'd like another drink.

Spitting back an almost disgusted laugh and ignoring his offer, Kit blurts out, "for good reason."

"Is it so wrong for me to be in a good mood?" Harrison rebukes with a fatherly tone.

"No, but if this is your version of a good mood, it's pretty annoying," Kit half-teases as he hides a confused smile. *I guess even the devil can be in a good mood*, he muses to himself before returning back to business. "Do you want me to call you a car to take you to the restaurant or will Sampson be retrieving you?"

Walking towards the window, Harrison gestures outdoors and exclaims, "It's fucking beautiful out, Kit! I'm going to walk!"

"I'll have Sampson pick you up in twenty," Kit definitively announces as he stands to exit. "I'll also have a psychiatrist meet you at the restaurant to check the sutures of your lobotomy when you arrive."

"Sounds like a wonderful time!" Harrison mockingly replies. "Everything you do is wonderful and you're the best employee in the building!"

Kit rolls his eyes and leaves with a final, "let me know when you get back to your home planet."

"Thank you, Sampson," Harrison acknowledges as he steps from the backseat of the SUV and onto the sidewalk. He arrives at the restaurant as the sky is waning from sapphire blue to soft rose. The streetlights blink to life and the sidewalks trickle with the bustling crowds pouring from their offices into the afternoon air.

Ken and Duncan loiter near the entrance of the restaurant as Harrison arrives. The pair's faces illuminate as they each light a cigarette. Crossing his arms and giving the two a bogus stern face, he reprimands the two.

"Smoking? In this day and age?"

Shrugging their shoulders and brushing off the scold, Duncan extends his cigarette to Harrison. "You want to bum one?"

Staring at the smoking cigarette with an almost angry brood, Harrison pauses before relinquishing. "Yeah, why not," he says, as he reaches into his suit pants to retrieve a small container of hand sanitizer.

As Harrison drops a small blob in his palm and rubs his hands together, Ken observes, "a little redundant, huh?"

"Not like it even matters," Duncan corrects. "We already have the cure for cancer," he continues as he lifts his chin in Harrison's direction and he sets a fresh cigarette to his lips before lighting the white paper and inhaling deeply with a satisfied sigh.

Their laughter fills the street as Harrison takes a steadying drag from the stick. "Anyone else here yet?" he asks, surveying the sidewalk surrounding the restaurant before blowing smoke into the changing sky.

Ken flicks his half-smoked cigarette into the street, blowing his final drag above him. "Not yet. We're actually going to be grabbing Mrs. Park from up the street."

"She got caught in some training seminar," Duncan chimes in to finish the thought. "She wants two handsome men to save her from the trenches," he says in a singsong tone, mocking a flirty women's voice.

"Well, at least one," Harrison wisecracks between the two as he flicks his half-smoked cigarette butt into the street and shoves his hands into his trousers. "I'll make my way to the bar and meet you boys back here in fifteen?"

"You got it," Ken confirms as they make their way down the street. "You know I'm the handsome one, right?" he prods at Duncan as Harrison ducks into the restaurant.

A teenaged hostess waits in the foyer of the restaurant as Harrison approaches and coolly rests an elbow atop her stand as she shuffles through a few papers before her.

"Anyone from the Bishop party arrived yet?"

Without looking up from her work, she drily answers, "I'm not sure, let me take a quick look, sir — oh my God. Hi, Cure—" she stops herself and feigns a cough. "Mr. Bishop."

A soft snicker escapes Harrison's nose at the reaction, "not a problem, Miss?"

"Miss Sarah. Wait, no. Miss Pearson," she says, flushing with crimson as she rushes her hands to her cheeks to hide her embarrassment.

Soothing her with a warm smile, Harrison consoles her with an understanding glance. "Not a problem, Miss Pearson." Her eyes grow to twice their size. "I'll be at the bar if anyone ever does arrive."

The joke does not register with Sarah as she stands motionless in confusion. Harrison dips in his ear slightly toward her, waiting for the laugh.

"Oh!" she says as a stiff laugh escapes her. "Good one, Mr. Bishop."

The restaurant is warm and inviting with shades of beige and cream. The wait staff prepares for the evening's dinner shift as they drape tablecloths across the lengthy tables and lay rows of silverware. The dining room appears desolate as Harrison makes his way to the bar. Spattered with a few patrons and an elderly bartender who is polishing glasses, Harrison stands near an empty bar stool.

The bartender peers up from his work and through his thick glasses, he squints to confirm the identity of the man before him. A polite smile crosses his face as the gentleman does not fawn over Harrison, but instead returns back to his work and throws out a playful, "what will you have, sonny?"

The casual question happily surprises Harrison as he pulls out a stool next to a younger man writing in a notebook and skimming through what appear to be contracts.

"What do you recommend?"

The older gentleman laughs at the question.

"A drink," he jokes without disturbing his work as a hidden smile causes his eyes to crinkle at the edges.

Harrison enjoys the bartender's witty banter and a carefree smile envelops his face.

"What is he drinking?" he asks, tilting his head to the seated man.

Leaning backward without looking, the bartender picks up a bottle of vodka. The clear bottle labeled with a sleek, red label has bold lettering. "Redbone," he comments dryly.

"Redbone and water it is," Harrison says as he dips his head to ask the man at the bar if he can join him.

"Seat's wide open," the man gestures with his pen as he pulls his sleeve back to examine his watch. "Past six so I should stop working anyway."

The man looks to be about early forties, handsome if he shaved his scruffy beard. His light brown hair and soft eyes that crease at the seams give him a look of someone who has been around the block a few times. His blazer is wrinkled and his collar is undone with his navy tie hanging askew from his jacket pocket. He looks as if he has had a rough couple of days in the office and is in major need of a drink.

"Harrison Bishop," Harrison says, introducing himself and reaching out a hand as he lands softly on the barstool.

"Alexander George," says the man as he grips Harrison's hand and pauses, recognizing the name. "Well I'll be damned, *the* Harrison Bishop," he says as a calm laugh escapes from him while he collects his work and starts filing it away into his briefcase, too exhausted to grovel over Harrison's presence.

"That's me. Last time I checked, anyway," says Harrison, his smile grazing his eyes. "Can I get you a drink while I wait for the rest of my group?"

Alexander drops his bag to the base of his stool and adjusts himself, settling into the seat.

"Why not? I don't have anywhere to rush off to," he says, his wry expression intriguing Harrison.

"A drink for my friend here if you wouldn't mind?" Harrison requests, raising two fingers to grab the bartender's attention. Turning back to Alexander, he undoes his top button and removes his tie, mimicking his look.

The two sit in silence for a moment as they wait for their drinks and savor their first sip as Harrison breaks the silence.

"So, what is it that you do, Alexander?"

"Alex, please," Alexander corrects. "I've recently broken into the software market. I've been consulting a few startups." His voice is mundane and stale with his apathetic response.

Harrison takes another sip and says, "that sounds fascinating. How are you liking it so far?"

"Startups can be rough," Alexander reluctantly admits, as he laughs at a memory that Harrison does not understand. Noticing the disconnect, he explains, "nothing is a guarantee, which can be rocky. But I'm hoping the risk is worth the reward."

"Well, I'm jealous," Harrison confesses. "I do miss the days of working a challenging day then coming home utterly exhausted and needing to hide away from the world." The idea causes both men to laugh in agreement.

"Enough about my day, I'm closing up shop for the evening," Alexander grins, dismissing himself from the topic. "What new undertakings have you been up to these days? Bishop Enterprises sounds like a madhouse from the gossip I hear," he says, taking a long sip of his drink as he leans into the bar enjoying the distraction.

"A madhouse indeed. We've been doing a lot of international investments as of late so I've had a fun time attempting to learn Mandarin and German the last few months with absolutely zero success," Harrison explains as the two laugh at the outrageous idea.

"Sounds like quite the misadventure," Alexander snickers.

"Yeah, I felt like an idiot in Beijing when the translator had to stop me about thirty seconds in to tell me that I sounded like I was having a stroke," he says, polishing off his drink and pushing the glass beyond his reach. "Another?" he invitingly asks of Alexander.

"Pull my leg," Alexander playfully agrees as he shakes his glass to measure its remaining contents. "Well, other than hindering the American-Chinese relations, what other exciting ventures do you have coming through the pipeline? Hopefully staying out of any bureaucratic roles."

Cordially laughing through the banter, Harrison swaps out his empty glass for a fresh drink as the bartender drops it before him.

"No, no. I don't have the stomach for that type of torture," says Harrison. He swirls a lime through the ice of his drink with his forefinger and reaches into the glass to delicately pull out the fruit and drop it on a bar napkin. "I've actually just signed off on an acquisition of The Rose Institute."

Alexander raises his drink to lips and knocks his head back with a final gulp. The ice ricochets off the glass and he snorts through his nostrils with a dry laugh, causing Harrison to perk at the reaction.

"That should be," he begins, but the words escape him as he presses his empty glass toward the bar with just a lingering forefinger and swallowing hard. "Interesting," he finishes, giving his head a slight shake.

Harrison wrinkles his eyes in confusion as he gives a harsh scratch to his five o'clock shadow.

"Interesting?"

Nodding his head with a subtle laugh, Alexander connects the dots for Harrison.

"How is Daisy? I haven't seen her in quite some time."

Who the hell is this guy? Harrison thinks to himself.

"You know Daisy?" he asks with an astonished tone, attempting to mask his annoyance.

"We're old colleagues," replies Alexander confidently, laughing eerily. "How long has this new venture been in the works?" he asks with a vaguely nosy tone.

Brushing the comment aside, Harrison says, "I've actually known her since college. It's a pretty big undertaking for the both of us," he explains, attempting to give an assured answer. "She was actually with me when I discovered Episcopus Aerobium."

"Oh, wow," Alexander surprisingly answers, the shock not relaying against his expression. "She must be delighted to be brought into such a large organization as yours."

Giving a subdued laugh, Harrison timidly admits, "not at first, but I think once we get to working like old times, it will be like riding a bicycle."

Cocking his head to the side, Alexander gives an inquisitive look.

"Old times?"

"We actually met about halfway through our undergraduate degrees at Northwestern," says Harrison, now settling into his own story. "I was nearly failing biology because I spent so much time worrying about my astronomy courses. I always told myself I was destined to go to space, so I initially started studying physics and engineering, but I couldn't understand biology for the life of me." He looks ahead but his sight is inside of his own mind as he recounts the memories. "Daisy was an intimidating genius who always seemed to wreck our class curve, so I attempted to butter her up and have her tutor me. Instead, she told me, 'If you're going to be this fucking stupid, maybe you deserve to fail,' which still scares me shitless to this day."

"Typical Daisy," Alexander says, raising a drink at the story and laughs at the thought of her torment.

Harrison raises a drink, too. "Typical Daisy," he says, taking a long drink and pausing at his own memory before he continues. "So, I told her if I aced the next exam, she had to tutor me for the remainder of the course. She begrudgingly said yes and in my hotshot mentality, I studied my beer bong-ridden ass off just to have this pretty girl teach me about cell structure and yell at me every weekday. But I aced the test and she ended up being such a great teacher that by the end of the course, I had switched my major to biology and we ended up working through our undergraduate degrees and eventually graduate school together."

Alexander lowers his line of sight to the table as he spins his drink on his axis.

"So, you fucked?"

The question stuns Harrison but only his eyebrows raise at the absurd question.

"No. We had this back and forth thing all through the years but she is one ferocious beast to tie down."

"She should have that written on her tombstone," Alexander comments as he hints at his own mysterious Daisy tale.

Of course I sat down next to the biggest ass in New Orleans, Harrison thinks to himself.

"Are you a friend of Daisy's?" he asks, feeling a bit intrusive but without care.

Alexander pulls his fresh drink toward his mouth slowly and says, "oh, I *know* Daisy." His words hold a heavy weight as he takes a long drag of his drink. Setting his elbows tenderly on the bar top, he clasps a hand over a fist and props his head, settling in for a story. "I used to work with Rushmore Testing and we were contracted with The Rose Institute on a few projects."

"I've never heard of Rushmore Testing. What type of work do they do?" Harrison asks, intrigued by his newfound stranger.

"Did," Alexander corrects. "We did embryonic genome testing."

Nodding at the clarification, Harrison pulls at a distant memory.

"Ah, yes. You had a great study about, I believe, restructuring a pig embryo for growing..." Harrison starts, but the resolution of the thought does not come to him as he snaps his fingers attempting to trigger the lost thought.

"A cow's lung," Alexander finishes as he takes another sip. "Yeah, that was a huge moment for us," he says, half-heartedly smiling at the memory. "That was about three or four years ago and we actually received a lot of national coverage on the advancement."

"Did Daisy work with you on that project?" Harrison asks, salvaging to connect the dots.

Alexander looks around, as if preparing to tell a secret.

"Well, I had a team of researchers working on the project when I met Daisy. She was this fresh Ph.D. candidate turned hot-shot exec traipsing through town and just hearing the words 'The Rose Institute' made me weak in the knees after about a dozen beers. So, me and my big mouth go spouting off about this new discovery and how we're going to save the world. Blah, blah, blah, you know?"

Harrison holds his stare as he narrows his gaze.

"Did you two date?" Harrison asks, still feeling intrusive.

"For a brief period. She swooped in right as we were on the brink of releasing our findings and told me she was looking to settle down. At one point, I invited her to some ridiculous bed and breakfast in Idaho and had her meet my family." Taking a hard drink from his glass, Alexander continues, "I bought a fucking *engagement* ring. I thought this girl was the love of my life and I got caught up in this whirlwind of sex and power and her extravagant life."

Harrison releases a minute snort as he laughs in agreement, saying, "she does have that effect on people."

"Yeah," Alexander agrees, but aggressively shifts to meet Harrison. "Until I find out that she had conspired with my executive team to absorb Rushmore Testing into The Rose Institute, laying off our entire staff and taking credit for the great pig-cow discovery." He pauses for a moment, then says, "so, once I'm out of a job, she hits me with a lawsuit for slander and proprietary rights on the findings, burying me with so many legal fees that I hit bankruptcy and ultimately wound up losing my home and almost everything I own." He slings back the remainder of his drink, his face stern. "I was shunned from my own industry, so now" – he shrugs his shoulders in disbelief – "now I'm working in startups with overly intelligent brats who spend all day combing *Reddit* or arguing over Python sets while they keep their faces so deep in a computer's screen they probably don't even know how to spell 'laboratory.' It's infuriating."

Taken aback, Harrison holds his stance.

"I'm sorry, man. I know Daisy can be a tough one," he says. He feels his sympathy is not warranted or appreciated, but he holds his ground.

"Tough?" Alexander scoffs at the comment. "The bitch had been planning everything for months. She just wanted me to fall for her so when the papers were drawn out, she could play me like a fiddle as her own power sponsor to the entire agreement. I was the ultimate long con in her career."

Releasing a tense breath, Harrison drops his shoulders and closes his eyes momentarily to collect himself in response to Alexander's words. His nostrils flare and he fakes a smile as he stands without his brain instructing his feet to do so.

"Another drink?" Alexander asks, noticing the strange shift in Harrison's stance.

Shaking his head and raising a hand to his forehead, Harrison declines.

"I'm not feeling so hot. I think I guzzled those drinks too fast and they're hitting my head bit tougher than I'd like," he lies.

Harrison hastily pays the bill while avoiding any further interaction with Alexander. His tousled hair haphazardly frames his face as he collects his things and quickly leaves. He flags down Sampson outside the restaurant just as Ken and Duncan are arrived with a few others.

"Did you have the dinner without us?" Ken jokes as he escorts an older woman into the foyer, but stops short outside with Harrison and Duncan.

"Or did we miss all the fun?" Duncan chimes in, accessing the strange look in Harrison's eyes.

Harrison wrinkles half his face with an unpleasant grimace and says, "drank a bit too much at the bar and it's not sitting well." He grasps his stomach as if he is in pain. "Going to go home and lie down for a bit." He begins walking through the traffic but calls back to the two as he arrives at the backdoor of the SUV, saying, "we'll meet up later," although his words are not promising.

Sampson adjusts the rearview mirror, the surprise of seeing Harrison this early easily hidden in his facial expression.

"Where to, sir?"

"Get Daisy Stone's office on the line," Harrison sternly instructs as he plunks into the backseat. "I am making new dinner arrangements for this evening."

Chapter Nine: **Cocaine**

"COURTNEY?" Daisy shouts through her open office door much more aggressively that she intends. Clearing her throat, she softens her tone. "Courtney? Can you come in here?"

Daisy sits at her desk, both elbows perched with her head propped up against one of her fists. Her free hand claps a generously poured glass of red wine and she delicately balances a burning cigarette between her index and middle fingers. Her eyes glaze over as she stares through her oversized tortoise shell glasses through the open office door. Her messy hair is pulled into an effortless bun and her cherry red lipstick hints at its origins while her childlike posture exposes her detached mind.

The office is somber in the early evening's fleeting sun. The drapes are drawn and the only source of light filling the space is the insignificant sunlight between the curtains and a single lamp from the corner of the desk. A vinyl album spins on her record player, long since playing its last song, filling the room with white noise. The humming creates an eerie effect as she stares through space until breaking her silence when she finally speaks again.

"Are you dead, Courtney?"

Peering around the corner with a concerned look and unsure of the state in which she will find Daisy, Courtney whispers, "I'm here, just sitting in on that conference call for you. Sorry, I didn't hear you." Her tone is quizzical as she scans Daisy's aloof state before perplexedly pointing. "Are you smoking in your office?"

Carelessly holding still, Daisy takes a lingering drag from the cigarette. Releasing the breath, she looks up to meet Courtney's troubled stare, shifting her wild eyes.

"I don't know what you're talking about," she lies with a salty deflection. "Can you reset the record, please?" she requests, taking another drag from the immobile cigarette.

Courtney begrudgingly obliges to the asinine instruction, taking an exaggerated step into the office and delicately moving the needle to the perimeter of the record as the music plucks to life through the speakers.

"Anything else you'd like me to do, *Miss Stone*?" says Courtney. Her words sting the air but are ultimately drowned out as the record rattles to life.

Daisy falls back heavily into her chair and pats the cigarette into a document on her desk.

"Now that you mention it," she coolly retorts as she crosses her arms and takes a heavy sip from her glass, "I need you to do a little research and figure out how the fuck I ended up working for Harrison Bishop." Courtney pauses, listening to Daisy's ill-humored joke, not sure how to respond. "You know, check Page Six for the colossal fuck up that is my career."

Daisy sinks lower into her chair as Courtney releases an audible breath and storms her way to the light switch, flipping the overhead lighting to life.

"What the fuck is your problem?" she lashes, the words intrusive as she attempts to knock Daisy out of her stupor. "Did you really work your ass off for all of these years to have some egomaniacal prick pull the rug out from under you?"

Pausing for an annoyed eye roll before regaining her slouched posture, Daisy sets her glass of wine atop the wooden desk.

"*The Post* article isn't going to print for two months," she exhales through crimson tinted lips. "I'll double your holiday bonus if you can guess what story they want to run with now."

Courtney takes her place in the doorframe and her breathing becomes relaxed as she takes an empathetic tone.

"I know you often see me as just an assistant, but I have some news for you," she says, her words deliberate and stern. "I received a call from someone by the name of Sampson about an hour ago requesting your presence with Mr. Bishop this evening."

Daisy purses her eyes and tilts her head to the side.

"You have my attention," she says, her voice dripping with curiosity as her mood instantly shifts.

"That's what I thought," Courtney reprimands. "I wasn't going to tell you as I thought, well, 'fuck Harrison,' but after your little" – she waves her hand toward Daisy's composure – "scene, I think there are better ways for you to handle this situation." She crosses her arms with an authoritative tone. "Now, as I see it, you have three options this evening. You can sit in your office and mope. You can find someone from maintenance to give you roof access and plummet to your own death. Or, and probably your best bet, you can get your ass out of that chair, take this situation by the balls, and do what you do best."

A proud smile tugs at Daisy's mouth and her eyes blink to life after Courtney's rousing speech. "Anything else, *Miss Lacelon?*" she mocks.

"Actually, yes. Slap on some lipstick and run a comb through your hair," she instructs as she makes her way from the office before turning over her shoulder to drive her point home. "There is nothing more harrowing to a man than being destroyed by a gorgeous woman."

The afternoon heat gently dissipates as twilight covers the quiet street. A few couples walk hand-in-hand lackadaisically down the sidewalk. Nearby, traffic lights change from red to green to yellow then back again.

Daisy swiftly exits the back door of her town car as she rolls back her shoulders to steady herself and thank the driver. Making her way to the passenger side rearview mirror, she hinges at the hips to lean forward, inspecting her reflection and delicately dabbing her lips with a burgundy lipstick that brings her cat eyes to life, completing her sultry look. Confidently, she regains her composure, grazes her hands softly against her hips to smooth her formfitting burgundy dress, and proceeds into the restaurant as the sound of her clicking heels reverberate throughout the entrance.

Wellington was a hidden cafe along the outskirts of town. Located inside of a refurbished home that is nearly a century old, the dining room had roughly a dozen tables in it. While its sensuous interior would normally be a place for romance, Daisy had no interest in a passionate meal with Harrison.

As Daisy enters the dining room, a young waiter in a black button-down shirt and a matching black tie greets her. She does not acknowledge Harrison's presence at the corner table. He has now risen to greet her while she exchanges pleasantries with the waitstaff.

"You look lovely, Miss Stone," Harrison says, greeting Daisy as she arrives at the table. He waves off the waiter to pull the chair out for Daisy himself. Although his warm smile pulls at his lips, she cannot help but notice his frazzled hair and awry jacket, indicating that he has spent the last few hours in disarray.

Daisy raises an eyebrow to acknowledge him but is not surprised by the compliment, as she can already sense his eagerness bubbling beneath the surface.

"I see your vehicle did not spontaneously combust on your drive here," she coolly spits as she fans her napkin atop her lap. "How tragic," she sarcastically adds.

Harrison returns to his seat, sitting back in his chair as his fervent emerald green eyes watch Daisy's every move. Delicately, he places his elbow on the table and leans into his fist then opens his mouth to speak, just as the waiter arrives.

"Welcome to Wellington, have you two dined with us before?" the waiter enthusiastically asks as neither Harrison nor Daisy turn to engage in conversation.

Keeping their gaze on each other, a devilish smile pulls at Harrison's face. He curls his lips, camouflaging his humor, and responds, "not in quite some time." He playfully toys with Daisy, but his comment does not produce the intended reaction. Turning his face to meet the waiter's and pulling his eyes at the very last moment, he changes the subject.

"The place is as beautiful as always."

The waiter begins listing off dinner specials as Harrison feigns interest and Daisy broods until the waiter concludes his speech.

"We'll take two dirty martinis," says Harrison. He then leans in to whisper, "I'll be lucky to get an entire meal out of this one."

The waiter replies with a friendly smile and a soft, "you two are so cute together," as he turns to leave.

Daisy purses her eyes and gnaws against her cheek.

"Please don't order for me," Daisy instructs, her tone pressing cool but seeping at the edges as she attempts to ignore the waiter's remark.

Ignoring the request, Harrison hides another charismatic smile.

"Just for the record, are we here as business associates or as friends?"

"We haven't been friends in years, Harry," Daisy scoffs as she crosses her legs and calmly rests her chin atop her delicate hand.

The seconds click by as the pair sits in uncomfortable silence. The waiter seats a table nearby and takes their drink order while making pleasantries. All the while, Daisy and Harrison wait for the other to break, two wild west gunslingers waiting for the draw, ready to kill the other at a moment's notice.

"I know you have a lot to say to me," Harrison says, breaking the tension as their drinks arrive and Daisy takes her first sip without shifting her gaze. "We may as well address the elephant in the room. Just get out what you want to say."

Daisy chuckles, her amusement surprising to Harrison.

"Harry," she starts, her tone seductive and enticing as she softly sets her drink on the table, causing Harrison to mimic her actions. "I have absolutely nothing to say to you." Her eyelashes flutter coyly in contrast to her cool words.

Harrison rolls his eyes as he again sits back into his chair.

"You have got to be kidding me, Daisy. After everything at the party?"

Regaining her height, Daisy leans into her chair and lifts her brows to casually laugh, "let's just put on happy faces so the boards know we won't murder each other and be on our way."

This has got to be a joke, Harrison thinks to himself, befuddled by Daisy's response.

"How the hell could you have *nothing* to say to me? Aren't you angry?" he demands.

"No," Daisy dryly responds, swirling her toothpick and olive through her drink.

"Do you hate me?" Harrison quips.

"Not one bit," she says, holding her composure.

"Do you want to yell at me?" Harrison asks, his tone turning from cool and charismatic to slightly panicked.

A breathy laugh escapes Daisy's deep lips.

"No," she says, shifting her eyes from Harrison's wild gaze to her drink and then back to him through her long lashes, playing with his head.

"What the hell, Daisy," Harrison sneers under his breath as he drops his glass so forcefully that it causes the neighboring tables to turn. Feeling uneasy, he shifts his weight and attempts to hide the outburst. "Then why are we here?"

"You called me," Daisy eloquently says as a smirk crosses her face, causing Harrison's nostrils to flare.

"Fine, then I'll start," Harrison announces but quickly comes to the realization that he doesn't have a point in mind. He searches for a moment before declaring, "from purely a business perspective, I am thrilled to have our organizations begin working together." Daisy holds her ground without a flinch. Harrison turns an ear in her direction for a reaction. Defeated by her stonewall demeanor, he continues, saying, "and although this may not be the venture you had planned, this is going to be extremely lucrative for both of our teams."

Holding her statuesque stance, Daisy doesn't waver as she continues to stir her drink.

"You know, I will stay here all night," Harrison threatens, anger permeating through his wavering cool tone.

Daisy's mouth pulls into a poorly hidden smile.

"No, you won't," she says. Laughter cracks through her subdued grin.

Harrison abruptly stands, feeling the full weight and attention of the narrow dining room. Adrenaline burns in his chest. A bump of cocaine coursing through his veins. He hinges forward, planting a clenched fist into the table and harshly whispers, "If this is all we're going to do, I'd rather play nice in front of the board members so we don't waste our time."

Oh, this ought to be good, Daisy muses as her wide eyes gleefully drink in the evening's entertainment. Leaning into his face until their noses rest an inch from each other, she breathes into Harrison's mouth, "prove it." Her voice is like honey, forcing Harrison's eyes to smolder.

A beat settles between the two just long enough for Harrison to press back, "good evening, Daisy," but his body holds his menacing stance. The pool of stillness across the table slowly fills with his empty threat just as Daisy's bright eyes fill with life and a hearty laugh erupts from her gaping mouth.

Their positions fall as Daisy dips forward slightly into Harrison as she clutches her stomach and genuine laughter fills the room, causing the nearby tables to turn and smile at what appears to be a romantic moment between the two. She reaches up to wipe a small pool of tears from her eye just as Harrison returns to his seat. His face is flushed, and he forces an exasperated breath through his nostrils.

"Is this a joke to you, Daisy?" Harrison furiously snaps. "Did you just agree to this so you could publicly mock me?"

Daisy attempts to regain herself but the laughter continuously emits from her now relaxed and cheerful demeanor.

"It's just," she takes harsh breath as the laughter continues to spill from her, "how the fuck are people scared of you?" Her laughter picks up again as Harrison's face splashes with confusion. "You're so full of shit!" She falls into the back of her chair and picks up a knee to her stomach as a single tear streams down her face.

Harrison adjusts his suit jacket and attempts to regain his composure while uncomfortably surveying the dining room. He observes a middle-aged couple holding hands across the table. A group of older gentlemen are playing cards and raising their rocks glasses in celebration. He takes a full breath and slowly releases the air from his lungs as he quietly waits for Daisy to conclude her tirade. Lifting his drink to drag a shaky sip, he breaks the moment and asks, "would you like to see my wine cellar?" His eyes are deep and serious. "I just had it remodeled and I think you'd love the ambiance."

Daisy raises her glass to her lips and a lighthearted laugh spills out of her mouth.

"I'd rather die than spend another moment alone with you."

Harrison's eyes perk at the phrasing as he raises his drink in unison once more with Daisy and their eyes lock as they finish their drinks simultaneously.

"Are you down for another?" he asks with his typical calm, charming tone.

An inviting smile fills Daisy's face as she drops her elbow atop the table and leans her chin into her palm. Harrison meets her across the table in anticipation of her next words.

"I know your secret," she says, her callous words not matching her sultry expression. Her eyes flutter with an amorous glow that draws him in like a moth to a flame. "I fucking *made* you, Harry."

Harrison cocks his head to the side and a sympathetic wash covers his face. He opens his mouth to say something, but Daisy pulls her hand from beneath her chin to stop him.

Turning her fist over, Daisy dips her head to rest on her hand with a playful smile.

"I'm not afraid of you," she says, her words cold and harsh, clattering around in Harrison's brain. "I see what you truly are and I have no problem playing this little game with you," she says. Her doe eyes come to life as she stands to press two clenched fists into the tabletop, mirroring Harrison's previous stance. She dips down to hover over Harrison until their noses graze. "I am going to destroy you. Heads will roll if you think for even a second that you will take this company away from me."

Her words pummel across his face and his eyes pang with a grimace. Daisy stands just as the waiter returns to their table.

"He's got the bill," she says as she adjusts her dress and ends the evening with a calm, "good evening, Harry." Grasping her clutch by the seam, she delicately knocks the bag against the table and leaves him with a parting wink as she turns to strut out of the restaurant.

Daisy stands outside of Wellington, loitering on the street as she waits for her town car to arrive. The evening has released a frigid breeze that hints at the soon to come winter months. Daisy knocks her head back against her shoulders, feeling the calming wind across her face. *If he didn't wish he was dead yet, he surely knows it's coming*, she congratulates herself. *Game one goes to Miss Stone*. She shakes out her shoulders as the black vehicle pulls up to the sidewalk, allowing herself to sink into her delicious victory.

"Miss Stone?" the driver asks as he walks around the front of the car to open the door.

"As I live and breathe," Daisy warmly confirms. A humorous grin fills the man's face as he opens the rear door.

She slips into the backseat of the car, giving the driver her address as he shuts the door.

"Daisy! Hold up!"

A familiar voice reverberates through the glass of the vehicle that causes Daisy to roll her eyes as the driver returns to his seat.

The driver clips his seat belt, turning over his shoulder to comment, "looks like you left your friend. Want me to open the door for him?"

Daisy releases a mild scoff and responds, "just run him over on your way out." Drooping her head to rest against the window to hide her face from Harrison, she waits for the driver to accelerate. Sensing the animosity, the driver flashes a coy smile through the rearview mirror as the window retracts into the door, causing Daisy to pick up her head and let out an irked, "oh, come *on*."

Harrison rests his hand on the roof of the vehicle and waves a quick thank you to the driver as Daisy crosses her arms.

"I thought this conversation was over," Daisy muses with a mundane tone.

Harrison surrenders a wry laugh that pulls at his dimples and infuriates Daisy.

"Not yet," he says, bending down and moving into Daisy's personal space with an enigmatic grin. "If we're going to do this, there has to be something I can do to make it worth your while," he says, his eyes now soft and sincere.

Daisy softly laughs and shakes her head at the audacity of the suggestion. Turning to meet his gaze, she eases her tone and says, "do you really think it's that simple, Harry?"

A familiar look fills Harrison's eyes as he hangs on her every word.

"I mean, after all these years I would like to think so," he says. "We're going to end up killing each other if we don't find some common ground."

"It's not like I can just walk in and run the show. I'm now *your* employee, which is the last place I ever thought I'd end up," says Daisy, thinking aloud.

"Why not?" Harrison asks, pulling her back into their conversation. "Why can't you run it?"

Daisy leans into him to whisper, "ecause you run your company, you idiot."

Harrison sets a heavy hand on the window's ledge.

"Exactly," he says. "It's my company and I want you to lead the merger."

Sarcastic laughter fills the car as Daisy reacts to the ridiculous statement, but Harrison doesn't budge. Realizing the seriousness in his tone, she turns to him, and says, "yeah, right," as her eyes slowly start to see the earnestness in his face. "Holy shit. You're serious?"

"Dead serious," Harrison drearily replies, still holding his stance.

Daisy pauses a beat as she waits for the "just kidding" moment to arrive. Sitting there in the silence, she reads Harrison's face but he's a slate wall of information.

"Fine," she finally says. "I'll do it, but I want it in writing."

Harrison's eyes flicker a piercing green and his lips curl in to hide his smile as his dimples carve through his cheeks.

"Anything else I can do for you, Miss Stone?" he asks with an alluring tone as he has finally gotten his way. He regains his height and drops his hands into his pockets with a confident stance.

"No," Daisy retorts as she shifts her weight against her seat. "But I would like to formally submit my resignation after the merger is complete."

Harrison's mouth drops open, bewildered by the comment.

"Daisy," he laments as he tilts his head in confusion. "Do you have any loyalty?"

"Not to you," Daisy concludes as she turns back to the driver and quips, "we can go now," before rolling up the window without turning back to Harrison.

The car pulls away from the sidewalk with a muffled roar and Harrison removes one hand from his pockets to run a hand through his tousled hair. He searches the street for an answer, but coming up short, he turns back to the restaurant and exhales a quiet, "well, fuck."

Chapter Ten: **Coping Mechanism**

The morning sun gleams through the floor to ceiling windows of Bishop Enterprises' conference room. A quickly depleting fog hovers across the view and gives way to the world below. The warmth of the day pierces through the moisture and heats the windows as condensation begins to pool at the base the sill. The office quietly hums as the Monday morning bustle begins to bloom.

The lengthy conference room table is adorned with pots of coffee and breakfast pastries as Daisy stands at the far end of the table, pointing into her palm and dictating a feverish speech about the structural layout of middle management.

"A tiered system will be most beneficial to give the appearance of cohesive organization through the transition," she announces.

Nearly two dozen employees are huddled around the conference table, layered in two rows like cows around a watering hole. The meeting's attendants are nose deep in tablets or notepads as they take notes and sip coffee. A redheaded intern releases an audible yawn that causes Daisy's eyes to dart in his direction, but he quickly snaps his mouth shut as he senses the eyes of the room drift toward him.

At the other end of the table is Harrison, sitting nonchalantly with an arm draped across the back of his chair and a pen rolling between his teeth, releasing muted clicking noises. Stopping only when he spots Daisy staring at him with one raised eyebrow, he pulls the pen from his white teeth and drops it to the table as she continues.

Daisy narrows her eyes discreetly as she continues on with her presentation until she delicately returns to her seat and adjusts her rose colored blouse, feeling every male in attendance caress her with their eyes.

"Any questions?" she asks with a stern yet sweet voice.

This was the first day of negotiations and planning between The Rose Institute and Bishop Enterprises, and Daisy, with the guidance of Charlie, had been on her best behavior all morning for her new coworkers.

"I want you to act as if you're Bishop Enterprise's grandmother," Charlie had previously advised her. "They're steering the ship and we do not want to be sent out to sea, so, best behavior."

Although she knew she would not be sticking around long enough to see the team cast out to sea, she kept the status quo and donned her most professional attire, topping off everything with a happy face.

"Have we determined the protocol for distributing managerial assignments that would not disrupt current workloads?" Harrison asks, his eyes focused on Daisy as the entirety of the conference room snaps their heads in his question. Still in his lackadaisical stance, his demeanor is youthful but his gray suit and serious tone give him a professional appearance.

"Yes," Daisy responds, the room's focus turning to face her again. "We're going to be pairing duplicate departments to categorize their workloads and then divide them amongst their teams to streamline the current workflow and maximize efficiency on upcoming projects." Daisy shifts her eyes to Molly who is seated to her right. Molly has her weight in her chin perched against a closed fist and raises her forefinger atop her lips in an attempt to hide as smirk in response to Harrison's question. She quickly rolls her eyes in agreement with Daisy's passive response.

"Are you concerned with the amount of time that could be wasted by duplicating teams, comparing current projects, and then dividing amongst them?" Harrison questions as the room turns their focus from Daisy back to him. "Wouldn't it be more beneficial to just—"

"Just start fresh with new teams?" Daisy finishes the question for Harrison.

Once again, the room reverses their attention back to her, a tennis match playing out across the conference room table. The two hold a steady glare as the conference room has front row seats to the match of the century.

"We did take that into consideration, but we didn't want to have teams split between two sets of projects during the transition. We would rather have a clear direction with a fresh start."

"I'm assuming you have seen better success with that approach in previous acquisitions?" Harrison asks, steadying himself to launch a lob on his side of the court as the audience continues to look on. Daisy prepares for his swing and the room once again turns to her.

"Exactly. Drawing the line in the sand between new and old gives clear direction to maintain efficiency, but more importantly, it increases morale with only minimal lag to regroup."

"Would you foresee any issues on the sales or marketing side, Miss Jordan?" Harrison asks as the audience swivels in its unexpected new focus.

Molly pauses for a moment as she feels the question landing in her lap and says, "oh, me?" A muffled laughter emits from the room as her head perks at the question. "As long as we have a definitive direction with research and development, our team can spin this as a positive," she quickly spouts. "We'll maybe even see some boost in revenue from buyers who are enthusiastic about the acquisition."

"Then if we are in agreement, I think it's a solid plan." Harrison confirms, his eyes still locked into Daisy.

"Good," Daisy agrees as she raises a playful eyebrow.

"Good," Harrison repeats as a peculiar tension fills the room.

Molly, quick to break the silence, says, "I think that calls for a break." Her eyes dart between Daisy and Harrison, who coyly pull their flirtatious stares. "Let's regroup and meet back here in fifteen," she announces as the room breaks and a muted roar fills the conference room with people erupting into conversation.

Molly hands a fresh cup of coffee to Daisy and says, "well that was some interesting breakfast entertainment." She suppresses a ridiculous grin as she impatiently waits for Daisy to explain herself.

"And what is that supposed to mean?" Daisy curiously asks, attempting to play dumb.

Rolling her eyes, Molly plucks a Danish from a tray of pastries and takes a bite.

"Oh, please. At the rate you two were going, we're lucky we didn't have to watch you two get to third base on the conference room table," she says too loudly, catching the eyes of an intern who conceals his laughter in a tablet.

Daisy snaps her head toward the giggle and barks, "you didn't hear that."

"Oh, come on, Daisy," Molly says, comforting her and pulling her back into the conversation. "You two have known each other for years. You're bound to have some sexual tension." She takes another bite from the Danish and tosses it onto a napkin just out of reach. "I'm just teasing. It's actually rather cute to watch you two finally get along."

Daisy relaxes her shoulders and turns back toward the conference table to collect her things. "You're the fucking worst," she mutters with a knowing grin.

"Now," Molly says, "let's chat about tonight." Her voice is giddy with excitement as she shimmies her shoulders at the change in topic. "I was thinking drinks at La Boisson and then a little dancing. Thoughts?"

"Drinks, yes, but dancing is a maybe." Daisy responds. "I have some, uh, business to take care of this evening."

"And who is this 'business' you speak of?" Molly pries, sensing the double meaning.

"Taylor Pierce. I have some questions I'd like to discuss with him about his financial issues after a few bad investments," Daisy relinquishes with a provocative smile.

"Hmm," Molly agrees with a devilish grin. "A little 'business' indeed."

Just outside the conference room door, Harrison flips through his phone perusing his email inbox.

"Harrison!" Ken calls down the long hallway, picking up his pace as he trots to meet up with him. "Duncan has been swooping in on the new Rose chicks all morning. Nearly had a cup of boiling coffee thrown in his face. It was amazing."

"Just like clockwork," Harrison laughs as he pulls Ken away from the conference room and toward the cafe down the hallway. "Speaking of, coffee?"

Peering over Harrison's shoulder, Ken scans the conference room before catching a glimpse of the pink blouse and the lioness's mane, realizing what he is avoiding.

"Ooh man, the Ice Queen. No wonder you're trying to wrangle me out of here," he laughs, causing Harrison to grab him by the elbow and drag him forcefully down the hall. "What? Don't want me to see your new girlfriend?" he chides in a singsong voice.

"How any woman has ever agreed to have sex with you is beyond me," Harrison quips as he shakes his head in irked amazement.

"I know, but your mother was a lovely woman. I could never say no," Ken retorts, finally pulling his arm free and walking on his own. "Okay, tonight. Let's get some plans made before I have to hop on this snooze fest of as sales call. You'd think that listening to a beautiful Russian woman on the phone would be just as splendid as sitting across from her, but the payout really isn't the same."

Ignoring the comment, Harrison chimes in, saying, "I was thinking drinks and then drinks and then maybe another round of drinks."

Ken turns on his heels to land about-face with Harrison, feigning a goofy salute.

"Aye-aye, captain! Drinking it is!"

Shoving his hands into his pockets and faking annoyance, Harrison waits for the show to end.

"Pick you and Duncan up at six?"

"I'll wear a red rose in my hair for you, *Mister* Bishop," Ken teases as he walks backward down the hall to depart, knocking into two men exiting a nearby office. "Pardon me, I was staring at the ever so lovely *Mister* Bishop," he continues has he mockingly curtsies in Harrison's direction.

Rolling his eyes and turning back toward the conference room, Harrison calls over his shoulder, "I don't know you, Kenny!"

>>>

Deep into the evening at La Boisson, Daisy and Molly are pressed against the sleek bar attempting to flag down a bartender. The scene has shifted from its respectable business facade as the lights have dimmed and the rowdy late-night crowd begins to file into the chic space. The music turns to a stiff beat that causes the crowd to sway with the sound, making it difficult for Molly to grab the attention of the nearby bartender. Eventually giving up, Molly leans into the bar top. Turning back to Daisy, she shouts, "I should have worn something with a lower cut. I'm never getting a drink!"

The man standing next to Daisy peers around her to look over to Molly and shouts, "this guy has been avoiding this end of the bar all night. Even if you were naked we still would be waiting."

Molly quickly assesses the man and half turns her eyes in a flirtatious annoyance back in his direction.

"Maybe he's into dudes. Undo a few of those buttons and we'll see if that helps," she shouts back with a camouflaged, sultry smile.

"Let me see what I can do for you ladies," the man answers and quickly pulls in a nearby cocktail waitress. The woman, too confused by the confrontation, quickly shifts into a charismatic smile as he spouts, "If I give you two hundred for four drinks, how quickly can you make them appear?"

The waitress gives an understanding laugh and agrees, taking their order and quickly slipping behind the bar to present four rocks glasses before Molly.

"Your boyfriend is quite convincing," says the waitress, laughing off the incident and slipping back into the crowd.

The man turns back to Molly and comments, "maybe by the end of the night we can see how convincing your boyfriend really can be," and the two tap their glasses with a subtle clink.

Without breaking eye contact, Molly introduces Daisy to the man but Daisy cannot make out his name with the echoing bass of the music.

"Just go have fun, kids," she laughs and ushers them out of her way. "I'll take care of your friend here," she says, motioning to the man's friend. Daisy taps him on the shoulder to introduce herself, but there is no need.

"Taylor!" Daisy exclaims as he turns around with an excited grin and pulls her into a friendly embrace. "What has it been?"

"Almost two years!" he eagerly replies and pulls her in for another hug. "Aaron, this is my old friend, Daisy. We met when I first moved to the city from Boston!"

"Well, well. Isn't that quite the love connection," Aaron jokes with a lascivious eyelash flutter as he presses Daisy and Taylor's shoulders together as if he is taking an imaginary photo.

Holding her glass to her lips, Molly flashes Daisy a knowing grin.

"Why, *yes*. Quite the coincidental connection," she says, a lone brow lifting at the fabricated luck as Daisy shrugs her shoulders with a coy chuckle.

"Now, if everyone wouldn't mind," Aaron announces to the group, "your dear friend Molly is in dire need of a waltz through the bar." He flashes Molly a wicked smile and scoops her up by the arm, her toes grazing the floor.

Molly tosses her head back with an elated laugh and calls back to Daisy, "I'll catch up with you later!" The two drift away through the crowd but not before Molly yells out a quick, "don't do anything I wouldn't do!"

"So, Aaron seems like a real charmer," Daisy says with a witty grin as she takes a long sip from her glass.

Taylor agrees with a throaty chuckle, saying, "he's quite difficult to keep up with some days," as he gives Daisy a once-over. "Doesn't seem so bad right now though," he continues, his eyes gleaming a boyish indigo.

Taylor Pierce was one of the first friends Daisy had made when she relocated to New Orleans from Illinois. His blue eyes and unruly brown hair gave him an adolescent look. He had grown into a handsome adult over the years, but he still possessed a youthful charm. His tall and lanky stance made him approachable and his easygoing personality was what had originally drawn Daisy to him.

"I know it's only been a couple of years but you look so..." The words escape Daisy as she looks him up and down. "Mature?" she says, finishing her thought, unsure of how the statement would resonate.

Taylor replies with a familiar smile and says, "I know. My mother says the same thing." He gives Daisy a slight jab in the arm with a bony elbow and flushes with excitement at what appears to be a coincidental connection.

Hidden away behind a corner cocktail table with only a small tea light illuminating their faces, Daisy and Taylor spend the next few hours catching up and reminiscing. Quickly falling into their old ways, she teases him like a brother.

"Like hell you and Misty ever hooked up! She was a solid ten and you were maybe a four with those God-awful cargo shorts!"

Nearly spitting out his drink, Taylor covers his mouth with a cocktail napkin, saying, "I thought I told you to burn those photos!" His fake anger causes Daisy to erupt into a fit of laughter. He continues, saying, "you know me too well, Daisy. I can't take you anywhere." He pauses briefly, collecting his breath before admitting, "I've wanted to call you so many times over the years but, I don't know. It always felt like our timing was off." His mouth pulls into a mix of laughter and pity.

Rolling her lips into a half-smile, Daisy confesses, "we never could time things, could we?" Her eyes glimmer with a rarely seen genuine sorrow. Shaking out her mind, she asks the questions she's been preserving all evening. "So, how's the job been? I've been talking your ear off all night with stories and I've completely forgotten to see how you're doing now," she lies. "You look like you're doing well," she prompts, attempting to pull a specific response.

"Eh," Taylor starts with a shrug, a bashful flush covering his face as he was hoping to avoid the question. "Times are...okay."

"Only okay? Last I heard, you were diving into synthetics research with HBH Discoveries." Daisy says, luring him into her trap.

"That's right, but we've been trying to compete with the times and transition into something more financially sound," Taylor answers with a short tone, taking a long sip from his drink. "We're about to go under, I'm afraid. A couple of bad research investments over the last year or so. You know how it goes," he says, shrugging toward Daisy with sheepish embarrassment.

Nope. I'm too smart to let that happen, idiot. Daisy thinks to herself as she fakes a shocked expression.

"How is that possible? You brought on something, like, two dozen of the best scientists in the biodegradables market."

"Three dozen," Taylor corrects her. "And when our lead developer brought on some less-than-adequate projects, our stock completely tanked." He shakes his head, taking a stabilizing drink at the thought. "I couldn't pay someone to buy us up now."

Jackpot, Daisy thinks.

"I wish there was something I could do to help. I know Rose is always in the market for our polymers division."

"If only," Taylor says, dryly laughing at the pipedream.

"You know what?" Daisy asks, clasping her drink and raising it before Taylor in a toast. "To making tonight as memorable as our friendship!" she exclaims, waiting for his mood to shift.

A familiar smile fills Taylor's face and cascades into his eyes.

"To old friends," he agrees as he taps Daisy's glass with his.

> > >

Daisy's back lands against the door of Taylor's apartment with a heavy thud. Leaning his weight against her in a passionate moment, the two embrace in a heated kiss and Taylor raises his hand into her hair as they make their way into the high-rise condominium.

"Your neighbors are going to get quite a show if we stay out here," Daisy laughs as Taylor kisses her neck and pulls at her back. "I'd say let's give them a free show, but I'm sure the parents of your building wouldn't love that idea," she continues to joke in a hushed whisper.

Pushing himself to an arm's length, Taylor regains himself.

"I guess I can behave until we're on the other side of the door," he says, adjusting his suit jacket and inserting his key. Presenting his best English butler's accent, he says, "after you, Miss Stone," waving her inside.

Once settled inside, Daisy sits perched on the edge of an overstuffed sofa in the living room. She admires the beautiful pieces of art adorned along the walls and the soothing tones of the room. *A woman decorated in here*, she muses to herself, well aware of the culprit.

"I love how you've decorated the place. It feels very homey."

Taylor appears through the kitchen carrying two scotch glasses, delicately dropping one in Daisy's waiting hand.

"Thank you, although I didn't do much of the work in here," he says, hinting at a decorator.

"Ah," Daisy comprehends with a mask of sympathy. "It's beautiful nonetheless."

Taking a long sip, a stillness falls between the pair. Daisy imagines what the room would have looked like if she had taken up a life with Taylor instead of spearheading her career all those years ago. She pauses for a moment to imagine herself living in the apartment with Taylor, picking out a living room sofa or brushing paint samples along the kitchen wall. *You made the right choice, Stone*, she tells herself. She rolls back her shoulders, regaining her confidence.

Taylor blurts out, "sorry about before," tearing Daisy away from her thoughts as he nods toward the front door. "Old habits," he admits with an embarrassed grin.

Turning in her lips, Daisy tries to cover a similar smile.

"You're right," she says, looking at Taylor with playful eyes. "I guess we haven't done that in a while." Looking back to her drink, she takes a shallow breath and then lunges at him, pulling his mouth into hers. Running a free hand through his hair, she entangles herself around him.

Taylor plucks her drink from her hand, drops both of the crystal glasses on top of the coffee table, and grasps Daisy by the thighs. Lifting her legs around his waist, he walks through the living room toward the bedroom, holding her mouth to his.

Laying Daisy down on his bed, Taylor undoes the top button of his shirt and kneels over her with a boyish charm.

"Old habits," he repeats, now with a wicked grin spread across his face that throws Daisy into a fit of giggles.

Between heavy breaths and ripping through clothes, the two continue to talk as if they are still catching up at the bar.

"I heard you were being acquired by Bishop Enterprises," Taylor says as he kisses down Daisy's stomach and she moans at the tickle of his breath.

Pushing him off of her and onto his back, Daisy straddles Taylor as she pins his shoulders into the bed.

"Not my idea," she admits with a sigh of annoyance before leaning into his neck and gently nibbling his ear. An audible breath emits from his throat at the sensation.

"I'm sure *the* Daisy Stone is more than qualified to handle it," he praises, the words with a trace of double entendre.

Daisy raises herself up to lift both her brows sensually. Making her way down his open shirt as she slowly kisses his abdomen, she pulls the trigger.

"I'm surprised you mentioned the business is going under," she says, her hands now unbuckling his belt, causing Taylor to moan at the action. "You had such an amazing reputation in the field. It was like you were an unstoppable force," she coos, giving the words a slight innuendo to mask her true intentions.

Shaking his head free from Daisy's distraction, Taylor finally plops on his elbow and asks, "you want the truth?" His eyes hint at a secret.

"Sounds juicy," Daisy comments with a salacious tone and works her way back up his stomach then returns to kissing his neck.

Attempting to hide the diversion, Taylor spits out, "I recently broke up with my CFO a few months back."

Continuing her game, Daisy nuzzles into his neck and questions, "did you two not get along?" She then switches to his other ear.

"Not exactly," Taylor hints. "We started dating about three weeks after she was hired and she treated the company just badly as she treated me." Daisy pushes herself up by her palms and puts on her best doe-eyed, inquisitive face. "If she wasn't screwing over the company, she was screwing me over," he further confesses.

Dropping her weight onto his chest, Daisy sets her chin atop his breastbone and longingly gazes into his eyes.

"That's terrible," she says, her voice soft and sincere. "You really had the road paved out for you to be something in the industry." She strokes his hair away from his eyes and grazes her thumb against his temple. "You're one of the most intelligent people I know," she confesses, an honest statement amongst her web of lies.

"There can only be one Cure All-Kid," he scoffs with a joking tone. The words cause Daisy to flinch slightly.

Daisy runs her hand through his hair once more before leaning forward to lightly kiss Taylor's lips.

"How about this?" she sweetly muses as she continues to kiss his stomach. "I'll speak with my president and see what I can do about a possible arrangement between The Rose Institute and HBH Discoveries."

Taylor begins to deny the request but Daisy dips a hand below his briefs, causing him to gasp. A smile forms ear to ear, as he mumbles, "If you think you can swing it."

"It's really the least I can do," she purrs, returning her lips to his stomach and lifting a devious brow. "Old habits."

"We'll take three vodka rocks and your phone number if it's up for grabs," Duncan touts to the cocktail waitress as he hands her his credit card.

"You'll have to max this out to get remotely close to my digits," the waitress replies without missing a beat.

"Oh, my credit limit is enormous!" Duncan bellows after the waitress, causing the nearby tables to turn and snicker.

Ken drops his glass of water to the table and scolds Duncan, saying, "come on, man. You know that has never worked."

Harrison, Ken, and Duncan are sitting down for drinks at Du Vin, a prestigious wine bar in the financial district that always seemed to be bustling with single executives and new divorcées. Duncan dragged the guys out at least once a month to search the town for an occasional conquest.

"Now that we have finally been pinpointed as the worst table in this place, Harrison, what was up with you hiding your one true love from me this morning?" Ken teases, knowing he will get a rise out of Harrison.

Harrison audibly sighs through his nostrils and attempts to change the subject.

"Why, thank you, Ken!" he overenthusiastically retorts. "The acquisition meetings have indeed been going very well."

Ken ignores Harrison and continues to press on.

"Any late-night meetings with The Oxymoron?" He asks, his face pitifully hiding an obnoxious grin.

"You're completely correct! The first set of transitions should be completed by the end of Q three and I think it's going to be a great opportunity for us to begin presenting to the finalized board members!" Harrison says, dodging him yet again.

"If you have sex with her on her desk, you are legally bound to tell us," Duncan chimes in, scanning the room for his lost waitress. Harrison tongues his cheek in annoyance. "I bribed some intern in legal to add in a few clauses."

Ken closes his eyes and turns to Duncan to smugly shake his head in disagreement. "Like anyone from legal would take a word you say seriously," he says.

"You'd be surprised what a few cases of scotch can buy in this town," Duncan says matter-of-factly. Turning back to Harrison, he joins in the cross-examination, saying, "seriously, you've been in a rather chipper mood these last few days. I can't help to see a correlation between your shift in character and time spent with the Ice Queen."

Harrison throws an unconcerned laugh back at Duncan.

"We're just old friends. It's nice to finally get along with her."

Their drinks arrive and Duncan holds out a forefinger to the group, saying, "put a pin in this for a moment." Turning back to his waitress, he continues his campaign. "There has to be something that I can say to entice you this evening." His voice is sincere yet playful.

Leaning into Duncan's side, Ken cuts into their moment.

"I happen to have it on good authority that bribery isn't out of the question," he says.

Turning back to the waitress, Duncan flashes an impressed look of content.

"He's not wrong," Duncan says as he gestures his thumb at Ken before she rolls her eyes and disappears into the crowd.

"So, back to your new lady," Ken says, jabbing back at Harrison as he passes out their drinks.

Releasing another superfluous laugh that doesn't reach his eyes, Harrison shakes his head.

"There isn't anything to tell. We've worked together in the past so we understand each other. End of story."

"Understand each other naked is more like it," Duncan ribs as he takes a long drink. Harrison lifts an eyebrow but he continues. "I've seen the way you look at her. If you think we've been friends for this long and I don't know your 'please fuck me' face, you are crazy."

Holding back his annoyance, Harrison grips his drink with a hearty grasp.

"I'd love to see you two say no to her," he laughs, now rolling the glass on an angle and circling the base along the tabletop. *Just fucking drop it*, he thinks to himself, feeling his blood pressure rise against his ears.

"I'd just love to get an invite to the party," Ken adds, sensing the irritation in Harrison's tone. "Just be careful, dude. The girl loves to prey on the weak."

Slinging back his drink, Duncan catches the eye of the waitress and holds his drink up to signal another round.

"He's not weak, he just hates it when he doesn't get what he wants."

Harrison mimics Duncan's actions and polishes off his drink.

"Please. There isn't anything I can't have."

>>>

"One hundred dollars says she slaps him," Ken leans into Harrison to whisper. The two are pressed against the corner of the bar, attempting to inconspicuously watch Duncan make his move on the waitress in the center of the bar. "I'll bump it up to two if she throws a drink in his face."

Harrison takes a surprised step back.

"And bet on our dear friend, Duncan?" he mocks with a facetious shocked tone. "Make it an even three hundred and you've got yourself a bet."

Reaching his hand out, Ken agrees.

"Deal!"

The two shake on their friend's fate and huddle close together to watch the show.

"Are you watching that guy out there who is about to crash and burn?" asks a redheaded woman who leans into Ken. "The one in that awful blue jacket?"

The redhead's eyes do not drift from the scene as her black-haired friend leans over to add, "she is light years out of his league."

"Oh, he's not going to last longer than five minutes," Harrison says as the group diligently watches the scene unfold.

"Do you mean here or in bed?" the redhead asks, still focused on Duncan.

Ken takes a step back from the cluster to take a look at the woman. Her tall and slender physique paired with her copper red hair might as well have been a bull's eye for him. Adding to the fact that she was dressed as if she had just come from her office and had an air of confidence that would have deterred most men, Ken could barely make out his next words. Opening his mouth to speak, she beats him to the punch and reaches out a hand.

"Stephanie Lenox."

Taken aback by the introduction, Ken squeaks out, "Ken Madison."

He half-smiles in a look of disbelief. A pause settles between the two as his brain reconnects with his surroundings. "My apologies, this is my friend Harrison," he says, taking a step back and gesturing toward Harrison.

"Harrison? As in Harrison Bishop?" Stephanie asks, her face slightly stunned.

Oh, fuck, Ken thinks to himself. *If he cock blocks me tonight, I swear to God I'm going to end him.*

"Yes, as in Harrison Bishop," says Harrison, attempting to turn the attention back to Ken. "And your friend?"

The black-haired woman takes a step from behind Stephanie to introduce herself. She eagerly moves forward to shake hands.

"Hello there! Maggie Austin."

While Maggie was a bit shorter in than Stephanie, her bravado gave the impression that she was running the show between the two, signaling that Ken's only way to Stephanie was through Maggie.

"What are you two ladies up to this evening?" Ken asks without peeling his eyes away from Stephanie.

"Just out blowing off steam after a long day," Maggie eagerly answers for the two and showcases two drinks, one clutched in each hand. "But now that we have your buddy to watch, things have taken a turn for the evening." She tilts her head in Duncan's direction and the group settles back to watch.

Stephanie leans subtly into Ken's shoulder to say, "there's no way she's into him. You know that, right?"

"I think he may have a shot," Maggie adds, taking a sip from one drink and then from the other. "See how she's leaning her hips into his?"

Ken tilts his head to one side and says, "I think you're right. If she wasn't interested, she would have been long gone by now."

"Maybe her handcuffed her to the table," Harrison dryly comments, then turns to the group. "I've seen him do it before."

The waitress leans her chest into Duncan, placing a delicate hand just above his heart. Throwing her head back, she releases a grandiose laugh that fills the bar. Duncan leans back and reaches out his arms, gesturing emphatically with his words. The waitress then leans forward pushing him away playfully and clutching her stomach with the other hand, keeling over in laughter.

"Well, shit," says Ken, releasing a defeated sigh. He quickly shifts his eyes back to Harrison, giving him a "What now?" look.

Clapping his hands together, Harrison swoops in to save him.

"Shots?" Harrison asks, his eyes darting between the group as he shrugs his shoulders. "You know, for Duncan."

>>>

Further into the evening, the bar's crowd doubled in size and nearly tripled in sound. The wait staff slowly started to remove the cocktail tables, creating a dance floor, and a DJ started playing, making conversation nearly impossible.

Knocking his head back to finish off his drink, Harrison drops his glass heavily on to the bar as he flags down a bartender for another drink. Leaning into his elbows, he partially listens as Maggie rambles on about a work story that included her receptionist sending the incorrect package to her marketing team. *Or maybe it was the sales team?* Harrison thought to himself. He had already forgotten.

The four had paired off rather quickly as Ken begged, "take this one for me?" forcing Harrison to roll his eyes and begrudgingly accept.

"Isn't that just hilarious?" Maggie asks Harrison, nudging him with her elbow and knocking him back into their conversation.

The bartender drops a drink in front of Harrison and he says, "put it on Mr. Madison's tab." Turning back to Maggie, he quickly recovers. "Totally hilarious!"

"But that's not the half of it!" Maggie continues as Harrison takes a deep drag from his glass.

"So, Maggie," Harrison interrupts, turning on his side to lean into the bar in hopes of a conversation that kept him awake. "How did you and Stephanie meet?"

Maggie's eyes light up at the question and Harrison immediately regrets asking.

"It's *super* funny! You're just going to die!" she eagerly spits back at him.

I really wish I could right now, he thinks to himself. Faking a laugh and nodding politely, he prepares himself for what he assumes will be another two-hour long story about a missing box.

"We met right after my divorce about two years back," Maggie begins and Harrison gives a look of sympathy in return. She takes a drink but stops herself short to waive off Harrison. "No, no! It ended up working out great!"

Harrison gives Maggie a confused look and asks, "great? Not a common phrase you'd hear from a divorce."

Maggie quickly peers back and forth for any eavesdroppers, before leaning in to whisper.

"Here's the thing, I caught him cheating on me twice, so I set him up to look like he had been beating me before we went into our divorce proceedings." She leans back with a smug arrogance in her eyes. She lifts her drink back to her lips and says, "he'll be paying me alimony until he's long dead."

Harrison reminds himself to blink and takes a sharp breath through his nostrils.

"Wow, that's quite a story there, Maggie."

Maggie's face continues its self-righteous tour as she leans into Stephanie's back and yells over the music, "steph! I just told Harrison about good ol' Jake!"

Stephanie flashes a half-engaged smile in return to Maggie as Ken grips her upper arm to whisper something in her ear before she emphatically giggles.

"Well, those two look preoccupied!" Maggie comments and gives Harrison a not so subtle once over. "If only we had something to pass the time while these two finished up," she says in a loud, sultry voice.

Harrison's deadpan expression wanes as he ponders over Maggie's question. His eyes light up and he flashes a charismatic smile.

"Oh, I have something in mind for us."

A soft echo rings through the wine cellar as Maggie's muffled screams are hindered behind a handkerchief gag. She is suspended by her ankles from a metal chain that connects to an eyehook in the cellar's ceiling. Her arms hang limp below her head and are bounded by a nylon rope.

Harrison stands from his crouching position, donning his typical black shirt and blue jeans as he regains his power. He pushes a lock of hair from his forehead with the back of his hand, leaving a long streak of crimson across his forehead. The weight of the day dissipates with a red-hot aura.

"You know, Maggie," he announces as he rubs his hands together in an attempt to clean the patches of blood from his palms. "It really is amazing what organs the body can continue to live without once they are removed."

Harrison plucks a serrated blade from a nearby bucket and examines the knife for cleanliness before wiping it along the outside seam of his jeans. Leaning forward, he braces his weight on Maggie's hip to keep her from swinging as he inserts the metal into the side of her already bloodied abdomen.

The sunlight pours through the windows of Déjeuner early on Saturday afternoon. The crisp fall day feels less cool with the blue skies and busy streets bustling with weekend energy. The restaurant feels airy with its baby blue table clothes and brightly colored flower murals. It was exactly what Daisy, Molly, and Amber needed after a night of rowdy debauchery.

Sitting together at a corner table, they sip on brightly colored cocktails and gossip about their night before. While they are put together for the stylish eatery, their red eyes hint at a rambunctious night

Amber Irving was one of The Rose Institute's best sales representatives. Although she was tiny, her boisterous voice and brass tone was exactly what was needed in a heavily male-dominated industry. There wasn't a man she couldn't outsell or a woman who wasn't terrified of her.

Delicately, Daisy strips her napkin free of its ring and lays the fabric across her lap.

"If you're not going to tell us about Aaron, I'll call Taylor and ask him myself," she jokes with a devious look in her eyes.

Molly rolls her eyes and tosses her napkin across her lap.

"What do you want? A fucking diagram?"

Narrowly avoiding spitting out her drink, Amber pulls her hand to her lips to stifle her laughter and drink.

"I mean, it wouldn't hurt," she says.

"You people are monsters," Molly teases, pulling a fresh croissant from a basket in the center of the table. Dropping the pastry on to a bread plate and reaching out for a pat of butter, she shifts the conversation. "I'll spill if you do," she directs at Daisy, lifting one delicate eyebrow.

Daisy's cheeks flush and she rolls in her lips to hide her smile.

"Oh, just the same old, same old."

"Fuck you," Amber calls out slightly more eager than she intends. "You can't hide the juicy details from us. I was the one who told you HBH was about to go under."

Lifting both hands in surrender, Daisy caves.

"Fine, fine. Told him I would, 'see what I can do,' and then," she looks over both shoulders for any onlookers before continuing. "Then we 'saw what we could do' all night long."

"Oh, God!" Molly exudes with a phony bothered tone. "You truly are the worst." Laughing off the terrible joke, she takes a bite of her croissant. "That explains why you're in a rather upbeat mood this morning," she remarks, waiving the half-eaten pastry in Daisy's face. "It's rather disgusting. Let me know when my passive aggressive friend is back."

Daisy releases a genuinely happy laugh.

"I know it's strange, but things have just been going so well with the merger and then this new project with Taylor and then Kennedy. It's exciting to not have to worry about the survival of my work life, you know?"

Shaking her head in disagreement, Amber chimes in, saying, "I wouldn't know. We let go of that cute intern on the sales team and I'm just waiting to get back into the swing of things."

"Didn't you call him 'sweet cheeks' during a meeting and drunkenly give him a raise during a happy hour?" Molly asks.

"*You* called him 'sweet cheeks.' *I* gave him the raise," Amber says, suppressing a laugh. "Judge me on your own time, Molly."

Leaning back into her chair, Molly crosses her arms and asks the table, "do you think I need to stop hitting on interns?"

"Not this conversation again," an irritated Daisy says, smirking at Molly.

"Speak of the devil!" Amber calls out, again, too loudly for their surroundings. Leaning into the table in a poor attempt to hide, she whispers, "It's Duncan and Ken!" She points to the door with a meek forefinger.

Molly shifts her eyes to Daisy with an entertained face, adding, "and it looks like Mr. Bishop is bringing up the rear."

Daisy shifts in her chair to catch a glance and upon seeing the trio and reacts with a muted "yikes."

Erupting into laughter, Amber says, "yikes isn't the half of it. Those guys look like they've had a rough morning."

Harrison's hair lay in disarray atop his head and Duncan had yet to remove his sunglasses. Ken looked as if he hadn't quite quit drinking from the night before as Duncan kept grabbing him by the shoulder in an attempt to hold him upright.

"What do you think would happen if I called them over?" Molly asks the table with a crafty look in her eyes. She pauses, shifting her eyes from Amber to Daisy and back to Amber. Molly braces for Amber's slight head nod before sitting up straight in her chair and calling out, "duncan! Ken! Harrison! Over here!" as she waives the group over to their table.

Daisy releases an exasperated breath before turning to Molly, saying, "I told you, I'm fine with him now." Then she leans into her to jokingly whisper, "your subtly really is your most redeeming quality."

Shrugging her shoulders, Molly blows off Daisy's comment.

"You are so beautiful and wise and funny and sweet. Hey guys!" She ends her sarcastic rant just as the guys arrive at their table.

"My, don't you ladies look lovely today," Duncan croons, still donning his horn-rimmed sunglasses.

"You guys playing *Weekend At Bernie's*?" Amber asks, thrusting her brow in Duncan's direction, pointing out his accessory with a mocking tone.

Peering through the windows into the bright afternoon, Duncan leans his head back to examine the light outside.

"I drank nearly an entire bottle of tequila in an attempt to take a waitress home last night. I think I'll need to get these glasses surgically fused to my face," he says groggily as he taps the rims of his glasses.

Molly raises a chin at Ken who has yet to greet their table.

"What's with him?" she asks.

Harrison raises his shoulders in defeat and says, "we can't find his apartment keys so he's stuck with us until we get ahold of a locksmith."

Daisy chuckles at the bunch.

"You guys are a disastrous superhero team."

"Ha, ha, ha," Duncan exaggeratedly laughs at Daisy. "We really just need to get some food in us before we kill someone." Running his fingers through his hair and releasing an irked breath through his nostrils, he asks, "does this place not have a hostess? We need to eat."

"There was a waitlist when we got in," Amber informs the disorderly group. "You may need to scavenge through the trash for leftovers," she teases, taking an exaggerated sip from her drink.

"How the hell are you drinking?" Harrison asks with a dazed tone.

"We've perfected the work-life balance that it seems Bishop Enterprises has yet to master," Daisy digs as her mouth twists into a poorly hidden smirk.

Still peering through the restaurant in search of the hostess, Duncan butts in.

"Oh, please. Once you're on board with us, balancing work will be a thing of the past." He lifts his sunglasses and exposes his bloodshot eyes. "Did the hostess die?"

Bursting through Duncan and Harrison's shoulders, Ken makes his appearance. "Well, well, well! Look who's here!" he half yells, causing the nearby tables to turn and glare.

"Ken, you've been here for, like, five minutes," says Amber with an amused laugh.

Ignoring Ken, Molly continues to rib the guys.

"Duncan, didn't you have to take a nap halfway through last Friday's sales meeting because you went too hard at Thursday's happy hour?"

"I think he actually fell asleep *during* the meeting," Harrison corrects with an entertained chuckle.

Duncan pulls in sunglasses down the bridge of his nose to haphazardly stare into Harrison's eyes.

"Dude, be cool. Also, once we're all together we can just make poor performance the norm and then we'll be all set," he says, pushing his glasses back into place smiling smugly at Harrison. "It'll be great for everyone."

Rolling his eyes, Harrison turns back to the group.

"That is not how I run my ship. I'd rather be great at work and even better after hours."

Pulling her drink to her lips, Daisy mutters into her drink, "so great he can't even run a merger himself."

The group snickers at Harrison's expense and he jams his hands into his trouser pockets.

"You know, Daisy, sometimes I need to step aside and let others attempt to make something of themselves."

Sensing the bickering about to erupt, the group quiets and Molly jumps in to save the day.

"Daisy, why don't you take Harrison and find that lost hostess." Her eyes dart to Duncan's. "Duncan looks like he may pass out if we don't get some food in him," she says, covering the urgency in her voice with a warm laugh as she pushes Daisy from her chair.

As she awkwardly rises from her seat, Daisy stands to adjust her sundress and glare at Harrison.

"Come on, let's go," she mutters as she brushes past his shoulder without waiting for him to speak. Once at the hostess stand, Daisy drops a heavy elbow atop the counter and searches for anyone to help her escape Harrison's presence.

Harrison stops behind Daisy, mimicking her actions while he searches for the hostess. Leaning forward, he begrudgingly whispers into her hair, "I was just joking, Daisy."

"Didn't realize you were moonlighting as a comedian, Harry," she mutters irritably. "Can't wait to catch your cable special."

Delicately dropping a hand against Daisy's shoulder, Harrison tugs her toward him, but she merely angles her ear to listen.

"Oh, come on. You never could take a joke."

Daisy snaps her head to face him.

"Don't start," she exclaims more forcefully than she intends. Realizing that a few people have turned to the commotion, she hisses at Harrison, "outside." She then storms through the foyer doors and out onto the street.

Harrison resentfully follows, noticing that Daisy is facing away from the door in her typical frustrated brood. Standing along her shoulder, he attempts to ease the tension.

"You know," he starts, speaking into the street, "if you keep worrying like this, you're going to have crow's feet by forty."

"You're unbelievable," Daisy huffs, grabbing him by the shirt sleeve and dragging him around the building into the alleyway. Whipping him before her, she plants him in an uneven stance that catches him off guard. "What is your fucking problem, Harry? Things have been going so well lately and you want to rile me up just for the sake of a joke?"

Harrison leans his head back and rolls his eyes into his head.

"Jesus Christ, Daisy. I let you run the fucking merger. I don't get to make a few jokes at your expense?"

Daisy's eyes pierce through Harrison as they shift from bright green to damped emerald.

"*Let* me?" she growls through her teeth. "You *begged* me to stick around and take over," she says, her eyes flashing as she angrily grips her hips.

With a disgusted look on his face, Harrison throws his hat in the ring as he feels the fight begin to build.

"Oh, my mistake. Would you rather have strong-armed me into the position per usual?" He demands, his tone becoming aggressive as his voice rises.

Releasing a harsh laugh in Harrison's face, Daisy crosses her arms and says, "I thought that's what I had done?"

"You're un-fucking-believable, Daisy." Harrison shouts as he grips his hands into fists and then combs both of his hands through his unruly hair. "Why is it always a fight with you?"

"Why do you always feel the need to one-up me?" Daisy spits before leaning into Harrison. "Afraid that you'll need to keep living off my work for the rest of your life?"

Harrison's nostrils flare with his heavy breath as Daisy continues to brood through him. The noisy street beyond the alley is full of life, but their private backstreet is another dimension of solitude and aggression.

"Fuck it," Harrison growls as he lunges forward toward Daisy. He claps a hand around the base of her skull and another at the small of her back, pulling her forcefully into his body as he plants his lips on to hers.

Instead of fighting, Daisy's hands grip at Harrison's back and she leans her weight into him as she feverously presses her mouth into his. Her hands move from his back and up his arms then eventually into his hair, where she roughly pulls it, forcing a moan from his throat.

As Harrison tugs at Daisy's thigh, he turns her back into the building and presses her into the cool brick. Pulling at her knee, he traces his fingers up her thigh and pulls her waist into his as they lose themselves in the moment, hidden away from the rest of the world.

What the hell am I doing? Daisy thinks to herself as she pushes both palms into Harrison's shoulders and forces him to step back uneasily onto his heels.

"Harry!" she yells, regaining consciousness.

"I didn't mean to," Harrison haphazardly answers with a hint of laughter as he runs two fingertips across his lips and lingers on Daisy's eyes with a bewildered look.

"Oh, fuck off," Daisy says as she runs her hands down her dress and combs her fingers through her hair. "If that is your form of a coping mechanism for dealing with me, try to keep it in your pants next time," she says, scowling before hurrying back into the restaurant.

>>>

Daisy and Harrison stand before the group as eight eyes judge the pair with barely hidden smiles. Daisy's dress is turned up at the hem and her hair is distraughtly pulled from her ponytail. Harrison's hair is equally revealing, frayed at the sides and his cheeks are rosy and flushed.

"Well, you two look like you were having fun," Molly comments as she presses her lips into an entertained hard line, holding back what appears a tremendous giggle as her cheeks puff from the pressure.

Duncan snorts half a laugh from his nose and pulls his hand to grip his chin.

"Find that hostess yet?" he asks.

Daisy crosses her arms and releases a long and audible sigh.

"Not yet," she says.

With that, the table erupts into laughter and she takes a seat with a heavy thud.

The afternoon sun gleams through the conference room windows, heating the space until it is muggy. The room is brimming with employees of both Bishop Enterprises and The Rose Institute. Half eaten sandwiches and empty bags of chip litter the long table while some employees take notes on laptops or write on legal pads.

Daisy stands at the far end of the table while she points to an oversized board on an easel.

"Okay, am I forgetting any other teams?" she asks the room, snapping a cap on a dry erase marker before turning back to the group. "I think that's everyone."

Molly sits to Daisy's right with both elbows propped on the table and gently taps a pen against her bottom lip.

"Did we forget the new HBH Discoveries team?" she asks.

Daisy eagerly turns back to the easel as she raises a hand to her temple to tap her head.

"Ah, yes!" she says, scribbling down another name at the bottom of the list.

At the opposite end of the table, Harrison leans back into his chair with both hands locked behind his head.

"Do we really need to list HBH as its own team?" he asks as the entire room swivels at the sound of his voice. "I mean, we could just loop them in with the plastics division," he says, releasing a hand to point to another name on the list.

"We thought of that already," Daisy answers as the room pivots, returning their attention to her. "We'll be incorporating that in the second phase of transitions as this is a much newer development."

Harrison releases his other hand to lean forward and drop his elbows against the table. The conference room rotates in preparation of his next statement.

"Do you think that will cause some disarray between the timelines of other teams?" he asks, now gesturing with his hands in a circular pattern. "Wouldn't it make more sense to just expedite their process?"

Before Harrison can even finish his thought, the room swings to Daisy for the return serve.

"They won't need as much guidance, as we'll be leaving their organizational structure as is, so it should work out," she says, her tone positive and confident as the room prepares for the lob into Harrison's lap.

"That works for me," Harrison concludes as he claps his hands together. "Any issues on the sales side, Miss Jordan?"

Molly shifts her gaze back to Daisy waiting for her response but when she's greet with Daisy's wide eyes, she realizes the question was directed to her.

"Oh, sorry," she stumbles. "Yeah, no issues, as it's not changing their current market focus."

As Daisy and Harrison continue their rally across the table, Molly thinks to herself, *déjà vu, much?* and shakes her head from the strange recollection.

This is the game that Daisy and Harrison played for months, a mind-numbing waltz of death, copulation, and utter confusion that left their world spinning and hazy. Daisy would ruin the lives of dozens of pliable men when Harrison would infuriate her. Then, Harrison would become so enraged by Daisy's success that he would kill any seemingly guilty person in his path. Once the pair was satisfied from their kills, they would return to their day jobs with a newly found vigor until they once again clashed and found themselves fighting in the streets or in each other's beds.

Molly relaxes her eyes as they flitter between the couple, now volleying across the conference room table.

Back and forth and back again. *They really are the worst couple*, she thinks to herself, releasing an offhanded chuckle as her focus shifts back into space. She presses the tip of her nose into the butt of her pen, tugging at the taught skin until her weight slips and she jolts herself out of the trance. A few heads turn at the subtle rustle causing Molly to blush. Raising her eyebrows in a sheepish eye roll she diverts the attention elsewhere by lifting her chin in the direction of the table and whispering with a subdued laugh, "these two would kill each other if we didn't put a table between them."

Chapter Eleven: **All Night**

Harrison runs both hands aggressively through his unruly hair with a frazzled look in his eyes as he forcefully sighs. "How is Singapore three months behind in production?" he demands, gripping his chin and forcing his eyes shut in exasperation. "We own the fucking production lines."

On the other side of Harrison's sprawling desk, an unamused man with a receding hairline and rounded glasses stands between two armchairs. He stares back into Harrison's angered stare with minimal concern. "Drug resistant antibiotics don't just sprout from the ground, Mr. Bishop," he retorts with a hint of sarcasm.

"I bet if I paid the ground as much as I'm paying you, we'd be harvesting antibiotic trees within the hour," Harrison answers, mirroring his mocking tone. Relaxing his shoulders, he closes his eyes and drops the weight of his head back against his shoulders. Speaking into to the ceiling, his eyes still tightly shut, he asks the question he knows will not provide an adequate answer. "How long can I expect, Barry?"

Barry lifts an index finger to adjust his glasses, the faintest smirk pulling at his lips.

"How honest do you want me to answer?"

Harrison releases a groan and rolls the weight of his skull to dangle against his shoulders before opening a single eye to Barry.

"Should I be sitting down?"

Harrison's corner office was brightly lit this afternoon. The floor to ceiling windows framed with emerald green blinds allowed the autumn day to filter across the charcoal concrete floors. The oversized furniture and minimalist metal desk felt less like an office space and more like an examination room, but Harrison felt at ease when surrounded by the deep tones and cool hardware.

Opening his remaining eye, Harrison braces himself for Barry's words.

"Give it to me straight, Barry."

A delicate knock on the door saves Barry from breaking the bad news. The glass door swings open and Kit peers his head through the opening.

"Miss Stone is here," he announces with a timid squeak. "Said something about, and I'm quoting here, 'breaking that bastard's balls in two' if I didn't allow her to speak with you." The blood rises in his cheeks noticing the audience.

Barry turns his focus back to Harrison, his smirk forming into a full grin.

"Mind if I stay and watch?" he asks, his ruthless enjoyment filling the room.

"You've had enough time to bust my balls today, Barry," Harrison relinquishes with a prepared sigh. "Might as well let someone else have a go at me," he laughs apathetically.

Kit parts his lips to excuse himself and escort Daisy into the room, but she brushes past him, gliding into the office unannounced.

"Afternoon, gents," she says without an introduction. "Which one of you is going to explain to me why I have a Brazilian diplomat denying me access to four of their research centers because they're still waiting on antibiotics from Singapore?" she demands as she crosses her arms defiantly.

Harrison raises his eyebrows. A smug smile fills his face as he returns his focus to Barry, who awkwardly adjusts his sweater vest.

"Let me introduce you to Mr. Barry Newhall."

Daisy reads Harrison's face raising her brow, knowing he has thrown an ill-prepared fighter into the ring with Muhammad Ali. A sweet smile fills her cheeks as she turns to Barry.

"Let's hear the issue, Gary."

"It's Barry, Miss Stone," he corrects with a slight crack. "Barry Newhall," he says, leaning forward and extending a hand to Daisy.

Shifting her hips, Daisy releases her arms from their staunch stance and, instead, digs both hands into her slim trouser pockets. Ignoring the correction, she continues with her interrogation.

"Listen up, Gary," she says, taking a challenging step forward that forces Barry's weight onto his heels. Her voice growls with a sticky-sweet seduction as she dips her chin and scrutinizes him through her lush eyelashes. "I don't know if you've ever had the opportunity to be on the receiving end of a diplomat's Portuguese beratement," she continues, each syllable from her lips pummeling into Barry. "But I'm more than happy to recreate it for you until I get a fucking answer as to why I am no longer allowed into South America."

Harrison rolls his lips inward hindering a smile and crams his hands in his pockets as he delightfully relishes in entertainment. Barry's eyes flicker to his desk in hopes of salvation, but he comes up empty handed when the only lifeline he receives is a mere "I told you so" look from Harrison.

A soft click of Daisy's heel echoes through the office as she takes a menacing step into Barry's personal space and harshly whispers, "give me the *new* timeline, Gary." Her cool breath hits him between the eyes. "A favorable timeline, if you don't mind," she harshly adds.

Swallowing hard, Barry breathes deeply through his nostrils and chirps a meager, "one month," just as a microscopic bead of sweat forms above his lip.

Daisy purses her jade eyes, surveying the response for honesty. Scrunching her baby pink lips to one side, she stares into Barry's trembling face. Finally, she dabs an open palm on his cheek in chastising approval.

"Let's make it three weeks and we've got ourselves a deal, Gary," she counters, her lioness eyes victorious.

Barry drops his eyes in defeat and says, "three weeks it is." His lips produce a line of agreement and he turns his rosy face toward Harrison, lamenting his goodbyes.

"Thank you, Barry. I'll speak with you later next week," Harrison definitively announces as Barry exits the office and Daisy holds her stance, turning only her line of sight to meet with Harrison.

"Have a great weekend, Gary," Daisy calls out, her body holding a satisfied stance that forces Harrison to shake his head in faux disapproval as a warm smile fills his face.

"You may have just knocked a few years off his life," Harrison says with an amused face of appreciation. He rarely had the chance to see Daisy in action and he relished the opportunity to not only witness the infamous torment, but also not to be on the receiving end of it. Her power was terrifying though impressive and left Harrison with a baffling desire to want to watch it all over again.

A coy smile tugs at Daisy's lips.

"If you want to make an omelet, you've got to crack a few eggs," she says, draping herself into an armchair across from Harrison's desk.

Imitating her actions, Harrison takes a seat.

"Well, how about that," he comments with an air of laughter. "Maybe it was the correct move putting you at the helm."

"Or maybe you just needed a woman like yours truly to do your job the right way," she says, satisfied. She flashes an entertained smile and shakes out an arm to check her watch. "Shit, it's almost seven. Do you want to grab a bite to eat?" she asks as she rises from the chair. "Doing half your job makes me hungry."

"It must be excruciating to participate in *actual* work instead of terrifying grown dimwits into selling off their company," Harrison counters.

"I mean, it really is," she says as a genuine grin fills her cheeks and causes Harrison's do to the same. "Come on, I'm buying," she says, coercing him out of his chair without further discussion.

A frazzled hostess stands before Harrison and Daisy, her eyes apologetic.

"I'm so sorry, Mr. Bishop. We didn't know you would be joining us this evening so there won't be a table for another thirty minutes." She looks down to a chart of tables before her. "I can ask some of the patrons to make room if you don't mind waiting a moment or two?"

Harrison tugs his mouth into a slanted thought of contemplation and turns to face Daisy.

"Well?"

Looking through the crowded restaurant, Daisy twists her lips into concentration. A waiter passes by with an elegant plate of salmon and fall vegetables fanned into an intricate pattern. Turning back to Harrison, her eyes glitter to life with another plan in mind. "I've got a better idea," she says. Turning back to the hostess, she thanks her for the offer and grabs Harrison by the hand, dragging him out of the chic restaurant.

Once outside, Harrison stands next to Daisy as she looks up and down the busy street.

"What's your plan here, Stone?" he asks with a perplexed inflection. "I've seen you cook before and I'm not sure my stomach is prepared for that debacle."

Feigning annoyance, Daisy turns to him with assurance and says, "oh, I know you're going to like this." She nudges a hip into him and leans her weight into his side. "Just like *all* of my decisions."

Still searching the street, Daisy takes a small step forward. Her mouth twists to one side as she surveys their options. Harrison digs a hand into his pocket, pulling out a pack of cigarettes and a lighter but is stopped short when Daisy's manicured hand grips his wrist in surprise.

"No time!" she shouts. "We need to make a run for it!"

Harrison feels his weight shift as Daisy breaks into a sprint down the crowded street with him in tow. Through happy hour groups and couples walking arm in arm, Daisy drags Harrison across the sidewalk. Quickly dodging pedestrians, he calls back with an apologetic, "excuse us!" to each person they nearly topple over in their mysterious chase. Daisy manages to hurdle each obstacle with ease, tugging at Harrison's slender fingers when he starts to lag behind.

"Daisy!" Harrison finally regains enough breath to yell. "Where are we going?" he asks as his oxfords echo with a muted clunk after each haphazard step.

Turning her delighted face to meet his, Daisy exposes a joyous smile as a few tendrils of her mousy hair cross her face.

"Just trust me!" she calls back, her voice fearless and enthusiastic.

Some things never change, Harrison thinks to himself humorously as he recalls their adventures in college. He remembers the times Daisy dragged him out of a lab and forced him into an impromptu road trip or a surprise concert in the middle of the night. She was always a bit of a mystery to him, but in a way, that excited him like nothing else he had ever experienced.

"Should we change into gym clothes?" he yells to her in a teasing tenor.

"And risk being the worst dressed couple?" Daisy retorts through hurried breaths. "I thought you were better than this, Harry!"

After what feels like an eternity of running through the street, but ultimately only accumulates to a mere four blocks, Daisy slams on the brakes and Harrison pummels into her back, their intertwined fingers still tightly wound. They find themselves away from crowd on a quiet street corner. A few cars hum at the traffic light and Harrison shakes his head, assessing their surroundings.

"This place is lovely!" he jokes, raising an arm to showcase the street corner. Taking a step forward, he speaks to a street lamp.

"Good evening, sir! I'll take the dinner special and the lady will have a," Harrison turns to Daisy in faux confirmation, "garden salad?"

A satisfied smile pulls at Daisy's rose lips as she lifts a chin, pointing behind Harrison.

"I'll do you one better," she smirks, waiting for his reaction.

Harrison's eyes squint with uncertainty as he turns over his shoulder to examine the sight behind him. A brightly colored food truck with an awning and plastic chairs sits kitty-corner to their location. Twinkle lights fill the space of the secluded side street and the smell of grilling hamburgers envelops Harrison's nostrils. Dipping into his knees, he turns back to a satisfied Daisy.

"Oh man," he groans with pleasure. "You *are* good."

Daisy grasps his bicep and begins dragging him across the street with an entertained smile.

"Yes," she agrees with an obvious tone. "But you're not that hard to impress."

Daisy delicately places a French fry across her top lip, curling her pout upward and holding the fry in place all the while her arms are outstretched as she balances. Harrison sits beside her at a white, plastic table near the food truck. Her legs are strewn across his lap, crossed at the heel, as she dangles a high heel from her toe.

The night has a slight chill beneath the truck's multicolored string lights and an engorged moon hangs low in the evening sky. The rustle of the food truck creates a world of its own along the hidden street corner.

Harrison swills his paper cup as he balances his elbow against the plastic table, his other hand hanging softly at the wrist from Daisy's ankle.

"It's really a shame your career has hindered you from exposing your many talents," he comments as he drops his cup before popping a fry into his mouth with a chuckle.

"I really am quite the multifaceted woman," Daisy agrees, dropping the fry into her lap. "You know, I actually had another career in mind when I was younger," she says, picking a single pickle out of her burger. Tearing a bite from the burger's edge she drops the morsel back on to the paper before picking up her drink to chew on her straw.

Gulping his soda, Harrison furrows his brow in thought.

"I actually remember that," he says.

"No way. I would have told you this nearly a decade ago."

"Nope, nope. I remember," Harrison presses as he sits up and closes one eye. "A race car driver?"

Dropping both hands into her lap, Daisy concedes. An astonished smile engrosses her face.

"How the hell do you remember that?"

Sitting back satisfied, Harrison crosses his arms in pride. A chuckle croaks from his mouth and he says, "there isn't much I don't know about you, Daisy. You have to remember that."

Daisy rolls her eyes upward and suppresses a smile.

"If that wasn't so charming, I could really hate you for it," she says. Her chin dips as she traces the outline of her hands with her bright green eyes. "I really thought I had the hand-eye coordination for racing. I guess I forgot the part where I'd have to, you know, nearly die every time I went to work," she says, smiling lackadaisically.

"Doesn't sound so different from what we do now," Harrison adds. "I think you're right where you belong," he says, his tone soft and sincere. "It takes a very specific personality to do what you do."

"Oh, please," Daisy scoffs. "No grown man appreciates being ridiculed by a woman half his age while giving up his company." She drops the paper cup on to the table as the ice rattles inside. "I mean, I don't make it easy on them, but that's really for my own enjoyment."

"You do tend to make some enemies along the way," he jokingly observes. "But I think most of them deserve it, so it cancels out."

Daisy purses her lips in thought.

"Well, you handled it in stride," she says. She pauses, letting her mind wander for a microscopic moment. "All in all, our current situation doesn't seem so bad." Her eyes flicker to meet briefly with Harrison's before returning to her lap.

"We really do spend a lot of time on a broad spectrum," Harrison laughs. "If we're not killing each other, we're..." his voice trails off until his eyes return to Daisy's. "Well, here."

"I think we were just meant to be enemies," Daisy concurs. "I think there's just a lot of...history. Yeah, that's the word."

Harrison rolls his cup in his hands, a thoughtful smirk balling within his right cheek that digs into his dimple.

"I secretly think you enjoy it," he says, waiting for Daisy's reaction.

"Oh, please," Daisy digs, knowing she is the butt of the joke. "This is purely business at this point."

A deep silence settles between the pair.

"Do you feel it still?" Harrison asks sheepishly, his emerald eyes sparkling.

Twisting her lips, Daisy turns her cheek to hide her expression.

"I don't know what you're talking about."

Harrison scans the food truck and looks up into the night sky, saying to no one in particular, "Maybe one day."

Raising a delicate brow, Daisy pops another fry into her mouth.

"You've never been one for subtle cues, Harry," she says, playfully lowering her face to hide her smile.

"Subtle?"

"The merger, the meetings, Wellington the other night," she says, her concealed smile booming through cheeks. *"Maybe one day,"* she says, mimicking Harrison's deep voice.

Rolling his lips inward against his teeth, Harrison disguises his smirk.

"I thought recreating our first attempted date would make you more cooperative to work with me," he says, shaking the ice in his paper cup before taking an empty sip through his straw.

Daisy nods to no one in agreement, repeating, "maybe one day."

A sting of dread settles in Harrison's stomach momentarily, causing his eyes to relax and his mind to float elsewhere.

"Maybe one day," he repeats to himself in a hushed voice.

<<<

Harrison's head slams into the concrete driveway as his older brother Tom straddles his torso. His weight digs into Harrison's stomach, forcing out a groan from the pit of his gut. Gary stands just over Tom's shoulder, watching on entertained.

Harrison's left eye and cheekbone are bruised and there is a noticeable tear across the arm of his tee shirt. He tries to collect himself, attempting to wriggle out of Tom's grasp.

"Don't kill him in the driveway," Gary says, kicking Tom lightly in the arm. "Mom will ground us if we get blood on our clothes again today."

Tom leans forward, his nose inches from Harrison's beet red face.

"You hear that, faggot? Don't get your fucking blood on me again," he barks. Regaining his height, he leans back onto his heels and looks over to Gary. "Wanna take few swings at him before knock this faggot out?"

"Get the fuck off of me, you idiot," Harrison croaks as he attempts to escape.

"Quick moving, faggot," Tom says as he grasps both of Harrison's skinny biceps in his bear-like grip, forcing both forearms beneath his knees.

Harrison screeches out a yelp of pain and winces at the pressure.

"Get the fuck off of me!" he yells more forcefully as the claustrophobia wraps around him like an unwelcomed blanket.

"Can you shut him up already? It's almost dinnertime and we don't have all night," Gary says, annoyed.

"Yeah, dude. Gimme a minute," Tom confirms as he lurches forward, both oversized hands aimed at Harrison's throat. "He told you to shut up!" he yells into Harrison's face. The rancid breath of someone who hasn't brushed his teeth in days pummels through Harrison's nostrils and forces through his face.

Harrison gasps for air, suffocating beneath Tom. A muffled "stop!" is all he can utter as his eyes bulge and turn cherry red from the lack of oxygen.

"I told you," Tom grunts as he tightens his strangle. "Just shut up. We're your family, *little bro*," he says with a sweetness that could only dictate hatred.

>>>

Daisy's straw gurgles as she finishes off the last of her soda. She shakes the cup to toggle the ice and returns the straw to her blush lips as the remainder of her drink echoes with a gurgle.

"Well, where to now, Harry?" she asks with an extra pep in her tone.

Harrison blinks his eyes to regain his mind. Scanning the corner, he realizes he hasn't made much of an effort to locate himself after their earlier jog.

"I'm actually not sure if I know where we are at the moment," he says. He turns to scan the dark street behind them, twisting his torso back toward Daisy. "Are we still in the financial district?"

Ignoring Harrison's need to control the situation, she thinks of their next move.

"I've got an idea."

"More rigorous exercise?" Harrison quips as he raises a single eyebrow.

"Not until later," Daisy retorts with a salacious tone. "I think this will be fun, but you gotta trust me." She grabs him by the wrist, drags him from the plastic chair, and again, they billow down the street.

Jutting down a nearby alleyway, the pair arrives at a dark door nestled between the back entrance of a delicatessen and a pharmacy. The worn metal door looks as if this could be an apartment, but the lack of windows hint otherwise. A subtle hum can be heard, almost as if a factory is operating nearby.

"Ready?" Daisy eagerly asks Harrison, who looks up at the building.

"To be murdered?" Harrison asks. He drops his head to meet Daisy's eyes. Sticking out both wrists before her, he adds, "make it quick," before feigning a flinch.

"Oh, come on, you big baby," says Daisy, scowling as she opens the door into a dim entryway with a single, unlit stairway leading upward.

"Ah, I see you *are* intending on killing me," Harrison comments. "Lovely."

Once they reach the poorly lit third story landing, the hum that they heard along the street has shifted into an almost deafening cacophony of sound. The ground shakes slightly with the noise and the bannister's nails rattle deep within the worn wood.

"You're gonna love this," Daisy says, just before swinging the entry door open with a fluid motion. Blue and lavender light flood the landing and the sound blasts across Harrison's face. Deep within what appears to be an apartment stands a small stage, overrun with a large brass band and a petite, brunette woman wailing away as she grips a nearby microphone stand by the neck. The lights from the stage wave across the room on toggling, unmatched stands where nearly one hundred patrons dance through what used to be living quarters and lean against the previous kitchen island. Although the space is packed with people dancing and drinking, the band surges through the open doorway, drawing the two inside.

Harrison leans into Daisy, shouting over the sound, "are you kidding me? How did you find this place?"

Daisy pulls herself to her tiptoes and drifts into Harrison's chest to be heard.

"You're not the only one with secrets, Harry."

An enormous smile fills Harrison's face as he digs his elbow into Daisy's bicep. Grabbing her hand, he shouts yet again, "I guess – when in Rome!" before dragging her off into the dancing crowd

Nuzzling their way deep into the audience, a new song bursts through the precarious speakers and Daisy's eyes light to life as she recognizes it. Harrison takes a few quick steps forward, holding tightly onto Daisy's hand as he swings her outward between a nearby couple. With a gentle flick of his wrist, he pulls her back into a swing move. Daisy's eyes spark with astonishment of the intricate move, her face an unseen fit of surprise.

"I had career goals outside of this life as well," Harrison yells over the music.

Daisy's mouth hangs slack.

"A *dancer*?" she shouts as she drapes both wrists across his shoulders and allows her hips to move to the upbeat tempo. "Absolutely incredible."

Harrison tugs at his lower lip as his dimples dig deep into his cheeks and he traces his hands across Daisy's hips until he nestles them into the small of her back.

"Do another," Daisy instructs as she leans into Harrison's chest, whispering a mere inch from his lips.

"You got it," he replies with a subtle wink. Without warning, he grips both of Daisy's wrists and takes a deep step backward. Pulling one arm into his stomach, he repeats his previous move of casting Daisy outward into the thick crowd. This time, instead of pulling her inward, he tugs at her wrist to instruct her to return and misses her retrieval to do a spin move of his own until he catches Daisy on the pass and pulls her in close for another embrace.

A full laugh escapes from Daisy as she drops her head backward and wraps her arms around Harrison's waist.

"Un-fucking-believable!" she yells in amazement.

Harrison grips Daisy's waist, an earnest look in his eyes that forces the pair to pause momentarily. Parting his lips to speak, a soft tone emerges.

"Dais—"

"Holy shit! It's him!" a nearby woman screeches through the crowd. "I fucking told you, Shannon!" The portly woman pushes a neighboring couple out of her path as she marches toward Harrison and Daisy, interrupting their intimate moment.

The woman reaches the two and presses her large body into their arms.

"Harrison Bishop!" she shouts over the music. "Take a picture with me!" she instructs, pulling a cell phone from her purse and extending her arm outward for an impromptu photo.

Harrison releases Daisy and lifts a hand to shield his face.

"I'm sorry, ma'am. I'm actually a little tied up at the moment," he says, his voice apologetic yet stern.

Another woman rams into the couple, exclaiming, "see, Shannon! I fucking told you!"

Shannon nudges her head between Harrison and the camera-wielding woman and releases a high-pitched scream, forcing Daisy to wince at the noise.

"Holy shit! You weren't kidding!"

Daisy glares through Harrison, instructing him to stop this intrusive behavior. Nodding in silent agreement, he turns to the women.

"Would you two mind? I'm kind of busy at the moment."

"With who?" Shannon scoffs, pointing a finger inches from Daisy's nose. "This bitch?"

Unamused, Daisy crosses her arms and taps an impatient finger atop her elbow, waiting for Harrison to correct the situation.

Shannon's friend doesn't miss a beat as she gives Daisy a once over.

"Listen Harrison, this prissy bitch doesn't hold a candle to me," she says as she places her hands on her hips and winks at him.

Harrison rolls his eyes and flashes Daisy a remorseful look.

"Ladies, thank you for stopping by, but I really do need to get back to my evening," he says as he holds back his building anger.

Without warning, Shannon pushes between her friend and Harrison, placing herself directly in front of Daisy, pressing her back into Daisy's chest.

"I don't give a *fuck* about this tiny bitch, Harrison. You're the one who's saved us all and I want to make it up to you." Her tone takes a forcefully sexual turn.

"Yes, yes. The Cure All Kid, I was there. I found TEA and saved you all. You can thank me some other time," Harrison says, blurting out what he knows the women want to hear as he lifts both hands in surrender, hoping to escape the confrontation.

Taking a step around Shannon, Daisy's eyes bulge in her skull as she yells, "are you fucking kidding me? Glad to see you haven't changed a bit, your majesty."

"Daisy, come on!" Harrison barks over the booming music still thumping over the speakers nearby. "You know I didn't mean it like that!"

Daisy flares her nostrils and waits for the women to retreat. Shannon steps yet again in front of Daisy, blocking her from the conversation.

"Harrison, ignore blondie. We're all the woman you need."

Harrison tongues his cheek and turns his eyes to the ceiling.

"Ladies, could you please give me a moment?"

He is too late. Daisy is already walking away, dropping both hands to her sides in defeat.

"It's cool, Harry. I guess we finally found the reason why we can't make things work," she says. She tugs at her handbag, fumbling for her cell phone. "I'll just see you at work," she says as she disappears into the crowd, stranding Harrison alone with his doting fans.

After months of their song and dance, Harrison and Daisy finally hit their breaking point in the late fall. The merger planning slowly came to a close with the finalization of the acquisition occurring at the beginning of the new year.

Late in the afternoon, Daisy dismisses the teams from the conference room for the evening. As people begin filing out of the room, Harrison walks in the opposite direction toward Daisy, who collects her things after scribbling a few final notes on a legal pad.

Molly rises from her seat and opens her mouth to speak to Daisy, but as Harrison hovers nearby. She snaps her mouth shut, shooting him a glance as if to say, "you're welcome, Bishop."

Once Molly is out of earshot, Harrison clears his throat but Daisy holds her composure. Waiting for a reaction, he tries his luck again and releases another phony cough in her direction.

Without looking up, Daisy says, "yes, Harry?"

Slumping his shoulders and sighing with annoyance, Harrison finally speaks.

"Can we chat?"

"I'm on my way out, actually," she says. Daisy stacks her papers into a neat pile and finally raises her line of sight to meet Harrison's eager, emerald eyes. "Make it quick," she says, strutting out of the room, causing Harrison to pick up his pace.

"Alright then," he begins much more hurried than planned. "Now that we're finally not at each other's throats, I figured it would be a good time for us to discuss your pretend exit strategy." His words feel ill-formed in his rushed state.

Keeping her steady pace, Daisy presses through the hallway.

"What on earth are you talking about?" she challenges bitterly without meeting his eyes.

"You know what I'm talking about. Finalized executive positions are due next week and we haven't even sat down to discuss this yet." His tone is concerned and confused. "This is *your* job, Daisy."

Daisy laughs dryly and shakes her head.

"No shit, Harry, but you already know my stance. I'm out once the ink is dry," she says, callously.

Harrison grips at her elbow and forces Daisy to swing around on one foot.

"What the hell?" she shrieks.

"Daisy, look at me!" Harrison demands. A few passersby turn at their tiff. "You're not leaving. I know you just said that in the heat of the moment but you can't just walk away from all of this!" he says, waiving his hands frantically.

Shaking her head and laughing at the scene, Daisy turns to walk into her office. Harrison holds his ground but grunts with exasperation and follows her into the dark room, slamming the door.

"Daisy!"

Searching around her desk, Daisy looks for an object but continues to ignore Harrison's antics.

"If you're going to throw a fit, would you either do it more quietly or shut up long enough for me to find my glasses?" she asked distractedly.

"This isn't a game, Daisy! This is our company. Mine *and* yours."

"I know that. However, I earned my spot at the table," says Daisy, unfazed. Locating her glasses on the shelf behind her, she picks them up and drops them delicately atop her nose. Looking Harrison straight in the eyes through her frames, she turns her tone. "You happened to steal my chair and spray paint your name across the back to claim it as your own." Her words batter and sting Harrison.

"That's not what I meant," he croons with a soft voice in an attempt to change the conversation, but Daisy is already ten steps ahead.

"Aren't you getting exhausted of all of this?" Daisy asks as she picks up a stack of papers, arranging them neatly, her voice returning to a careful attitude. She waives her hand in the air in a circular pattern. "All of this fighting and hooking up and fighting and on and on. It's fucking exhausting."

Her body language feels different to Harrison, more rigid and structured than their typical back and forth. Taking a stabilizing breath, he shoves his hands deep into his pockets and straightens his back.

"I could do this with you for years, Daisy."

Daisy pauses to peer at him over her glasses.

"Oh, God," she murmurs, clearly irritated. "What for? What is your end game here, Harry?"

Instead of answering, Harrison opens his mouth to respond but closes his lips and instead watches Daisy move through her office, her natural confidence that he always admired about her in full effect. His eyes trace the dozens of trophies that line the walls behind her as if shouting her praises. He clenches his breath, feeling his rough heartbeat pound against his sternum.

A moment passes without a sound and finally Daisy turns to stare at Harrison.

"Well?" she asks, not sure of the peculiar look in his eyes. "Is that it?"

Harrison glances at Daisy just as the words come pouring out of him uncontrollably.

"I think I'm in love with you," he says. The words seep out of him like honey with such genuine resonance that he is not quite sure if they are his own. "You're the only person I care about and even further, the only person I can't seem to win over."

Daisy holds her breath briefly. She looks to floor in thought and returns her vivid green eyes back to Harrison's. The tense air sits between them as Harrison waits for her next words, but they do not come. Instead, Daisy erupts into a fit of laughter so intense that she leans forward to clutch her stomach. Her deep, palpable laugh freezes Harrison in time. She drops a hand to her desk to stabilize herself from the hilarity and flings her papers onto the desk.

"That's fucking hilarious!" she spouts between laughs. "Absolutely comical!"

Stunned by the reaction, Harrison squeaks out, "I'm glad you find it so funny." He furrows his brow, and taking a more serious tone, he tries again. "I'm being serious, Daisy. I'm in love with you."

Closing her eyes and continuing her episode, Daisy shakes a hand at Harrison.

"No, no! Not again!" she exclaims, grabbing the back of her chair for support.

Staring down, Harrison traces the grain in the wood floors with his eyes. When he was a boy, he would search across the stars in the night sky for hours when he snuck out to lie down in his front yard. Completely disconnected from the world, his eyes would glide along the heavens and he would feel at peace with himself. Repeating the motion now, Harrison didn't feel the stabilizing effect that he was hoping would wash over him.

"Is that it?" Daisy asks, breaking Harrison's train of thought as he moves his eyes to meet hers. "I have a lot to get to tonight, so if you don't mind," she says, hinting for him to leave.

Harrison's eyes follow the same pattern as his pupils caress the trophies and plaques behind Daisy. He tilts his head to one side as he examines row after row of awards and acknowledgements broadcasting her life's work.

"Are those up there because of Episcopus Aerobium?" he asks, the words once again tumbling out of his mouth, too quickly to retrieve.

Daisy pauses as she glares at Harrison, finally landing on a moment of connection. She removes her glasses and drops them to the table. Following his line of sight, she looks over her shoulder to the wall behind her.

Turning back to face Harrison, Daisy drops her shoulders and straightens her spine.

"I don't need a fucking trophy to know that you're a fraud, Harry," she spits across the office.

Mimicking Daisy's stance, Harrison puffs his chest and lowers his shoulders.

"If you really had invented it, I don't think we'd be in this position," he says, his words like molasses and his eyes tightened into a stare that burns a hole through her. Without further discussion, Harrison slowly turns and opens the office door to flood the room with light, leaving Daisy frozen, her jaw hanging along its hinges.

Chapter Twelve: **Coaster**

"Drink up, sweetie," the cheery nurse instructs of a teenage Lily. "The last thing anyone with pneumonia needs is a bout of dehydration." Her grandmotherly coo eases Lily in the uncomfortable room as she tips a flimsy cup towards Lily's pale lips.

An adolescent Daisy perches at the foot of Lily's bed, squeezing her feet with an eager smile.

"She's right. The sooner you feel better, the sooner we can go home," she says. The hushed tones of a respirator slowly drown out her words as the dull room digs its suffocating talons into her throat. She harshly swallows as she attempts to ignore her discomfort.

Although Lily had spent nearly half of her life in and out of the hospital with lymphoma complications, Daisy could never overcome the menacing presence she experienced whenever she would visit her sister. The bleak severity of the white walls and the sharp smell of alcohol that lingered with a slow strangulation seemed to follow her even after she was home. After painting herself with her happiest smile for her sister, she would hide away in her bedroom, unsure if she would ever experience the day when Lily would finally return home for good.

Reaching forward, Daisy grips Lily's cold hand.

"Summer is only a few months away. If you're feeling up to it, Susan said that you could come with Mom and Dad and me to Brighton Beach on Lake Superior. But no way they'll agree to it if you're shriveled up like a raisin from dehydration," she jokes with a playful grin. She squeezes her sister's chilly hand again.

Lily coughs dryly into her shoulder. She takes a long sip from the paper cup and hands it back to Susan as she turns to leave.

"I'm not dumb, Dais. I know Mom and Dad aren't letting me out of here," she says. Her tone is somber but assured. "I can't even get out bed. Like they would let me go to the beach," she sputters before coughing again into her yellow hand.

Daisy sits up straight, tightening her jaw at the truth behind Lily's words. She hated how her sister knew too much about her diagnosis and how her parents barely attempted to play the part of a concerned family.

"You know that's not true, Lil," she lies with an irked smile. "Mom and Dad just want to see you happy. I know they haven't been around much, but who would you rather spend your Friday afternoons with? Me, or Mom and Dad arguing over what to watch on the TV?"

"Why don't you hang out with your friends?" Lily croaks before another cough. "You're here every weekend. Don't you have prom coming up next weekend? You don't need to baby me."

Daisy's lips flatten into a harsh line as Lily's mature words internally infuriate her.

"Yes, but I want to make sure my baby sis has fun on the weekends, too. You should have a normal life just like everyone else," she says, although her upbeat words do not reflect in her eyes.

Lily shakes her head softly and says, "look, I know my life isn't normal. Probably won't ever be normal." She squeezes Daisy's hand in return with a meager tug as the corners of her lips finally perk up. "But I'm happy you're here."

A heartfelt smile grows across Daisy's face. "Of course you are. I'm your favorite sister," she teases as she reaches for the bulky television remote.

Rolling her eyes, Lily coughs again before saying, "you're my *only* sister."

"Yeah, still technically your favorite, though," Daisy chuckles before sweeping her legs beneath her, settling into the drab comforter. "Should we pop in a VHS? I picked up some new ones on the way over."

Lily clumsily sits up in bed and props a pillow behind her back. "Daisy? Are you there?"

>>>

"Daisy?" Molly repeats again in confusion. "Daisy? Are you there?" she asks, waving a hand in front of Daisy's face. "Earth to Daisy?"

Shaking her head of the memory, Daisy blinks her eyes and clears her throat noisily.

"Y-yeah, sorry. Just zoned out for a second," she says. Her brow glitters with a trail of sweat from the daydream and she grips her fingers into her palm, attempting to regain her thoughts.

Daisy scans the sidewalk as the streets bustle with the hum of a Friday workday coming to a close. The flood of happy hours and the excitement for the weekend draws the town out for the final days of warm weather, as the fall chill slowly seeps into the city.

Molly loops her arm through Daisy's and soothes her.

"A couple of drinks out with the girls will help you get your head on straight," she says. The two walk arm in arm as they make their way into the bar, a few of their other colleagues scampering in behind them. Molly continues, saying, "I know just the thing to cheer you up." A playful grin pulls at her icy blue eyes.

"A Lorazepam and a bottle of wine?" Daisy sarcastically asks, the joke not resonating on her face.

"And a cute bartender as the cherry on top," Molly confidently adds as she swings Daisy through the entrance. She has rounded up every fun-loving woman in the office in an attempt to salvage the week for Daisy, hoping that copious amounts of alcohol and dancing can fix the mess Harrison Bishop created.

A few of the girls settle around a cocktail table in the center of the room, giving them a pristine view of the bar for later on in the evening. Crowded with the post-work masses who have started undoing their ties and letting down their hair, the atmosphere turns lively. It was exactly what Daisy needed after these last few months.

"This place has one of the most lethal Long Island Iced Teas I've ever had," Amber announces to the table as the waiter arrives, stopping him before he can even list the specials. "I'm going to take a stab in the dark and say that's where we should start," she says. She surveys the table, waiting for someone to object. Three sets of eager eyes and raised brows instruct her to turn to the waiter with a smug smile. "Eight, please," she says.

"Now that Amber has decided to get us all good and drunk," Emily teases, "someone give me some good news on the guys from Bishop Enterprises. There has to be at least one man on their roster who isn't completely disgusting."

Emily Murray may have been one of the only women on the IT team. She was as quiet as a church mouse, but when she teamed up with Amber, it was like Doctor Jekyll and Mr. Hyde. She was notoriously known for starting a game of strip poker with the executive team at a holiday party then going home with Charlie's pants, wallet, and the keys to his pool house. Her tight curls and wide eyes gave her an adolescent look, but her captivating voice demanded attention when she deemed a room worth her time to speak.

"They have some new guy in accounting that I was checking out at the team structuring meeting this week," Molly comments while looking over a menu. Looking up to the table she announces, "yeah, I don't know why I'm going to pretend like we're gonna eat anything other than empty calories."

"His name is Jonah, or Joe, or Jacob, I think," Daisy says. "He's the one who was checking out that intern's ass and you gave him a thumbs up when you caught him."

Molly gives an overly exaggerated wink to Daisy, saying, "love that guy."

"Anyone who isn't willing to spend the rest of their career fighting off human resources?" Emily mocks.

"Oh! What about Duncan what's-his-face?" Amber adds.

"Lyon," Molly answers just as their drinks arrive, giving the waiter a disappointed look as he drops a drink in the center of the table "Did you really need to get two for each of us?"

Amber nudges Molly in the side with her elbow and blows her a kiss. The waiter hides a quiet laugh and Amber blows him a kiss as well, handing him a tip.

"Who the hell is Duncan Lyon?" Emily asks.

Plucking the lemon from her drink and popping it into her mouth, Daisy squints her eyes at the sour bite and says, "Harrison's buddy." She removes the fruit and drops it back into her drink, swirling the brown concoction with the obnoxiously long straw. "He was the one who broke the overhead projector with a golf club that you had to replace a couple weeks back."

"Oh, *that* Duncan Lyon," she says. The table laughs at her annoyed response before she adds, "could be worse. I'll see if he needs anything else fixed next week."

"Speaking of Harrison," Amber inquires with a lascivious tone, "you two had quite the rendez-vous the other day. How amazing was it?"

Daisy takes a long sip from her drink, coolly replying, "just the usual Harrison bullshit."

"Bullshit?" Emily asks with a confused look. "How is that possible? I thought you'd be over the moon to be working with him?"

"Why?" Daisy asks, clearly annoyed.

"Because it's *Harrison Bishop*. The guy basically saved the human race. And you get to spend ten hours a day with him and that beautiful smile," says Amber.

Emily leans in with a girlish laugh to hit Amber on the shoulder, saying, "the guy is beyond dreamy, Daisy."

Daisy rigidly sits up straight on her stool, stabilizing herself. Sensing the looming debacle, Molly quickly shifts the conversation, saying, "enough about work. We're here for much more important business." Spotting their waiter as he passes by, Molly grabs his tie and drags him into her personal space. Stunned by the close proximity and Molly's deathly good looks, he opens his mouth to speak but barely croaks a measly, "yes?"

"We're going to need another round of these, plus a round of tequila, sweetheart," she says, batting her eyelashes for an added effect. He musters a silent head nod as Molly kisses him on the tip of nose before sending him on his way.

Emily delicately places the butt of her drink on top of her head and cautiously removes her hands as she steadies the glass.

"It would be much more impressive if I had a straw that could reach my mouth," she announces as she attempts to hold still.

"Stop moving," Amber instructs as she pops a cherry into her mouth and rips the stem from between her lips.

Daisy and Molly have their heads placed in the palms of their hands with their elbows perched along the cocktail table, each with a straw of their Long Island Iced Teas dangling in their mouths.

"No fucking way she makes it," Daisy whispers to Molly.

Molly leans her head onto Daisy's shoulder in a drunken slump and says, "I'll give you fifty bucks if she misses."

Daisy's drunk eyes half-close in laughter as she says, "make it one hundred if she spits it into her eye."

Still holding the cherry between her teeth, Amber turns back to the pair.

"I saw her catch a cherry in her tits in Cabo. It was spectacular. Now shut up!"

"I'm going to drop it if you don't hurry up!" Emily squeals, trying to hold in her laughter.

"Do you ladies need anything else?" the waiter interrupts just as Amber plants her hands on the table to steady herself.

"You're just like my ex. Terrible timing when I'm at my peak performance," Amber says through the cherry. Leaning back into her stool ever so slightly, she spits the cherry into the air, drifting over the table, and it delicately plops into the glass with a muted *tink*. The group bursts into cheers and Amber takes a bow. "Thank you, thank you!"

"So, more tequila?" the waiter jokes until he senses the eyes of the table have slowly turned to an offended glare. "Oh, you really want more?"

"Pay up," Daisy demands, turning her hand out before Molly.

Molly digs into her handbag and changes the topic.

"Speaking of exes, whatever happened with Sam?"

"I can't believe you haven't heard," Amber says as she rolls her eyes. "The motherfucker told me he was in Reno visiting his dying grandmother. He leaves town for two weeks and I barely hear anything from him." Settling into the story, she props her chin on the knuckles of her closed fist. "Turns out, he was in Vegas taking full advantage of every strip club's amenities within a five mile radius of the strip."

"What a fucking prick," Molly says, taking a sip of her drink as the rest of the table groans disgustedly.

"Okay, Amber," Emily chimes matter-of-factly. "If you're going to tell that story, you have to tell the whole story." She holds back a hearty chuckle.

Daisy and Molly's eyes light up as Daisy demands, "what did you do next, Amber?"

Stirring her drink and avoiding eye contact, Amber says, "I may have taken his company credit card and subscribed to every porn website I could find online." A devilish smile fills her face as she looks up at the table.

Emily cocks her head to the side and says, "How many websites?"

Releasing a sigh through one corner of her mouth, Amber groans, "thirty-two." The group erupts into laughter.

Holding her maternal stare, Emily digs deeper.

"*And*?"

Amber smiles and says, "and then I maxed out the credit card by ordering a few male escorts to his office." The table topples over with laughter and Amber attempts to catch her breath to finish, saying, "I didn't even stick around long enough to see if he got fired!"

The waiter returns with a tray of tequila shots and a glass of limes.

"Anything else, ladies?"

"Just drop off the bottle off on your next trip over, honey." Molly says as she flashes an enticing smile.

The waiter tucks his tray under his arm and feigns a look of concern.

"I'm not going to give you the microphone. I shouldn't have to remind you that this isn't a karaoke bar."

Molly crosses her arms and pouts her lips.

"But you promised," she quips in a baby voice. She waits for the waiter to leave and leans into the table to confess, "I can't remember if he gave me that microphone because I promised to hook up with him or if we actually did."

Emily raises her shot to the table exclaiming, "to terrible exes!"

"Here, here!" Amber agrees as they clink glasses and quickly gulp down the drinks.

Daisy pops a lime into her mouth and turns to Molly as she offers a flash of a green smile. Pulling the rind from her teeth and dropping into the shot glass, she turns back to the table.

"I have you beat with terrible exes," she says, her face flushed in her drunken daze.

"This ought to be good," Amber excitedly says as she cozies into the table.

"Oh, yeah. It's a roller coaster. So, in college I never really dated because I was spending so much time on schoolwork. I mostly just had flings or random hookups to blow off steam," Daisy explains. "Blah, blah, blah. Fast-forward a few years to graduate school when I'm selected for a research grant and I get to pick two assistants from the university to help me out."

"Is this about that dreamy guy you went to Spain with?" Molly interrupts with a wicked grin.

Daisy blushes at the memory and says, "oh God, no. He was delicious, though."

The waiter returns with the bottle of tequila and delicately places it in the center of the table as if it is an award. Molly mocks a curtsey in her seat. "Thank you, kind sir," she touts with a horrendous British accent.

"So," Daisy begins again, "the first one I pick is this girl who seemed to have her shit together. She was so attentive and polite when I met her, but jump ahead, like, six months and all she does is break my glassware and show up stoned out of her mind." She pours herself a shot and places it before her. "The other is this little prick who had sucked up to my adviser and I was forced into bringing him onto the team. Turns out he was this idiot who I had hooked up with a couple of times with during undergrad. We had dated back and forth, but he was just a fun fling and nothing serious, so I figured he was just there to get a recommendation from someone he knew and move on."

Daisy reaches for Molly's shot glass and begins filling its contents. "Instead, he spent all of his time studying outside of my research requirements and doing his own studies and it drove me fucking insane." She drops the glass in front of Molly. "During the winter of my second to last semester, I was working on growing an antibiotic substitute that I figured would be kind of a bust, but I wanted to use it as a stepping stone to get into real oncology work."

Amber extends a finger to slide her shot glass towards Daisy and asks, "because of what happened to your sister?"

Molly and Emily's eyes dart toward Amber and then to Daisy at the insensitive remark. Feeling the unwelcomed attention, she corrects herself. "Sorry. I didn't mean for it to come out like that," she sheepishly apologizes.

Reaching for Amber's glass, Daisy pours her shot and says, "yes, because my sister had cancer." The words are heavy as she drops the drink before Amber. "Anyway, I'm laying out a tray of petri dishes and this idiot kid is supposed to take the samples that I've laid out and recreate the process I've written out to compare my work. I tell him, 'just follow the process I've written out and we'll compare the findings tomorrow,' hoping he can listen to the most basic instruction in the history of mankind."

Emily hands her shot glass over to Daisy and groans, "I thought this story was about an ex?"

"I'm getting there," Daisy says, laughing off the obvious comment as she fills the glass. "Turns out he hadn't listened to a word I said and instead of testing the second batch of samples, he tests my first set with a new process and comes rushing over to me telling me how one of the original samples tested positive for the bacteria using his method."

Handing the glass back to Emily, Daisy drops the bottle in the center of the table. "I spent the remainder of the afternoon explaining that he had contaminated my original sample and that he needed to do what I instructed. So on and so forth," she says, raising the glass to her lips. She pauses and gazes through the table recalling the memory. "The kid ends up taking the tainted sample with him and running his method the following semester when I've moved onto a new project." Discarding the thought from her mind, she swings back the drink. "Turns out, that sample ended up being the Episcopus Aerobium bacteria and guess who went on to save the fucking world?" she says, picking up a lime from the table and popping it into her mouth.

The table falls silent and eyes dart back and forth while the dots connect internally.

"Holy shit," Molly finally says. "*That's* how you and Harrison met?"

Dipping her head down into her drink, Amber releases an incredulous laugh.

"What?" Daisy asks with a dumbstruck face.

Swirling a lime in the liquor, Amber doesn't lift her gaze to meet Daisy's.

"Sounds to me like you're a little pissed he, I don't know, stole your thunder," she says.

Emily lifts her shoulders in understanding and says, "I mean, it doesn't sound like you *actually* dated, and how can you even hate him?" Her eyes are sincere and sympathetic. "He did go on to cure *every* known disease on the planet, Daisy."

"Shouldn't we just be appreciative?" Amber adds with an apathetic tone. "Yes, it sucks, but look at all the good that came from it," she says, her inflection positive and reassuring but causing Daisy's blood to boil.

"Put yourself in his shoes," Emily says. "If you had discovered TEA off of his discovery, you would have done the exact same thing. We all would have," she admits.

Daisy grinds her teeth in a furious rage as she bottles her anger internally. *You've got to be fucking kidding me*, she thinks to herself. *Even my best friends are on his side.*

"I know, I know," she finally succumbs. "Just felt like I had a bit more at stake."

The front door of the bar swings open, funneling in the crisp, fall air. A group of drunk men clamber into the bar. as nearby patrons yell to close the door.

"Alright, alright!" Duncan yells over the crowd. "We're going, you animals!"

Emily perks up on her stool and says, "look! It's the guy who broke the projector!"

Daisy sits statuesque in her seat as her eyes lock with the only other green pair in the room. *You've got to be fucking kidding me*, she thinks to herself.

Molly's eyes follow Daisy's line of sight. "His timing really is impeccable," she comments with indignation for her friend.

"Impeccable." Daisy agrees, her lips popping with each syllable.

<<<

A much younger Harrison leans in the doorway of the laboratory as a youthful Daisy stands with her back to him. Being mindful to not enter the laboratory with his street clothes, he slings his lab coat over his forearm as he surveys the situation in front of him. The room is eerily quiet for this early in the day. The morning sun plays off the walls, although the room feels cool without the bustle of students and staff throughout the building. The smell of solvents and freshly mopped floors fill the laboratory while the air between the pair is dense, slowly filling with anger.

Daisy's hands sit directly in front of her, her arms bent slightly at the elbows as she leans into the dark granite of the workbench. Her head drapes down and she takes in a deep breath, the smell of bleach and dryer sheets calming her slightly, although her face twists into a melancholy mask. Her nose and eyes are a matching shade of pink from rubbing the tears off of her cheeks. Her hair is pulled into a messy ponytail.

"I..." Harrison starts, not quite knowing where his thoughts are leading. "I really wish I knew what to say." His voice lightly quivers as he continues, "I know there isn't anything I can say to change this, but..." His voice trails off again. He lifts his eyes to the ceiling and searches for the right words to relieve the palpable anxiety. He runs a hand through his hair as he collects his thoughts, but begins spitting out his hurried words, saying. "I mean, you know I've—"

"No. No, Harry. You *don't* know," Daisy snaps, far angrier than she knew she could sound. "You think you know, but that's the thing, you never really do," she says through clenched teeth as she slowly raises her head to look up into the workbench shelving before her. Her eyes drift over the cases of pipettes and test tubes lining each shelf as she reaches out a delicate finger, tracing over the edges of the nameplate in front of her. "DAISY STONE," written out in professional lettering, stares back at her and she skims each individual letter of her first name, as if reminding herself of who she is at this moment. She releases the thoughts she has bottled up inside since she heard the news that Harrison's discovery was being picked up by a major research facility.

"You think you know how this feels, but..." she continues to glide her now trembling finger over the S and on to the T. "That's all you can do, think. You haven't done anything worthwhile in your entire life." She continues to graze the O and N. "You're just a sad boy who wants to spend his entire life thinking for everyone else." She stops her quivering finger to finally rest on the E.

Daisy spins her head to meet Harrison's gaze. She shifts her weight, removes a shaky finger, and grasps the edge of the workbench at her sides to stabilize herself. "You're nothing more than that. Full of ideas and wishes and pipedreams." She continues as her voice rises and she feels herself bursting at the seams. Holding his stare, another long pause sets between them. She grits her teeth between her slightly parted lips as she holds back whatever anger is pooling in her throat, stopping herself from continuing.

"Daisy..." Harrison says again, attempting to salvage the situation. "I – I really don't know," he murmurs in an exasperated, low voice.

She closes her eyes again, feeling the sting of tears. *Don't fucking cry in front of him. He doesn't deserve it*, she thinks to herself, trying to hold her ground.

"Of course you don't know. You never fucking knew. You didn't think of anyone but yourself, time and time again," she says, breathing loudly through her nostrils.

"But, congratulations. You finally won. You finally beat me," she says with animosity and defeat as one single tear streams down her face.

"Daisy…" Harrison says again with a deep, throaty hum, knowing he's losing her. "Don't let this be how we leave things." He takes a step off the doorframe and positions himself directly in front of her. Taking two steps forward until he is just out of arm's reach, he dips his knees and lowers his head. He attempts to meet her fluttering gaze as she tries to hide her tears.

Daisy pushes herself from the workbench and takes a full breath until she steps forward and fills the gap, regaining her strength to hold her own. Her shoulders drop in a proud defeat, despite her poignant glare.

"Goodbye, Harry. I hope it was all worth it."

Daisy reaches out an arm and pushes Harrison to the side, causing him to fall back on to one leg.

Regaining his stance, Harrison opens his mouth to speak, but Daisy is already gone. Taking a few steps forward, he drops his weight into the doorframe and he watches her press down the hall.

>>>

Harrison presses his mouth into a hard line as he attempts to smile at Daisy, who is reeling from the memory.

"I think I've had enough for the night," she announces to the table. "Let me know how much I owe you, Mol," she says, standing up and collecting her handbag.

Molly's eyes flitter between Daisy and Harrison, trying to assist. "Do you want me to come with?" she asks.

Emily hops off her stool with Daisy in a peppy step.

"I'll come with you! I'll chat up Duncan and see what these guys are up to," she says, unaware of the boiling tension between Daisy and Harrison.

"Perfect," Daisy says with a cold tone, still holding Harrison's stare.

"Be back in five!" Emily announces to the table as she maneuvers through the crowd, creating a path for Daisy behind her. She stops before Duncan and greets the guys while Daisy continues toward the door.

"Come on, Daisy," Harrison pleads, sensing her anger from their fight had not blown over. Daisy presses between their group, hurriedly shifting through the crowd. He turns over his shoulder to call after her, "are you really just going to leave?"

Daisy does not turn around, but releases an exaggerated laugh and continues through the front doors of the bar.

Once outside and amongst the busy street of rushing traffic, Daisy drops her head back into her shoulders and closes her eyes. She shakes her head of the moment and digs her hand into her purse, retrieving her phone.

"Daisy?" A familiar voice calls from behind her. An irritated stare on her face indicates that she knows the voice all too well.

Continuing her text, Daisy speaks into her phone.

"You know I don't want to talk, Harry," she says. She releases another phony laugh. "We've already talked." Completing her text, she drops her cell phone back into her handbag and looks both ways before taking a confident step into the street. She strides through the bustling street and onto the road's median ignoring the oncoming traffic.

"Jesus Christ!" Harrison calls out after Daisy as she narrowly avoids being crushed to death by a pickup truck. Yelling over the sound of the traffic, he calls after her, "are you really willing to die to avoid talking to me?"

Looking over her shoulder, Daisy calls back to Harrison, "with my luck, you'd just bring me back to life."

Oh, for fuck's sake, Harrison thinks to himself.

"Well, here we go," he assures himself as he mimics Daisy's actions and pushes through the busy street before him, barely avoiding being hit by an electric car.

Daisy turns on her heel, her arms crossed across her chest and glares into Harrison's deep emerald eyes as he pants for breath. The cars continue to zoom by and a few honk as they spot Harrison.

"What the fuck do you want me to say, Daisy?" he asks as he digs his hands into his trouser pockets. "I've done nothing but attempt to make up for lost time over these last few months and we get into a couple of fights and—"

"There are not enough days in a lifetime for you to make up for what you did to me, Harry," she says. Turning back to the road, her tone shifts from anger to disappointment. "The only reason you are, well, *you* is because you're a fucking liar." She turns back to meet his gaze, driving the point home. "But, you already knew that."

Dropping his head and kicking a small stone in the grass, Harrison coughs out a pitiful laugh. "You don't think I already know that? The only reason I ever worked on that fucking project was because I wanted to spend more time with you. I was completely in—"

Daisy raises a hand before him, cutting him off from his next word.

"I *really* do not want to hear it again."

Harrison drops his hands to his side, defeated.

"You're the only one who has ever rejected me, Daisy," he says. His head shakes in anger and bewilderment. "I could not care less about the approval of anyone else, but I can't seem to get things right with you."

"That's the problem, Harry," Daisy growls as she takes a step toward Harrison. "This isn't about you. You know that TEA was my outlet to saving my sister. To find compensation for what happened to her. But somehow you've made it about you trying to beat me."

Parting his lips, Harrison opens his mouth before releasing a slow breath.

"I didn't mean to make it about me," he says, his defeated tone reflecting in his eyes. "I really thought I was helping you."

Daisy releases a laugh from her nostrils that barely tugs at the corners of her mouth just as a car pulls up to a stop in the center of the street.

"Well, I guess we're really repeating history then," she concludes as she takes a step toward the car. "You didn't mean to turn me into a monster, but I guess you just bring it out in me." She stops at the driver's side to call back to him, "goodnight, Harry," as she leans down into the open window and plants a quick kiss on Kennedy Thomas's lips. She swiftly scampers around the car and into the passenger side where she drops inside as the car speeds away into the evening.

Well, great, Harrison thinks to himself as he shoves his hands into his pockets and stares into the street. As the last few months wash over him, he tongues his cheek and stands in this spot for what feels like an eternity until he reaches into his breast pocket to produce a packet of cigarettes. With a shaky hand, he attempts to light the stick. After a few attempts, he lights the paper and takes a full breath before leaning back onto his heels to blow a plume of smoke into the sky, where he can see a looming moon above his head. *Should have killed her when I had the chance.*

"Harrison Bishop?" a voice calls to him from across the street, pulling Harrison from his thought. "Oh my God! It's really you!" the voice continues on as he takes another drag of his cigarette and returns his eyesight to level ground, landing on a curvaceous brunette just across the road.

Harrison blows another puff of smoke before him as he pulls together a mischievous smile that does not touch his eyes. Taking a step into the traffic, he flicks the cigarette butt into the median and clenches a shaky hand into a hard fist.

Chapter Thirteen: **Clint Eastwood**

A ghostly chill fills the hallway leading toward the wine cellar. The reverberation of a woman's muffled screams creep their way up the wooden stairs and into the evening air just long enough for Harrison to slam the entrance door behind him with an emphatic crash.

The woman's screams die down until all that remains is her heavy breathing as Harrison finally appears within her line of sight. His faded black tee is slightly tucked into his weathered blue jeans as he tilts his head to the side with a crazed stare. The curvaceous brunette sits before him, bound at her wrists and ankles in the stained, wooden chair. A red and white patterned handkerchief pulls tight between her teeth, soaked with saliva.

Harrison gives the woman a once over as she attempts to speak through the restraints, but he ignores her unintelligible words. His typical cool demeanor shifting into a malfunctioning version of himself, he crosses his arms and anxiously taps his fingers against his biceps as he searches the room for his next move. His eyes, cloudy and dark, sink into his skull as profound bags dig beneath his eyes.

Running a haphazard hand through his hair, Harrison takes an unsteady step forward and paces the room before selecting a wooden kitchen chair along with a Louisville Slugger baseball bat. Returning back to the woman, he swings the chair in reverse of her and sits before her with both arms draping across the back of the chair. Plopping his arms atop each other, he drops his chin to settle on his forearm as he breaks his silence.

"Candice, is it?"

Candice attempts to answer but her faint voice causes her eyes to shift, and rethinking her move, she nods her head in agreement.

Harrison purses his stare, a slight shake in his hands, and stares into Candice's eyes. "I've never had anyone down here who didn't deserve it," he muses to himself. An unsure smile tugs against his lips. "So, why are you down here?"

Candice's eyes widen and her forehead wrinkles at the statement. She attempts to speak, as if to bypass the restraints, but Harrison stands from his chair to remove her from his line of sight.

"They always want to talk," he says, dropping the bat to the cement floor with a heavy clunk. "But nobody is fucking listening to me."

Another forcible muffle echoes from Candice's gag but Harrison raises a single finger, indicating her to cease.

"You know, I bought a boat a few years back?" he asks as her face displays further confusion with the statement. "Yeah," Harrison continues with a dry laugh as he paces. His brow begins to freckle with sweat. "I bought this extravagant yacht thinking it would be a great escape from reality and, hey, maybe something to eventually take the family out on the ocean one day," he continues in a humorous tone that feels more eerie than funny.

"So, I take this enormous boat out into the harbor with a few colleagues and a dozen crew members for an afternoon party," he says. Continuing his path, Harrison crosses back and forth before Candice, haphazardly moving his arms from a crossed position to his pockets, then through his hair again. "Our director of sales had even brought along Clint Eastwood. Apparently they were family friends, but he gave a nice little toast thanking us for our recent gala benefiting Cedars-Sinai Medical Center's oncology renovations. Anyway, we have a lovely afternoon in the early spring as the winds have just shifted to push up from the equator and bring a warm breeze to the day." Harrison stops in his tracks, closing his eyes and raising his shoulders with a full breath, as if he had transported himself to the edge of the boat. He could almost feel the breeze washing over him, but he jolts back to reality and continues to pace.

"Then," says Harrison as his eyes dart open with a wild glare and his tone changes from subdued hysteria to a subtle rage, "this cocksucker, Melvin Windsor, tells me how he had the exact same model as mine but had just traded it in for the 148-foot model." Walking to stop behind Candice, Harrison says, "can you believe it?" as she strains her neck to turn to face him. "I mean," he says as he advances his pacing, now circling her as if a shark enclosing on its prey. "He's on this enormous vessel having a lovely time with his friends and colleagues, and he has the fucking nerve to say he has a *bigger* boat. Like it was vital to our existence that we discuss his upgrade."

Standing alongside Candice, Harrison looks down to her.

"He was gloating about his giant boat while on another *giant boat*," he exclaims, a look of disgust in his wild eyes as he shakes his head in disbelief. "Fucking Clint Eastwood just laughed along with him," he mutters to himself rhetorically.

Peering through the wooden door, Harrison continues. "I took a look out on to the ocean and had to ask myself, 'I've gained so much but yet have I really grown at all?' And the answer was pretty obvious." Turning back to

Candice with a look of remorse as a single bead of sweat trickles down his brow, he answers to himself, "the greed had consumed me and I had stopped growing toward the person I wanted to become."

Harrison takes two confident steps to stand before Candice as he rubs his hands together. He massages his fingers between his hands with such force, his hands turn a ghastly white as he stares into the depths of Candice's eyes. Then, he lifts his right arm to shoulder level and pummels his clenched fist into her cheekbone with an audible *crack*. She releases a deadened scream beneath the handkerchief and attempts to pull her hands over her face, but the restraints lock her in place.

Harrison leans over to place his hands on each knee and angles himself just out of Candice's face.

"I would love to say that this was about my childhood, but I'm a product of my adulthood," he says, his glistening teeth and eager eyes a frightening mix as Candice haphazardly breathes beneath her bindings. "I have become a monster. The entire world has gotten so lost in greed that we've forgotten about survival," he continues as he pulls back his arm yet again to connect with Candice's jaw. She releases another stifled scream and again reactively pulls at her restraints, whimpering pitifully in distress.

Standing up, Harrison looks beyond Candice and ignores her screams as his face shifts from anger to a soft confusion.

"I was just trying to get to her," he says to himself, visibly shaking now. "You wanted to be close to her and although it took some time," he nods his head in agreement as he crosses his arms in front of him in an approving stance, "you are completing what you set out to accomplish."

Looking back to Candice, Harrison flings his arms outward in exasperation, causing her to flinch at a potential hit. He releases a shaky laugh and says, "I mean, it's endearing!" His voice is forceful as he rocks his head incredulously. "I saved the fucking *world* for her," he shouts at Candice as he cocks his left arm over his shoulder and swings to connect with her temple again.

Candice's skin breaks and a heavy stream of blood trickles down her cheek. Harrison watches the blood roll down, a steady ooze, and he presses a single finger into her cheek to stop the droplet, letting it pool atop his finger.

"I guess we're all human," he quietly muses as he stares at the crimson bead. His eyes dart from the blood to Candice's squinting eyes. "Some of us more than others, though," he snidely remarks, and again, triggers his right arm to land a solid punch to her nose, creating another *crack* that releases a steady tide of blood through both her nostrils.

Manically laughing as he wipes his hands against each other, Harrison attempts to remove the blood from his knuckles but spreads the sticky liquid along his forearms. He stretches out his hands, examining the mess, and pulls them both to his head to soothe his frazzled hair. Crimson streaks through his amber hair as his onyx eyes fall out of focus.

"I just don't get it," Harrison growls. Staring past Candice in reflection, he again swings for a punch but his heavy fist only skims her nose. He stutter-steps as his balance hinges and his wild eyes open to stare into Candice's face for an answer. His mouth gapes at the miscalculation and he clenches his fists tightly. Standing up straight, he stares at his hands with an intensity that causes Candice to hold her breath.

"If it's not one thing," he steadies himself, "it's another."

Rotating his focus, Harrison makes his way to the back of the cellar to open a drawer from the shelving unit. Pulling the handle with a fluid rush, he jams his hand into the cabinet, then marches to his previous stance.

Tugging at her restraints, Candice watches Harrison anxiously, knowing his anger has taken a new turn. She begins to speak, still restrained by the gag, repeating her hurried words. He reaches his right hand out to land a single forefinger atop her mouth, instructing her to stop. As he lifts his bloodied hand, a new wave of sensation lingers against her jaw. A heavy set of brass knuckles, cool to the touch, causes her to reactively scream beneath the fabric.

"Do you know why humans worship idols and gods instead of looking to each other for guidance and strength?" Harrison asks with a deliberate tone.

Candice hesitantly shakes her head.

"Because we'd rather pray to these mythical figures to save the world instead of building up our neighbors to do the same," he says, his word oil-slick as he pulls his right arm against his ribs and lashes Candice across the eye socket. The skin around her eye tugs and a cut flab hangs from her brow as the blood washes over the left side of her face. Leaning forward, he comments on his own monologue, saying, "It's fucking disgusting." Pulling back his left arm, he batters his hand into Candice's teeth with such intensity, her head knocks into the wooden chair and her skull bounces like a tennis ball.

Regaining his height, Harrison stands and weaves his fingers together as he clasps his hands. Stretching his bloodied hands before him, he cracks his spine; shaking his shoulders, he releases his hands and allows the metal from between his fingers to clatter to the floor. "In all honesty, though," Harrison resumes with a lighter tone, "if we can't even bother to look to our fellow man for aid, why are we even trying to save ourselves at all?" He shoves his hands into his pockets and produces a pack of cigarettes and a small matchbook. Placing the cigarette between his lips, Harrison further questions Candice.

"Let me ask you this: If I told you I could give you anything you want in the world, would you be happy?"

He reaches out to her face and tugs at the bloody handkerchief as two teeth drop from behind the fabric and fall on to the wooden seat.

Candice takes a full breath, forcing her shoulders back. She forces a labored gasp, swallows the blood between her remaining teeth, and lifts her eyes to meet Harrison's.

"You already have," she says, her eyes sincere and chilling. "I was diagnosed with stage four cancer up until the TEA discovery."

A rush of hot air filters through Harrison as he flares his nostrils. Shoving the pack of cigarettes back into his pocket, he rips a match from the matchbook and tugs the terracotta tip against the rough paper with an unsteady hand. Pulling the trembling flame to the cigarette, he lights the paper to release a gratifying plume of smoke before him. "Of course," he adds, as he drops the matchbook to the floor.

Sucking a full breath from between his bloodied fingers, Harrison relishes his moment with his cigarette.

"You know," he starts again before lifting the filter from his lips and examining the white paper spotted with Candice's blood. "These used to kill us." He knocks his thumb against the filter as a spattering of ash drifts to the floor like dirtied snow. "But now we survive everything, thanks to me, so I'm forced to kill you." His tone is eerily assertive as he returns the now-crimson paper to lips.

Another drag of air from the filter crinkles against the ash as Harrison tucks the cigarette between his incisors. He dips to his knees to retrieve the wooden baseball bat at his feet, expelling the dusty smoke from his nostrils and repeats to himself, "all thanks to me."

Gripping the bat, he pulls it above his right shoulder, instinctively bringing his left knee toward his chest. Swinging, he releases the wood into Candice's temple with a raucous *crack* as her forehead splits in two, releases a spattering of blood against the cinderblock walls.

Chapter Fourteen: **Hell Of A Life**

Hints of winter drifted through the breeze, and although it had only dropped a handful of degrees, the wind and cold turned the streets into a frigid tundra to most New Orleans residents. The looming thunderstorm that hung above the city created a desolate pressure as the lightening skirted the city's parameter. The crisp air lashed through street as the party-goers arrived in front of The Lapham Theatre.

The untimely weather arriving on the day that, in the final months before the merger between Bishop Enterprises and The Rose Institute, Harrison decided to throw an elaborate celebration to thank the employees and blow off some steam from the grueling months of work.

Stepping out of the town car and on to the street, Harrison stands to adjust the bowtie of his tuxedo as Sampson calls after him, "do you need notes for your speech?"

Peering back inside, Harrison flashes a pleasing smile. "I don't think I'll be in any capacity to give a speech this evening," he says, his laughter enveloping the cabin as Sampson hides his smirk.

Harrison spots Duncan standing alone near the entrance, fervently swiping through his cell phone, shaking his head. His bowtie hangs undone beneath his tuxedo, his collar not yet fastened.

"You lost?" Harrison jokes.

Without looking up from his phone, Duncan continues rummaging through the device. "I invited this gorgeous blonde to the party a couple weeks back but I can't remember her name or number for the life of me," he says. His fingers pick up speed as his brow furrows. "I got a note from my secretary that she had accepted the invitation but I never put two and two together and I don't have a way to get in touch with her, let alone find out her name."

Harrison releases an amused cackle. "You have one hell of a life, my friend," he exasperatedly jokes.

Scoffing at the remark, Duncan rolls his eyes and says, "you're one to talk."

His pouty attitude forces another laugh from Harrison.

Ken casually struts toward the pair as Harrison calls out, "Ken, you have to hear what our *brilliant* buddy Duncan has done." He leans back into his heels at the waiting joke with eager eyes.

Finally peeling himself away from his phone, Duncan darts his eyes to look up to Harrison and facetiously squints.

"You know I got a 1400 on the SATs. I'm sorry I forgot *one* girl's name in my life."

"Oh, this ought to be good," Ken chimes in just as Molly makes her way to meet the trio in a floor length, light blue evening gown that accentuates her thin frame.

"Thank God," Molly chimes in with an exhausted tone as she props her clutch underneath her arm. "At least three humans who aren't old enough to tell me where they were the day Kennedy was assassinated."

"We really are quite the pleasant bunch this evening," says Ken, chuckling at her misery.

Curling her lips inward to suppress her laughter, Molly turns to Harrison.

"Great party. Food's great," she says, her eyes glistening with humor.

"Let's just get inside before you start busting my balls, Molly," Harrison says, narrowing his eyes with faux anger and gesturing for the group to make its way inside.

> > >

The party-goers slowly begin to fill the ballroom of The Lapham Theatre, and the immense space begins to boil over with excited guests and the buzzing of alcohol. The theatre, a piece of history in the heart of downtown, is embellished with intricate detail of the early twentieth century and has forty-foot ceilings of delicate tiling. It was a mesmerizing hideaway in the city and the perfect backdrop for Harrison to close the books on a whirlwind of a year.

The group loiters around the edge of the bar of the ballroom while they impatiently wait for their drinks. Ken nudges his shoulder into Duncan's and leans in, whispering, "what do you think my chances are with Molly?"

Duncan distractedly searches around him for his mysterious date and loudly answers, "dude, I don't care who you bang, just help me find my date."

Sighing heavily and dropping both elbows on the bar to twirl a napkin between his fingers, Ken sighs. "One of us should get laid tonight. At least I'd be doing it with an actual human," he mocks at Duncan's expense.

Turning to drop a heavy palm on to the bar in annoyance, Molly turns to Harrison.

"What's with the service, Bishop? More than thirty seconds for a martini?" she demands, raising her brow with a phony discontent. "Is this the kind of company you plan to run? Because I won't stand for it." Her mouth pulls at the edges and her eyes are light with laughter.

"So, no date tonight, Molly?" Harrison quips with the same smug smile. "If only your jokes could produce a man for the evening."

Molly lets out a satisfied laugh. "Don't we all," she says as the bartender starts dropping martinis in front of the ravenous bunch. Raising a glass to the bartender, she adds, "If this martini is strong enough, maybe I'll just take this nice fellow home."

Lifting his drink to his lips and pausing a beat, Ken comments, "I think we'd all take him home if we had enough martinis."

"I would love to see which of us is able to score first with..." Molly leans forward to read the bartender's name tag. "Mister Steven, here," she says, taking a generous sip of her martini.

Plucking an olive from his drink, Ken retorts, "and if I lose do I just get you as the consolation?"

"Get a room, you two," Duncan interrupts. "We have much bigger problems here, people."

"I didn't realize it takes a village to get you laid," Molly says, as she hands Duncan his martini.

"A village isn't nearly enough," Harrison joins. "He once had to pay off an entire bar staff to keep every dude away from this beauty in Seattle."

Still distracted as he searches through the crowd, Duncan points a heavy finger at Harrison and says, "she was worth it and you know it."

"Where the hell is Daisy?" Molly asks as she plucks an olive off her toothpick. "She told me she has some juicy gossip for me that I'm just dying to hear."

Turning only his eyes to meet Molly's, Harrison squints and pulls a long sip. "What kind of gossip?" he asks in his best nonchalant tone.

"Oh, please. You're old news," Molly says, brushing off Harrison's question. "She over being mad at you. I think you two just spending all this time together got the best of her," she added with an unconcerned shoulder shrug.

Old news? Harrison thought to himself. Playing off the comment, he shook his head. "Yeah, felt like we were an old married couple for a few weeks."

"An old married couple featured in a male enhancement drug commercial," Ken adds as he wiggles his eyebrows at Molly with a devilish grin.

"I'm not nearly drunk enough to deal with you idiots yet," Molly says with an incredulous laugh. Turning to look into the sea of party-goers, she lets out a sigh of relief. "Oh, thank God. She's here!" she proclaims as she raises a boney arm to waive her over. "And she brought Kennedy. Now this party can really get going!"

Ken and Duncan lock eyes, then both look to Harrison. The two narrow their eyes with a furrowed brow, as if to ask, "who?" Harrison returns the same face and shrugs his shoulders.

"Kennedy Thomas?" he asks in an undetached tone as Daisy and Kennedy make their way through the crowd to join the group at the bar.

"Yeah. He just became president of Mendl Research Laboratories," Molly says.

"Didn't we acquire them, like, four months ago?" Duncan asks with confusion.

"Yep," Molly says. "Who do you think caught two fish with one hook?" She raises her glass to the couple just as they arrive. "My, my. Don't you look stunning!"

Daisy drapes her arm lackadaisically through Kennedy's and pulls her shoulder to her cheek to flutter her eyes at Molly.

"Only for you," says Daisy.

Daisy dons a floor length, charcoal gray evening gown. The high neck and long sleeves make it appear to be modest from the front, but the completely open back reveals much more risqué intentions. *Take a look at what you still can't have*, Daisy says to herself as she catches Harrison looking at her out of the corner of her eye. "So, what are we drinking?"

"Nothing is strong enough for tonight," says Duncan as he knocks his glass backward, takes a dramatic gulp, and polishes off his drink.

"He's upset that his date is imaginary," Harrison comments. "Hey there, Harrison Bishop," he says to Kennedy, introducing himself as he leans forward with a makeshift cool tone, quickly covering his eagerness.

Laughing at the unneeded introduction, Kennedy greets Harrison and then the rest of the group with a relaxed smile. Although he is wearing a tux, he is surprisingly at ease with Daisy by his side while going through introductions. Harrison could feel the blood pinching his cheeks as he watched Kennedy's tranquil composure.

"Martinis? Let me grab another round," Kennedy offers, gliding through the group to flag down the bartender.

Molly takes the opportunity to get cozy with Daisy and demands, "okay, okay. News!"

A mischievous smile fills Daisy's face.

"Are you sure you don't want to wait a day or two?" she says with a mischievous smile.

"Just remember that I'm stronger than you and I could take you in a fight," Molly threatens as she drops her weight to the side with attitude.

Daisy giggles and finally caves.

"Fine! If you insist," she relinquishes and tucks her clutch under her right arm to drape her left hand in front of Molly, exposing a monstrous diamond ring.

Molly's eyes grow twice their size as she bends at the knee to drop her eyes down to Daisy's hand.

"You have got to be fucking kidding me!" she squeals as the guys turn at the commotion.

Kennedy flashes an ecstatic smile from the bar as Duncan and Ken snap their heads to face Harrison who murmurs under his breath, "you have got to be fucking kidding me."

"Is your sole intention of this event to never serve me a drink?" Duncan says, standing at the bar with the palms of his hands pressed into his eye sockets. Pity and sadness tremor against his voice as he drops his tone. "I said *two* gin martinis and *three* vodkas. I can come back there and shake them myself it helps."

An unimpressed waiter stares at Duncan with a single brow raised as he hurriedly pours a drink into a rocks glass.

"I got you next, man," he says, his tone scoffing with indignation. "Take a look around, we're pretty busy."

Rolling his eyes through his head, Duncan says, "yeah, and it would be a lot better if I had a drink to enjoy during the waiting."

A thin blonde in a floor length red dress arrives at his side and hides a snicker of laughter at his obvious discontent. Draping her sleek bag over her shoulder, she eyes him slightly and orders a vodka tonic. The bartender nods in confirmation, immediately pulling a bottle of vodka from the shelf behind him and pours.

"Oh, come *on*, man!" Duncan yells as the bartender meets his eyes with an unamused glare. "She's been here, like, ten seconds!"

"Maybe the attitude slows down his process," the blonde suggests as she slides a folded bill toward the bartender, tipping him for the quickly produced drink. Turning to face Duncan and leaning into the bar, she continues her beratement. "You catch more flies with honey," she snidely remarks.

Taking an irked step back, Duncan drops his hands on to the bar in defeat.

"Yeah, yeah. You and this bartender really are doling out the insight today," he says. Shifting his eyes in an angry scowl, he looks back at her. "You two really do make a lovely couple."

The blonde takes a sip from her drink and lets out a relaxed laugh that further annoys Duncan.

"We've been talking about opening a B&B together, but we're not sure if we're ready for the commitment," she says sarcastically. "We'd rather work on opening up more poorly operating bars that keep out people exclusively named Duncan Lyon."

Still leaning into the bar through his heavy-set palms, Duncan turns to face the mysterious annoyer.

"Do I know you?"

Raising a single brow, the blonde smirks while squeezing a lime into her drink.

"I mean, you did attempt to pay that entire bar staff to keep the guys away from me long enough to invite me to this event, so yeah, I think so."

Regaining his height, Duncan stands dumbstruck before the woman. "No fucking way," Duncan says as he regains his height, looking a little dumbstruck. "You're my date?"

"Don't tell me you forgot already," the blonde pleasantly laughs. "I guess I should have called you personally instead of doing a secretary to secretary transaction." Reaching her arm out to shake his hand, she introduces herself. "I'm Olivia."

Crossing his arms before him, Duncan gives Olivia a once-over and nods his head with a befuddled laugh.

"Olivia, if I had remembered you were this beautiful, I would have bought that entire bar and held you hostage."

Tilting her eyes, a sincere smile fills Olivia's face and she turns back to the bar.

"Okay, let me win over this bartender and get you a drink."

>>>

Harrison stands outside The Lapham Theatre with his bowtie undone, smoking a cigarette. His head is tilted back to face the night sky as the soon-to-be winter air whips against his face. His eyes caress the dense clouds as he attempts to search for the stars, but when he comes up short, he releases a long breath of smoke that melts into the clouds above him.

"Mr. Bishop?"

Harrison hears a familiar voice behind him but doesn't shift his stance. It isn't until Kit reaches his side and lightly taps him on the shoulder with a meek, "Harrison?" that he returns his mind to the world around him, before turning toward the voice.

"Yes?" Harrison asks taking another long drag from his cigarette.

Kit's eyes dart across Harrison's face in an attempt to examine his mood. Unsure of his state, he asks the absurdly vague question, "you okay?"

Harrison smiles but the only feature of his demeanor that shifts is his mouth.

"Just fine, buddy. What can I do for you?"

"Well, you left in quite a rush," Kit responds with a confused tone. "I just wanted to let you know that everything is ready for the toast in a bit. We got someone from Rose to make the speech," he says, his eyes still attempting to read Harrison. "Charlie Meyer?"

Taking another drag from the cigarette before tossing the butt before him, Harrison confirms.

"Yes, he'll do great," Harrison says as he steps forward to smother the flame.

Kit pauses, realizing that Harrison is not himself.

"I'm sorry, but are you sure you're okay?" Kit asks, his eyes sincere and concerned.

"Yeah, thanks Kit," Harrison says as he closes his eyes and reluctantly nods his head. He lifts his collar and begins to retie his bowtie. "Just some stuff from the merger isn't going as planned. But yeah, Charlie will be great."

Taking a step back as if to leave, Kit gives one last shot at connecting with Harrison.

"You know," he begins with a fatherly tone echoing in his young voice, "if things aren't going how you want with the merger, why not just pull a Harrison and take charge?" His scrawny arms dig into his pockets as he shrugs his shoulders. "I know it isn't fun relinquishing control, but maybe you need to do some things yourself."

Shaking his head, Harrison pushes off Kit's advice.

"Thanks, bud. I just really need to take a break from the game I think," Harrison says. He looks at Kit, his face wrinkling in pain. "I think I'm getting a little too old for this league."

Kit laughs off the comment and says, "I don't think so, Mr. Bishop. We've just seen all your plays. It's time to turn these guys on their heads and show them what you're made of," he says in friendly confidence.

Harrison stares at Kit, not seeing him, but staring through him to heed his words.

"You're right," he agrees and shakes his head.

"I am?" Kit asks, cocking his head to the side.

Harrison's eyes flash to life and he drops a heavy hand atop Kit's shoulder, causing him to flinch slightly.

"Kit, I'm going to buy a bigger boat!" Harrison announces. He squeezes Kit's shoulder, causing him to release a minor squeak. Leaning in, he points a finger just inches from Kit's nose. "You're a fucking genius," he says, and releases his shoulder to jog back into the theater.

Calling after Harrison, Kit shouts in confusion, "what boat?"

> > >

The applause subsides as Charlie waives down the crowd.

"Thank you, thank you!" he warmly acknowledges. "And an even larger thank you for staying decent until at least ten o'clock!"

The crowd breaks into laughter as he begins to settle in for a speech thanking the two companies for all of their hard work and dedication to the merger.

Charlie is donning an ill-fitting tux that is about two decades too old and a festive pair of glasses, lined with gold sequins and jewels. He awkwardly jokes with the crowd and although he has good intentions, he is not cut out for the emcee role.

"In all sincerity, I want to take this time to thank those of you who have spent your evenings, weekends, and even holidays with these two groups to bring our families together. You could say it was a *family* affair!"

The crowd groans but a few throw out some pity laughs.

Bounding up the stairs two at a time, Harrison makes his way on to the stage. The audience cheers at the new face and a handful of party-goers call him out by name. Charlie turns to find the source of the ruckus, and when landing on Harrison, he turns back to the crowd.

"And a man who needs no introduction, Bishop Enterprises' very own Harrison Bishop!" he exclaims taking a staggering step back at the welcomed intrusion of his speech.

Grabbing a microphone from a nearby stand, Harrison flips the device to life and greets the crowd.

"Thank you everyone!" He unconsciously reaches a hand into his breast pocket for the prepared note cards. *Fuck,* he thinks to himself realizing he is on his own. "I don't typically give these speeches, as I'd rather let Charlie here wow us with his jokes while I set up shop at the bar," he absentmindedly confesses, but the crowd erupts into laughter in response to his honesty. Awkwardly laughing along with the group, he continues. "Nobody tell human resources, please." A charming yet awkward smile fills his face.

Harrison searches through the crowd in search of a particular face, but feels unsettled with the spotlight blinding him. Reaching a hand to his forehead to shield his face from the light, he continues his impromptu monologue. "I'm so glad to see each and every one of you here tonight. I genuinely believe that this incredible undertaking would not be possible without the hard work and dedication of every person's time and talents." Slowly turning to scan the crowd, he finally lands on a set of sharp green eyes.

Daisy has her arm draped over Kennedy's shoulder and her chin perched upon her hand. Her other hand holds a glass of champagne that she rolls between her thumb and forefinger. She swirls the glass's contents methodically as her eyes pierce through Harrison. His throat buckles as a choking sensation stuns him momentarily at the sight. The memory of Tom gripping his neck between his massive hands. His thumbs pressing through his esophagus.

Harrison swallows as he shakes the thought from his mind and continues.

"This merger isn't just a business move to me," he says. He swallows hard and takes a deep breath. "I'm incredibly excited to see our two groups come together to really make something of this world. To continue to save humanity and to better mankind even further."

Holding her stance, Daisy doesn't shift or react to the words, continuing to rotate her drink between in fingers, her eyes holding Harrison's steady. Harrison drops his makeshift shade and allows the beam to blare across his eyes.

"I know the potential that we all hold, and while sometimes it feels like one or more of us laid a lot of the road on their own, there are still many miles to go and I cannot do it alone. I need every single one of you."

An excited applause fills the theater. Harrison releases his stare into the bright light to survey the room but lands again in the spot where he can feel Daisy's emerald glare. "At the end of the day, this room contains the most important minds of this generation and I'd be a damn fool to let any of you go," he says, letting out an exasperated chuckle through his nostrils. "I really am nothing without all of you."

Dropping his hands to his sides, the audience bursts into cheers and applause. Harrison aches to peel himself away from the stage at the uncharacteristic and sentimental speech. Knowing there is one last task at hand, he continues. "And with that, I want to thank all of you for your work over these last few months, because we certainly have many more adventures ahead." Pausing again for clapping, Harrison holds up a hand to drive his point home. "I do have one final surprise, which should be quite exciting for everyone in attendance." His voice is more eager than he intends. "It is with great pleasure that I announce that when The Rose Institute finally merges into Bishop Enterprises, the role of president will be transferred from myself to Miss Daisy Stone."

A beat settles amongst the theatre as confusion and excitement crash together. Harrison reaches out a hand in

Daisy's direction as applause fills the space and people turn their heads to face each other unsure of her name. All the while, Daisy holds her stance while her glass of champagne still circles its pattern until she delicately lifts the glass to her lips to take a lingering sip.

Kennedy leans his face down to Daisy's and excitedly raises his shoulder to congratulate her. Feigning a smile, Daisy stands up and waives her hand to the crowd, turning her face with a phony smile.

Oh, he's good, Daisy thinks to herself as her eyes burn against her lids with every blink. *Really fucking good.*

"Let's get that crazy woman up here for a speech!" Harrison calls out into the crowd, returning his hand to his forehead to get a clear view. His eyes are a menacing black as his smile turns into somewhat of a snarl before the crowd. Once again spotting Daisy, Harrison turns his body to lock eyes with her.

Daisy delicately and slowly makes her way to the stage. Spotting Molly along the way, she raises her brows in an attempt to shout her thoughts. Molly mouths, "what the fuck?" with her face tangled into a confused grin. Shrugging her shoulders, she continues her stretch through the crowd and applause.

Harrison takes a few paces toward the edge of the stage as Daisy arrives and reaches out a hand to provide her with the microphone.

"How about a speech, Miss President?"

Gripping the microphone, Daisy tugs at the plastic but Harrison continues his hold.

"Un-fucking-believable," she says through her teeth, holding her plastered smile.

With an equally fake grin, Harrison spits through his teeth, "If you play with fire, you get burned." He releases the microphone, forcing the pull into Daisy's abdomen.

Turning to face the crowd, Daisy dons her most professional smile.

"Thank you, everyone! It really has been a coaster since our merger with Bishop Enterprises, but I am truly grateful to be standing here today," she says. Turning over her shoulder to face Harrison, he holds his satisfied smirk and crosses his arms as his eyes burn a hole through the back of Daisy's skull.

A plume of dust grows behind the car on the drive toward Harrison's home. The night sky is nearly to the brink of dawn as a few glimmers of red pierce along the eastern horizon and the dark road hums through the tires into the cab as Kennedy drives Daisy to Harrison's estate.

Kennedy grips Daisy's hand and pulls her wrist to his lips to gently kiss her skin.

"I'm proud of you, Daisy," he says, his voice soft and tender. "You really are amazing."

Daisy rests her head back into the seat and turns to lock eyes with Kennedy.

"I think you're just my good luck charm," she croons, the words not reaching her eyes. "Thanks again for the ride, I know you're probably exhausted."

"Exhausted from my first full night with my fiancée?" Kennedy's eyes flutter to life at the word. "Are you sure he's even home? The place looks desolate." He leans his head forward in an attempt to see between the dripping trees.

"Duncan told me that Harrison and he were heading to grab some late night food before heading back here. They're probably sprawled out on the couch watching reality TV or something," Daisy answers with a nonchalant tone. "I want to pop in quick and thank him again for everything tonight," she says, her words eloquently rushing through the lie. "I had no idea he was going to announce the promotion tonight, so it's the least I can do to thank him." *Or show up at his house and kick the ever living shit out of him*, she thinks.

"It's nice to see you two so close still after all these years," Kennedy says, a warm chuckle coming from his throat.

"It really is," Daisy agrees with a seeping tone. "I couldn't ask for anything more." The double meaning clamors through her teeth like broken glass.

Once outside the car, Daisy dips her head back inside and says, "you can stay if you want, otherwise I'll just get a ride with Molly. She texted me saying she's heading home in a bit, so she can swing by and pick me up."

"I'm pretty beat, just come on over if you want afterward," Kennedy calls, blowing a kiss to Daisy as she waves goodbye and slams the door without further discussion.

As Daisy climbs the steps of the estate, her mind recounts Kennedy's proposal, his lavish display of red roses and a string quartet in her living room when she arrived home from work earlier that week. Her mouth perks at the memory of him on one knee and declaring his love for her after all these years. How she felt a hole form in her chest as she wished her sister were there to experience this memory. How she loved the idea of Kennedy more than the man who knelt before her. A single tear pooled in her eye as she answered, "absolutely, yes," before he pulled her into a tight embrace while she imagined the look on Harrison's face when he heard the news.

Reaching the entrance, Daisy knocks heavily on the door hoping to make a scene.

Wake up, motherfucker, she thinks, but to her surprise, the door shifts on his hinges and swings inward. She turns over her shoulder as the dust from Kennedy's car billows softly against the estate lawn. Turning back toward the entrance she comments to herself, "well, this is convenient."

Once inside, Daisy squints in the dark foyer. Stretching out her arms, she walks blindly, hunting for a light or a lamp until her hip connects with the massive entry table.

"Shit!" she yelps.

Hugging her hip, she continues to search for a light until she notices a faint glow through the back hallway. She follows along the walls until she arrives in the kitchen, the source of light coming from the refrigerator where the door hangs ajar.

Daisy grabs the handle of the refrigerator and pulls the door open further to peer inside, rummaging through its contents as it softly purrs.

What type of food does a high-functioning sociopath eat? she ponders as she opens a drawer and plucks a grape from a bag, popping it into her mouth.

Slamming the door shut, Daisy turns and places both hands on the marble countertop, pressing her weight into the stone.

"Harrison?" she yells, tipping her head to one side and waiting for a response. The silent hum of the refrigerator continues, but no Harrison. *He probably went home with someone*, she thinks. *I hope he gets a venereal disease.*

Leaning back on to her heels, she peels her hands off the table to examine the remnants of the heat from her palms against the stone.

"Harrison?" She calls again holding her breath and waiting for a response in the muted silence.

Hunger aches against her abdomen as Daisy begins to open a few cabinets in search of a snack while she waits for Harrison to return home.

"Where the fuck does he keep his food?" she thinks out loud. "There has to be something here." Searching for the pantry, she opens a few cabinets before landing back at the kitchen island. In the silence of Harrison's home, Daisy stands at the marble slab and contemplates her next move. *Do I stay and kill the kid or do I just cry and make him feel like a monster? I could turn on the waterworks in a heartbeat. I feel like screaming wouldn't do any justice. Maybe just slap him and get out all my anger. Oh, when like when Don Corleone slaps Johnny Fontaine—*

Her thought is cut short as she hears a faint scream seeping through the kitchen floor. She snaps her head toward the sound.

The estate again falls silent as Daisy perches against the edge of the countertop. Then, another stifled scream pricks at her ears as her face darts toward the source. She takes a step toward the back of the kitchen, following the noise to the rear of the house. Tiptoeing, Daisy reaches an open door with a set of worn, wooden steps that lead down into what she assumes is the basement. Bracing herself, she pauses again to listen for a sound, but all she can hear is the thumping of her own heart in her ears.

Gripping the cool walls, Daisy carefully places a fragile step against the staircase and dips her head in search of the source of the noise. *If you break your neck down here and Harrison has to save you, you will never hear the end of it*, she cautions herself.

Nearly halfway down the stairs, a faint light traces the bottom step and there is a distinct clinking of metal that bounces along the concrete and cinderblock. The walls seep with a cave-like film and an eerie coolness surrounds Daisy as she descends further into the basement.

Once Daisy's heels finally land on the cement floor, she squints to understand the scene painted before her, the hairs on the back of her neck starting to prick. Through the open door, Daisy purses her eyes to block out the intense light in the dim hallway. Her eyes adjust as she spots what appears to be a man suspended at his wrists and a metal chain attached to a hook in the ceiling. Reverberating music pumps through the door and drapes around Daisy, pulling her forward toward the spectacle.

Daisy spots Harrison leaning forward into the man, whose mouth is loosely bound by what she makes out to be a red handkerchief. His unbuttoned dress shirt hangs limp against his bloodied chest and a plastic name tag that says "Steven" lays askew, spattered with blood.

I haven't seen him out of a suit since college, Daisy thinks to herself, appraising Harrison's typically unseen tee and jeans. Taking another stealthy step toward the door, Harrison murmurs what Daisy makes out to be, "elton John."

"Elton John?" Daisy whispers to herself.

Harrison rubs his hands together and runs his fingers through his hair, blood streaking across his neck and ears. Looking up into the man's eyes, he asks, "who would be so impolite to Elton John?" but the man's eyes do not meet his. Shifting his head to one side, Harrison shouts up to the man, "do you even know who Elton John is?" as his eyes widen in reaction to the disturbance behind him. "What are you looking at?" he demands.

Harrison turns over his shoulder, but stops short at the man's source of intrigue.

Daisy casually leans against the doorframe, her arms draped before her waist and her legs crossed pristinely at the ankles. She drops her head to rest against the frame and looks up into the man's eyes, then down to his stomach. There is an open wound with nearly two feet of intestines hanging limp across his hips. Blood trickles down his legs, creating a small stream pooling on the floor of the cellar. She returns her eyes to the man's face before musing to herself, *The bartender?*

The room falls still as Harrison's deep eyes stare into Daisy's vivid jade glare. His chest rises and falls until he inhales deeply to brace himself for her next words, but her face is stone-like, identical to the moment he announced her promotion. The Oxymoron in the flesh. Impossible to read, and Harrison too afraid to speak.

Breaking the silence, Daisy picks herself up from the doorframe to stand upright before Harrison and the bartender. Again, holding this stance, he waits for the next move but all that comes is a sharp exhale of a single laugh through her nose as the edge of her lips tugs at a smile.

"You know," she finally speaks, her words dripping like honey, "if you play with fire…"

Harrison swallows hard, releasing his breath as his heartbeat doubles its speed in his chest. He waits for her to complete the phrase, but Daisy doesn't finish, an unfinished melody hanging in the air in hopes of a resolution. Daisy tucks her clutch under her arm and turns to ascend the cellar steps back into the chilly night air.

Part Three: **Winter**

Chapter Fifteen: **Hey Kids**

The elevators open to the top floor lobby of Bishop Enterprises. The sleek interior whirls with life as a stoic Daisy steps out.

"Good morning, Miss Stone," a nearby reception says as Daisy glances in her direction and politely smiles, a devilish pinch in her eyes.

Rolling back her shoulders and shaking out her hair to cascade across her shoulders, Daisy prepares for her triumphant return. *Showtime*, she thinks to herself and takes her first steps through the lobby while her heels echo through the hall as the newly christened president of Bishop Enterprises. She had selected a pair of sleek, black pants and matching jacket today to go with her favorite white oxford. Paired with a bold red lipstick, she was now ready to take on the world – and more particularly, Harrison.

The halls reduce to a slight murmur as Daisy makes her way through the corridors and the shift in energy does not go unnoticed. She can feel her vibrato intensify with each conversation cut short by her presence and every hushed hum behind her back.

"I heard she bought him out of the job," a chubby man mutters to a neighboring employee behind a cubicle wall.

Shaking his head, the other man says, "no way. I heard he had given her an ultimatum to take the job because they were afraid that she was going to try to push him out and sell out the company secrets."

Daisy stops short and takes a step backward. Whispering loudly under her breath, she leans toward the pair.

"Hey kids," she says, her voice seeping with reprisal between the two as they slowly turn in hopes to not find Daisy as the source of the chilling call. "I heard that I earned the position by being exquisitely qualified and deserving of the role." The two men stand wide-eyed as Daisy raises a lone brow, releasing a slight chuckle.

Continuing her march to her destination, Daisy recounts the previous week of what led her to this position: the proposal, the jealously, the intestines. She continually tried to rid the memory of what she saw, but all of her thoughts seemed to be situated in a pool of blood. Her cool demeanor and newly found pride did not leave a trace of the incidents after the event, but this secret lingered on her face. She had achieved her ultimate goal after these last few months; she had found a way to bring Harrison crumbling to the ground.

Daisy arrives at the corner conference room where she had had so many back and forth debates with Harrison during the last few months. The air engulfs her as she observes her new sense of power and poise, and the room immediately becomes silent as she crosses the threshold of the doorway.

"Hello everyone. Are we ready to get started?" she asks the staff as she drops her belongings at the end of the table in a spot that appears to already be occupied.

Multiple sets of eyes move across the room and Daisy detects that she is the source of the commotion. Moving the things from her desired seat, she sits down and asks the man to her right to collect the untidy pile she created.

Harrison stands at the opposite end of the room, frozen with a confused stun. He senses the eyes of those around him shifting from Daisy and on to him, as she had not yet acknowledged him. Watching her diligently, he clears his throat to make his presence known, but Daisy does not lift her focus. He adjusts the sleeve of his black suit, rolling back his shoulders before adjusting his matching tie, but his tension lingers in his stance. Daisy lifts her eyes to scan the room, waiting for the meeting to begin. Her face cold and stern, she lands on a pair of identical emerald eyes across the table. Now holding Harrison's gaze, she does not retreat, but instead lifts a brow with a knowing glance that pulls against her catlike eyes.

<<<

Ribbons of daylight filter through the eastern windows of La Nuit's dining-room-turned-all-night-happy-hour by The Rose Institute's staff. Charlie stands with a microphone to his lips and an arm outstretched in Daisy's direction, her face inches from Kennedy's, while their fight boils over in the background.

"It is with great pleasure that I announce The Rose Institute has been acquired by Bishop Enterprises!"

Snapping her neck toward the distorted words, Daisy growls like a lioness, "what the fuck," far too loudly for her moment of spotlight.

Gritting her teeth and clenching her fist in an attempt to control her anger, Charlie pulls her in for a congratulatory hug and demands a speech.

"Give the crowd a quick speech!" he booms over the microphone that resonates through the crowded restaurant.

As Charlie jams the microphone into Daisy's hand, she can feel her mind whirling without substantial thoughts. Images and sounds blur past, leaving her mind in a tailspin as the scotch she shared with Courtney clouds the world around her with an uneasy haze. Kennedy's laughter frames the moment with his gleeful snide. This was Daisy's first monumental promotion at The Rose Institute, but she felt as if she was walking on thin ice with a spider web of cracks leaching out from her with every step she took. She saw Harrison's face as she stormed angrily out of the laboratory at Northwestern.

Daisy feels her weight slide out from her feet as her eyes glaze over, falling into Charlie's arms. Her mind blanks into a slate board of emptiness until Charlie bellows through her ear with a boisterous, "whoa there, Daisy!" tapping her playfully on the cheek to spring her back to life. "Almost lost you there for a moment!" His eyes are earnest and full of joy, which only angers Daisy further. "Let's hear a couple words from the woman of the hour! The woman who put The Rose Institute on the map!"

The anger drops momentarily as Daisy furrows her brow and turns to face Charlie, far closer than she would prefer to be in this moment.

"What do you mean 'woman of the hour?' I didn't do anything," she said, her voice trailing off through the applause while celebratory champagne passes through the crowd.

Charlie releases his fatherly chuckle and lifts a bear-like hand to his glasses to return the frames along the bridge of his nose. His fingers leave behind a spattering of prints across the crystal clear glass.

"Harrison told me all about the deal you pulled with him," he says proudly. "He told me how you had been berating him for months with offers until he finally caved."

He must be drunk, Daisy thinks to herself. *I haven't spoken to Harrison since the first week I moved to New Orleans. He obviously must be mistaken.* Opening her mouth to correct Charlie, she was too late to question him further.

Turning back for an eager handshake with a nearby coworker, Charlie dips his head into Daisy to comment, "he told me how you two were best friends back in the day and how you had been hoping to go into business together since college. I even saw the adorable heart you drew above the 'i' in your signature!"

The realization sets in as to what Harrison has done as Daisy grips the microphone with a heavy hand, her face as blank as her mind. *He couldn't let me have this*, she thinks to herself. *He couldn't let me have this one fucking thing without stealing it from under me.* A steadying breath fills her lungs and she raises a second hand to keep the microphone from shaking.

"Thank you, everyone," she begins, her voice a barren stream of emotion as she gives herself a moment to carefully pull her words together. "I know this is a huge announcement and endeavor for our team…" Her pause makes the crowd hang on every word. "But the next steps will be crucial in solidifying out place in the industry."

"Calm down, everyone," Daisy finally says as the group releases a unified sigh discerning no noteworthy battle would take place before them. "Let's take our seats and we can get started."

She pulls a few items from her bag and takes a seat at the far end of the table – Harrison's seat at the table.

Harrison's belongings slowly migrate to him at the other end of the conference room and he thanks those for passing them along. Feeling agitated, he pulls a chair from the table and takes a seat, immediately examining the scene from the opposite end of the room. *View sucks over here*, he says to himself.

Pushing back from the table to rise, Daisy authoritatively stands before the group and says, "today's meeting has been a long time coming. My apologies from both teams for putting this off for so long, but I was with the board almost all day Sunday and we have finally determined our arrangements for our new executive team moving forward after the merger."

A few audible breaths fill the room and quick eyes move with the notice of the dreaded announcement. It was evident that no one was prepared, let alone excited to hear who would be left standing once the calendar turned. "This isn't an easy decision for this organization, but moving forward," Daisy begins, the majority of the attendees holding their breath, "it appears that not all of you are fit to move forward with our new structure."

Dread immediately fills the room, realizing what Daisy is relaying. A few members lean back into their chairs and dip their chins into their chests. One woman raises a hand to shield her face from the expected tears forming in her eyes. The man to her right pulls a clenched fist to cover his mouth then exhales loudly in frustration.

"Mind you, this is not due to performance, but just a new corporate structure," Daisy further explains, her speech obviously well prepared and eloquently scripted. Of course, the corporate words do not ease the tension of the room.

What the fuck is she doing? Harrison thinks to himself, his eyes flashing to a few nearby co-workers. Leaning into an elbow perched atop the conference room table, he extends a hand upward to grab Daisy's attention.

"Are you saying that we will be *cutting* executive team members, Miss Stone?" his voice accusatory and uncertain.

Puffing her chest, Daisy nods with a parental glance. "That is exactly what I am indicating, Mr. Bishop. We simply do not need to retain duplicate roles within this team," she says, her tone prepared and steady, well equipped for this type of a reaction.

"Correct me if I'm wrong, and I highly doubt that is the case, but I specifically recall a contractual clause to keep all existing Bishop Enterprises executive members in place for at least three years post acquisition," Harrison explains, a low growl building in his throat.

"Well, Mr. Bishop," Daisy sternly begins. "Amendments have been made to that contract and reallocations have been made as we look forward," her corporate jargon a thin veil of her true meaning.

"Reallocations, my ass, Daisy." Harrison nearly shouts across the table, returning Daisy's unwelcomed forehand to his serve. Closing his eyes in an attempt to compose himself as he recounts his surroundings, he continues with a heavy finger pushing through the conference room table. "You don't have that type of pull, *Miss Stone*."

"Unfortunately, *Mr. Bishop,* I now do," Daisy finishes the conversation, exposing her long con. "Now, on to next steps," she says, continuing with the meeting, but Harrison has already mentally left the building.

Fire my own team? Who the fuck does she think she is? Harrison thinks to himself as the meeting continues without him. *This wasn't how this was supposed to play out.*

"The new chain of command will be as detailed," Daisy says, pulling a stack of papers from a manila folder. "The listing can be found within this new organizational chart."

Harsh swallows echo throughout the group as the neatly bound booklets holding the future for the conference room slide down the table. Handing each booklet down the row one by one, the tension building further at the mundane task, sighs of relief or groans of defeat ring throughout the expansive room. The conference room's massive space seems to slowly shrink by the minute.

The man to Harrison's left puffs his cheeks releasing a breath of relaxation after locating his name listed near the end of the chart.

"Here you go, man," he says in a freed tone as he hands the final booklet to Harrison.

"The listing may seem a bit unique to some of you, but I have discussed this extensively with the board over the last couple of days and we have come to a formal decis—"

"Where the *fuck* am I, Daisy?" Harrison lashes. The crowd drops their eyes to their papers without reading a single word. Tossing the papers in front of him, Harrison presses all ten fingerprints into the table and begins to slowly stand. "What the *actual* fuck, Daisy?"

Without flinching, Daisy tilts her head to one side. *Bingo*, she thinks to herself. *You don't have that kind of pull*, she mockingly repeats in her mind. *Well, now I do, you ass. If you want to go against me, you will feel the full wrath of Daisy Stone.*

A now motherly expression paints Daisy's face.

"*Mister Bishop*," she begins as her tone indicates that this isn't the time nor the place for this conversation. "If you have a grievance with the list, we can discuss it at another time."

"Oh, fuck that," Harrison barks. "I put you in charge of this this," he says, tossing the book into the center of the conference room table, the slide of the paper a deafening graze amongst the enraged silence. "*This* is what I get?" The room suspends in time, too terrified to move as World War III plays out across the table. "I fucking *made* you, Daisy. Don't you forget that," he says, his words harsh and malicious while they resonate through the hushed conference room.

Daisy holds her cold disposition, every atom of her body well-prepared for this backlash and soaking up every ounce of her revenge she has so badly desired after nearly a decade of anger. Leaning forward, she drops both sets of knuckles atop the table to speak directly to Harrison.

"If you'd like an answer, let me put it to you in a way that you'll understand," she says while a slight snarl forms on her ruby lips. "This isn't something that should be shocking to those in this room. We are two large organizations and not everyone will be needed once we have become one and, frankly, if you are offended by this revelation you must not have been paying attention." Her words collide, breaking Harrison's face as he understands their true meeting.

Harrison grits his teeth and pulls a shallow breath. *No way*, he tells himself. *No way she could have known I would have put her in that fucking chair*. Opening his mouth to speak, Daisy raises a palm to stop him.

"For now," Daisy halts him, "please have some respect for the rest of this team and let us continue with the remainder of the meeting. Do I make myself clear?" This wasn't a question, but a warning to not cross her. Her eyes recount the blood pooling on the cellar floor. "Do I make myself clear?" she asks again, her tone more forceful and demanding.

Say it, Harrison tells himself. *Just fucking agree and get this charade over with*.

"Crystal."

A wicked smile of agreement pulls at Daisy's lips, wrapping neatly around her cold eyes with feverish glee. "Good, I was afraid you were going to disembowel me for a minute there," she laughs, feeling the dart of Harrison's eyes burning through her. "Now, where was I?"

Chapter Sixteen: **Revenge**

A soft patter of glasses clinking chimes through Daisy's office as Molly, Amber, and Emily toast her. The group cheers with a rambunctious, "to Daisy!" in celebration of her promotion, her latest kill in what could only be described as a manifesto of men who had finally met their match.

The group sprawls across the office, draped across the oversized chairs and office furniture. The drapes are pulled back to expose the windows, allowing for the afternoon sun to shine through the windows. This was a rare view for Daisy, as she hadn't seen the true color of her office furniture in months. Bottles are scattered on top of a nearby bar cart and an ashtray holds a lingering burning cigar. Emily delicately dangles off the edge of the desk. Both of her shoes are kicked off and her toes caress the wood floor in a circular pattern.

"So, how terrible was the meeting?" Amber asks, taking a long swill from her glass.

Molly's face morphs into a look of confusion.

"Terrible? Imagine telling an ex that you're firing him *and* taking his job," she says as she takes a sip of champagne. "It had to be nearly pornographic."

"Oh, it was delicious," Daisy says, flashing a grin at them. "Better than porn if I'm being honest," she says, reaching behind her ear to press against her glasses and wiggle her frames in Molly's direction.

"Ha!" Molly exclaims. "Fucking knew it."

Amber scoots her rear toward the end of an armchair and in a fluid motion, turns on a dime to sit reversed. Her legs are outstretched across the back of the chair, her hair dangling softly across the floor. "Tell us every gory detail," she says, her face turning pink from the rush of blood. "Graphic descriptions are encouraged."

Pulling her knuckles beneath her chin and fluttering her lashes, Daisy feigns a phony Southern accent to complete her charade.

"It was quite something, I must say," her poorly constructed pronunciation slipping from her lips. "I had to shade myself from the sun, the heat was too intense for my fair complexion."

An embarrassed laugh escapes Molly's lips as she shouts, "boo! You suck!" cupping her mouth to echo the sound and tease Daisy's Southern accent.

"I don't know," Emily chimes in to sarcastically defend Daisy's honor. "Pretty accurate to me."

Daisy stands from her desk chair and steadies herself as the champagne toggles her head.

"Okay, okay," she says, taking another sip from her glass before placing it back on the wooden surface. "It was fucking *beautiful*. Better than any moment I could have ever dreamed," she begins, although she knows the truth behind her words – her well-planned and finally fulfilled fantasy was real life.

"What did he say?" Amber asks, her face turning a concerning wine hue and forcing Emily to twist a single forefinger in her direction, instructing her to bring her head back above water. Shaking her head to release the bubbles, she presses. "What did you say? Tell us *everything*!" Her words are giddy with a tipsy slur.

"Here's the beauty of it all," Daisy begins, leaning forward in anticipation. "I didn't even tell him, he was forced to read the executive layout to discover that he wasn't even considered to stay." A vindictive grin drags across her catlike eyes and the excitement warms her face.

Molly's mouth hangs slightly in amazement.

"You evil genius," she whispers, tapping her champagne glass to her rose lips. "He's going to be gunning for you now."

"On what grounds?" Emily asks with an obvious tone. "It's not like he works here any longer," she says, her words hanging in the air as she reads the room, concerned she took things too far.

A beat idles between the women as they wait for a response, but they quickly erupt into a fit of laughter, knowing the corporate boys club they had hated for years is finally behind them. The lioness herself took on the pack leader to not only defeat him, but destroy him using his own tail as the noose.

Dropping a heavy elbow against the back of her desk chair, Daisy dips her chin into her palm, watching her friends gleefully revere in this new chapter of their lives. *After everything*, she thinks to herself, *we're finally here and it truly feels as good as I imagined*. Her words were like silk as she replayed the morning's events. Harrison's anger playing on a movie theater screen across her mind on a constant loop. Briefly, the image of the bartender in chains from the cellar flashes against the screen until she suppresses the moment from her mind.

Daisy took a moment to watch her friends gleefully enjoying their moment of salvation in her office. She looked back on the years of pain they endured from being amongst

CAVALIER: A Novel

the minority of women in their careers. The jokes and ridicule that they brushed off in hopes of promotions and better salaries. She felt the weight of her career begin to lift from her shoulders as the power rippled through her veins.

"Did he cry?" Amber asks, interrupting Daisy's daydream. "And even if he didn't, can you just say he did so we can publicly berate him?"

"Like a blubbering baby," Molly chimes in to build the lie. "He cried and then he was so upset that he had to run out of the room and when he did, he tripped on the way out and his pants fell down."

"One hundred percent accurate," Daisy says, raising her glass in faux approval

"Miss Stone?" Courtney calls from the other side of the office door. Her knock is lost amidst the laughter and commotion. "Hey Daisy? Are you okay?" she asks, her voice flushed with confusion.

"Yeah?" Daisy calls, waving a hand above her head instructing her to enter, her voice equally disoriented. "What's wrong, Court?"

Courtney peers around the door as she presses her weight again the frame.

"Just checking to see why you're in here – thought you'd be at your meeting but I can see you're obviously up to something much more fun," she says, her voice hinting at the ladies' mischievous activities.

"Hold on. What are you talking about? It's nearly six o'clock," Daisy asks with a baffled tone.

Standing to turn her head slightly, Courtney opens the door further to enter the room. The scent of cigar smoke and alcohol burns her nostrils. Shaking a hand before her mouth to brush the odor, she chokes out, "the board meeting. I figured you'd be there but I can tell you're dealing with a 'family emergency,' so I'll let you ladies be," she says in an upbeat tone, subtly winking as she overly pronounces the phony excuse she and Daisy had cooked up years ago.

Mimicking her stance, Daisy straightens her back and tilts her head to the side in confusion.

"Okay, now I'm really confused. What exactly are you talking about?"

Three additional sets of eyes turn to watch Courtney with a perplexed glance. Scanning the room quickly, Courtney's tone takes a harsher tone. "Th—the board meeting happening at Bishop Enterprises? Harrison's giving some presentation."

The same sets of eyes now shift their focus from Courtney's perplexed face to Daisy's, as it slowly smolders with anger.

"What *kind* of a presentation?" Daisy growls, the words like a venomous snake.

"I couldn't hear much of anything," Courtney begins to squeak out, her voice hinting at her anxiety of being the bearer of bad news. "I was turning in that old filing cabinet you hated on the fifteenth floor for the upcoming renovation and—"

"Back to the point, Courtney," Daisy says, cutting her off as her outrage builds.

"I saw the board members walking into the room while Harrison was preparing for what looked like a presentation. I assumed he was trying to wiggle his way back into good graces after what happened."

Courtney barely finishes her thought before Daisy pushes past her in a whirlwind.

"Oh, he is," she snarls, the door slamming behind her in a thunderous crash.

$$>>>$$

Coughing faintly into his clenched fist, Harrison steadies himself as he takes his place at the far end of the conference room table. He had only willingly been the center of attention to this group twice before, once amidst a cheating scandal of which he was the other man, and once when members of a local church group protested outside their offices when he was given the Cure All Kid moniker. The prior had been a hilarious joke to him, but that was not taken in the same regard to the board members.

However, this instance was much different. Harrison had willingly called the board members together to plead for his survival in hopes of retaining some grasp of his career, but more importantly, to hold on to Daisy.

The fifteenth floor was not a location that the board members frequented. Nestled between the executive offices of the sixteenth and seventeenth floors and the dining facilities of the fourteenth, the fifteenth floor was considered the closet of Bishop Enterprises. It was the lackluster storage facility that housed one drab conference room that was saved for high-profile legal battles and firing "at risk" employees, as to guarantee nothing of value would be destroyed on the way out of the office. Its dull lighting and wooden decor felt claustrophobic and dated.

Adjusting his tie, Harrison welcomes the group before thanking everyone for meeting on such short notice. His swears to himself that he will never wear a black suit again. *I look like I'm going to my own funeral*, he muses before he paints his best boyish grin in an attempt to start on a good note. The faces staring back reflect a melancholy glare, knowing well that this is a desperate man's plea to not be sent out to sea. His heartbeat reverberating against his eardrums, he steadies himself before the storm.

"This should come as no shock to those here today, but Bishop Enterprises is not just a company to me. Hell, I loved it so much that I threw my own name up on the building like a pretentious idiot," Harrison begins as the room opens up with an unamused laugh. "This organization has become so much more than curing the common cold. I come in every day so incredibly grateful for the things that we've accomplished. I've stopped looking at this group at its present state and I do nothing but think about what our next steps will be into the future. But more importantly, I think about how we will do it together," he says, his words ringing a verbal orchestra only he could construct. His eyes beam with their subtle amber of genuine honesty that was seen so infrequently, and his hands move wildly, pulled from their typical pocketed homes and gesturing with intensity.

"I wake up every morning and tell myself that I have the best team of employees coming into this office," Harrison says as he stretches out his arms to showcase the room, but he pauses as he remembers his location. "Well, maybe not *this* office," he jokes. The room sputters with life and eagerness at his words. "But we get to stand together as the world's best minds pool together to tackle the truly deadly elements of our globe. Cancer, disease, even death itself is no longer a concern because we've yet to find a problem we haven't completely obliterated."

A motherly woman in the center of the table pulls an elderly hand to her chin as a warm smile pulls at her lips. Her eyes prick with a hindered smile.

"With all of this," Harrison continues, taking a moment to let his lyrical words settle amongst the group, "I can't sit idly by and watch the great potential of this marvelous organization go by the wayside. I've invested my entire life's work into Bishop Enterprises. It's so much more than blood, sweat, and tears. The walls are literally built with my sweat and blood."

A few heads nod in agreement and newly found pleasant smiles stare back at Harrison. Feeling the grip of the room, he presses further. "Marlin," he says while gesturing toward an older man in a chocolate brown suite in the back of the room. "I was there the day you invested your first check into our immunology research lab in upstate New York. You told me that I needed to double the check before the end of the quarter or you would…" Harrison takes a moment to let Marlin conclude the story.

"Or I'd push the check through your mouth and make you lay a golden egg," Marlin says, the room snickering with a gleeful humor.

"And Nancy," Harrison continues gesturing to a slim woman in a robin's egg blue blazer and matching reading glasses. "I was there the day you demanded we shift funding toward tuberculosis research. You had asked if there was any way we could help erase the pain that you had felt after your son had passed away."

Nancy grips at a delicate crucifix along a gold chain hanging softly against her chest.

"Simon would be very proud to see what you've accomplished in his honor," she says, her words squeaking out in an attempt to hold back her tears.

Taking an eager step forward, feeling he's finally won over the room, Harrison rests a heavy hand on the man to his immediate right.

"And Allen," he begins before he is quickly cut off.

"We get it, Mr. Bishop," an angry man interrupts from the far end of the room, instructing him to halt the show. Louis Bradford was one of the most senior board members and most difficult to win over. His posture proving that he was the deciding factor in his case, Harrison knew he would not go without a fight. "Get to the point or let us go. This room is more depressing than a dinner party at Marlin's," he says, a stubbornness hinting of a recurring issue amongst the board members.

He was not wrong. The room's wooden panels and yellow lighting gave it a sickly ambience that unsettled most and knowing he had done just what he came here to accomplish, Harrison asks the staging question that should land him on the bull's eye.

"So, I have to ask. Is there nothing left for me to do here? I know Miss Stone is more than qualified to serve as president, but I cannot stand on the sidelines here," says Harrison. Understanding he could not simply come out and ask for his old role, Harrison knew to lowball the group and push his way up until he resumed his seat at the table.

"That really isn't for you to decide, Mr. Bishop," says Louis. He stands to present his answer, knowing that the others in the room have little to no say on the matter. "We made our decision based off of *your* recommendation for Miss Stone to move forward in *your* role and what would be best suited for everyone moving forward, not just the boyish vision that you have for the team."

"But it really is so much more than leading," Harrison begins, only to be blocked as Louis raises a hand, stopping him before he can continue.

"It is more than leading, and it's what will make this company money," he says, his words as harsh as granite. "If you told me today that your latest discovery would bring back our old pup Monty, I would be excited. But my next question would be 'How much is this going to cost me?' followed by 'How much am I going to gain?'" Each word is a menacing dagger through Harrison's heart as he can feel himself slipping from between Louis's hairy knuckles. "As much as you want to believe in humanity, our *only* goal is providing a paycheck at the end of the day, and we need a leader who puts zeros on the checks."

Before the guillotine finally slices through Harrison's neck, Daisy clamors through the far end of the conference room.

"What the hell is going on in here?" she shouts forcefully. Clearing her throat and starting again, she asks with a more dignified tone, "I'd like some explanation as to why there was a board meeting called and I was not included."

Gotcha, Harrison thinks to himself as a demonic smile pulls at his eyes, forcing his dimples deep into his cheeks.

"Just laying out my case to the board as to why I should still be here come January," Harrison explains with an air of self-righteousness.

"Well, we've seen more than enough of you over the last few years to know that you're not a good fit, Mr. Bishop," Daisy lashes through her ruby lips and champagne-soaked eyes.

"Enough out of you two," Louis calls as if a father scolding his children. "You two obviously have a long history, but this is the board's decision and I will not tolerate you two bickering instead of acting like adults," he says. He puffs an expansive breath through his lips and his cheeks billow against the pressure.

Daisy folds her arms across her chest, but notices her childish this stance. Instead, she removes her hands and shoves them into her trouser pockets, catching Harrison as he performs nearly the exact motions.

"Harrison," Louis begins, turning to address him. "Your playboy lifestyle is no longer conducive to our plan moving forward. You and your buddies gallivanting around town and dragging the Bishop name through the mud has not gone unnoticed, and we cannot in good reason continue to play damage control week after week," he says, his tone pulling at Harrison's throat like bile rising in his mouth.

A callous snort pushes through Daisy's nostrils, causing a few board members to turn and purse their lips at the rude response.

"Don't even get me started on you, Miss Stone," Louis barks, turning to face her with his wide shoulders. "Don't think we haven't recognized this charade of buying up every nearly-viable company with a frail corporate structure. While your acquisition spending has brought in a fair share of new profits, the money we're wasting just to feed your ego will come to a halt this January."

The words knock the air from Daisy's lungs as she and Harrison exchange embarrassed glances, knowing they are both in the wrong. They quickly shift back to their bitter tones once they reflect on what led them to this situation. The engagement and the blood. Episcopus Aerobium and the years of perpetual animosity.

"Daisy, Harrison," Louis begins, taking the time to address each of them individually before his decision. They each hold their breath for the final judgment. "We feel that Harrison would be the best candidate in the presidential role moving forward."

A silent grasp deadens against Daisy's throat as she attempts to breathe, feeling her stomach flip within her abdomen. She begins to open her lips to speak, but she knows there is nothing she can say to sway this colossal vote.

"Harrison is the face of this company and the founder of TEA," Louis explains further. "The organization, the industry, this vile room would not exist if he hadn't made this discovery. He is what the people know and love about our products, and despite his showboating demeanor, he is why people come back to work with us time and time again."

Daisy could feel everything slipping away, the room melting into a psychedelic landscape of synthetic wood grain, her eyes begging to release their tears as she holds in every drop with as much strength as she can muster.

"Ultimately, Harrison is the reason we see the sales and growth that keep us afloat, and we cannot bear to lose that type of buy-in with our clientele and stockholders. Daisy will stay in her role as vice president of mergers and acquisitions, but you are on thin ice, Miss Stone," Louis concludes.

The room slowly begins to file out through the plywood door, leaving only Harrison and Daisy among the turned chairs and scattered coffee cups. They hold their pose for what seems like hours. The only sound filling the space is their blinking and staggered breathing, as if they had returned from running a half marathon. A clear winner and a clear loser.

"How could you fucking do this?" Daisy demands, her voice full of resentment. She stares Harrison dead in his emerald set of eyes, her eyes so dark, they've become black in the vexing light. "You just had to take what isn't yours. You just *had* to complete your plot of revenge," she says, the words slinking through her teeth like venom.

With a glower so intense, Harrison could feel himself burning a hole through her forehead.

"Maybe it was time for your powers over me to subside, Daisy," he says, his words sticky to the touch as he turns his frame to address her fully. "Your time is up, but I have a consolation prize to make it up to you."

Taken aback by his words, Daisy furrows her brow in confusion.

"Define prize," she says, her hatred perked with curiosity.

"A gift for you," Harrison reveals, his voice husky and enticing. "Something waiting for you in my wine cellar."

Chapter Seventeen: **Radar Love**

Harrison grips his hands around the leather of his steering wheel, careful to extend then curl each finger individually in a lucid exaggeration.

"You ready?" he asks, his voice throaty as he narrowly hides his eager expression.

"Let's get this over with," Daisy says, dropping into the passenger seat with an irked sigh.

She was no stranger to Harrison's surprises over the years. He had popped up from time to time once they had parted ways, after the initial explosion of TEA, and she expertly dodged his advances like a seasoned boxer until one minor mishap landed her in his bed for an extended weekend. Beyond that, she kept a close eye on him, knowing how easy it was to fall back into his trap.

"Nothing could surprise me at this point, Harry," she declares as she closes the door, the sound of their surroundings vanishing the moment they are alone.

Watching her carefully, Harrison waits for her to yell, fight back, or retaliate, but Daisy sits patiently next to him with her hands dutifully placed in her lap. "Last chance to run," he reminds her, coming to the uneasy realization that she followed much more easily than he had anticipated. She was the only person who was able to make him feel this way, a spinning top dipping its edges as its spin concludes.

"Just fucking drive," Daisy mutters with the attitude of a preteen child.

Delicately placing a hand against the back of Daisy's seat, Harrison reverses out of his corporate parking spot, the car purring to life beneath their feet. Tonight, Harrison drove his two-seater sports car, a petite vehicle with an iridescent navy finish that sparkled in the parking garage's fluorescent lighting. It was perfect for a romantic date night, a Sunday drive, or blackmailing an old friend.

Harrison and Daisy pull into the evening with an exaggerated hum of the engine. The road is quiet with the majority of the population retreating inside, as the cool air had engulfed the city. An eerie shift in the scenery unfolds as a spatter of fog begins rolling in across the gulf and into Lake Pontchartrain. They slowly filter across the streets and between the buildings like a squid's tentacles slinking through the night.

Feeling her eyes relax and her mind trail elsewhere, Daisy mentally exits the vehicle. Her focus wanders as she reflects on her whirlwind of a day. From the promotion, to Harrison's execution, to the termination of her own position, the last twenty-four hours were something she'd prefer to move past as soon as Harrison had finished his song and dance.

Daisy feels her tongue tense and drops her jaw to relax her chin. A microscopic cut has formed along the roof of her mouth, her tongue caressing the sore skin again and again until her saliva stings of iron. Softening her tongue across the base of her mouth, she attempts to ignore the pleasurable pain and stares through the windshield before her.

All the while, silence drills through Harrison like an unrelenting drum. Typically favoring the radio or any noise to fill the car while driving, this muted black hole begins playing tricks on his mind as he can hear every movement coming from Daisy in a cacophony of sound. The subtle *thick-thick-thick* drips against his ears as Daisy drags her tongue across the roof of her mouth.

Releasing an irritated sigh, Daisy reaches forward to switch the antique radio to life. Deliberately turning the dial, she lands on each clear station to examine its content before moving on to the next.

Thank god, Harrison thinks to himself, watching her meticulous work. His mind flashes back nearly a decade as he remembers watching Daisy work in the laboratory, her color-coded pens and calculated note-taking. Nearly identical in her career, his mind wondered in awe at how she had turned from overbearing tutor into such a ravenous empress. It was as if he had front row seats to the blooming of the illustrious corpse plant, although she had a much more pleasant odor.

Daisy selects a station and sits back in her seat, the *thick-thick-thick* now drowned out by the bluesy voice of the radio host as she turns to face out of the darkening window. The city lights begin to dim as they inch closer to Harrison's estate.

"Hey there, all you foxy guys and gals," the host says, his voice reminiscent of a '70s late night radio program, complete with neon posters and beaded curtains. "This next one is for all you lovers just knowin' what's in store for you tonight," his not-so subtle double-entendre forcing Daisy's eyes deep inside her head. "Here's Golden Earring's 'Radar Love.'" The soothing host begins fading out as the ghostly chords drag the fog from the swampy road across their path, a smoky serpent slithering into the night.

"I know I'm wasting my breath here," Daisy breaks her silence, her voice indifferent and wondrous, "but have you found an end goal with all of this, Harry?" she asks as she swivels her head to face Harrison's face.

His Adam's apple visibly shifts as he swallows, and Harrison takes a shallow breath in response to the question. The radio titillates to life with the song's snare drum, shifting the tone of the car. "I've been pretty open with my thought process here," he answers as he looks her directly in her green eyes, muted by the car's dark interior, before turning his sight back toward the road. "I laid out my feelings for you and you made your response loud and clear."

"*Feelings*?" Daisy repeats with an unpleasant snide. "Yeah, your *feelings* are quite something." Her tongue returns to the roof of her mouth, the pain gripping as her jaw tenses from the satisfying prick.

"Yeah, my *feelings*," Harrison repeats with over-exaggerated attitude. The music of the car picks up as the vocals hum to life. "You must have forgotten about feelings after all these years, but your sociopathic meltdown should be quite the event any day now."

Daisy exudes a dry laugh and knocks her head into her seat before turning a blank face toward Harrison. "I'm glad to see your comedy career is alive and well," she says, turning back to the windshield. "Have you ever taken a moment to realize that maybe it was you I couldn't stand to be around? Maybe your charming personality was just as tiny and futile as, well, other things?" she asks, her voice trailing off as her line of sight shifts toward Harrison's trousers.

The speakers bump to life as the chorus pummels through the interior. Harrison grips the steering wheel as he sits upright to speak over the music, saying, "oh, I'm sure, Daisy. After all these years, you absolutely *hated* sleeping with me." His tone mocking and exaggerated, he adds "You really pulled the long con on me!"

Daisy sits up in her seat to fight back, the music breaking against her voice and forcing her to nearly shout, "yep! That's it. The good news is that your laughable performance always gave me such a great workout from spending the next day talking over every mistake with the girls that now my abs are made of steel!"

"You act as if we were married," Harrison growls with palpable angst. "I thought we were just fooling around. You know, having some fun on the side!" He shouts, his astonished tone turning incredulous.

"Is that why you were willing to throw it all away once I got over you?" Daisy ridicules before crossing her arms and turning her focus out her window.

The chorus fades away and the next verse quietly drains through the car. Both Daisy and Harrison relax their muscles then melt back into their seats. Daisy's tongue returns to her wound and she flicks it against her peeling skin.

Harrison curls in his bottom lip to press his teeth angrily against the skin at the sound of Daisy's insistent, clicking tongue. He briefly closes his eyes as he drags in a heavy breath through his nostrils, his chest rising and falling with a minute whistle.

Tucking her hair delicately behind her ear, Daisy softens her shoulders in a moment of collection. Reminding herself that this would all be over soon, she pulls a thin breath through her lips, exhaling in a steady pattern. She blocks out the world around her and attempts to ignore every fiber of Harrison.

Booming drums and slinky guitars pick up yet again throughout the vehicle as another chorus swirls between the brooding pair. The air tilts once again as the two stand at the starting line, waiting for the gun to fire.

"Don't pretend as if the last few months were just a charade to you," Harrison breaks with a snotty remark, knowing the exact reaction he will pry out of Daisy.

Clenching her teeth, Daisy feels herself begin to snap like a rubber band. She is unable to control herself as the words pouring out of her: "My Oscar is going to look beautiful behind my desk because I've been putting on the performance of the year."

"Oh, don't get me started on your precious trophy case," Harrison spouts. "You chastise me for my showmanship while you have a monument to your success that you force your poor receptionist to polish once a week so you can feel superior with your overbearing shrine to the great *Miss* Stone."

"I have never ordered Courtney to do such a thing! And you know that us hooking up was merely a way for me to force you into forking over your *precious* company. Another *trophy* for Courtney to polish, if you will," Daisy huffs.

"Ha!" Harrison lashes back, leaning forward into the steering wheel as they turn on to the estate's drive.

"Oh, you want to talk receptionists?" Daisy sputters back. "That poor Kit. All he's ever wanted was for you to help him succeed in his career, but instead all you do is have him cover for you and your buddies after traipsing around town and breaking up board members' marriages!"

"Mrs. Linnwood came onto *me* with her marital troubles," Harrison retorts, angered. "How was I supposed to know that her husband held ten percent of our stock? I merely helped satisfy her needs."

"You say 'satisfy' as if that is something you could ever accomplish," Daisy spits as the chorus quiets to a mere cymbal and bass line.

Harrison presses the weight of his calf into the accelerator as they hit the halfway mark of his drive. Knowing the road by heart, he is able to push the car past ninety and then over a hundred as his outrage now takes control. His blood boils with rage and his heart spits pure adrenaline. This was not the evening he had in mind, and knowing what awaited at the estate, the situation was due to get much messier.

Pummeling toward the house as the final chorus erupts to life, Harrison floors the gas, pushing both himself and Daisy firmly into their seats until they arrive at the front steps with an audible *sckreek* across the gravel driveway. The abrupt halt throws their bodies like a pendulum, first forward into the dash and then back into their seats with an audible thump.

Daisy hastily exits the car, but Harrison is not willing to let the battle die just yet. He opens his door, the keys still dangling in the ignition while the driveway floods to life with Frans Krassenburg's rough vocals. Standing with one foot firmly planted on the drive and another still lingering inside, he stands to balance himself atop the car. "You know, I met your little friend Alexander," he catcalls after her, forcing her to stop mid-step and turn on her heels to face him with a seething look in her eyes that only fuels him further.

"I'm sure he had an outrageous story for you," Daisy responds with an unbelieving tone. "He always did have a vivid fantasy of what we were. You two really would hit it off quite well. I'm glad to see you've finally met your psychotic other half."

Stepping from the still-running car, Harrison bashes his way up the estate steps. "I'm sure I wasn't dreaming up the *dozens* of men you seduced and swindled over the past decade, Daisy. We both know my imagination isn't that good," his tone accusatory, even edging on humor.

"Why the fuck are we here, Harry?" Daisy demands with a hoarse roar while neither acknowledges the allegations echoing across the front lawn. Her weight falls to one hip as she folds her arms angrily across her chest. "Let's see the grand finale of the evening."

>>>

The cellar door is propped with a spare cinderblock as the uneven lighting floods through the doorframe. The air is sticky with the withering humidity of the earth, and a slight gust from inside the estate slides across the wooden steps and down the cement floor.

The moment is still with only a few sounds clashing together in a hushed symphony of chaos. The hum of the light fixture, slowly purring with the electrical current of the bulb. Harrison and Daisy's steady and focused breath. And Kennedy's muffled choking noises, muffled into his gag and reverberating through his wine-colored cheeks.

Daisy leans against the doorframe in a familiar stance to the last time Harrison saw her here. She stands against the opposite wall now, her bicep pressing into the frame, arms leisurely hanging before her abdomen. Her ankles are neatly crossed with one toe tucked behind a heel to prop her foot properly behind her. Her lips purse in concentration as she appraises Kennedy.

Kennedy sits in the wooden chair, bound by ragged ropes at his ankles and wrists. There is a blue and white spotted handkerchief tidily tied against his molars to keep him quiet. His brow drips with sweat and his eager eyes are crazed with emotion as he attempts to scream out to Daisy. His hands turn a ghastly shade of plum as he tugs beneath the rope. From time to time, he moves large portions of his body in an attempt to break free, continually coming up short as he is gripped further into the wooden posts.

Harrison stands in the doorway, his back and head leaning into the opposite door frame from Daisy as he watches her reaction across the bridge of his nose. He is cool and relaxed as his face slowly shifts into a perplexed expression attempting to read her mind. His legs are stick-straight as he digs both hands into his pockets, and his index finger taps against his thigh beneath the fabric as Golden Earring replays in his mind and he begins to quietly hum the tune beneath his breath.

Continuing to audit the situation, Daisy's ears prick at the sound of Harrison's breath, as if a lioness hunting her prey. Clearly recognizing the rhythm, Daisy's voice croons to life as she hums along. Her muffled purr along, the words absorbed then lost against her closed lips.

Harrison continues his breathy song, beginning to sway his shoulders in time to the unheard music, unsure if the excitement or catchy tune is moving him. Daisy continues to sing along, her voice sweet and curious. She hums softly to herself. She opens her mouth as if to speak, but instead exhales a heavy sigh. Her cheeks puff in a gust of air as she turns to face Harrison with a barren look of instruction, as if her eyes as speaking for her to ask, "what next?"

$$>>>$$

Harrison and Daisy stand opposite each other across the kitchen island, both of their hands digging into the granite countertop as Harrison leans forward, shouting into Daisy's face.

"What did you expect me to do, Daisy? You showed up *engaged*!" Harrison roars, the over-pronunciation of "engaged," booming in an appalled tone.

"There are literally thousands of things you could have done besides this!" Daisy yells back, now leaning across the counter, her nails seeking to drill through the stone. "What do you want me to say? That this was all a ploy to trick you into making me president?"

"No need to say it when it's the truth," Harrison spits back into her face, standing matter-of-factly, easily seeing through her plan. "You were never good at camouflaging your intentions."

"Seeing as I was made president, I think I know how to twist you around my skinny little finger," Daisy mocks as she twists a finger in the air. "It wasn't that difficult to spot your weaknesses and prey on them."

Kennedy's muffled screams filter through the open cellar door, briefly pulling their attention away from their feud as they quickly return to their argument.

"You sure do have a lot of experience with that," Harrison responds as he rolls his eyes at the interruption. "I'm sure the other men you've deceived over the last few years were more than happy to put a ring on your finger in hopes of winning over the oh-so-wonderful *Miss Stone*," Daisy's name spoken as if it were a curse.

"I didn't even need to get a ring from you before you signed over your entire company, Harry." Daisy snarls, already feeling his next move. "If you've got such a read on me, why did you drop me in the driver's seat the second you saw a rock flashing across my hand?" she demands, her words ringing more truth than Harrison would like to admit as she flips her hair away from her neck, her skin red-hot beneath the shadow.

A muffled shout erupts from the cellar door. Kennedy has broken free from his muzzle and begins choking to life, his voice ascending the basement stairs, causing both Harrison and Daisy to shift their attention only momentarily before returning to the ring.

"It should come as no surprise to you that I didn't make my way into this business by playing nice," Daisy begins again, ignoring Kennedy. "You'd be surprised just how much more difficult I'd have to fight to get to where you are today."

Harrison scoffs before lunging forward to yell into Daisy's face, "by ruining the lives of every weak man along the Gulf Coast? Please, tell me how this is a noble feat you've accomplished in your career." He claps his hands, pulling his clenched fists to his chest. "Please, please, please. Teach me your revolutionary ways!" he calls, feigning a pleading face.

Again, Kennedy's cries writhe from the cellar door. Neither Harrison nor Daisy turns to face the commotion. Instead, they both roll their eyes in annoyance, offended that someone would disrupt their conversation.

"At least I *earned* my career," Daisy lashes, knowing the real battle had only begun with the addition of TEA to the conversation. "I'm sure it's very difficult to build such an empire while you're stealing my life's work. Tell me all about your burdensome pathway to all of this!" she shouts, stretching both arms lengthwise to draw attention to Harrison's massive kitchen.

"You didn't even think I completed the sample, Daisy!" Harrison booms in full timbre, repeating his side of the debate that he had held close for all of these years, his hoarse voice cascading through the colossal kitchen and reverberating off the metal appliances. "You told me that didn't follow your *precious* instructions and nearly demolished your experiment! If you want to take ownership, own up to the fact that you can't write out simple experimental protocols!"

Daisy removes her weight from the island and stands up straight, her face seething with anger as her eyes pierce through Harrison. "Is that what you want to think?" she demands, her tone harsh and eerily quiet, elastic and menacing. "That you're in the clear due to a fucking technicality?" Each syllable reverberates against her teeth.

Another shriek clamors through the cellar door and echoes through the kitchen, followed by a helpless "Someone help me!" in Kennedy's rugged, dwindling voice.

"Are you really so spoiled that you think you're owed the rights to TEA just because you happened to be along for the ride? If that's the case, I won a couple hundred at the horse track last month. I should probably send a residual check along to the jockey," Harrison scoffs, his joking tone smoldering with anger.

"I confided in you. I told you about what happened to Lily and you *still* felt the need to try to one-up me!" Daisy screams, her words holding a sincere weight that knocks Harrison onto his heels.

Harrison's eyes soften as he drops his shoulders, pausing for a moment.

"Is that what you really think? Daisy, I wanted to help you. I was there through that entire project trying to help you find that goddamn bacteria, but you and I both know you were looking in the wrong place. No, I didn't follow your instructions, but I always just assumed you would see what I had done and figure it out on your own. Do you think I'm that much of a monster that I planned on all of this? That I would try to come between you and your sister?"

"Enlighten me then, Harry," Daisy bellows, her voice hitching in her throat. "If you're so certain that TEA is your discovery, why tag along with me after all these years?" she demands, the genuine question peeking through the argument like a ray of hope to a conclusion.

"Do you want me to tell you again?" Harrison roars through clenched teeth, again gripping the edge of the granite in hopes of breaking off a slab to throw at Daisy. "Are you really *this* obsessed with men pining after you?"

Kennedy screams yet again, releasing a reverberating "Is anyone there? Help me!" Both Harrison and Daisy turn with disgusted faces at another interruption, completely oblivious to the scene.

Daisy laughs back her answer, enthralled by the anger she is unraveling like a thread from inside Harrison. "So, which is it? You love me or you want to destroy me because you have this perpetual need to prove that you didn't steal TEA from me? I'm delighted to get deeper into that twisted mind of yours, Harry."

"You know the only power you've had throughout your pathetic career has been what I've let you keep," Harrison spits, his words like hot oil splattering across Daisy as only her eyes react to the comment.

"Then why is my fiancé hogtied in your torture chamber?" Daisy quickly shoots back into Harrison's equally bitter expression.

Breaking their commotion, Kennedy releases another gut wrenching wail that crashes through the kitchen and snaps the pair's attention toward the open door.

"Shut up!" Harrison and Daisy scream in unison, still amazed at the audacity of Kennedy for inconveniencing their evening. The sound from the basement stifles into only slight rustlings and murmurs as he continues an attempt to break free.

Turning back to Daisy, Harrison lifts both hands in a sign of defeat and shakes his head as if to say, "what's his deal?" but she is already there to flash an equally irritated expression.

Resuming their battle, Daisy digs further into Harrison in hopes of an answer that will satisfy her insatiable hunger. "So, which is it?" her voice more composed now, but still teetering with fury.

"What do you mean?" Harrison asks as he begins to cave into the conclusion of the fight.

"Do you love me or do you love having power over me?" she asks, a matter-of-fact uptick in her voice. "What's the reason that I'm here?"

Harrison tongues his cheek as he mulls over the question, then says, "you know it's not that easy, Daisy." He knows his vague response isn't going to suffice.

"Well, then let's play this scenario out for you," Daisy commands. "Since we're already here, show me this *gift*," she says, the final word holding a strange texture as it rolls through the room.

"I—" Harrison begins, stunned by the request. "What?" he asks, unsure if he heard Daisy correctly.

"Show me what you were going to do to Kennedy," Daisy reiterates definitively.

Harrison turns his face slightly and purses his eyes.

"Are you sure?" he asks.

"Absolutely," Daisy agrees. "If you went through all this trouble, there must be some significance." The words ring with unease like an unfinished melody, waiting for the final chord to satisfy the tune.

A sliver of Harrison's tongue emerges as he presses the tip into his top lip in thought, surveying Daisy for a hint of her next move. *Is she bluffing?* He thinks to himself, sizing up her bet.

Breath forcefully rushes out of Daisy's nostrils as she impatiently crosses her arms. "Well?" she asks, laying her cards on the table.

Pulling his shoulders upright, Harrison outstretches a long arm toward the cellar door, welcoming Daisy to this evening's performance.

"Ladies first."

Chapter Eighteen: **Wicked Games**

The muffled slide of rope against rope hisses through the cellar as Harrison wraps a bowline knot around Kennedy's wrist. The graze of the twine creates a deafening roar in comparison to the hushed basement. Wrapping the rope across the thinnest portion of the wrist, Harrison then brings the loose end through the eye and around the existing tether to wrap again through the loop.

Daisy patiently sits across the narrow cellar watching Harrison prepare for the final show. The chair she occupies is identical to Kennedy's, however, free of years of bloodstains, the spice of the wood lingering in the air with a faint oak scent.

Harrison, donning his standard black tee and worn jeans, returns to the back corner of the room once the first knot is completed to pull the rope taught. He pulls against Kennedy's wrist, then against a fisheye hook above the seat, and then once more along the far end of the cellar where the remaining rope is tethered around one final hook. Harrison's precision and movements are of those of a fisherman preparing for the day's catch.

The eerie silence intensifies as Kennedy attempts to speak or scream, muffled by what is now two handkerchiefs choking against his mouth. Becoming wary that he may break free once again, Harrison added the additional gag in hopes of keeping his concentration in a solid state, as this the new set of eyes watching his every move has him jarred.

Daisy glides her tongue against her lips, feeling the moisture coat the parched surface as she exhales, the anxiety building in the pit of her stomach – the sour feeling after citrus or witnessing your fiancé murdered before your eyes. Kneading her glistening lips against each other in a fluid motion, she pops her lips causing a faint echo that breaks Harrison from his task momentarily and he shifts eyes in her direction.

Intertwining her fingers, Daisy places her clasped hands daintily atop her crossed legs. The warmth of her palms swelter compared to the frigid air, agitating her until she releases her fingers to set one hand upon the other. Her restlessness exudes by the second as she watches the scene unfold.

Once Harrison has suspended both of Kennedy's wrists, he produces a pocket knife from the back of his ripped jeans. Leaning over to release both ankles, he catches a glimpse of Daisy's stone face. Brushing his amber hair from his eyes, he regains his height. His demeanor hinting at his insecure state with only a feeble exhale to indicate his thoughts as he collects himself, Harrison cuts Kennedy free from the remaining binds to the chair.

Kennedy's rapidly beating heart and the hum of the single lightbulb hanging from the ceiling are the only sounds Daisy can hear. A moment passes as both Harrison and Daisy hold their composure, the stillness before the storm quieting a city in a beat of desperation.

A circle forms between Harrison's lips as he exhales slowly, balancing himself, before taking an assured step to the back of the cellar to wrap one rope skillfully around his wrist. He repeats the same action with the opposite rope. Another steadying breath rushes between his lips as he digs his fists into his shoulders to propel forward and lift Kennedy's arms above his head into a standing position until his feet only graze the floor by his toes. Kennedy's muffled screams reverberate off the walls, forcing Daisy to flinch at the sound.

Clearing his voice in a nervous tick, Harrison lightly kicks the wooden seat from behind Kennedy and into the far wall. Turning to face Daisy with a set of nearly black eyes, he pauses before asking, "are you ready?" His voice is gruff with uncertainty.

Daisy presses her lips into a hard line, and instead of showing her emotions by speaking, chooses to nod her head once in agreement as she quietly holds her breath. Her eyes flash briefly from Harrison to Kennedy, distraught and defeated. His muffled screams fade away as if they were mere whispers in the night.

"Okay," Harrison confirms, although the word falls on the cusp of a question. With minor hesitation, he lunges forward, his full weight of his right forearm and bicep colliding with Kennedy's chest as an immense wail tries to escape Kennedy's mouth. Returning to an upright position, Harrison turns over his shoulder to expose only one half of his face, waiting for Daisy's response. He shifts his weight, then moves one foot slightly to showcase his handy work for her approval.

The pocketknife that was once hidden Harrison's jeans now sits at a tidy ninety-degree angle, hanging from just below Kennedy's ribs as a dark pool of blood begins to seep through the fabric of his shirt. The circumference grows at a steady rate as both Harrison and Daisy hold their breath until she drops her shoulders as if to instruct, "continue."

Harrison grits his teeth as he prepares himself internally. He attempts to realign his demeanor, as he never thought he would make it this far into the evening. Gripping both hands to release their power and then sprawl each finger independently to test his senses, he makes his way to the far end of the cellar toward the shelves of metal bins. Tugging softly at a wire handle, a scrape against the wood brings Harrison back into reality. A stillness rests momentarily after the clatter until he dips a hand inside to examine its contents. Instead of selecting an item and returning the bin, he scoops up the edges of the metal between his strong hands. His arms clench at the weight until he drops it to the floor with a crash near Daisy's seat, the sound shocking, although she only reacts with a mere jolt.

Harrison leans forward to submerse a hand into the bucket as Daisy leans her head toward the contents to peer inside. As Harrison selects a single chef's knife and returns to a standing position, Daisy's eyes trace row after row of cutlery filling the bin, nearly to the brim. Kitchen knives, steak knives, serrated blades, paring knives – dozens of blades glaring back at her with the polished shine of the light bulb against the cool metal.

Turning back toward Kennedy, an eruption of screams echo from beneath the fabric but do not hinder Harrison from his next move. Kennedy's eyes widen at the sight of the blade and he shakes, attempting to break free, visibly in pain from the initial attack, and clearly fearing what will happen next.

Skillfully, Harrison rests a heavy hand atop Kennedy's right shoulder to steady his next move. His eyes tracing slowly over Kennedy's abdomen, he reaches a hand upward to drag a forefinger from his collarbone and down until he meets the base of his sternum. The knife juts out of his clenched fist as he locates his next target.

A quick flip of Harrison's hand turns the blade inward to readjust his grip. The butt of the blade presses gently into Kennedy's chest, verifying the location. Harrison again flips the blade against his palm in a fluid motion to face the knife tip toward the spot, and with agile precision, he forces the blade through the fabric.

Tears stream down Kennedy's cheeks, mixing with the sweat against his brow as he faintly attempts a scream. His eyes dart through Daisy, pleading for her salvation, but her cool demeanor clenches as she sits by idly.

Jesus Christ, Daisy thinks to herself as she holds composure. She shifts her attention to Harrison, who takes a step back to admire his work. His hair starts to fray from his typical tousled look.

"How long have you been doing this?" Daisy asks, her voice not as sturdy as she hoped, but she ignores the intonation realizing that this is the least of her worries.

Taking a step forward to select another blade, Harrison does not turn to face Daisy. Dipping a bloodstained hand into the bucket, he selects a twelve-inch serrated bread knife.

"About seven years or so," he says, glancing upward for her reaction. "Maybe a bit longer."

Daisy chooses not to respond, absorbing the answer. Her mind reflects backward to when the first time would have been. She recounts her first few years at The Rose Institute as a carefree and cocky consultant, her vibrato and charisma so young and carefree that the memory tugs at her eyes with an almost smile.

Harrison then returns to a standing position and turns back toward Kennedy. Another howl gets lost in the background of the moment as the blade slowly slides between a pair of his ribs on his right side. A gurgle comes from Kennedy's throat with the excruciating pain of each divot of the blade.

Swallowing hard, Daisy asks another question.
"How do you get...them...down here?"

Her eyes linger on the new blade hanging from Kennedy with a smear of blood as the weight of the grip visibly tugs against his skin.

Harrison reaches a bloodied hand to his face, wiping a line of sweat from his jaw, the motion flecking blood across his neck until he wipes his palms along the front of his shirt.

"Sampson," he bluntly replies. "He typically uses a tranquilizer until he can get them into the chair."

Harrison selects a thin boning knife with a bright blue grip from the bin, pulling his other hand to the blade to press the pad of his thumb against the tip. A microscopic dot of blood pools at the wound and he lifts his thumb into his mouth, sucking the blood against his teeth.

"Some are so eager to be selected that they come willingly," he continues with an air of disgust.

Selected, Daisy repeats to herself internally, the ache of the word leaving her ill.

Harrison turns back to Kennedy and places a hand atop his navel. He then lifts his dress shirt, exposing his taught stomach, rising and falling in a heavy breath sprinkled with trails of blood. Pressing a thumb into his navel, he traces Kennedy's right side to locate the large intestine. The boning knife then replaces his thumb as Harrison slowly inserts it, lightly tugging the blade upward until he softly lands at the base of Kennedy's ribcage. Harrison's eyes shift to Kennedy's face to watch him wither in pain. The blood leaks from the wound, soaking his trousers, a spout of eerie red sap from a maple tree.

As Daisy watches Harrison's jaw clench with the motion, her mind continues to reel. "Who cleans up when you're done?"

Daisy's question breaks Harrison's concentration. Harrison releases the blade from his grip, the weight of the handle forcing another cry from Kennedy. Wiping his palms against his jeans, Harrison's eyes cascade from blade to blade to ensure he has hit the precise pain points and veins.

"Also Sampson," he says, his voice aloof as he focuses on the task before him. "He removes the bodies and hoses down the cellar. For messier jobs, he calls in a cleaning crew."

Daisy nods with understanding, her face still indecipherable as Harrison turns to her before selecting another blade.

"Do people know they are here?" she asks as he plucks a wide chopping knife. He stands before her, feeling an additional question on the cusp of her lips. "Or do they simply go missing?" she finishes, only a narrowed eye broadcasting her emotions.

Turning back to his prey, Harrison passes over the examination of Kennedy's body for a spot, but instead he simply drives the blade into his chest with a hefty grunt. His breathing ragged from the effort, he speaks directly into the knife's grip as he steadies himself.

"Most are listed as missing," he answers with a slight waver. "Some are being investigated by the New Orleans Police Department. Sampson makes those issues go away from time to time," Harrison says, swallowing hard as he acknowledges something he's hidden for quite some time.

Without waiting for another blade, Daisy presses on with her questioning.

"Do the police know about..." her voice trails off before she returns her line of sight to an already forgotten Kennedy. "All of this?"

Kennedy's eyes close as he slowly succumbs to the excruciating pain.

"Not at all," Harrison says with a saddened breath. He wipes his hands against each other in an attempt to clean them, then presses his lips into an anguished line. "Not one bit," he repeats before selecting another blade and hurriedly slamming his full body into Kennedy, leaving behind only a handle dangling from his kidney. The motion feels hurried and angry rather than the deliberate intent Daisy witnessed earlier.

"Does anyone else know?" she asks, breaking the moment with her even voice, not waiting for Harrison to regain his composure.

Harrison grips Kennedy at the waist, leaning forward to straighten out his back while he drops his face to floor in defeat. He rests his head on Kennedy's sternum, hearing his faint, remaining heartbeats.

"No," he responds as if he is finally beaten, his breathing now ragged and harsh, the moment visibly taxing.

Opening her lips to continue her impromptu questioning, Daisy pauses to drag and uneven breath.

"How do you choose them?" she asks, the question leaving a sour taste in the air.

The only reaction Harrison provides is his clenched fists that force a half-hearted scream out of Kennedy's throat.

"How did you choose Kennedy?" Daisy presses, knowing she does not want to hear the answer.

Harrison clears his throat as if to speak, but takes another audible breath before answering.

"I only choose people who deserve to be punished, who have gotten away with far too much," he says. The room is still as Harrison attempts to collect himself. His shoulders rise and fall in another jagged breath as Daisy's questions rise like venom through his veins.

"How did you choose Kennedy?" Daisy repeats, knowing she should not ask. The ring of his name hovers like stale cigarette smoke.

The silence that follows without an answer from Harrison is deafening, more intense than the screaming or the clattering of knives. The shift in the room grips Daisy's posture as she holds her breath. Only her eyes move as she examines Harrison. Her eyes periodically shift to Kennedy, but his limp body and quiet heartbeat indicates that he won't be alive much longer.

Still unwilling to provide an answer to the question, Harrison grips even tighter on to Kennedy's body like a lifeless buoy. Anger begins to seep from every pore of his body as he tells himself, *you should have just had Tom and Gary kill you.*

Ask, Daisy thinks to herself. *Just ask the question.* Parting her lips to speak and releasing a small breath, Daisy murmurs the question that has been gnawing at her since the last time she was in this room.

"Why do you do this?"

Harrison chews against his cheek, knowing he would have to answer this question at some point. His rehearsed words are monotonic and brut.

"I'm not the idol that the world has played me out to be," he says. His rushed tone builds as he stands upright to look Daisy in the eyes. "I'm not a man on a throne or a king of the people." He stretches out his hands before him in an exhausted gesture.

Daisy purses her eyes and tilts her head to one side. "Why do you do this?" she asks again, ignoring the answer.

Blood heats in Harrison's face in indignation.

"I don't want to be their *idol*," he nearly spits back into Daisy's face. The rise and fall of his shoulders are much more visible with his outrage as he expects her to understand. After all these years, she should understand the pain in his life.

The only response he receives is Daisy narrow eyes, miniature slivers pulling the truth from Harrison. Blowing a harsh puff through his nostrils, he turns toward the cellar shelving. Moving swiftly before her to crouch down to a bottom drawer, he continues his lie.

"I didn't choose to be in the spotlight – that's what people tend to forget. I simply put the..." But he stops mid-sentence, avoiding the word "discovery." Reaching into the drawer to remove an oversized object, he stands and turns to face Daisy. His voice more composed, he says, "I was thrown into this life. I was happy to spend my days plugging away in a lab and living my mediocre life." His hurried words expose his anxiety as he nears his breaking point.

Daisy watches Harrison walk toward her with a strange eagerness. His body tense and shaking at every move, she gets a glimpse into a world that she may very well be the only person to witness. Her eyes soften as she accesses his features: his deep eyes and sharp jaw; the splattering of blood and disheveled, amber hair that trails along his temples. She wanted to understand her friend. Maybe even her oldest friend. Her heart pleads to let him in, but the blockade that stood between them was so much more than Kennedy's now lifeless body.

Harrison watches Daisy, her earnest gaze focused on him. Yet again, he waits for her approval. He holds his stance as her eyes trace his face, then to the streaks of blood and sweat that line his hair, his clothes, his hands, the cellar floor. The mix of dread and misery hangs in the air like a plume of smoke, choking the air from their lungs in hopes of survival.

The sight of the gun finally shakes Daisy from her trance. The gray metal is splattered with traces of old, dried blood, blood belonging to those she would never know. The trigger gleams in the yellow light as its soft silver hue bursts through the room like a beacon in the night.

The metal rattles with Harrison's shaking hand as he cocks the gun, silently praying for Daisy to stop him. *Open your fucking mouth and tell me what to do*, he thinks to himself, completely lost in the unplanned moment. He senses his temples beating with each pound of his heart until he finally snaps.

"Say something, Daisy!" he shouts so forcefully that Kennedy jolts with life, only to droop yet again at his own weight.

Daisy's tongue sits atop her front teeth, contemplating her next words before breathing out her initial question.

"Why do you do this?" she asks, almost in a whisper, although her eyes are wide and shouting for the truth.

Without an answer, Harrison pulls the gun from where it hangs against his thigh and up toward Kennedy's lifeless face. His unblinking eyes glare through Daisy as he parts and then closes his lips. He presses them into a hard line to stop them from shaking and pulls the trigger. Kennedy's skull jolts backward, hanging limp along his shoulders, the blood spattering the cinderblock walls in a mosaic of blood, bone, and skin. The wound seeps crimson from what remains of his skull.

Daisy closes her eyes to avoid the sight of Kennedy's mangled face as he is finally put out of his misery. The noise of the gunshot pierces her, and her chest tightens. A harsh swallow drives through her throat as the sadness burns in her ears until she releases the pain through her pale, cracked lips.

Harrison drops the gun to the floor and Daisy can't help but stare at it, allowing her mind to shift elsewhere. She thinks back to their fight the night that she stole Kennedy's company and a punch of agony fills her lungs at the thought of her sealing his fate.

Taking a step toward Daisy, Harrison moves in hope of a reaction, but her face is lifeless. He takes another hesitant step until he stands before her, his voice shaking her back to reality.

"Daisy?" he asks with a meek voice. "Are you okay?"

His voice bitterly rings in her ears. The black pupils of Daisy's eyes are the only response Harrison receives as they dart to his face, her deposition a ghastly bleakness as she feels herself turning inward. Her lungs release a burning breath through her nostrils as Harrison drops to his knees before her, her legs still crossed, drawing her attention at the ache in her muscles.

"Please say something," Harrison pleads with wild eyes. "Anything," he tacks on in hopes of a response. Daisy merely stares into his face as he reaches his two bloodied hands to lay atop her own. The blood is sticky to the touch and leaches through her fingers then into her lap.

The talons of Harrison Bishop had dug as far as they go into Daisy's life. Still maintaining her perplexed composure, she looks deep into his eyes in search of answers, but still, even after nearly a decade, she comes up short. She moves both of her hands from his grasp, sliding her fingers in the palms of each of his hands. The blood paints her fingers and wrists and stains her lap with the crimson life of what used to be Kennedy.

In this moment, Daisy gives into the realization that she is no better than Harrison. He may physically kill, but she had taken countless men's lives in the wake of her career. Her eyes pricked at the thought and she parted her lips to speak as Harrison's eyes flittered to life in the hope of hearing her sweet voice.

A moment passes as Daisy comes up short. The words she wishes she could speak are not the words that need to be said, so instead, she delivers a dazed, "are we done here?"

The words slap Harrison in surprise.

"Y-yeah," Harrison squeaks, stunned by the question. He releases her hands and sits back on his heels. "Sampson is upstairs. He can get you a fresh set of clothes and take you home," he answers with a defeated sigh.

Daisy stands, pushing her seat backward with the back of her knees, her height now towering over Harrison as he sits, still pleading for her approval. Effortlessly sidestepping him, she walks forward to lay a light hand against Kennedy's heart. Her face is somber with a touch of agony.

"This thing," Daisy finally speaks with a hushed whisper. "These are quite the wicked games we're playing, Harrison," she finishes with a defiant voice. Turning over her shoulder, not removing her hand from Kennedy's chest, Daisy looks into Harrison's eyes with an unforgiving glance. He shifts his eyes away, the pain of her words like fire against his ears.

As Daisy exits the cellar, making her way back upstairs, Harrison holds his stance. Taking his time to rise, he allows his eyes to trace the cellar walls. He looks at the splatter of blood and bone across the wall. The knives still hang limply from Kennedy's body. This is the mess he had created in his life.

Chapter Nineteen: **Ever Since New York**

The chandelier in Harrison's dining room is obnoxious, to put it politely. The gaudy structure is comprised of tendrils dripping elongated crystals in every direction. The intricate webbing of lights and wiring funnels into the primary focus of the nearly softball-sized crystal enveloped in its center like an oversized pearl. He sits at the end of his twenty-four-seat chestnut dining room table, which is accented with an ornate border of deep walnut that mimics the chandelier's twisting talons. The walls, hand-painted with coils and flutterings of gold against navy seeps of gaudy wealth, engulfing the room in a rich swaddle of nonsense.

The over-the-top lightening casts on to the tabletop, surrounded by intricate decorations. Harrison despised everything about this room. The way it showcased his wealth. The way he never felt at ease when sitting at the bulky table. Most importantly, the way he hadn't selected a single item. He had hired an interior decorator when he purchased the home and the man appeared in a whirlwind, demanding he purchase every extravagant monstrosity under the sun.

Drinking whiskey from a smudged rocks glass, Harrison spins the tumbler along its rim in hopes of destroying the lavish wood's surface. His face still smattered with remnants of Kennedy, he looks up into the chandelier and cocks his head as he imagines the light fixture swinging like a giant pendulum. Swaying the full length of the dining room table as if the estate was rocking on its heels until the wiring snapped and rocketed toward him, destroying him a single blow. His mind continues to wander as he envisions his own death. The paramedics attempting to revive him. Sampson giving his statement. The eulogy read by, well, no one. Not a single person would come forward to claim his body and he'd rot atop the embalming table. His eyes perked at the idea of himself decaying in the soil.

Instead, the chandelier stands perfectly still, mocking Harrison until he glares through the wire and crystal structure like an angry child.

"Fucking chandelier," he mutters under his breath in an irritated growl.

"What did the chandelier ever do to you?" Sampson asks smoothly from the main entrance of the dining room. The blinding light of the room washes out his features as Harrison remembers that he has not bothered to turn on any additional lights. After leaving the cellar, he plucked a bottle of whiskey from the bar cart, picked up a glass, and stormed into the one room guaranteed to make him hate what he had become. He was a gaudy fragment of a man, now covered with the traces of his mistakes.

"I want to smash it to the ground with a baseball bat," Harrison responds before downing the remainder of his drink in a single gulp. Reaching out to the bottle of whiskey to refill his glass, he returns his empty eyes to Sampson. "I'll let you take the first swing if you'd like," he says, the joke not registering on either of their faces.

Taking a step inside the dining room, Sampson is flooded with light. He is donning his typical sports coat and trousers as Harrison takes the time to admire his dear friend – his salt and pepper hair and the deep-set bags under his eyes, the way he always reminded him of a sitcom father, ready to reprimand his children and then sneak them dessert when their mother wasn't looking.

A dry laugh is all that Sampson can muster, his most sincere form of bonding.

"Even if we turned that glass atrocity into dust, there would be another in its place by the end of the week," he says, the certainty in his voice burning in Harrison's ears. Taking an additional step forward, he stands behind a high-backed dining chair and grips the elegant wood by its shoulders. "I'd ask how you're doing, but that appears to be a loaded question."

Harrison acknowledges the statement with a gentle shift of his eyes.

"Loaded indeed," he murmurs before downing another glass with a gulp. "Did I ever tell you the story about why I brought you on, Sampson?" Harrison asks, his tone unnerving and strange, even for Sampson.

"I remember you having a..." Sampson answers as he searches for a polite term. "a tussle with a man."

Raising a humorous set of brows, Harrison nods in agreement.

"When Bishop Enterprises first started to gain traction in the industry, my publicist Jordan booked me a thirty-six-city worldwide promotional tour by the decision of the newly appointed board members," Harrison says. Reaching for the bottle of whiskey, he pauses, then pours himself another glass. "They told me point blank that my position as president was merely a title and a way to put someone young and vibrant before the public in hopes of drafting a new generation of employees – but, more importantly, investors. Basically, to look and sound pretty before the cameras."

"Children should not be seen or heard unless spoken to," Sampson comments in his paternal purr. "My father used to tell us that during holidays when he wanted us kids to put on a good face and pretend our family was picture perfect."

"Precisely," Harrison agrees before taking a subdued sip of his drink. He relaxes, grateful to have Sampson's composure to ease him. "They sat me down and gave me speech after speech and approved comments and what to wear and who I could to talk to and what to do with my hands if I was interviewed. I felt like an astronaut adrift in space. I could see the shuttle of humanity floating nearby, but the crew wouldn't pull in my tether. Hell, I still use the prepared statements like my life is one long script."

Sampson grips the seat back as he considers sitting. He had seen Harrison in a multitude of bizarre scenarios before, but vulnerable was one on his list that was foreign. Instead, he shifts his weight slightly and acknowledges the metaphor.

A wry laugh croaks deep within Harrison's throat.

"I remember when they unveiled the Cure All Kid poster and I was so excited to have my name written out for the world to see. I felt like a rock star." A disheartened smile tugs at his eyes, but his stare remains somber. "Jordan had slapped me on the back and told me, 'kid, you're going to make us a fucking fortune with those dimples,' like I was a prized pig at a fair." Still rolling his glass along the rim, Harrison marinates in the moment before taking another sip and returns his eyes to Sampson. "The night that the 'tussle' occurred, I was on stop thirty-one of the tour and the entire charade was beginning to weigh on me. I remember being completely giddy visiting New York City for the first time in my life. I had seen pictures in magazines, but they don't do the city justice," he says. His words are a warm blanket of sincerity that slowly drained from his eyes. "But all I was allowed to think about were the buzzword speeches. The disingenuous investors. The interviews scripted to sound 'casual.' I could feel myself spiraling minute by minute when all I wanted was to enjoy that moment in time."

Feeling the shift in Harrison's tone, Sampson tugs at the seat back with a muted scuff and sits lightly in the chair.

"Go on," he instructs as Harrison stares blankly into his eyes.

"Jordan had promised some Russian shareholder that I would be opening a new research facility in St. Petersburg once we began opening locations internationally, but this guy was so outraged by the fact that we would make him wait. He nearly spat at me when he told me, 'I spend your annual revenue for your little Bishop Enterprises three times a week,'" says Harrison, attempting a Russian accent. "So, I repeat note card number 102: 'My sincerest apologies for the inconvenience. This disruption to our roadmap will personally be my top priority moving forward to see that we can continue our business venture.'" His stage voice sings in full, mocking vibrato.

Sampson's lips press into a harsh line as Harrison's words land heavily against his shoulders. The picture of the young Harrison he met was like a son to him and it saddened him to imagine the pain he endured before he came along.

"I had asked the conference members if we could take a few days off. Maybe even go home and rest for a week, just to recover before the remainder of the tour. But they insisted we press on because we had created such a buzz in the industry." Harrison progressed as the words hung on his lips like anchors. "But it wasn't about me or TEA or helping people at that point. It was about the investments that we brought in and the money at stake. I was a cartoon character to them and I kept telling them, 'I need a change of pace for just one day,' but they didn't care."

Taking another sip, Harrison balloons his cheeks as he releases a gust from his lungs. "I could feel myself unraveling at the seams. So, one night I walked out the back of the banquet hall and into an alleyway behind the building to smoke a cigarette. I remember being able to see a glimpse of Central Park from between the brick walls and I imagined just running away. Sprinting down the street and running as fast as my legs would take me. But instead I stayed in the alley and smoked my lonely cigarette for a few minutes of sanity." A genuine smile glints across his eyes momentarily. "Jordan always hated that I smoked. She thought it gave the impression that I couldn't be trusted. I thought it just further proved the point that TEA was working."

Harrison dips his chin and stares into his drink, pausing before his next sentence. "This guy is dropping a couple of garbage bags into a nearby dumpster and asks to bum a cigarette. As I'm lighting it, he recognizes me and flips out. He asks why I'm here and if he can take a picture, yadda, yadda, yadda." Now rushing his words, he can feel the heat rising in his esophagus, a memory he wished to forget. "He was telling me how TEA had cured him of his pneumonia and all he wanted to do was thank me. He kept throwing himself at me for a hug and asking to take pictures. I—"

He coughs, stopping himself short to choke a lump of air into his desperate lungs.

"I just snapped."

Finally raising his eyes to meet Sampson's, Harrison looks into his dear friend's face and concedes to his dark past. "I kept telling him that I was still a person and I wasn't any different, but he didn't care. He kept coming at me and thanking me until it just snowballed. I wasn't Harrison any longer. I had become *the* Harrison Bishop. I was barely human. Just a name and a face and an oversized dollar sign."

His lips part as if to continue but he waits for Sampson's approval. Gently closing his eyes to nod, Sampson gives him the go-ahead and Harrison resumes.

"I pushed him, thinking he would get scared off, but he was almost happy?" he says, the words coming out as a question. "His face exuded complete ecstasy and it sent me across the edge. I lunged at him, grabbing him by the throat, and I pressed and pressed until there was nothing but a limp shell of a man between my fingers. It felt so good to finally have control to – I don't know – release the anger and aggression and emotions that had dug their way so deeply into my life that all I could do was explode. And now, ever since New York, I've been haunted by the ghost of the life I could have lived." His words soften to a slowed whisper. "It is my *only* source of control."

The air settles as Harrison releases a definitive breath. Staring through his glass he imagines drinking the entire bottle in a single gulp. The weight of the chandelier impaling him with a blow to the face. A meteor landing directly on top of the dining room and crushing him through the soil of the earth. But none of this happens. The two men sit quietly and let the story marinate.

Sampson exhales as he stands to rise from his seat. Calmly, he strides out of the dining room, leaving Harrison painted with confusion. The thuds of his shoes echo in the cavernous silence. Harrison sits back in his seat, unsure if he will return.

Sampson arrives in the same condition he exited, this time a clean rocks glass in his hand. Returning to his seat, he slides the glass toward Harrison in a smooth motion.

"If we're going to share our first kills, you might as well not drink alone."

This is the longest sentence Harrison had heard from Sampson in nearly a decade. He quickly masks the shock on his face as he pours his friend a drink and then tops off his own with the brown elixir.

Sampson takes a sturdy breath. His shoulders lift with a stern intent before taking a sip.

"During the Gulf War, I was a soldier within the 101st Airborne Division. We were a highly specialized Army division charged with combat air assaults in Iraq," he says, his eyes glazing over as his mind strays. Shaking his head briefly, he takes another sip and continues. "We were under the impression that it was to a be a quick in-and-out, then we'd return to base and wait for further instructions. We cut off the supply route between the Iraqi and Basra forces and an all-out battle broke out. We went wild in the streets, in a rush of pure chaos. After four days of combat, we retained hundreds, if not thousands, of prisoners," he says. Raising his drink, he takes a hearty gulp and looks harshly into Harrison's eyes. "We lost sixteen men that day. A simple task that should have lasted one day nearly bled us dry in the sand." His face is a stone fixture as he opens up further. "I had gotten word that my buddy Sammy had been wounded in battle and went to the infirmary to visit him. He was tied up with tubes and a breathing contraption and I could see his heart withering away on the monitor. Just a pathetic sputter of life that beeped over and over until my body could barely handle the sound. He could hardly speak, but he managed to get out the words 'end it' beneath the bandages."

Stopping short, Sampson shifts his weight in his seat and returns his focus toward the room, the ostentatious room that somehow made both men feel so small. "He couldn't handle the pain and the life he would go on to live if he even made it back in one piece," Sampson says. He takes another pause before he nods his head in affirmation. "I had to help him. He was suffering beyond imagination and for what?" The sudden uptick in his tone surprises Harrison. "For a battle where he was only a mere pawn? The worst of it was I had to see his picture plastered throughout town like a goddamn martyr to their cause, but I knew the truth. We were played like an expendable force and Sammy was nothing more than a worthless chess piece."

Harrison opens his mouth to speak but decides against the intrusive response, closing his lips sternly.

"What I'm saying is," Sampson begins to conclude as he turns toward Harrison with a surprisingly positive expression. "Some of the roles we play in our lives are not our first choice." His voice is sincere and full of intention. "But that doesn't mean we cannot succeed from the hands we are dealt."

"What about those of us who play our hands poorly?" Harrison asks with an air of humor.

"Even a pair of twos can win at poker," Sampson responds, mimicking his banter.

A warm smile returns to Harrison's face as he rolls Sampson's words around in his mind like marbles, the realization that although his actions are not justified, at least someone in this world understands his misery.

"I'm assuming all of this," Sampson breaks the silence, tipping his glass toward the Jackson Pollock across Harrison's face, "is because of Miss Stone?"

Harrison allows the hurt acceptance to wash over him.

"Afraid so, but it was long overdue. Our history and chemistry – it's..."

Harrison stops himself short, musing his next word.

"Complicated?" Sampson finishes with a soft laugh.

"To put it lightly," Harrison says with an equal laugh. "It was bound to fail, and I think I'm finally accepting that. She was the last bridge I had to burn and I threw gasoline into the flames."

"Give it time," Sampson suggests with his fatherly tone. "You'd be surprised how time has a way of putting perspective on a situation."

The men sit again in their silent moment as they ruminate in the first serious conversation they may have ever had. A hard swallow fills Harrison's throat as he finally speaks.

"You may not know this, but when I was younger, two of my foster brothers used to beat me up pretty badly," Harrison says, his eyes pricking as he turns to face Sampson. "They loved to torture all of us, but they were especially fond of bludgeoning me until they knocked me out or sent me to the emergency room. One of them was particularly fond of choking me and slamming my head into our cement driveway," he says, lifting his bloodied hands to his neck with a timid pantomime. He pauses again as his hands land against his throat before drifting down his chest. "I've been thinking back on those memories quite often lately," he confesses as a lump forms in his throat. "The weight of Tom suffocating the life from me was truly terrifying, and at times, when I feel like I've lost all control, my mind will almost transport me back to that moment. I can feel my soul being squeezed out of me by his massive hands, and even though I've become this horrendous man, I can still pull this frightening emotion from the pit of my stomach. It almost – I don't know – comforts me?" he says, dragging a heavy breath. Then he finally admits, "something so gruesome can somehow make me feel so human."

Sampson furrows his brow in thought, sighing and then asking, "as if you can feel the life in your veins when you know it shouldn't be there?" A knowing look in his eyes flashes briefly to Harrison in reassuring sympathy.

"Like walking away from a car crash that you know you shouldn't have survived," Harrison says, stifling an inappropriate chuckle. Harrison presses his legs against the chair, slowly rising.

"Thank you for this, Sampson. It's nice to finally have someone who..."

He pauses as the word "understands" lands uneasy in his mind. *Comprehends? Appreciates?* Harrison weighs in his mind.

Sampson lifts his drink with no intentions of leaving.

"Say no more," he acknowledges before taking a sip. "It can be nice to just have someone."

Harrison stands at the foot of his bed, still donning his blood-spattered ensemble. His arms are crossed as he intently views the vast painting above his headboard. Two opposing styles of artwork, one of lightness and one of dark, colliding together in a disarray of colors and textures.

"It's a bit heavy-handed," Harrison says to himself.

Propping up one foot along the comforter, he continues to contemplate against the painting with a newly found eye. Forcing his weight into the ball of his foot, he lifts his body to now stand atop the bed in line with the painting.

"I fucking hate it," he mutters.

Taking a few shaky steps along his fabric walkway, he reaches to grasp the heavy frame at the base of the painting. Then, leaning into the wall, he lifts the structure until he hears the soft *clink* of the frame's hook releasing the nail. Holding his composure, he steadies himself before releasing his fingers as the painting comes crashing to the floor beneath the headboard.

Harrison returns his gaze to the wall, admiring the blank space. A smile jerks at his lips and digs his dimples into his cheeks. The fresh slate he had been looking for all these years was finally before him.

Jumping from the bed and onto the floor, Harrison releases a satisfied breath as he makes his final decision.

"One last kill," he tells himself. "One grand finale and I'll leave this world behind for a fresh start," he says.

Reaching for the bedside lamp, Harrison pauses momentarily, looking at the blank wall.

"A blank wall," he comments to himself. "Still a bit obvious."

Chapter Twenty: **Hello**

The streets are slick as the evening rain ceases. An oil spill creeps through the city while its dampness clings to the air as Daisy opens her window in the backseat of a dingy cab. Her softly curled hair begins to billow, framing her face in the breeze, and her eyes fall into a placid happiness when faint droplets splatter against her skin. Streetlights flicker to life as the cab glides across the city, and waves of people filter into the streets in celebration of New Year's Eve.

Typically, Daisy would jump at the opportunity to drunkenly roam through the city with her girlfriends, but tonight she could feel her neck flush with heat at the idea of forcing a smile while making small talk. Nearly a month had passed since her showdown with Harrison, and her skin pricked with every flash of Kennedy's withering face.

"Please roll up the window, Miss," the driver says to Daisy without turning to face her. His eyes linger in the rearview mirror with an unamused stare. Her oversized, emerald studs flash a piercing green light against the mirror and force a cringe from his eyes.

Pursing her lips and holding back an eye roll, Daisy does as she is told and presses the button to close the glass. She presses her face on to the cold window in hopes of soaking up one last bit of evening rain across her cheeks.

Adjusting the long sleeves of her favorite floor length black dress, Daisy rolls back her shoulders and prepares to put on a happy face. *It is sad about Kennedy*, she rehearses in her mind. *We just were going our separate ways. It's tough right now, but I have my career to keep me grounded.* The lie was almost real enough that she believed it herself.

Her mind felt adrift as she thought of the wave of lies she had built up around her life beginning to sway. The house of cards that built up the aura of Daisy Stone was so intricate that she had forgotten what she had actually become underneath her manmade shell. *He had told me he wasn't happy with where we were going, that he wasn't ready to settle down just yet. He needed to explore his full potential and I couldn't stand in his way.* Each lie settled atop another neatly folded card.

Daisy leans her head back into the worn leather and allows her eyes to glaze over as she envisions a world outside of her own. A universe where she had allowed herself to tear down her facade and be with someone who truly loved her. A man of innocence, free of her lifestyle – Taylor Pierce, perhaps. He had always had a genuine fondness for Daisy that was remarkably pure and earnest.

As her mind wanders further, she imagines a suburban home with a three-car garage and a basketball hoop in the driveway. She arrives home from her job as a nurse or a teacher and is greeted by Taylor in the driveway, his clear blue eyes closing before her own as he plants an eager kiss against her cheek. Their children scurry in circles around their ankles as they hold each other in a tender embrace. His strong hands grasp her waist and he brushes a lock of her mousy hair from her face with a slim finger.

As Daisy presses her cheek into Taylor's palm, she forces her eyes into a harsh line with a wince of pain. Taylor chokes a muffled cough against her hair as Daisy stands her ground, her weight against his narrow chest. Coughing again, a gurgle of blood overflows from his mouth, spilling down his chin, the oozing red turning a sickly black in the bleaching sun.

"I'm sorry," Daisy whispers as she deliberately pulls a long, serrated blade from Taylor's abdomen, the teeth of the knife shining an eerie onyx. "Just one more," she calmly insists before sliding the blade just above the previous wound.

"Looks like we're a bit backed up on the Ten," the cab driver abruptly announces as Daisy's eyes dart from her daydream. "I'll see if I can find a shorter route if you'd like," he says, his burly face not turning to meet her own.

"I'm in no rush," Daisy says coolly. "Whatever is easiest for you."

Daisy opens her purse, reaching into its contents to pull out a gold compact. She momentarily examines her complexion before pausing to practice her sad but composed pout. Watching her features frown but lift at the edges, she closes the compact and drops it back into the bag before dropping her elbow into the car door to prop her chin atop her palm.

Daisy replays the scenario in her mind, swapping out Taylor's thin frame and baby blues for Harrison's charismatic eyes and sharp jaw. His dimples dip when she walks toward him, her arms opened for an embrace while the harsh daylight blinds her in the reverie's haze. Instead of children, Lily follows behind him angelically. Her blue eyes flutter as her bright hair billows in the light. When Daisy steps forward, bypassing Harrison, she is unexpectedly stunned as Lily shoves a similar serrated knife into her stomach, the full blade pressing its weight into her like a baton through a door. Her sweet face remains stoic in her fantasy.

"Who would act so crude to Elton John?" she says, the intonation unnerving.

Daisy's eyes burn from the continued loss of focus and she blinks heavily to wet her fuzzy eyes. The sting of the cab's musky air leaves a film across her line of sight as she shakes away the strange thoughts as they linger with a sour taste in the pit of her stomach before her mind returns to the physical world around her.

$$>>>$$

Molly glides a cherry red tube of lipstick across her lips, smacking them together in the process. Dabbing the center of her lips with the soft pad of her ring finger, still grasping the tube between her thumb and forefinger, she looks over Daisy's ensemble while lackadaisically leaning into a festively decorated bar.

"You're like a hot widow who's looking to do more than mourn at the wake," she says, her words lascivious, momentarily pulling Daisy from her brooding funk. "I love it," she finishes with a playful wink.

Amber holds three drinks between her haphazard fingers. Her nails painted an obnoxious shade of gold glitter and Daisy feigns a fit of blindness as she approaches.

"Amber, your nails are atrocious," she jokingly calls before plucking a drink from her hands.

"Figured I'd do a little peacocking this evening," Amber responds as she waves her hand. "You look killer, though," she compliments Daisy in return, her word choice ringing in Daisy's ears like a dog whistle.

"Well, thank you. Figured I'd do a little peacocking of my own," Daisy answers with a wiggle of her hips. She told herself that if she could not be her vibrant self, she would dress the part and wait for the rest of her to catch up.

Slamming her champagne in a single swallow, Molly turns to Daisy to cut the fat from the conversation.

"Okay, now that we're done with the bullshit, how are you actually doing?" she asks, her voice a motherly croon.

"Not great. It's been hard without Kennedy these last few weeks," Daisy says, the honesty in her voice holding her lie in place.

"Has he called at all?" Amber asks as she hands her drink over to Daisy. "Drink up," she instructs before twirling a glittering finger in a circular motion toward a nearby bartender, signaling another round.

A smirk of gratitude tugs at Daisy's face in appreciation of her friends' solidarity.

"He hasn't. I've wanted to so many times, but I don't know how to reach him," Daisy says, her words continuing to seep into her playing cards as she metaphorically sets another one atop the pile.

Amber grasps Daisy's bicep with a squeeze of comfort, as if she is checking fruit for ripeness.

"We're obviously here if you need anything. Boys, booze, or shopping, you tell us your vice and we are there," she says, her words defiant and exactly what Daisy wanted to hear. "But right now, I need to find that bartender because I need a drink." Amber's voice trails off as her eyes scan the bar, leaving Daisy with her full drink.

"Do you want me to get mind-bogglingly drunk and sign us up for karaoke?" Molly inquires, her not-so-subtle pry at a joke.

Daisy immediately drops her friendly facade and turns a suspicious face to Molly, apprehension flooding her face.

"I just feel off, that's all. Like I've dropped a hundred pounds in a single day and I'm not used to my new body."

"Well, let's open the flood gates a bit," Molly encourages. "I know this probably isn't the right place, but it's only ten o'clock and there will be crying girls all over the place soon enough. You're pretty much covered for the next few hours if you want to let it all out," says Molly. This was Molly's forte – pulling the raw emotion from any conversation is what people loved about her.

A moment popped into Daisy's mind as she remembered Molly arriving at a black tie event in the early years of their friendship. She had arrived in a pair of flats, blue jeans, and a leather jacket. Any other person would have been utterly mortified, but Molly merely convinced a nearby set of party-goers to loosen their ties and kick off their heels. The warm memory pierced Daisy's eyes and curled her lips into a smile.

"I'm just," Daisy begins, but cuts herself short. Her tongue delicately balances against her top lip as she carefully selects her words. "I'm not quite sure what I'm doing here."

The ambiguity in Daisy's comment leaves Molly to turn her head in thought.

"Here?" she asks, looking through the bar. "This place has a great martini, but if you're not up to going out tonight we can all go somewhere else. Or home if you'd like?" she suggests, her hurried pace causing anxiety to build in Daisy's throat.

"No, with my life, I guess," Daisy says. "I know that sounds so high school, but I've been stewing about everything in my life over the past weeks and I'm just…"

"Lost?" Molly finishes with an inquisitive tone.

"Exactly. Kennedy and I didn't work out. Harry and I aren't speaking. Taylor has been—"

"Wait, Taylor? As in Taylor *Pierce*?" Molly asks, her eyes mere slivers in a judgmental stare.

Gnawing at her cheek, Daisy attempts to brush off the interrogation.

"I was just thinking about him on the ride over. He was always so sweet to me and after everything the last couple of months, having someone who genuinely loved me felt..." Daisy's words trail off, but Molly's unapproving scoff speaks for her.

"Okay, I get it. Obviously, that's probably not a great path to explore," Daisy says, caving as she polishes off one of her drinks. "It was just a thought."

Crossing a pair of slinky arms before her, Molly merely raises a knowing brow before taking a noisy sip of her drink. Her face turns into a subjective grin.

Amber arrives with another round of drinks, breaking the silent duel between Daisy and Molly.

"What did I miss?" she asks, reading the strange vibe between the two.

Molly is a statuesque force as she reaches a sinuous arm toward Amber to snatch a drink from her grasp.

"Daisy has been thinking about giving Taylor Pierce a call," says Molly, her intonation biting his name like a carrot snapped between her molars.

Handing a drink to Daisy, Amber squints in confusion.

"Didn't you buy him out and then demote him to regional sales manager or something?" she laughs back with a dry cackle that doesn't reach Daisy's face.

Turning a sour glare to Amber, Daisy sneers in annoyance, saying, "he was generously compensated for his work with the transition of HBH Discoveries."

A singular cough of a laugh erupts from Molly's throat.

"Don't give us that M and A bullshit, Daisy. We know you better than this." Molly's words are stern with a friendly note that chimes against Daisy's ears.

"What do you want me to say, Mol?" Daisy spouts. "You knew I always liked him, even when I first moved here, but business is business." Daisy's voice is aggressive and her blood is simmering.

"To be completely honest," Amber chimes in with an unsolicited opinion, "I thought you always *liked* Harrison, so," her casual tone destroying Daisy's reasoning.

"What the fuck does Harry have to do with this?" Daisy snaps.

Holding a hand up to pause the potential scuffle, Molly jumps to Amber's side and says, "what I think she's implying is that you tend to *like* guys but you typically don't act on the emotion." The uptick in Molly's voice attempts to spin the conversation. "You tend to put business before pleasure," she says, the maternal tone returning to her voice and throbbing in Daisy's ears.

Daisy opens her mouth to speak but the words are lodged in the pit of her throat. Snapping her teeth closed, she looks around in hopes of her next words resembling an actor calling for a line. Releasing a sigh acknowledging their honesty, Daisy droops her shoulders in defeat.

"So, what are you saying? I should have never taken this job and just stayed at home and played house?" she asks. A singular card topples from the pile with a breath of wind.

Mimicking Daisy's stance, Amber drops her defense and says, "of course not. I guess I'm just suggesting you work on separating your personal and professional lives."

Sensing the sadness creep through Daisy, Molly chimes in with a softer tone.

"Look at how you and Harrison turned out. You two never could separate your feelings from your work and it got – well – messy."

"I don't really think that was your fault though," Amber adds as she turns a half-closed eye to Daisy. "Harrison just as bad as you are when it comes to separating life from work."

"Taylor was more cut and dry," Molly agrees as she turns to Amber, cutting Daisy off from her own conversation. "He drew a deep line in the sand between the two."

Daisy feigns a cough for attention. "I'm right here," she says.

"Sorry, your love life is interesting," Molly says through her pearly white teeth. "You're really playing both sides of the coin. You should have your own reality show," she says, her sarcasm reigning the conversation.

"My brain hurts. Could we just make a Venn diagram and bring a visual to the discussion?" Amber jokingly suggests.

Daisy's face turns sour as their jokes permeates.

"I don't want to be known for my interesting love life," Daisy says, rolling her eyes and sipping a hefty swallow from her glass. Daisy turns to examine the bar, realizing the place is nearly packed. Her eyes land on a familiar blonde woman slinked around the back of a taller man. "Do we know her?" Daisy asks of the pair without turning back to the conversation.

"Oh my God, is that Duncan?" Molly squeals as a nearby couple turns to laugh at the outburst. Ducking her head in embarrassment, she continues. "I think that's Olivia! Duncan brought her to Harrison's party. I nearly drank the bar out of vodka with her."

Amber steps forward to see the scene for herself, as if viewing an ancient artifact with her own eyes.

"No way. That party was more than a month ago," she says as Duncan grips the blonde in a full embrace and plants a quick kiss against her cheek. "Whoa, you're right," Amber concedes.

"They look…" Daisy begins as she sets her weight into her hip, watching Duncan with a surprised expression.

"Happy," Molly says, finishing with an inquisitive deviation. "I mean, I knew she was cool when I was with her, but I didn't think she was cool enough to settle him down for a couple of weeks." Molly laughs with a trace of amazement.

The group settles for a moment as they watch the couple's poorly hidden love, another quick peck on the cheek followed by a cute nudge of embarrassment at the public affection. Olivia taps Duncan playfully on the bum and he squeezes her around the shoulder before planting his lips on her forehead.

"He deserves it," Amber says, as a sly smile fills her face.

"Maybe now he'll be bearable during meetings," Molly snidely adds as she nudges Amber in the elbow.

"This isn't heaven," Amber teases.

Disconnected from the world around her, Daisy continues to watch the couple's veiled romance. The sparkle in Duncan's eyes illuminates every time Olivia touches him. She grips his suit jacket as she leans forward in a full laugh, her opposite hand covering her gaping mouth.

The jagged feeling stirring in Daisy's stomach causes her to loop one arm across her torso, holding her in place. Her scalp prickles and the emptiness that she had ignored for weeks screamed from deep within her lungs. Attempting to pinpoint the enveloping emotion, she allows the image of Harrison leaning into Kennedy's lifeless body to replay in her mind. The only image that pulled a resembling emotion. The mix of drinking orange juice after brushing your teeth. The initial drop of a roller coaster. The defeated sighs of Harrison into Kennedy's limp body.

Daisy holds her restless composure as she leans toward Molly and Amber, her face continuing to watch the romantic pair.

"Do you think we'll ever have that?" she asks.

Their eyes perk at the question, as they are pulled from their conversation.

"What?" Amber asks, the first to break the silence. "A relationship?"

"A moment where we're not completely infatuated with ourselves," Daisy says. Her eyes pinch with a warm-hearted sputter.

"Not for a long time," Molly blissfully scoffs, her nurturing tone a serene wasteland of knowledge. "We're too focused on our careers, and more importantly, our own selves."

Amber contorts her smile into an accepting nod and says, "once we've completely dismantled the patriarchy, we can all take a well-deserved vacation."

"Well, I'm sick of waiting," Daisy states as she finally turns to address the group.

"Waiting for Duncan?" Amber jokes.

The comment doesn't register.

"I need to get out of here," Daisy says, dropping her glass heavily against the bar top.

"Wait, does this have to do with Taylor or Harrison?" Molly challenges with a perceptive smirk.

An unconcerned face paints Amber's eyes as she asks, "does it matter at this point? Whatever you're planning to do, it isn't a good idea."

But Daisy had already mentally left the building. Tucking her purse underneath her arm, Daisy gives a final wave to the two.

"I'll catch up with you guys later," she says before she slips her way through the glittering New Year's Eve crowd.

>>>

Daisy grips the drab car seat before her as she thrashes her spine into the backseat of a cab. Forcing a grunt so loud that the cab driver turns to check in on her, he asks, "lady? You okay?"

"Fine," Daisy retorts like an angry child. "Just drive."

"Lady, I can't just drive in circles for hours," the bald man explains. "You need to give me an address at some point. I'm going to run out of gas."

Rolling her eyes, Daisy shrugs her shoulders in confrontation.

"Can't you tell I'm having a bit of a life crisis here?" she asks, tucking a ringlet of hair behind her ear and pressing her forehead against the headrest in front of her.

"Trust me, lady. My rate doesn't include a therapy session," the man mocks, eyeing her through his rearview mirror.

"How about this," Daisy offers before dropping both biceps atop the front seat. "I'm going to tell you a story and then at the end of it, I'll give you two addresses and whichever you are closer to at that time, that will be my destination."

Narrowing his eyes, the man attempts to understand Daisy's end goal.

"Boy troubles?" he asks with a nosy inquiry.

"Life troubles," Daisy says without further discussion.

The man furrows his brow and gives Daisy a once over. Determining she is not a threat, he obliges. "I'm going to charge you double the fair, so keep it brief."

Curling her arms around the headrest, Daisy leans her cheek against the leather of the headrest.

"When I was a little girl, I read a book about a boy who could change into animals," she says, her voice fanciful and forcing the man to roll his eyes. Noticing the action, she pauses the story. "Either listen to the story or I'm living in this backseat for eternity."

"Sorry," the man apologizes. "Please continue your little girl story."

Shifting her eyes in an unsure glance, Daisy continues.

"So, I came home from school and told my dad that I was going to start turning into animals," says Daisy. Her face perks as the memory washes over her. "He was always so sweet with me. He played along and asked me 'What kind of animal are you going to be?' and I told him that I was going to be a hawk because they were ferocious and people were scared of their talons."

"Makes sense," the driver snidely comments.

Ignoring the quip, Daisy resumes, saying, "he asked why someone so small and sweet would want to be such a frightening predator, and at that age, I never really understood why being feared wouldn't be, you know, positive. In my kid brain, the concept of relationships and kindness was so unknown that all I could see was the way kids would bow down to me that I was so blinded by the rest of the picture."

Pausing at the memory, then turning to face the cab driver, Daisy asks with an honest tone, "do you remember that feeling? Where your world was the *entire* world. If you could only see to the end of the driveway or to the other side of the park, then that was the universe to you?"

"I have a little boy who always tells me that the basement is another planet," the man begrudgingly says with reluctant warmth. "He makes me wear a space helmet because he's worried I won't be able to breathe."

Daisy's lips loop into a sincere smile.

"Exactly. Their perspective is so youthful and full of hope that, even today, I still imagine the ludicrous idea of 'What if I had become a hawk?' What if I got up in the morning, packed a bag, and went off to my job as a hawk?"

A wry laugh escapes both of their mouths at the image. Then, a beat of understanding settles between the pair. The cordial compassion engulfs their adult world and takes them back to a moment of adolescent wonder. For a moment, they weren't grownups doing grownup things – they were children playing dress up. Wearing their mother's high heels and awkwardly clacking down the stairs. Trying on Dad's tie and having it drag against the floor like a tail between their feet.

Daisy returns to the present.

"I guess what I'm trying to say—" she begins, before she is quickly cut off by the blaring horn.

"Get out of the fucking way, you jackass!" the cab driver howls as he swerves to miss a car barreling from a side street and into traffic. Throwing both hands into the air then charging both hands into the steering wheel again, the horn pierces Daisy's ears. She closes one eye at the forceful noise.

"You okay, lady?" the man asks without turning to see Daisy's face.

"Yeah, just fine," Daisy awkwardly answers.

"Okay, you were trying to say—" the man starts, again but interrupts himself: "This *fucking* jackass is going to get us both killed!" he screams with another forceful deploy of the horn.

Equally annoyed with the disturbance, Daisy instructs the driver to "just tail him until he gets out of your way."

Her dismissive tone like an old friend.

"Oh, you better believe I will," the man says before slamming on the gas until he is mere inches from the car.

Daisy squints her eyes in an attempt to see the driver, but she cannot make out the shape through the foggy windows.

"This asshole," she chimes in with the driver. "Just because he has a fancy car..." she starts to chide before realizing she had seen this fancy car before.

"Some arrogant dickhead who thinks just because he has money that he owns the road," the man shouts with another blare of the horn.

"Yeah, that's him all right," Daisy agrees under her breath as a hurried anxiety fills her lungs, adrenaline burning. "My destination is wherever that car is going," she spits at the driver. His face painted with confusion. "I'll give you an extra hundred if you tail him the entire way."

Another aggressive throttle of speed lurches the car forward as the man sees the money dangling before his eyes. Weaving in and out of traffic and gunning through red lights, Daisy uses every spare breath, encouraging the man to drive faster, ensuring he keeps a close distance to the vintage sports car.

As they zip through the traffic, avoiding collision after collision, Daisy rolls down her window and sticks her head out in an attempt to see Harrison.

"Fuck," she murmurs as she awkwardly lands in the seat after coming up short. "An extra two hundred if you get him to pull over."

Three red lights, six avoided accidents, and one woman narrowly hit, Harrison turns on his blinker as he signals to turn into a parking lot.

"Oh, *now* he uses a turn signal," Daisy exclaims, the cab driver scoffing in agreement.

Before the cab can come to stop, Daisy hurls a wad of hundreds at the driver and forces open the door, sprinting toward Harrison's humming car. Shouting over the roar of the engine, Daisy calls after Harrison.

"Harry! What the *fuck* are you doing?" Her voice crackles as she attempts to yell across the full length of the parking lot.

Daisy's breathing staggers until it clamors against her chest as she storms toward Harrison's car. The blue lighting of the building's signage covers the parking lot in a surreal lilac hue. "NEW ORLEANS POLICE

DEPARTMENT" shines like a beacon in the night sky. The whirling and clatter of the New Year spinning amongst the street fell into absolute silence as Daisy froze. Stunned by the vibrant sign, her head droops to her shoulder as if it was a mirage in the desert.

Swiveling her head on its hinges to verify her location, Daisy gawks as her eyes trace her surroundings with row after row of squad cars and police vans that line the back rows of the parking lot.

Harry, she thinks to herself striding toward Harrison's car, picking up speed.

The driver's side door of Harrison's car swings open as Daisy plants her feet, still meters away from the vehicle. Another moment of stillness encases her as she waits for Harrison, unsure of the state she will find him. The only noise in the city is an echoing boom of the blood in her ears, the thumping bass of her own heart.

"Let's go," Harrison sputters as only his head and shoulders emerge from the car before being tugged back inside. A grunt of anger roars through his teeth before he shifts his weight back inside the car and then, rocking back into the night, he materializes from inside the cabin.

Daisy does a double-take, as all she can make out of Harrison is his unruly amber hair. He's not in his typical suit, but a gray tee and jeans with no shoes. The clothing choice springs Daisy's eyes to life as she remembers the outfit. He has swapped out his standard tailored suit for an old gray tee, bloodied pants, and tired face indicating that he has come directly from the cellar. The box of knives flash before her eyes.

Tracing the spattering of blood down his face and cascading across his shirt, her eyes stop as she comes upon a new addition to his ensemble: a youthful, brunette girl in a sparkling top being dragged by her hair out of the sports car. She has an open wound on her forearm, leaching blood against the soft fabric of her skirt. There is another laceration against her chest where a flash of silver showcases what appears to be a nail of some kind.

"Harry?" Daisy croaks, unsure if the words leave her lips.

Harrison freezes at the sound of Daisy's voice. The blood pulses in his arms and the shake of his adrenaline forces his grip around the girl's hair. He shifts his weight from foot to foot as he attempts to steady himself.

Dropping the girl but tightening his grip within her hair, she tumbles from the driver's seat and onto the asphalt of the parking lot with a dull cry. Standing upright, Harrison turns to face Daisy. His face is a determined wash of ambivalent emptiness as he drags a full breath through his nostrils. Raising a clenched fist to his mouth, the girl's blood oozing across his wrist and forearm, he clears his throat before meeting his eyes with Daisy's.

An apathetic look in his emerald green eyes is all he relinquishes as he casually asks, "hello. How are you doing this evening?"

Chapter Twenty-One: **Mitsubishi Sony**

"Your home is fucking amazing," the brunette woman says in a sleazy tone as she steps into the foyer. "I can't believe you live this far outside of town. Don't you get lonely?" she asks, finally turning toward Harrison, acknowledging his presence.

The woman looks to be about twenty-five. Harrison had forgotten to ask when he picked her up at the club. Leaning against the opposite wall from her in the dimly lit foyer, his dark eyes caress over her in appraisal for his evening's grand finale. Her drunken sway and sparkling top made her an obvious target, but she had solidified her fate when she had confessed to him that she had recently broken into a small boutique, stealing hundreds of dollars worth of jewelry, then hit an elderly woman and her grandson with the getaway car on her joyride out of town. She was wearing an oversized set of earrings this evening that flashed in the minimal light. *One of her many souvenirs of the crime*, Harrison thinks.

"It's not so bad," Harrison says confidently. He reaches up to undo his tie, a sultry look in his inky eyes that the woman misreads as lust. "It's nice to have the company of someone as beautiful as you," he says, his words an elegant poem compared to her drunken chatter.

The woman flashes a bashful smirk and nonchalantly walks through the foyer, examining Harrison's home. There were oversized paintings and decorative vases that had been placed throughout the space. She observes everything as she is transfixed by the thought of being in the home of *the* Harrison Bishop. Her hand glides across the oversized table in the center of the room as she turns her attention toward Harrison, attempting a sensuous trot in his direction. His eyes fixate on her neck like a hungry wolf.

"So, you really live out here *all alone*?" she asks again, the question leaving a stale taste in Harrison's mouth from the over-pronunciation.

Holding his pose, Harrison watches his prey plead for his approval.

"My bodyguard stays in the guest house from time to time," he says, his tongue tracing along the pointed edges of his teeth. "But I've asked him to spend the night away this evening so we could…" he trails off, winking.

The woman's mouth crashes into his. She twists her thin arms around his neck, one eager hand pulling at his tangled hair. Harrison drapes a single arm around the small of her back, apathetically holding his position. Although this evening was to be his final kill, he does not feel his usual vigor that typically enveloped him before a slaughter. His mind felt soggy, as if he had soaked his brain in syrup. He could feel his cloudiness dragging him down as he attempted to shake it off. *Get it together*, he told himself. *This is your last one and you need to make it count.*

Gripping the woman's shoulders, Harrison pushes her weight off of his own and holds her at arm's length to study her face. Her wild eyes and flushed cheeks – he'd seen this face countless times in the past, but his sights linger on the pounding blood beneath her neck. With a mix of adrenaline and power, he smells the scent that is very familiar to him, but it doesn't invoke his typical thirst.

Harrison leans forward to plant a faint kiss on the woman's mouth.

"I'm going to go change out of these stuffy clothes," he whispers with a musky voice. "When I get back, we can grab a bottle of wine from the cellar and make ourselves a bit more comfortable," he says, his words like velvet, but his eyes a barren void.

As Harrison makes his way to his bedroom, he takes his time to ensure he is prepared for the night's festivities. *Whatever is left in your fucked up mind, you better get it out tonight. Tomorrow, you are Harrison Bishop, the goddamn Cure All Kid, and you will play that part until you die.* He hesitates at the notion of him dying, realizing that by the day he would pass, Bishop Enterprises would most likely have solved that problem. *You will take her into the cellar, use every tool in that godforsaken room, and get it out of your system.*

The soft thud of Harrison's heels against the hardwood flooring begins to evaporate as a larger thumping sound rattles through his skull. The rush of adrenaline and nerves pulsates through his limbs, seeping from his spine like venom. *Once I am through with this one, I will never look back on this life*, he reminds himself as he swings open his bedroom door, floods the room to life with a switch, and marches toward the closet to retrieve his uniform, careful to avoid the sight of the blank wall above his bed.

Tugging his jeans over his hips, Harrison reaches for his bottom drawer of black tees but hesitates when he sees the worn fabric staring up at him. He stretches his hand outward, feeling his muscles tense and relax at his command, then grips the drawer just above to expose a larger array of rarely used tees. Digging through the pile, he closes one eye, feeling with his long fingers for a particular touch.

"Gotcha," Harrison utters as he finds a faded gray shirt and clasps it between his fingers. The fabric was not as worn as his black tees, but it was one of his old favorites. "MITSUBISHI SONY," the faded lettering spells out in a futuristic font hinting at the shirt's age.

"Okay, I'm ready," he tells himself as he pulls the shirt over his head and expels a puff of breath through his quivering lips.

Harrison locates the woman standing in the doorway of his dining room peering with oversized doe eyes at the chandelier.

"Is that a real diamond?" she asks without turning as she hears the soft echo of Harrison's bare feet against the floor.

The mention of the chandelier rattles through Harrison's skull with an irritating hum. Choosing to ignore her, he sets a delicate hand against her bicep.

"How about that wine?" he asks.

"I can't even imagine the dinners you've had at this table!" the woman bellows, turning to face Harrison, her eyes now ravenous and hungry. "Oh my God, and the *parties*!"

Pushing his lips into a focused line, Harrison grips both of her shoulders between his full hands. He opens his mouth to ask her to stop, but turns his head as he notices the traces of a gold chain resting along the woman's collarbone. Releasing one of his hands, he delicately raises his forefinger to lift the fine chain from beneath her top and into the light. A golden 'E' dangles from the far end of the chain and Harrison lifts his face in confusion.

"For my name," the woman explains, but Harrison purses his eyes further, unsure of the source. "Ella?" she states, the uptick morphing her name into a question.

"I didn't notice the necklace earlier," Harrison says with a persuasive lie. "It's quite beautiful, Ella," he says, repeating her name in an attempt to commit it to memory, knowing he can leave it behind soon enough. Shaking out his eyes and returning to his task, his confidence returns and he takes a step backward, extending an arm in the direction of the cellar.

"Shall we?"

Ella releases a throaty moan as Harrison binds her wrists with a vibrant blue rope. His eyes are laser focused as hers move excitedly throughout the cellar.

"This is quite the kinky place," she observes in a sultry tone. "I like it," she tacks on, seductively.

"Yeah, it's quite romantic," Harrison adds, his focus on completing his intricate knot. A sparse spatter of sweat frames his hairline as he breaks his concentration to run a jittery hand through his hair. Feeling the tremor, he clenches both fists and clears his throat before momentarily returning his eyes to Ella's energetic face.

Too fucking happy for my liking, he remarks to himself as he flares in nostrils in annoyance. "Let's see what we can do about that," he responds to himself aloud. Rearranging his face into a haphazard yet charming smile, he struggles to pull himself together. With a shaky grasp, he begins again with the knot between his fingers. The loops uneven and loose, he releases a guttural cough to release his aggression.

"You okay?" Ella asks, showing no sign of nerves as she spots Harrison's uneasy hands. "We can just fool around if—"

"Please stop talking," Harrison snaps. His eyes are harsh and black, seething with a building temper.

Ella's face jerks as she is taken aback by the interjection, but she relaxes and gives Harrison an accepting smile. Her eyes trail the back wall of the cellar, gliding along the drawers and shelves of materials. Landing on the open paneling, she recognizes the outline of the record player.

"Do you want to put on some music? That could make it fun."

Tonguing his cheek, Harrison ignores the comment as he finishes the knot with a forceful tug of the rope.

"Stay here," he instructs before retrieving the suspended rope from the far corner of the cellar. A momentary flash of Daisy's presence in the room stuns him and he forces a harsh swallow through his throat to suppress the memory. Her ghost pumps hot through his veins.

"You're in for a special treat tonight, Ella," Harrison begins as he omits the thought. "Tonight is a big night for me and my career." His voice is poignant yet abrasive, and his deep eyes slant with a lingering sadness as he turns to face Ella, guiding the rope to her methodically.

"Well, some congratulations will be in order for you, it seems," Ella says with a lascivious smile.

Harrison completes his expert knot with its newest addition and returns to the corner of the room, turning proudly before his mark.

"I am going to kill you tonight, Ella," he says. His words lose their strength as they shake through his teeth. Gripping the rope with a heavy fist he continues, "I am going to kill you slowly and painfully and when I wake up tomorrow, I will start my life fresh." His eyes force a melancholy glare.

Pursing her lips, Ella reads Harrison without movement. She blinks slowly, once, twice, and then a third time before curling one half of her face into a smirk.

"I'd let you do anything to me," she says, her words as thick as molasses, permeating through Harrison. She leans forward slightly to substantiate her point: "Absolutely anything."

Another unyielding swallow forces itself through Harrison's throat before he gives a heave of the rope and stretches Ella's arms until her toes graze the ground. Securing the rope, Harrison begins his classic speech.

"I have a fascination with idols," he recites. "These individuals who we put in towers and allow to dictate our lives haven't earned their place at the table. You see, Ella, idols are merely an escape for our mundane lives. A reasoning behind our weaknesses and the reason we falter within society."

Ella eagerly listens with her smug smirk still painted across her face as Harrison glides forward with his resilient stride. Unnerved by her composure, he pushes himself, saying, "I am not one of these people, Ella. I am not some Earthbound god or a savior to you." His temples throb with the violent beating of his heart.

Inches from Ella's nose, Harrison glowers down on her in hopes of intimidation. Any source of worry or fear would fuel his fire, but she simply parts her lips and traces her tongue across her teeth. Landing on a pointy incisor, she presses the flesh of her tongue into the tip. Her pompous smile fills her eyes as Harrison watches the pink skin press until it is near its breaking point.

"Do you think this is funny?" Harrison spits into Ella's face. "I am not the hero this world needs. I am not the fucking Cure All Kid," he shouts. His bottom lip trembles and his hands grip their strength before releasing the rope.

Ella continues to relish in Harrison's attention, sucking in the scent of his anger with a subtle sneer. "You can be whatever you want to be for me, Harry," she says, her words glinting off her tongue like a sparkler in the night.

The nickname igniting something within Harrison, he reaches toward her face and grips Ella by the back of her hair. His fingers roam through her wild, dark mane and he dips his grimace into her, lashing his words carefully: "Don't you *dare* call me that."

Releasing Ella's head and taking a few steps back, Harrison shakes, nearly in convulsions, and makes his way to the back of the cellar. The blood turns over in his muscles, and his hands grasp the bins as he looks for his weapon. *Just finish this*, he grounds himself. *Just finish her off and go to bed.*

A sharp breath exhales through Harrison's lips as he pulls out the drawer and retrieves a handful of items. The metal clatters together as Ella excitedly watches.

Turning to face her, Harrison rattles a handful of metal stakes in his left hand, each the size of a pen. The metal creates a resounding clank of holiday bells as he twists a hammer in his opposite hand. "

"I'm going to drive these camping stakes into your body, Ella. The pain will be excruciating and you will bleed out for hours while I continue to hammer spike after spike into your porcelain skin," Harrison says, his words deliberate. However, she holds her composure easily.

"I already told you, *Harrison*, you can do anything you want to me," she says, her expression spattered with certainty as she lifts a single brow in anticipation of Harrison's next move.

Harrison walks until he is face to face with Ella. The cellar is a void of sound beyond the hum of the light and the soft pat of his feet against the cement floors. His breathing is rugged and unsettled until he lands his nose just above her own, delicately placing the tip of the stake just below her collarbone.

"Are you ready?" he asks rhetorically, mainly to himself.

Ella nods in understanding and pulls her lips inward to brace herself for the blow. Harrison drags a jagged breath, holding it within his chest. Without warning, he raises the hammer, grits his teeth, and lands the blow atop the metal stake. Ella releases a bloodcurdling scream and grips at the rope holding her in suspension.

Blinking his eyes to life, Harrison peers back into Ella's eyes in hopes of validation, but she discharges a heavy sigh and shakes her head.

"Another," she demands, the veins in her neck pulsating with visible pain as a trickle of blood encapsulates the first stake.

"What do you mean, 'another?'" Harrison barks before setting a stake against her suspended forearm and burrowing the muted metal into her clenched muscle. Ella's head knocks backward as she releases another scream. "Is that what you fucking want?" he yells over her tortured yells.

Ella suspends her head against her shoulder blades, the weight of her skull tearing at her neck until she props her head onto her shoulders to glare into Harrison's eyes. Her face fervently awaits his next words. "Abso...lutely....anything," she breathes through labored gasps.

Grabbing hold of the first stake, Harrison grips the cool metal and twists it against Ella's skin. He tears her flesh as blood streaks across her abdomen. Harrison glares into her eyes, attempting to read her next move as she holds back her cries. He contemplates his next action, his mind stuttering beneath the surface. Killing Ella with a single blow of the hammer. Gutting her like a fish and leaving her to rot in the cellar. Slitting her throat and watching as the blood slowly pools on the floor. His options are an endless massacre but he simply drops his weapons with a noisy clang.

"Is that it?" Ella asks, her panting breath still confident as she rolls back her shoulders in preparation for the next blow while her iridescent top muddies from the trails of sticky blood.

Harrison lifts his brow and releases the weight of his head onto his shoulder. A puzzled look reads her every breath until he breaks his silence and turns toward the back of the cellar to retrieve a single serrated blade. Reaching above Ella's suspended hands, he saws against the plastic cable until her feet drop to the floor. Dropping the blade, Harrison straightens his spine and clears his throat. "You are free to go," he says before taking half a step backward, indecipherably motioning toward the open cellar door.

Ella mimics him and cocks her head to one side, attempting to understand Harrison's actions, her face a quizzical mosaic of emotions until she finally selects her thought to speak aloud. "You can finish if you like," she says, the hopeful inflection in her voice forcing Harrison to glare his eyes at the asinine request.

"*Finish*?" Harrison seethes. "You'd rather die than go free?" he asks, his words lashing without a single blow.

"Being killed by Harrison Bishop would be an honor," Ella touts with a proud vibrato. Dipping her chin into her chest, her eyes collapse into a smoldering scowl. "Give me your worst."

Without hesitation, Harrison grips Ella by the binding against her wrists. Lugging her against his weight, he marches toward the steps of the cellar. Bounding the stairs two at a time, he drags Ella along the rugged wood planks. Ella yelps in pain with every crash against the staircase, but she does not cry out for him to stop.

Once Harrison has landed within the back of the kitchen, he continues his hurried pace toward the garage with Ella still in tow. "Do you want me to stop yet?" he yells, his voice reverberating throughout the vacant estate as Ella streaks blood across the hardwood, her fresh wounds opening and spilling on to the polished floors.

"I'm, all, yours, Harrison," Ella croaks against the floor.

Once inside the garage, Harrison continues to drag Ella against the concrete. "Un-fucking-believable," he murmurs to himself. "Does everybody in this Godforsaken town *want* to be killed by me?" he asks, his voice echoing against the metal of a dozen neatly arranged sports cars and oversized SUVs.

"Are all...of these...yours?" Ella gasps, drooling blood. "You must...be worth...a fortune!" she continues to croon through her fragmented breathing.

Harrison grips the rope against Ella's wrists and lashes her weight against the side of a black town car, her body colliding with a crash before dropping to the concrete and convulsing at the pain. "Shut up," he shouts, leaning over her through clenched teeth. Towering over her as he regains his height, he throws her into the passenger seat of the furthest car and shouts, "we're going for a ride," before slamming the door of a navy sports car that lingered with Daisy's scent.

Chapter Twenty-Two: **Sound And Color**

Harrison tightens his grip through Ella's hair, forcing her to wince in pain. Her eyes are stained pink from the blood of her head wound and tears stream down her cheeks amidst her bizarrely happy appearance. Her eyes drift with a puzzled focusing between Harrison and Daisy and then back to Harrison, reading the mood between the brooding pair.

The quiet evening has fallen into a muted buzz while the show develops against the backdrop of the New Orleans Police Department. The cars zip along the street and a noisy group of partygoers cheer along the sidewalk as they pass, unaware of their destructive wreckage.

Opening his mouth, Harrison looks as if to speak but releases only a miniscule breath. Instead, he dips his head to his bloodied hands and his face curls with an unseen ache. Shaking his head, he raises his face to meet Daisy's fervent green eyes and delivers a meager, "I know I should say something."

Daisy drops her shoulders and tilts her head to one side as she appraises Harrison. The parking lot lamps drown him in a blue hue, his unruly hair bleached by the unnatural lighting that dances to life with every breeze against his face.

"What are you doing here?" Daisy breaks her silence with a hurried whisper. "D-do you realize what is going to happen when you barge through those doors?" she asks, her catlike eyes open wide with tears pooling near the edges. Drawing in Harrison, she growls, "what are you trying to prove, Harry?"

Shaking his head in acknowledgement, Harrison's eyes glaze over as he stares through Daisy and plays out the next few moments in his mind. He imagines himself walking through the front doors of the station. Being handcuffed and fingerprinted. Sampson bailing him out of jail. Calmly reading the paper on the car ride home, his own face littered across the front page.

Harrison stares into Daisy's face, clearing his throat and straightening his shoulders in confidence. "I know exactly what I'm doing," he answers, although his voice has lost its timbre and fades without confidence. "If you play with fire," he starts, but his voice falters before he can complete his next words.

A moment passes as Daisy eagerly braces for Harrison's next move, but it does not come. He swallows hard, his throat shifting at the uneven motion. His gaze falls to Ella, her wild eyes holding his stare as he collects the will to move his feet, but his body has cemented them to the asphalt. His mind races as his heartbeat fills his ears before perking to life with a faint *tick-tick-tick* of Daisy's lighter illuminating her face against a cigarette.

Pulling a shaky drag, Daisy sucks a full breath into her chest before returning to Harrison. "Walk me through this, Harry," she says, her voice calm but her demeanor still rattled. "Why are you here?" Her sincere eyes grasp like talons through Harrison.

Raising and dropping his shoulders in dismay, Harrison shakes his head as he chokes the words from his stomach. "I want to be done with this life. I told myself that I'd have one last run and then go into the office tomorrow like nothing had happened," he says, his voice chopping like waves against a ship.

Pulling another puff from her stick, Daisy crosses her arms as she listens. "But now?"

"But now," Harrison repeats as he inspects his arms, his chest, and notices a trail of blood along his right foot. His head tilts to one side trying to determine the source. "Ella was too *eager*," he continues, the word draining like poison from his teeth. He shakes her knotted hair within his hand, raising her and dropping her once again against the asphalt. "She *wanted* me to do it and I couldn't have this any longer. I couldn't have another person wanting me to do these horrible things to them. I am not their fucking savior!" he shouts, his voice vibrating against the nearby buildings.

Daisy scans their surroundings for onlookers but the street is quiet. The faint bark of a dog cascades across the lot with a shadowy echo. She pulls another drag from her cigarette, the ashes tugging with an extended crackle until they collide with the filter. She drops the cigarette to the ground and suffocates the embers with her toe. "So, what? You're going to turn yourself in?" she asks, her words glinting with an air of sarcasm.

"I'm going to get what I finally deserve," Harrison corrects. "I'm a monster, Daisy. You more than anyone should know that." His eyes burn like coals as his neck flushes with the heat of his words.

"I see," Daisy acknowledges, her eyes glassy as she processes. She digs her hand back into her purse and produces another cigarette. Placing the clean filter between her cherry lips and clenching it delicately between her teeth, she ignites the lighter. Her face flashes to life with the brief flame before it quickly disintegrates without lighting the paper.

"What? Are you a chain smoker now?" Harrison asks, his words frank and his face bursting with disapproval.

Still clenching the cigarette between her teeth, Daisy purses her eyes before speaking through the filter. "Yeah, because that's the issue we're dealing with here," she says, the sarcasm now fully developed against her throaty tone before striking the lighter again. "Lucky for us though, you've ensured that we can all live forever," she mocks again before releasing a puff of smoke above her head with a straightforward tone. "Harry, I may be your only friend at this point. I'm not going to coddle you and tell you why all of *this* is a bad idea," she says, waving her cigarette in an outline of Ella.

"I need to do this," Harrison announces with an unsure defiance. "I need to feel human again. I need someone to hate me as much as I hate myself." His eyes search for relief, but without Daisy's approval, the anger rises again in his mouth and he tightens his grip around Ella's hair as another squeal of pain emits from her throat. He tenses his body and pulls her weight into his chest.

Swinging Ella against his side, Harrison heaves her head to land against his hip and begins his ascent into the precinct. Ella latches herself on to Harrison's arm in an attempt to raise herself to her feet, but does not have the strength and trails behind him, her bare heels sliding across the pavement and then the concrete stairs. A trail of blood seeps from her skin and oozes against the asphalt as if she's leaving a slug's trail.

Watching wide-eyed, Daisy hurriedly rushes after the pair, lifting the hem of her gown as she sprints after them. Flinging her cigarette into the night, she reaches out for Ella as if to save her. Each step of the stair releases a screech of pain from her as her body collides with the cement. Watching as a patch of red prints her remnants as a roadmap with each connection against the surface.

When Daisy reaches for Ella in an uneven gesture, she misses her foot with an instant just as Harrison reaches the door and yanks the handle, flooding the steps with light. Taking a step back, she raises a hand to block the light from her face as the lively sounds of the precinct slam into her with a cacophony of cheery sound. Dropping the hem of her dress, she takes a skeptical step into the precinct for what would come next.

The heavy-set doors of the police station glide close as the trio moves haphazardly toward the receptionist desk. No one is in immediate sight. Harrison and Daisy look to each other for a moment of preparation before he gives her a subtle nod of understanding, then sets his free hand upon the desk. A smear of blood lingers as his hands shake and Ella pulls herself to her feet along his side. His hand is still tangled against her hair, forcing her to lean in a lopsided stance.

A few men in uniform sit toward the back of the room around a small table, throwing cards toward the center. One takes an exaggerated sip of a can of soda before standing to hold the tin out toward the others, offering them a drink. Another woman nearby raises her hand asking for a soda as she leans against a table. A miniature television sits across from her as she watches a news program, the steady voice blurring with the sound of a printer dropping papers into a bin.

"Hello?" Harrison asks in a fearful and edgy tone. His eyes shifting across the room, he prepares himself for who would be the first to discover him and call for backup. He raises his shaking chest in anticipation.

The man walking to retrieve the sodas notices the group and quickly apologies before setting down the empty can as he hustles toward the receptionist desk. There is a warm tone in his voice as he apologizes a second time before reaching into his pocket to produce a set of wire glasses.

"We gave Lynn the evening off to go celebrate and we're not the best at manning the front. What can I do..." he starts, but trails off as his eyes follow the path of blood from Harrison to Ella and then to Daisy's clean and elegant ensemble. "You folks okay?"

"I'd like to turn myself in," Harrison announces with a strong and an almost certain voice. His brow furrows and his jaw visibly rattles against its hinges.

The man turns over his shoulder to yell backwards to the lounging officers, "I need a med kit over here!" He begins to scurry around the desk to land at Ella's side, holding her in his arms and peering against her collarbone to inspect the protruding stake.

Daisy hops backward to provide space for the officer, unsure of her next move. Her eyes fervently watch the man before turning her line of sight to Harrison, his face lost in ambivalent haze.

"Jesus Christ," he mutters under his breath before turning his face up toward Harrison. "*Jesus* Christ!" he shouts more forcefully. "Are you Harrison Bishop?"

Harrison curls his lips inward with a dissatisfied glare. "I need to report a *crime*," he repeats, his strength waning as he loses his power.

The officer holds Ella in his arms, her limp body trailing stamps of her blood along his navy uniform until she rests her head against his shoulder. "Let me just get your friend some medical attention and then I'd be delighted to assist you, Mr. Bishop. I almost didn't recognize you outside of a suit," says the officer. He begins to scamper with Ella's weight into his side toward the woman watching the television who has made space for Ella near the table. She pulls out a chair, guiding Ella into the seat.

The television continues its mundane voiceover. "In breaking news," the host announces with an urgent tone, "a new strain of the flu has been wreaking havoc throughout South America." The woman turns around to mute the sound but the screen flashes with a banner indicating "Widespread Panic Over Fatal And Untreatable New Strand Of Influenza."

Harrison's eyes dart to Daisy's. The mix of panic and anger, the dissonance of emotions leaves her staggering in bewilderment. Taking a step forward, she narrows her eyes to scan the television. A new banner flashes across the screen: "Prescribed Antitoxin Escalating Death Rates In Brazil and Chile."

Watching Daisy move, Harrison releases the tension in his hands and stands dumbfounded in his tracks. His bloodied hand slides from the desktop to land at his side, leaving a streaky path of blood. "What's happening?" he whispers.

Daisy shakes her head as she watches the television behind the officers. Harrison's eyes turn to Ella as one officer braces her and the other places a snow white strand of gauze around the bulging stake. Her face narrows at the sensation but relaxes once someone places a bandage atop the cotton.

A wave of heat comes over Harrison, a passion of impatience and exasperation as he if is going to vomit. The surge of anger fills his lungs as he braces for the action, much like Ella bracing for the application of gauze. Instead, a roar forms against his cheeks and his words boom as if he is not within his own mind. "I tried to kill her!" he shouts, his eager words turning the face of every officer in the room. He takes a surprisingly confident step toward the desk. "I took her into my cellar and attempted to kill her."

A moment passes as eyes dart from person to person in a whirlwind of connections. The identification of Harrison. The bloodied woman being bandaged. His clothing soaked with blood.

The officer applying the dressings to Ella's wounds stands and turns to face Harrison. His eyes narrow as he processes the statement and lifts an arm toward his gun. Instead of anger, the officer's face lifts and a guttural laugh pours from between his rosy cheeks. "Yeah right!" he yelps between snickers and turns toward the female office who has leaned forward with a similar laugh as she shakes her head in disbelief.

"I'm serious!" Harrison shouts ardently. "I tried to kill her and I've been killing people for nearly a decade," he admits, the words ringing in his molars like loose fillings.

The female officer is the first to erupt further with an overriding cackle. She looks toward the male officer who knocks his head backward to release his laughter into the ceiling.

"I'm *sure* you have, Mr. Bishop. You nearly *killed* me four years ago when I was cured of my prostate cancer!" he exclaims, slapping a heavy hand against his stomach.

Harrison darts his eyes to Daisy who mirrors his confusion and astonishment. Her cheeks fall a ghostly white as he turns his face toward the officers and then to a nearby corkboard. A faded missing person poster shows the friendly face of Harrison's long lost victim, Brandy.

"This girl," he bellows, pointing a bloodied finger. "I captured her from work and took her to my home and murdered her with a knife."

A fresh babble of laughter blooms throughout the room with a pungent humor. Harrison clenches his fists and turns back toward Daisy, who is now frozen in time.

"I'm serious! I took a six-inch deboning blade and gutted her like a trout!" he barks, his screams lingering with a spittle of saliva against the corkboard. "You *need* to arrest me!" he demands, but his pleas are drowned out against the laughter.

"Okay, okay, Mr. Bishop," says the officer, raising both his hands in surrender, his voice a serious transition until he turns back toward the female officer. "Let me get *right* on that and *arrest* you," he says, his sarcasm emphasized with an over-exaggerated eye roll that leaves Harrison's nostrils flared in anger. Turning back toward Ella, the officer kneels down to her side feigning a doting parent.

"Miss? Did *Mister Bishop* attempt to kill you this evening?" he asks, the singsong tone in his voice leaving Harrison's teeth gritted in fury as he visibly clamps his jaw.

Ella turns her wide eyes up toward Harrison, her high brows painting a sincere wash of hope on her face that Harrison internally prays will produce the response he so desperately desires.

"Of course not," she laughs with a rough cough. "These two found me near the outskirts of town and saved me from a man in a baseball hat who was trying to assault me," she lies, her tone full of gratitude. "I owe my *life* to Harrison," she says. Her angelic eyes curve at the edges with a sultry glower.

Harrison raises his hands against either side of his neck and presses his full strength against his esophagus. A shade of plum rises in his cheeks from the lack of oxygen, Tom's phantom weight slowly pulls the life from his body. His composure dwindles as his astounded demeanor forces his face to Daisy, her own hand raised to her throat as she grips at her delicate skin, attempting to process the evening.

This isn't happening, Daisy tells herself as the room spins by in a chaotic blur. *How is he getting away with this? He has taken everything from me and yet they are still worshiping him like a god.* Her eyes smolder as she watches the girl excitedly adjust her bandages and a few of the police officers eagerly rush to thank Harrison. The pain seeps through her lungs like hot tar as the sound and color of the room punch the air from her lungs.

The female officer watches the pair and takes an assertive step forward.

"We would like to thank you, Mr. Bishop. And you, too, Miss?" she asks Daisy.

Daisy swallows hard against her palm as she shakes herself into reality.

"Miss Stone," she chokes.

"Miss Stone," the officer nods in understanding. "On behalf of the entire New Orleans Police Department, we'd like to thank you for your bravery and courage this evening." She looks over her shoulder at an innocent looking Ella, one corner of her mouth tinged in humor. "This woman is extremely lucky to have been found by such selfless individuals as yourself. Can I grab you a towel and get you both cleaned up?"

Ignoring the question, Harrison avoids the female officer and turns back toward the male officer.

"This isn't what is supposed to happen," he growls, his expression shifting from confusion to anger.

"You're correct," says the male officer, nodding in agreement. He turns to look for an object nearby. "We will need your statements and photos for evidence, but other than that," he lifts his earnest eyes to Harrison, "you are both free to go."

"Free to go?" Daisy whispers without comprehension.

"Yep! Free to go," the officer gleefully repeats. "Quite the cavalier gentleman you have with you this evening, Miss Stone. You are very lucky to have found someone as admirable as Mr. Bishop."

"Keep on saving the world, son!" the male officer calls after Harrison with an eager wave of his hand.

Harrison turns over his shoulder, his eyes crazed as he provides a meek wave in response. Holding the door for Daisy, he waits until she stops just outside the glass doors.

A moment passes as Harrison and Daisy stare into the parking lot, the chill of the evening billowing her dress and ruffling his bloodstained hair. The driver's side door of the car still hangs ajar with a soft purr of the motor idling beneath the hood.

Harrison digs both of his hands into the pockets of his jeans, clears his throat, and then pauses again in hopes of the glass doors swinging to life with a SWAT team to arrest him. He patiently waits for the chandelier of his dining room to impale him in the face and crush him in on impact.

Daisy senses her shoulders drop and loses control of her arms as they slip from their knot across her chest, falling to her sides. Her handbag's chain chimes with a soft clatter before resting with its gentle swing. *If I was a hawk*, she rambles internally, *I could fly away from this place and never return.*

A police car pulls into the lot. It slows at the sight of the strewn vehicle, but continues when the driver spots Harrison and Daisy standing on the stairs. The air falls still as the roar of the squad car's engine turns off.

Releasing a dampened cough from his throat, Harrison turns his face to Daisy's, who does not meet his eyes.

"What do we do now?" he asks. His words float like dust, the particles clinging to their skin.

Without acknowledging Harrison, Daisy holds her stare forward.

"Looks like we can go anywhere," she says, her voice an aloof tone of wonder as she takes a meager step forward. "But for now, I'd like you to take me home," she instructs before turning to face him with a stern brow. Her eyes are an eerie shade of black. Harrison nods in understanding as they make their way toward the whirling car.

Once inside, Daisy leans back into the leather seat. Her lids close and blink to life at the weight of her exhaustion. Harrison grips the wheel while his eyes canvas the bloodied streaks across the wheel, the console, and gear stick.

Daisy reaches a somber hand outward, as if to grab Harrison's wrist. Instead, she wipes the pads of her fingers against the stereo, cleaning the blood from its screen. She then turns the knob slowly, allowing a momentary pause when a radio station comes into focus. Once she lands on a suitable selection, she turns her vacant face toward Harrison.

"Let's go," she commands before dropping her weight back into the seat with a heavy breat

348

Epilogue

Harrison stands in the doorframe of the cellar, propped against his outstretched arm. He crosses a dress shoe before his leg and lands the toe against the cement floor with a *thump*. His tongue traces the sharp edges of his teeth until he presses the tip into an incisor and winces slightly with the pain.

The motionless cellar sits before him, still painted with Ella's blood. The metal stakes are sprinkled amongst the pools of dull, dried blood, and the hammer sits upright, its weight burrowing against the mallet. Taking a step forward, Harrison kicks the bulky metal and it clatters across the floor with a resounding echo. Kneeling down, Harrison picks up a clean stake and examines it between his thumb and forefinger before turning it over in his hands and pressing the weight of his thumb into the point. He flips the metal until it lands within his grip, then places it sturdily behind his right ear.

Flipping the switch, he extinguishes the single light in the cellar. The hushed hum of the bulb falls silent and his eyes adjust to the darkness. Grasping the door handle without needing the light to locate the metal, he tugs at the wooden door and closes the room behind him.

Walking through the hallway, he makes his way toward the stairs and begins bounding up the steps until he lands just before the door. Turning to peer down into the darkness, he dips his hand into his pocket and produces his cell phone. Pressing the buttons as they flood his face with the soft blue lighting, he locates a number and a muted dial tone fills the corridor. He raises the phone to his ear and he climbs the remaining steps, the ringing subdued against his cheek.

Closing the entry door behind him, Harrison leans his full weight backward and drops his head back into the wood. He props the phone against his shoulder as he digs a hand into his pocket to product a small bottle of hand sanitizer when a voice finally answers on the other end.

"Hello?" a gruff male voice says. "How did you get this number?" The clattering of a restaurant can be heard on the recipient's line. Vibrant chatter and clinking glassware rustle in place of his silence.

"This is Harrison Bishop," Harrison announces confidently as he squirts a dollop of the clear liquid into his hand, the smell of alcohol stinging his nose. "Is this Jopling?"

The man coughs aggressively into the phone then hushes someone on his end. "It might be," he says, as a clang of silverware ripples against an expensive plate before Jopling begins chewing assertively into Harrison's ear.

Harrison clears his throat.

"I heard you can make people disappear. Is this correct?" He narrows his eyes and rubs the remainder of the liquid between his hands before adjusting his tie nervously.

Jopling takes a gulp of liquid before continuing to chew into the phone.

"For a price. What's your offer?" Another gulp. More chewing.

"Money is no concern. Just tell me when, where, and what to bring," Harrison says, the rudeness piercing his eyes with an irk.

"Six a.m.," Jopling instructs. "Bring yourself, one suitcase, and a vehicle." He swallows audibly as he forces down his bite and releases a poignant laugh. "Have a nice life, Mr. Bishop."

The story continues with **DESPERADO**

Visit KMDudley.com for updates

Acknowledgements and **Thank Yous**

Thank you to my friends for encouraging this ludicrous obsession. An even bigger thank you for not forgetting about me on the nights when I skipped trips to Pourman's to stay in and write.

Thank you to Abbey and Shelby for reading the madness of my first drafts and the biggest thank you I can muster to Allison for taking my words and make them coherent.

Thank you to Sydney for your ominous and whimsical aesthetic.

Thank you to black coffee, white wine, and diet cola for fueling my brain when I did not have the will stamina to do it alone and to Matt and Oliver for cheering me on.

A special thank you to my dog, Maverick, after he learns how to read.

About the **Author**

K M Dudley is not an award-winning writer, singer, or comedian. However, she does have an insatiable fascination with true crime and would like to remind everyone to stay out of the park after dark.

Born and raised in the Midwest, she and her Australian Shepherd, Maverick, recently relocated to the San Francisco Bay Area. Although she spends her days in the software sector of Silicon Valley, by nights and weekends, she alternates between white wine and black coffee to write fiction and solve the mystery of the Zodiac Killer.

Her debut novel is CAVALIER.

Visit KMDudley.com to learn more.
Twitter: @thekmdudley
Instagram: @thekmdudley
E-mail: thekmdudley@gmail.com

Made in the USA
San Bernardino, CA
13 February 2018